A Study Guide to Jules Verne's

Around the World in Eighty Days

With explanatory footnotes and comprehension questions

✓ **Unabridged edition**
✓ **Includes 185 comprehension questions with answers**
✓ **Includes over 525 explanatory footnotes**
✓ **Supports vocabulary building**
✓ **Ideal for 11 plus preparation**

Explained by
Dolly Jain

Other books in the **Classics: Explained for the young readers** series:

The Wind in the Willows: Explained for the young readers
    Kenneth Grahame, Dolly Jain

The Railway Children: Explained for the young readers
    Edith Nesbit, Dolly Jain

Robinson Crusoe: Explained for the young readers
    Daniel Defoe, Dolly Jain

Treasure Island: Explained for the young readers
    Robert Louis Stevenson, Dolly Jain

The Prince and the Pauper: Explained for the young readers
    Mark Twain, Dolly Jain

Frankenstein: Explained for the young readers
    Mary Shelley, Dolly Jain

Pride and the Prejudice: Explained for the young readers
    Jane Austen, Dolly Jain

The Hound of the Baskervilles: Explained for the young readers
    Robert Louis Stevenson, Dolly Jain

The Adventures of Tom Sawyer: Explained for the young readers
    Mark Twain, Dolly Jain

All rights reserved. No part of this publication maybe reproduced, stored in a retrieval system, or transmitted, in any form or by any means, electronic, mechanical, photocopying, recording or otherwise, without the prior permission of the publishers.

Independently Printed by Dolly Jain

dolly_jain@yahoo.com

A Study Guide to Jules Verne's

Around the World in Eighty Days

With explanatory footnotes and comprehension questions

About the original book

Around the World in Eighty Days is an exciting adventure story about Mr. Phileas Fogg, a rich Englishman who bets half of his fortune that he can travel around the world in eighty days. The story is about his journey as he crosses land on elephants and railways, and sails across boisterous waters on steamboats and sledges, and faces adversaries with unperturbed calmness. But can he complete his trip within the given time?

About this edition

This 'explained' edition of classic literature not only includes the complete, unabridged text but also provides comprehensive support to aid readers. Footnotes on each page offer assistance with vocabulary and comprehension, ensuring a smoother reading experience. Furthermore, each chapter concludes with comprehension exercises featuring inference, information retrieval, and vocabulary testing questions.

This enhanced edition offers support in various forms. A built-in glossary assists with both archaic and challenging modern English words. Additionally, explanations are provided for idioms, phrases, and other literary devices found in the original text.

Annotations offer contextual information, including references to other literary works, locations, and customs. Summaries are provided for lengthy paragraphs and complex sentences, facilitating comprehension.

By pairing the original text with explanatory footnotes, this edition ensures continuity in reading while enhancing the overall reading journey.

A Study Guide to Jules Verne's

Around the World in Eighty Days

With explanatory footnotes and comprehension questions

Explained by
Dolly Jain

Contents

Chapter 1 1
Chapter 2 6
Chapter 3 10
Chapter 4 17
Chapter 5 22
Chapter 6 26
Chapter 7 31
Chapter 8 35
Chapter 9 40
Chapter 10 45
Chapter 11 50
Chapter 12 58
Chapter 13 65
Chapter 14 71
Chapter 15 77
Chapter 16 84
Chapter 17 89
Chapter 18 95
Chapter 19 100
Chapter 20 107
Chapter 21 113
Chapter 22 120
Chapter 23 126
Chapter 24 132
Chapter 25 138
Chapter 26 144
Chapter 27 149
Chapter 28 155

Chapter 29 163
Chapter 30 170
Chapter 31 177
Chapter 32 183
Chapter 33 188
Chapter 34 195
Chapter 35 199
Chapter 36 204
Chapter 37 208
Answers to comprehension exercises 212

Chapter 1

IN WHICH PHILEAS FOGG AND PASSEPARTOUT ACCEPT EACH OTHER,
THE ONE AS MASTER, THE OTHER AS MAN

Mr. Phileas Fogg lived, in 1872, at No. 7, Saville Row, Burlington Gardens, the house in which Sheridan[1] died in 1814. He was one of the most noticeable members of the Reform Club[2], though he seemed always to avoid attracting attention; an enigmatical personage, about whom little was known, except that he was a polished man of the world. People said that he resembled Byron[3]—at least that his head was Byronic; but he was a bearded, tranquil Byron, who might live on a thousand years without growing old.

Certainly an Englishman, it was more doubtful whether Phileas Fogg was a Londoner. He was never seen on 'Change[4], nor at the Bank, nor in the counting-rooms of the "City"; no ships ever came into London docks of which he was the owner; he had no public employment; he had never been entered at any of the Inns of Court[5], either at the Temple, or Lincoln's Inn, or Gray's Inn; nor had his voice ever resounded in the Court of Chancery[6], or in the Exchequer, or the Queen's Bench, or the Ecclesiastical Courts[7]. He certainly was not a manufacturer; nor was he a merchant or a gentleman farmer. His name was strange to the scientific and learned societies, and he never was known to take part in the sage deliberations of the Royal Institution[8] or the London Institution[9], the Artisan's Association, or the Institution of Arts and Sciences. He belonged, in fact, to none of the numerous societies which swarm in the English capital, from the Harmonic to that

---

[1] Sheridan refers to Richard Brinsley Butler Sheridan, an Irish dramatist and politician. He died on 7th July 1816.

[2] The Reform Club was a social club founded in 1836, in Pall Mall, London. The palatial clubhouse was designed by Charles Barry, an eminent architect.

[3] 'Byron' refers to George Gordon Byron, one of the greatest British poets.

[4] 'Change refers to the London Stock Exchange, located in the City of London.

[5] The Inns of the Court serve as the professional associations for the barristers in London. Traditionally, barristers were trained at the four Inns of Court: The Honourable Societies of Lincoln's Inn, Inner Temple, Middle Temple and Gray's Inn.

[6] In earlier days, civil disputes were heard in equity courts, such as the Court of Chancery and Exchequer Courts.

[7] Ecclesiastical Courts are Christian courts with jurisdiction mainly over spiritual or religious matters.

[8] The Royal Institution is an independent charity dedicated to the world of science.

[9] The London Institution was an educational institution, particularly noted for its teachings in chemistry, until its closure in 1912.

of the Entomologists[10], founded mainly for the purpose of abolishing[11] pernicious[12] insects.

Phileas Fogg was a member of the Reform[13], and that was all.

The way in which he got admission to this exclusive club was simple enough.

He was recommended by the Barings[14], with whom he had an open credit. His cheques were regularly paid at sight from his account current, which was always flush.

Was Phileas Fogg rich? Undoubtedly. But those who knew him best could not imagine how he had made his fortune, and Mr. Fogg was the last person to whom to apply for the information. He was not lavish, nor, on the contrary, avaricious[15]; for, whenever he knew that money was needed for a noble, useful, or benevolent purpose, he supplied it quietly and sometimes anonymously. He was, in short, the least communicative of men. He talked very little, and seemed all the more mysterious for his taciturn[16] manner. His daily habits were quite open to observation; but whatever he did was so exactly the same thing that he had always done before, that the wits of the curious were fairly puzzled.

Had he travelled? It was likely, for no one seemed to know the world more familiarly; there was no spot so secluded that he did not appear to have an intimate acquaintance with it. He often corrected, with a few clear words, the thousand conjectures advanced by members of the club as to lost and unheard-of travellers, pointing out the true probabilities, and seeming as if gifted with a sort of second sight, so often did events justify his predictions.[17] He must have travelled everywhere, at least in the spirit.

It was at least certain that Phileas Fogg had not absented himself from London for many years. Those who were honoured by a better acquaintance with him than the rest, declared that nobody could pretend to have ever seen him anywhere else. His sole pastimes were reading the papers and playing whist[18]. He often won at this game, which, as a silent one, harmonised with his nature; but his winnings never went into his purse, being reserved as a fund for his charities. Mr. Fogg played, not to win, but for the sake of playing. The game was in his eyes a contest, a struggle with a difficulty, yet a motionless, unwearying struggle, congenial[19] to his tastes.

---

[10] 'Entomologist' is someone who studies a branch of zoology that deals with insects.
[11] 'Abolish' means to put an end to something.
[12] 'Pernicious' means damaging or to have a harmful effect.
[13] The Reform Club is a private members' club in central London.
[14] Barings Bank was a British merchant bank. It collapsed in 1995.
[15] 'Avaricious' means very greedy and materialistic.
[16] 'Taciturn' refers to a very quiet and un-talkative person.
[17] Mr. Fogg seemed to know enough about world geography to correct the guesses made by others. Whether or not he had actually travelled or simply read about these places is not certain.
[18] 'Whist' is a classic English card game. A Whist player should be good at strategising and have a good memory for counting cards.
[19] 'Congenial' means something that is suited to one's nature.

Phileas Fogg was not known to have either wife or children, which may happen to the most honest people; either relatives or near friends, which is certainly more unusual. He lived alone in his house in Saville Row, whither none penetrated.[20] A single domestic sufficed to serve him. He breakfasted and dined at the club, at hours mathematically fixed, in the same room, at the same table, never taking his meals with other members, much less bringing a guest with him; and went home at exactly midnight, only to retire at once to bed. He never used the cosy chambers which the Reform provides for its favoured members. He passed ten hours out of the twenty-four in Saville Row, either in sleeping or making his toilet[21]. When he chose to take a walk it was with a regular step in the entrance hall with its mosaic flooring, or in the circular gallery with its dome supported by twenty red porphyry Ionic columns[22], and illumined by blue painted windows. When he breakfasted or dined all the resources of the club—its kitchens and pantries, its buttery and dairy—aided to crowd his table with their most succulent stores; he was served by the gravest waiters, in dress coats, and shoes with swan-skin soles, who proffered[23] the viands[24] in special porcelain, and on the finest linen; club decanters[25], of a lost mould, contained his sherry, his port, and his cinnamon-spiced claret; while his beverages were refreshingly cooled with ice, brought at great cost from the American lakes.

If to live in this style is to be eccentric[26], it must be confessed that there is something good in eccentricity.

The mansion in Saville Row, though not sumptuous, was exceedingly comfortable. The habits of its occupant were such as to demand but little from the sole domestic, but Phileas Fogg required him to be almost superhumanly prompt and regular. On this very 2nd of October he had dismissed James Forster, because that luckless youth had brought him shaving-water at eighty-four degrees Fahrenheit[27] instead of eighty-six; and he was awaiting his successor, who was due at the house between eleven and half-past.

Phileas Fogg was seated squarely in his armchair, his feet close together like those of a grenadier[28] on parade, his hands resting on his knees, his body straight, his head erect; he was steadily watching a complicated clock which indicated the hours, the minutes, the seconds, the days, the months, and the years. At exactly half-past eleven Mr. Fogg would, according to his daily habit, quit Saville Row, and repair to the Reform[29].

---

[20] Mr. Fogg lived in a house in Saville Row, a street in Mayfair, London, famous for being expensive and very fashionable. He lived alone and did not attend to any guests.

[21] 'To make one's toilet' is a general term meaning to get ready, brushing hair etc.

[22] Ionic columns are designed in one of the three original styles of Greek architecture. They are made of porphyry, a reddish coloured igneous rock containing conspicuous crystals.

[23] 'Proffer' means to offer something by holding it out.

[24] 'Viand' is an archaic term for an item of food.

[25] A 'decanter' is a bottle used to store and serve wine.

[26] 'Eccentric' refers to a person who behaves in an odd or unusual way.

[27] 'Fahrenheit' is a measurement of the temperature of something.

[28] A 'grenadier' is a specialised soldier.

[29] 'Repair to Reform' means that Mr. Fogg moved from his residence in Saville Row to the Reform Club.

A Study Guide: Around the World in Eighty Days

A rap at this moment sounded on the door of the cosy apartment where Phileas Fogg was seated, and James Forster, the dismissed servant, appeared.

"The new servant," said he.

A young man of thirty advanced and bowed.

"You are a Frenchman, I believe," asked Phileas Fogg, "and your name is John?"

"Jean, if monsieur pleases," replied the newcomer, "Jean Passepartout, a surname which has clung to me because I have a natural aptness for going out of one business into another. I believe I'm honest, monsieur, but, to be outspoken, I've had several trades. I've been an itinerant singer, a circus-rider, when I used to vault like Leotard[30], and dance on a rope like Blondin[31]. Then I got to be a professor of gymnastics, so as to make better use of my talents; and then I was a sergeant fireman at Paris, and assisted at many a big fire. But I quitted France five years ago, and, wishing to taste the sweets of domestic life, took service as a valet here in England. Finding myself out of place, and hearing that Monsieur Phileas Fogg was the most exact and settled gentleman in the United Kingdom, I have come to monsieur in the hope of living with him a tranquil life, and forgetting even the name of Passepartout."

"Passepartout suits me," responded Mr. Fogg. "You are well recommended to me; I hear a good report of you. You know my conditions?"

"Yes, monsieur."

"Good! What time is it?"

"Twenty-two minutes after eleven," returned Passepartout, drawing an enormous silver watch from the depths of his pocket.

"You are too slow," said Mr. Fogg.

"Pardon me, monsieur, it is impossible—"

"You are four minutes too slow. No matter; it's enough to mention the error. Now from this moment, twenty-nine minutes after eleven, a.m., this Wednesday, 2nd October, you are in my service."

Phileas Fogg got up, took his hat in his left hand, put it on his head with an automatic motion, and went off without a word.

Passepartout heard the street door shut once; it was his new master going out. He heard it shut again; it was his predecessor, James Forster, departing in his turn. Passepartout remained alone in the house in Saville Row.

---

[30] Jules Leotard, a French acrobatic performer, popularised the tight-fitting garment that covers the torso.

[31] Charles Blondin was a French acrobat known for crossing Niagara Gorge on a tightrope.

4

Comprehension exercise 1:

Q1) Why did Phileas Fogg live such a secluded life in Saville Row?
a) Because he was grumpy.
b) Because he preferred solitude and had specific routines.
c) Because he was afraid of public spaces.
d) Because he had no friends or family.

Q2) How did Phileas Fogg come to be a member of the Reform Club?
a) He inherited the membership from his family.
b) He was recommended by a prominent financial institution.
c) He bought his membership through a large donation.
d) He was sponsored by the Barings due to his financial credibility.

Q3) What did Phileas Fogg do with his winnings from playing whist?
a) He used them to fund his extravagant lifestyle.
b) He saved them for his retirement.
c) He donated them to charitable causes.
d) He invested them in various business ventures.

Q4) What was Phileas Fogg's attitude towards charity?
a) He was indifferent.
b) He donated anonymously and generously.
c) He only donated to scientific societies.
d) He preferred to invest in his own business ventures.

Q5) What does the word "enigmatical" mean in the context of the passage?
a) Mysterious
b) Predictable
c) Boisterous
d) Insignificant

Chapter 2

IN WHICH PASSEPARTOUT IS CONVINCED THAT HE HAS AT LAST FOUND HIS IDEAL

"Faith," muttered Passepartout, somewhat flurried, "I've seen people at Madame Tussaud's as lively as my new master!"[1]

Madame Tussaud's "people," let it be said, are of wax, and are much visited in London; speech is all that is wanting to make them human.

During his brief interview with Mr. Fogg, Passepartout had been carefully observing him. He appeared to be a man about forty years of age, with fine, handsome features, and a tall, well-shaped figure; his hair and whiskers were light, his forehead compact and unwrinkled, his face rather pale, his teeth magnificent. His countenance possessed in the highest degree what physiognomists[2] call "repose in action," a quality of those who act rather than talk. Calm and phlegmatic[3], with a clear eye, Mr. Fogg seemed a perfect type of that English composure which Angelica Kauffmann[4] has so skilfully represented on canvas. Seen in the various phases of his daily life, he gave the idea of being perfectly well-balanced, as exactly regulated as a Leroy chronometer[5]. Phileas Fogg was, indeed, exactitude[6] personified, and this was betrayed even in the expression of his very hands and feet; for in men, as well as in animals, the limbs themselves are expressive of the passions.

He was so exact that he was never in a hurry, was always ready, and was economical alike of his steps and his motions. He never took one step too many, and always went to his destination by the shortest cut; he made no superfluous gestures, and was never seen to be moved or agitated. He was the most deliberate person in the world, yet always reached his destination at the exact moment.

---

[1] Passepartout is confused by Mr. Fogg's cold response and sarcastically compares him with the wax statues of famous people at Madame Tussaud's.

[2] A 'physiognomist' is a person who is able to judge a person's character from their facial character.

[3] 'Phlegmatic' means calm or unresponsive to excitement or emotions.

[4] Angelica Kauffman was a Swiss artist remembered as a history painter.

[5] The 'Leroy chronometer' refers to a clock developed by Pierre Le Roy (1717-1785), a French clockmaker. His developments in clockworks are considered as the foundations of the modern precision clock.

[6] 'Exactitude' means the quality of being exact or accurate.

He lived alone, and, so to speak, outside of every social relation; and as he knew that in this world account must be taken of friction[7], and that friction retards, he never rubbed against anybody.

As for Passepartout, he was a true Parisian of Paris. Since he had abandoned his own country for England, taking service as a valet, he had in vain searched for a master after his own heart. Passepartout was by no means one of those pert dunces[8] depicted by Moliere[9] with a bold gaze and a nose held high in the air; he was an honest fellow, with a pleasant face, lips a trifle protruding, soft-mannered and serviceable, with a good round head, such as one likes to see on the shoulders of a friend. His eyes were blue, his complexion rubicund[10], his figure almost portly and well-built, his body muscular, and his physical powers fully developed by the exercises of his younger days. His brown hair was somewhat tumbled; for, while the ancient sculptors are said to have known eighteen methods of arranging Minerva's[11] tresses, Passepartout was familiar with but one of dressing his own: three strokes of a large-tooth comb completed his toilet.

It would be rash to predict how Passepartout's lively nature would agree with Mr. Fogg. It was impossible to tell whether the new servant would turn out as absolutely methodical as his master required; experience alone could solve the question. Passepartout had been a sort of vagrant[12] in his early years, and now yearned for repose[13]; but so far he had failed to find it, though he had already served in ten English houses. But he could not take root in any of these; with chagrin[14], he found his masters invariably whimsical and irregular, constantly running about the country, or on the look-out for adventure. His last master, young Lord Longferry, Member of Parliament, after passing his nights in the Haymarket taverns, was too often brought home in the morning on policemen's shoulders. Passepartout, desirous of respecting the gentleman whom he served, ventured a mild remonstrance[15] on such conduct; which, being ill-received, he took his leave. Hearing that Mr. Phileas Fogg was looking for a servant, and that his life was one of unbroken regularity, that he neither travelled nor stayed from home overnight, he felt sure that this would be the place he was after. He presented himself, and was accepted, as has been seen.[16]

---

[7] 'Friction' is a phenomenon that slows down motion.

[8] 'Pert dunce' refers to a person who is very stylish or attractive in appearance but slow to learn.

[9] Moliere is a French dramatist, regarded as the greatest French writer of comedy.

[10] 'Rubicund' refers to a healthy reddish colour often associated with outdoor life.

[11] Minerva was the Roman goddess of wisdom, arts, trade and strategy.

[12] A 'Vagrant' is a person who wanders idly from place to place and does not have an established residence.

[13] 'Repose' is a state of resting after exertion or strain.

[14] 'Chagrin' is distress caused by disappointment or failure.

[15] 'Remonstrance' is a complaint to someone about something.

[16] Passepartout sought a master whom he could serve with respect and dignity, someone characterised by stability and consistency in their daily routines.

At half-past eleven, then, Passepartout found himself alone in the house in Saville Row. He began its inspection without delay, scouring it from cellar to garret[17]. So clean, well-arranged, solemn a mansion pleased him; it seemed to him like a snail's shell, lighted and warmed by gas, which sufficed for both these purposes. When Passepartout reached the second story he recognised at once the room which he was to inhabit, and he was well satisfied with it. Electric bells and speaking-tubes[18] afforded communication with the lower stories; while on the mantel stood an electric clock, precisely like that in Mr. Fogg's bedchamber, both beating the same second at the same instant. "That's good, that'll do," said Passepartout to himself.

He suddenly observed, hung over the clock, a card which, upon inspection, proved to be a programme of the daily routine of the house. It comprised all that was required of the servant, from eight in the morning, exactly at which hour Phileas Fogg rose, till half-past eleven, when he left the house for the Reform Club—all the details of service, the tea and toast at twenty-three minutes past eight, the shaving-water at thirty-seven minutes past nine, and the toilet at twenty minutes before ten. Everything was regulated and foreseen that was to be done from half-past eleven a.m. till midnight, the hour at which the methodical gentleman retired.

Mr. Fogg's wardrobe was amply supplied and in the best taste. Each pair of trousers, coat, and vest bore a number, indicating the time of year and season at which they were in turn to be laid out for wearing; and the same system was applied to the master's shoes. In short, the house in Saville Row, which must have been a very temple of disorder and unrest under the illustrious but dissipated Sheridan, was cosiness, comfort, and method idealised. There was no study, nor were there books, which would have been quite useless to Mr. Fogg; for at the Reform two libraries, one of general literature and the other of law and politics, were at his service. A moderate-sized safe stood in his bedroom, constructed so as to defy fire as well as burglars; but Passepartout found neither arms nor hunting weapons anywhere; everything betrayed the most tranquil and peaceable habits.

Having scrutinised the house from top to bottom, he rubbed his hands, a broad smile overspread his features, and he said joyfully, "This is just what I wanted! Ah, we shall get on together, Mr. Fogg and I! What a domestic and regular gentleman! A real machine; well, I don't mind serving a machine."[19]

---

[17] A 'garret' is an attic room.
[18] 'Speaking tubes' are pipes through which conversation may be conducted.
[19] Passepartout remarks that a life without family and friends, without music and dance, without chit-chatter is lifeless, like a machine. He compares Mr. Fogg's life to that of a machine, but also concludes that this does not bother him.

Comprehension exercise 2:

Q1) How does Phileas Fogg's behaviour towards his servants contribute to his character?
a) It shows that he values their opinions and input.
b) It suggests that he is demanding and expects perfection.
c) It indicates that he is generous and lenient.
d) It implies that he is indifferent and uninterested.

Q2) What is the significance of the card hung over the clock in Phileas Fogg's house?
a) It contains instructions for the servant's daily routine.
b) It lists the rules and regulations of the Reform Club.
c) It displays Fogg's schedule for the day.
d) It provides information about upcoming social events.

Q3) How does Passepartout react to the discovery of Fogg's daily routine?
a) He is surprised by its complexity.
b) He is impressed by its precision and detail.
c) He is disappointed by its lack of spontaneity.
d) He is confused by its inconsistency.

Q4) What is the meaning of the term "repose" as used in the text?
a) Chaos and disorder
b) Rest and tranquillity
c) Energy and activity
d) Excitement and enthusiasm

Q5) How would you define the word "vagrant" as described in Passepartout's backstory?
a) A person who travels aimlessly or wanders without a home
b) A wealthy and influential individual
c) A skilled craftsman or artisan
d) A servant or domestic worker

Chapter 3

IN WHICH A CONVERSATION TAKES PLACE WHICH SEEMS LIKELY TO COST PHILEAS FOGG DEAR

Phileas Fogg, having shut the door of his house at half-past eleven, and having put his right foot before his left five hundred and seventy-five times, and his left foot before his right five hundred and seventy-six times, reached the Reform Club, an imposing edifice[1] in Pall Mall, which could not have cost less than three millions. He repaired at once to the dining-room, the nine windows of which open upon a tasteful garden, where the trees were already gilded with an autumn colouring; and took his place at the habitual table, the cover of which had already been laid for him. His breakfast consisted of a side-dish, a broiled fish with Reading sauce[2], a scarlet slice of roast beef garnished with mushrooms, a rhubarb and gooseberry tart, and a morsel[3] of Cheshire cheese, the whole being washed down with several cups of tea, for which the Reform is famous. He rose at thirteen minutes to one, and directed his steps towards the large hall, a sumptuous apartment adorned with lavishly-framed paintings. A flunkey[4] handed him an uncut Times[5], which he proceeded to cut with a skill which betrayed familiarity with this delicate operation. The perusal of this paper absorbed Phileas Fogg until a quarter before four, whilst the Standard, his next task, occupied him till the dinner hour. Dinner passed as breakfast had done, and Mr. Fogg re-appeared in the reading-room and sat down to the Pall Mall at twenty minutes before six. Half an hour later several members of the Reform came in and drew up to the fireplace, where a coal fire was steadily burning. They were Mr. Fogg's usual partners at whist: Andrew Stuart, an engineer; John Sullivan and Samuel Fallentin, bankers; Thomas Flanagan, a brewer; and Gauthier Ralph, one of the Directors of the Bank of England—all rich and highly respectable personages, even in a club which comprises the princes of English trade and finance.

"Well, Ralph," said Thomas Flanagan, "what about that robbery?"

"Oh," replied Stuart, "the Bank will lose the money."

"On the contrary," broke in Ralph, "I hope we may put our hands on the robber. Skilful detectives have been sent to all the principal ports of America and the Continent, and he'll be a clever fellow if he slips through their fingers."

"But have you got the robber's description?" asked Stuart.

---

[1] An 'edifice' is a large, self-imposing building.
[2] 'Reading sauce' is a spicy sauce that goes well with fish, beef, or poultry.
[3] 'Morsel' is a small quantity of food.
[4] A 'flunkey' is a steward or a butler.
[5] 'Uncut Times' refers to a copy of the Times newspaper that has not been trimmed or had its pages separated. It implies that the newspaper was fresh and had not been read or used yet.

"In the first place, he is no robber at all," returned Ralph, positively.

"What! a fellow who makes off with fifty-five thousand pounds, no robber?"

"No."

"Perhaps he's a manufacturer, then."

"The Daily Telegraph says that he is a gentleman."

It was Phileas Fogg, whose head now emerged from behind his newspapers, who made this remark. He bowed to his friends, and entered into the conversation. The affair which formed its subject, and which was town talk, had occurred three days before at the Bank of England. A package of banknotes, to the value of fifty-five thousand pounds, had been taken from the principal cashier's table, that functionary being at the moment engaged in registering the receipt of three shillings and sixpence. Of course, he could not have his eyes everywhere. Let it be observed that the Bank of England reposes a touching confidence in the honesty of the public. There are neither guards nor gratings[6] to protect its treasures; gold, silver, banknotes are freely exposed, at the mercy of the first comer. A keen observer of English customs relates that, being in one of the rooms of the Bank one day, he had the curiosity to examine a gold ingot[7] weighing some seven or eight pounds. He took it up, scrutinised it, passed it to his neighbour, he to the next man, and so on until the ingot, going from hand to hand, was transferred to the end of a dark entry; nor did it return to its place for half an hour. Meanwhile, the cashier had not so much as raised his head. But in the present instance things had not gone so smoothly. The package of notes not being found when five o'clock sounded from the ponderous clock in the "drawing office," the amount was passed to the account of profit and loss. As soon as the robbery was discovered, picked detectives hastened off to Liverpool, Glasgow, Havre, Suez, Brindisi, New York, and other ports, inspired by the proffered reward of two thousand pounds, and five per cent on the sum that might be recovered. Detectives were also charged with narrowly watching those who arrived at or left London by rail, and a judicial examination was at once entered upon.

There were real grounds for supposing, as the Daily Telegraph said, that the thief did not belong to a professional band. On the day of the robbery a well-dressed gentleman of polished manners, and with a well-to-do air, had been observed going to and fro in the paying room where the crime was committed. A description of him was easily procured and sent to the detectives; and some hopeful spirits, of whom Ralph was one, did not despair of his apprehension. The papers and clubs were full of the affair, and everywhere people were discussing the probabilities of a successful pursuit; and the Reform Club was especially agitated[8], several of its members being Bank officials.

Ralph would not concede that the work of the detectives was likely to be in vain, for he thought that the prize offered would greatly stimulate their zeal and activity. But Stuart

---

[6] 'Grating' is a frame of parallel bars or crossbars often used as a protective covering.
[7] An 'ingot' is a solid block of metal.
[8] 'Agitated' means disturbed or upset.

was far from sharing this confidence; and, as they placed themselves at the whist-table, they continued to argue the matter. Stuart and Flanagan played together, while Phileas Fogg had Fallentin for his partner. As the game proceeded the conversation ceased, excepting between the rubbers[9], when it revived again.

"I maintain," said Stuart, "that the chances are in favour of the thief, who must be a shrewd fellow."

"Well, but where can he fly to?" asked Ralph. "No country is safe for him."

"Pshaw[10]!"

"Where could he go, then?"

"Oh, I don't know that. The world is big enough."

"It was once," said Phileas Fogg, in a low tone. "Cut, sir," he added, handing the cards to Thomas Flanagan.

The discussion fell during the rubber, after which Stuart took up its thread.

"What do you mean by `once'? Has the world grown smaller?"

"Certainly," returned Ralph. "I agree with Mr. Fogg. The world has grown smaller, since a man can now go round it ten times more quickly than a hundred years ago. And that is why the search for this thief will be more likely to succeed."[11]

"And also why the thief can get away more easily."

"Be so good as to play, Mr. Stuart," said Phileas Fogg.

But the incredulous[12] Stuart was not convinced, and when the hand was finished, said eagerly: "You have a strange way, Ralph, of proving that the world has grown smaller. So, because you can go round it in three months—"

"In eighty days," interrupted Phileas Fogg.

"That is true, gentlemen," added John Sullivan. "Only eighty days, now that the section between Rothal[13] and Allahabad, on the Great Indian Peninsula Railway[14], has been opened. Here is the estimate made by the Daily Telegraph:

---

[9] 'Rubber' refers to a game of cards, often used in the phrase "rubber of bridge" or "rubber of whist," which indicates a series of games played until one side has won a certain number of points or rounds. The conversation about the robbery carried on between the series of games.

[10] 'Pshaw' is an expression of disbelief and contempt.

[11] The physical size of the world has not diminished, but rather, advancements in communication technology and transportation systems have significantly reduced travel times between different parts of the globe. This suggests that, in terms of accessibility and connectivity, the world has metaphorically 'shrunk'.

[12] 'Incredulous' means unwillingness to admit or accept something.

[13] Rothal is most probably a fictional place as it can't be found on today's map of India.

[14] The Great Indian Peninsula Railway, established in 1849, was India's first passenger railway. It ceased operations in 1951 when it became part of the Central Railway of Indian Railways.

From London to Suez via Mont Cenis and Brindisi, by rail and steamboats	7 days
From Suez to Bombay, by steamer	13 "
From Bombay to Calcutta, by rail	3 "
From Calcutta to Hong Kong, by steamer	13 "
From Hong Kong to Yokohama (Japan), by steamer	6 "
From Yokohama to San Francisco, by steamer	22 "
From San Francisco to New York, by rail	7 "
From New York to London, by steamer and rail	9 "
Total	80 days."

"Yes, in eighty days!" exclaimed Stuart, who in his excitement made a false deal. "But that doesn't take into account bad weather, contrary winds, shipwrecks, railway accidents, and so on."

"All included," returned Phileas Fogg, continuing to play despite the discussion.

"But suppose the Hindoos[15] or Indians pull up the rails," replied Stuart; "suppose they stop the trains, pillage the luggage-vans, and scalp the passengers!"

"All included," calmly retorted Fogg; adding, as he threw down the cards, "Two trumps."

Stuart, whose turn it was to deal, gathered them up, and went on: "You are right, theoretically, Mr. Fogg, but practically—"

"Practically also, Mr. Stuart."

"I'd like to see you do it in eighty days."

"It depends on you. Shall we go?"

"Heaven preserve me! But I would wager[16] four thousand pounds that such a journey, made under these conditions, is impossible."

"Quite possible, on the contrary," returned Mr. Fogg.

"Well, make it, then!"

"The journey round the world in eighty days?"

"Yes."

"I should like nothing better."

"When?"

---

[15] The term *"Hindoos"* refers to Hindus, followers of Hinduism, which is the predominant religion in India.

[16] 'Wager' means to officially place a bet or gamble on something.

"At once. Only I warn you that I shall do it at your expense."

"It's absurd!" cried Stuart, who was beginning to be annoyed at the persistency of his friend. "Come, let's go on with the game."

"Deal over again, then," said Phileas Fogg. "There's a false deal."

Stuart took up the pack with a feverish hand; then suddenly put them down again.

"Well, Mr. Fogg," said he, "it shall be so: I will wager the four thousand on it."

"Calm yourself, my dear Stuart," said Fallentin. "It's only a joke."

"When I say I'll wager," returned Stuart, "I mean it."

"All right," said Mr. Fogg; and, turning to the others, he continued: "I have a deposit of twenty thousand at Baring's which I will willingly risk upon it."

"Twenty thousand pounds!" cried Sullivan. "Twenty thousand pounds, which you would lose by a single accidental delay!"

"The unforeseen does not exist," quietly replied Phileas Fogg.

"But, Mr. Fogg, eighty days are only the estimate of the least possible time in which the journey can be made."

"A well-used minimum suffices for everything."

"But, in order not to exceed it, you must jump mathematically[17] from the trains upon the steamers, and from the steamers upon the trains again."

"I will jump—mathematically."

"You are joking."

"A true Englishman doesn't joke when he is talking about so serious a thing as a wager," replied Phileas Fogg, solemnly. "I will bet twenty thousand pounds against anyone who wishes that I will make the tour of the world in eighty days or less; in nineteen hundred and twenty hours, or a hundred and fifteen thousand two hundred minutes. Do you accept?"

"We accept," replied Messrs.[18] Stuart, Fallentin, Sullivan, Flanagan, and Ralph, after consulting each other.

"Good," said Mr. Fogg. "The train leaves for Dover at a quarter before nine. I will take it."

"This very evening?" asked Stuart.

---

[17] 'Mathematically' here means precisely, without wasting time in between.
[18] 'Messrs.' is used as the plural of Mr. before the names of two or more men.

"This very evening," returned Phileas Fogg. He took out and consulted a pocket almanac[19], and added, "As today is Wednesday, the 2nd of October, I shall be due in London in this very room of the Reform Club, on Saturday, the 21st of December, at a quarter before nine p.m.; or else the twenty thousand pounds, now deposited in my name at Baring's, will belong to you, in fact and in right, gentlemen. Here is a cheque for the amount."

A memorandum of the wager was at once drawn up and signed by the six parties, during which Phileas Fogg preserved a stoical[20] composure. He certainly did not bet to win, and had only staked the twenty thousand pounds, half of his fortune, because he foresaw that he might have to expend the other half to carry out this difficult, not to say unattainable, project. As for his antagonists[21], they seemed much agitated; not so much by the value of their stake, as because they had some scruples[22] about betting under conditions so difficult to their friend.

The clock struck seven, and the party offered to suspend the game so that Mr. Fogg might make his preparations for departure.

"I am quite ready now," was his tranquil[23] response. "Diamonds are trumps: be so good as to play, gentlemen."

---

[19] An almanac is an annual publication that lists the important events for the coming year, including information on weather, tide tables, religious festivals etc.
[20] 'Stoical' means calm and unemotional.
[21] 'Antagonist' means the contender or the opposer.
[22] 'Scruple' means reluctance on grounds of conscience.
[23] 'Tranquil' means calm and peaceful.

A Study Guide: Around the World in Eighty Days

Comprehension exercise 3

Q1) Based on the conversation among the members of the Reform Club, what can be inferred about their social status?
a) They are all commoners with modest incomes.
b) They are influential individuals with substantial wealth.
c) They are government officials with limited resources.
d) They are intellectuals with academic backgrounds.

Q2) What is included in Phileas Fogg's breakfast at the Reform Club?
a) Pancakes and maple syrup
b) Cereal and fruit
c) Broiled fish and roast beef
d) Omelette and toast

Q3) How does Phileas Fogg spend his time before dinner at the Reform Club?
a) Reading newspapers
b) Playing cards
c) Engaging in conversation with club members
d) Taking a leisurely stroll in the garden

Q4) How does Phileas Fogg plan to travel around the world?
a) By boat and horse-drawn carriage
b) By train and hot air balloon
c) By steamship and railway
d) By bicycle and camel

Q5) What is the meaning of the term "scruples" as used in the text?
a) Doubts or hesitation about the morality of an action
b) Small decorative items or ornaments
c) Agitated or restless behaviour
d) Rich and elaborate furnishings

Chapter 4

IN WHICH PHILEAS FOGG ASTOUNDS PASSEPARTOUT, HIS SERVANT

Having won twenty guineas at whist, and taken leave of his friends, Phileas Fogg, at twenty-five minutes past seven, left the Reform Club.

Passepartout, who had conscientiously[1] studied the programme of his duties, was more than surprised to see his master guilty of the inexactness of appearing at this unaccustomed hour; for, according to rule, he was not due in Saville Row until precisely midnight.

Mr. Fogg repaired to his bedroom, and called out, "Passepartout!"

Passepartout did not reply. It could not be he who was called; it was not the right hour.

"Passepartout!" repeated Mr. Fogg, without raising his voice.

Passepartout made his appearance.

"I've called you twice," observed his master.

"But it is not midnight," responded the other, showing his watch.

"I know it; I don't blame you. We start for Dover and Calais[2] in ten minutes."

A puzzled grin overspread Passepartout's round face; clearly he had not comprehended his master.

"Monsieur is going to leave home?"

"Yes," returned Phileas Fogg. "We are going round the world."

Passepartout opened wide his eyes, raised his eyebrows, held up his hands, and seemed about to collapse, so overcome was he with stupefied astonishment.[3]

"Round the world!" he murmured.

"In eighty days," responded Mr. Fogg. "So we haven't a moment to lose."

---

[1] 'Conscientiously' means in a careful way that involves a lot of effort.

[2] Dover and Calais are two port towns in the UK and France respectively, only 26 miles apart across the English Channel.

[3] Passepartout was bewildered and unable to understand Mr. Fogg's words.

"But the trunks?" gasped Passepartout, unconsciously swaying his head from right to left.

"We'll have no trunks; only a carpet-bag[4], with two shirts and three pairs of stockings for me, and the same for you. We'll buy our clothes on the way. Bring down my mackintosh and travelling-cloak,[5] and some stout[6] shoes, though we shall do little walking. Make haste!"

Passepartout tried to reply, but could not. He went out, mounted to his own room, fell into a chair, and muttered: "That's good, that is! And I, who wanted to remain quiet!"

He mechanically set about making the preparations for departure. Around the world in eighty days! Was his master a fool? No. Was this a joke, then? They were going to Dover; good! To Calais; good again! After all, Passepartout, who had been away from France five years, would not be sorry to set foot on his native soil again. Perhaps they would go as far as Paris, and it would do his eyes good to see Paris once more. But surely a gentleman so chary[7] of his steps would stop there; no doubt—but, then, it was none the less true that he was going away, this so domestic person hitherto!

By eight o'clock Passepartout had packed the modest carpet-bag, containing the wardrobes of his master and himself; then, still troubled in mind, he carefully shut the door of his room, and descended to Mr. Fogg.

Mr. Fogg was quite ready. Under his arm might have been observed a red-bound copy of Bradshaw's Continental Railway Steam Transit and General Guide, with its timetables showing the arrival and departure of steamers and railways. He took the carpet-bag, opened it, and slipped into it a goodly roll of Bank of England notes, which would pass wherever he might go.[8]

"You have forgotten nothing?" asked he.

"Nothing, monsieur."

"My mackintosh and cloak?"

"Here they are."

"Good! Take this carpet-bag," handing it to Passepartout. "Take good care of it, for there are twenty thousand pounds in it."

---

[4] A 'carpet-bag' is a travelling bag, a popular form of luggage in the 19th century.
[5] A mackintosh is a waterproof coat, whereas a cloak is an overcoat worn over indoor garments.
[6] 'Stout' means strong and sturdy.
[7] 'Chary' means hesitant or cautious about surrounding risks and dangers.
[8] The duo planned to circumnavigate the globe, traversing various countries and regions. The phrase "Which would pass wherever he might go" implies that British Pounds would be universally accepted in all those locations.

Passepartout nearly dropped the bag, as if the twenty thousand pounds were in gold, and weighed him down.

Master and man then descended, the street-door was double-locked, and at the end of Saville Row they took a cab and drove rapidly to Charing Cross. The cab stopped before the railway station at twenty minutes past eight. Passepartout jumped off the box and followed his master, who, after paying the cabman, was about to enter the station, when a poor beggar-woman, with a child in her arms, her naked feet smeared with mud, her head covered with a wretched bonnet[9], from which hung a tattered feather, and her shoulders shrouded in a ragged shawl, approached, and mournfully asked for alms.

Mr. Fogg took out the twenty guineas he had just won at whist, and handed them to the beggar, saying, "Here, my good woman. I'm glad that I met you;" and passed on.

Passepartout had a moist sensation about the eyes; his master's action touched his susceptible[10] heart.

Two first-class tickets for Paris having been speedily purchased, Mr. Fogg was crossing the station to the train, when he perceived his five friends of the Reform.

"Well, gentlemen," said he, "I'm off, you see; and, if you will examine my passport when I get back, you will be able to judge whether I have accomplished the journey agreed upon."

"Oh, that would be quite unnecessary, Mr. Fogg," said Ralph politely. "We will trust your word, as a gentleman of honour."

"You do not forget when you are due in London again?" asked Stuart.

"In eighty days; on Saturday, the 21st of December, 1872, at a quarter before nine p.m. Good-bye, gentlemen."

Phileas Fogg and his servant seated themselves in a first-class carriage at twenty minutes before nine; five minutes later the whistle screamed, and the train slowly glided out of the station.

The night was dark, and a fine, steady rain was falling. Phileas Fogg, snugly ensconced[11] in his corner, did not open his lips. Passepartout, not yet recovered from his stupefaction[12], clung mechanically to the carpet-bag, with its enormous treasure[13].

Just as the train was whirling through Sydenham, Passepartout suddenly uttered a cry of despair.

"What's the matter?" asked Mr. Fogg.

---

[9] A bonnet is a hat tied under the chin.
[10] 'Susceptible' means someone who is easily influenced by someone or something.
[11] 'Ensconce' means to place or hide someone or something securely.
[12] 'Stupefaction' is a state of being astonished or confused.
[13] The 'treasure' referred to is the twenty thousand pounds in notes that were rolled in the carpet-bag.

"Alas! In my hurry—I—I forgot—"

"What?"

"To turn off the gas in my room!"

"Very well, young man," returned Mr. Fogg, coolly; "it will burn—at your expense."[14]

---

[14] Mr. Fogg responded that Passepartout would have to pay for the gas used to heat his room while the pair was away travelling around the world.

Comprehension exercise 4

Q1) What can be inferred about Phileas Fogg's character from his actions at the railway station?
a) He is generous towards those in need.
b) He is indifferent to the plight of beggars.
c) He is cautious with his money.
d) He is impulsive in his decision-making.

Q2) How does Passepartout feel about Phileas Fogg's sudden decision to embark on a journey around the world?
a) He is excited and eager to travel.
b) He is confused and bewildered.
c) He is indifferent and uninterested.
d) He is apprehensive and fearful.

Q3) What time did Phileas Fogg leave the Reform Club?
a) At seven o'clock
b) At twenty-five minutes past seven
c) At eight o'clock
d) At twenty minutes before nine

Q4) What does the word "stupefaction" as used in the text mean?
a) Elation
b) Confusion
c) Comprehension
d) Excitement

Q5) Which word could best replace "susceptible" in the sentence: "Passepartout had a moist sensation about the eyes; his master's action touched his susceptible heart."
a) Resilient
b) Impervious
c) Vulnerable
d) Insensitive

Chapter 5

IN WHICH A NEW SPECIES OF FUNDS, UNKNOWN TO THE MONEYED MEN, APPEARS ON 'CHANGE

Phileas Fogg rightly suspected that his departure from London would create a lively sensation at the West End. The news of the bet spread through the Reform Club, and afforded an exciting topic of conversation to its members. From the club it soon got into the papers throughout England. The boasted "tour of the world" was talked about, disputed, argued with as much warmth as if the subject were another Alabama claim[1]. Some took sides with Phileas Fogg, but the large majority shook their heads and declared against him; it was absurd, impossible, they declared, that the tour of the world could be made, except theoretically and on paper, in this minimum of time, and with the existing means of travelling. The Times, Standard, Morning Post, and Daily News, and twenty other highly respectable newspapers scouted Mr. Fogg's project as madness; the Daily Telegraph alone hesitatingly supported him[2]. People in general thought him a lunatic, and blamed his Reform Club friends for having accepted a wager which betrayed the mental aberration[3] of its proposer.[4]

Articles no less passionate than logical appeared on the question, for geography is one of the pet subjects of the English; and the columns devoted to Phileas Fogg's venture were eagerly devoured[5] by all classes of readers. At first some rash individuals, principally of the gentler sex, espoused[6] his cause, which became still more popular when the Illustrated London News came out with his portrait, copied from a photograph in the Reform Club. A few readers of the Daily Telegraph even dared to say, "Why not, after all? Stranger things have come to pass."

At last a long article appeared, on the 7th of October, in the bulletin of the Royal Geographical Society, which treated the question from every point of view, and demonstrated the utter folly of the enterprise.

Everything, it said, was against the travellers, every obstacle imposed alike by man and by nature. A miraculous agreement of the times of departure and arrival, which was

---

[1] The Alabama Claim refers to the international dispute between the US and the UK, where Britain paid US$15.5 million for damages caused by the attacks upon Union merchant ships by Confederate Navy raiders during the American Civil War.

[2] The Daily Telegraph had to support him, because it was them who had published the 'Round the World' itinerary at the first instance.

[3] 'Aberration' is the state of deterring from normal or moral standards.

[4] The public thought Mr. Fogg had lost his mind, but they blamed the other participants in the bet for allowing him to gamble such a large amount on an impossible task.

[5] 'Devour' means to eat or consume something eagerly so that nothing is spared.

[6] 'Espouse' means to support a cause.

impossible, was absolutely necessary to his success. He might, perhaps, reckon on the arrival of trains at the designated hours, in Europe, where the distances were relatively moderate; but when he calculated upon crossing India in three days, and the United States in seven, could he rely beyond misgiving upon accomplishing his task? There were accidents to machinery, the liability of trains to run off the line, collisions, bad weather, the blocking up by snow—were not all these against Phileas Fogg? Would he not find himself, when travelling by steamer in winter, at the mercy of the winds and fogs? Is it uncommon for the best ocean steamers to be two or three days behind time? But a single delay would suffice to fatally break the chain of communication; should Phileas Fogg once miss, even by an hour; a steamer, he would have to wait for the next, and that would irrevocably[7] render his attempt vain.

This article made a great deal of noise, and, being copied into all the papers, seriously depressed the advocates of the rash tourist.[8]

Everybody knows that England is the world of betting men, who are of a higher class than mere gamblers; to bet is in the English temperament. Not only the members of the Reform, but the general public, made heavy wagers for or against Phileas Fogg, who was set down in the betting books as if he were a race-horse. Bonds were issued, and made their appearance on 'Change; "Phileas Fogg bonds" were offered at par or at a premium, and a great business was done in them. But five days after the article in the bulletin of the Geographical Society appeared, the demand began to subside: "Phileas Fogg" declined. They were offered by packages, at first of five, then of ten, until at last nobody would take less than twenty, fifty, a hundred!

Lord Albemarle, an elderly paralytic[9] gentleman, was now the only advocate of Phileas Fogg left. This noble lord, who was fastened to his chair, would have given his fortune to be able to make the tour of the world, if it took ten years; and he bet five thousand pounds on Phileas Fogg. When the folly as well as the uselessness of the adventure was pointed out to him, he contented himself with replying, "If the thing is feasible, the first to do it ought to be an Englishman."

The Fogg party dwindled more and more, everybody was going against him, and the bets stood a hundred and fifty and two hundred to one; and a week after his departure an incident occurred which deprived him of backers at any price.

The commissioner of police was sitting in his office at nine o'clock one evening, when the following telegraphic dispatch was put into his hands:

Suez[10] to London.

Rowan, Commissioner of Police, Scotland Yard:

---

[7] 'Irrevocable' means impossible to change.
[8] 'Advocates of the rash tourist' refers to Mr. Fogg's supporters.
[9] 'Paralytic' means to be affected by paralysis.
[10] Suez is a port city in the northeast of Egypt, located on the north coast of the Gulf of Suez.

I've found the bank robber, Phileas Fogg. Send with out delay warrant of arrest to Bombay.

Fix, Detective.

The effect of this dispatch was instantaneous. The polished gentleman disappeared to give place to the bank robber. His photograph, which was hung with those of the rest of the members at the Reform Club, was minutely examined, and it betrayed, feature by feature, the description of the robber which had been provided to the police. The mysterious habits of Phileas Fogg were recalled; his solitary ways, his sudden departure; and it seemed clear that, in undertaking a tour round the world on the pretext of a wager, he had had no other end in view than to elude the detectives, and throw them off his track.[11]

---

[11] Mr. Fogg's calm demeanour was now misconstrued as that of a criminal. His reserved way of life was confused with that of a robber attempting to evade detection.

Comprehension exercise 5

Q1) How did the public react to Phileas Fogg's wager to travel around the world?
a) They unanimously supported him.
b) They were divided in their opinions.
c) They considered it a brilliant idea.
d) They dismissed it as impossible.

Q2) What effect did the telegraphic dispatch about Phileas Fogg have on public perception?
a) It confirmed their suspicions about him.
b) It absolved him of any wrongdoing.
c) It caused confusion and uncertainty.
d) It generated sympathy towards him.

Q3) Who was the only remaining advocate of Phileas Fogg after the decline in public support?
a) Lord Albemarle
b) The commissioner of police
c) A member of the Reform Club
d) A representative from the Geographical Society

Q4) What does the term "aberration" as used in the text mean?
a) A deviation from the norm or expected course
b) A state of confusion or bewilderment
c) A sudden burst of energy or enthusiasm
d) A formal agreement or contract

Q5) What is the meaning of the word "paralytic" in the context of the text?
a) In a state of paralysis or immobility
b) Extremely active or energetic
c) Highly esteemed or respected
d) Prone to making rash decisions

Chapter 6

IN WHICH FIX, THE DETECTIVE, BETRAYS A VERY NATURAL IMPATIENCE

The circumstances under which this telegraphic dispatch about Phileas Fogg was sent were as follows:

The steamer Mongolia, belonging to the Peninsular and Oriental Company, built of iron, of two thousand eight hundred tons burden, and five hundred horse-power, was due at eleven o'clock a.m. on Wednesday, the 9th of October, at Suez. The Mongolia plied[1] regularly between Brindisi[2] and Bombay[3] via the Suez Canal, and was one of the fastest steamers belonging to the company, always making more than ten knots[4] an hour between Brindisi and Suez, and nine and a half between Suez and Bombay.

Two men were promenading[5] up and down the wharves[6], among the crowd of natives and strangers who were sojourning at this once straggling village—now, thanks to the enterprise of M. Lesseps[7], a fast-growing town. One was the British consul at Suez, who, despite the prophecies of the English Government, and the unfavourable predictions of Stephenson, was in the habit of seeing, from his office window, English ships daily passing to and fro on the great canal, by which the old roundabout route from England to India by the Cape of Good Hope was abridged by at least a half. The other was a small, slight-built personage, with a nervous, intelligent face, and bright eyes peering out from under eyebrows which he was incessantly twitching. He was just now manifesting unmistakable signs of impatience, nervously pacing up and down, and unable to stand still for a moment. This was Fix, one of the detectives who had been dispatched from England in search of the bank robber; it was his task to narrowly watch every passenger who arrived at Suez, and to follow up all who seemed to be suspicious characters, or bore a resemblance to the description of the criminal, which he had received two days before from the police headquarters at London. The detective was evidently inspired by the hope

---

[1] Ply means to carry on busily, steadily or regularly.

[2] Brindisi is a city in southern Italy, on the coast of the Adriatic Sea and is a major port of trade.

[3] Mumbai, formerly known as Bombay, lies on the Konkani coast on the western coast of India. Bombay was a major seaport on the Arabian Sea.

[4] Knot is a measure of speed.

[5] Promenade means walking or strolling in a leisurely way.

[6] A wharf is a landing area to which a ship may be moored to load or unload.

[7] Mr. Lesseps was a French diplomat and the developer of the Suez Canal, which joined the Mediterranean and the Red Seas. This canal brought in trade and instant business to the neighbouring villages and towns too.

of obtaining the splendid reward which would be the prize of success, and awaited with a feverish impatience, easy to understand, the arrival of the steamer Mongolia.

"So you say, consul," asked he for the twentieth time, "that this steamer is never behind time?"

"No, Mr. Fix," replied the consul. "She was bespoken yesterday at Port Said, and the rest of the way is of no account to such a craft. I repeat that the Mongolia has been in advance of the time required by the company's regulations, and gained the prize awarded for excess of speed."

"Does she come directly from Brindisi?"

"Directly from Brindisi; she takes on the Indian mails there, and she left there Saturday at five p.m. Have patience, Mr. Fix; she will not be late. But really, I don't see how, from the description you have, you will be able to recognise your man, even if he is on board the Mongolia."

"A man rather feels the presence of these fellows, consul, than recognises them. You must have a scent for them, and a scent is like a sixth sense which combines hearing, seeing, and smelling. I've arrested more than one of these gentlemen in my time, and, if my thief is on board, I'll answer for it; he'll not slip through my fingers."[8]

"I hope so, Mr. Fix, for it was a heavy robbery."

"A magnificent robbery, consul; fifty-five thousand pounds! We don't often have such windfalls[9]. Burglars are getting to be so contemptible[10] nowadays! A fellow gets hung for a handful of shillings!"

"Mr. Fix," said the consul, "I like your way of talking, and hope you'll succeed; but I fear you will find it far from easy. Don't you see, the description which you have there has a singular resemblance to an honest man?"

"Consul," remarked the detective, dogmatically[11], "great robbers always resemble honest folks. Fellows who have rascally faces have only one course to take, and that is to remain honest; otherwise they would be arrested off-hand. The artistic thing is, to unmask honest countenances; it's no light task, I admit, but a real art."[12]

Mr. Fix evidently was not wanting in a tinge of self-conceit.

Little by little the scene on the quay became more animated; sailors of various nations, merchants, ship-brokers, porters, fellahs, bustled to and fro as if the steamer were immediately expected. The weather was clear, and slightly chilly. The minarets of the town loomed above the houses in the pale rays of the sun. A jetty pier, some two

---

[8] Mr. Fix comes across as an impatient, arrogant and conceited man.
[9] 'Windfall' means an expected or sudden advantage.
[10] 'Contemptible' refers to a person deserving hate and detest.
[11] 'Dogmatic' means characterised by very strong opinions.
[12] Mr. Fix boasts of his skill at picking out cheats among honest men, based solely on their facial expressions.

thousand yards along, extended into the roadstead. A number of fishing-smacks and coasting boats, some retaining the fantastic fashion of ancient galleys, were discernible on the Red Sea.

As he passed among the busy crowd, Fix, according to habit, scrutinised the passers-by with a keen, rapid glance.

It was now half-past ten.

"The steamer doesn't come!" he exclaimed, as the port clock struck.

"She can't be far off now," returned his companion.

"How long will she stop at Suez?"

"Four hours; long enough to get in her coal. It is thirteen hundred and ten miles from Suez to Aden, at the other end of the Red Sea, and she has to take in a fresh coal supply."

"And does she go from Suez directly to Bombay?"

"Without putting in anywhere."

"Good!" said Fix. "If the robber is on board he will no doubt get off at Suez, so as to reach the Dutch or French colonies in Asia by some other route. He ought to know that he would not be safe an hour in India, which is English soil.[13]"

"Unless," objected the consul, "he is exceptionally shrewd. An English criminal, you know, is always better concealed in London than anywhere else."

This observation furnished the detective food for thought, and meanwhile the consul went away to his office. Fix, left alone, was more impatient than ever, having a presentiment that the robber was on board the Mongolia. If he had indeed left London intending to reach the New World, he would naturally take the route via India, which was less watched and more difficult to watch than that of the Atlantic. But Fix's reflections were soon interrupted by a succession of sharp whistles, which announced the arrival of the Mongolia. The porters and fellahs rushed down the quay, and a dozen boats pushed off from the shore to go and meet the steamer. Soon her gigantic hull appeared passing along between the banks, and eleven o'clock struck as she anchored in the road. She brought an unusual number of passengers, some of whom remained on deck to scan the picturesque panorama of the town, while the greater part disembarked in the boats, and landed on the quay.

Fix took up a position, and carefully examined each face and figure which made its appearance. Presently one of the passengers, after vigorously pushing his way through the importunate[14] crowd of porters, came up to him and politely asked if he could point out the English consulate, at the same time showing a passport which he wished to have

---

[13] In 1873, when this book was authored, the Indian subcontinent was ruled by the British Crown, and hence considered English soil. The long independence movement finally led to the partition of India (into India and Pakistan), and creation of the Republic of India in 1947.

[14] 'Importunate' means to be persistent in an annoying way.

visaed[15]. Fix instinctively took the passport, and with a rapid glance read the description of its bearer. An involuntary motion of surprise nearly escaped him, for the description in the passport was identical with that of the bank robber which he had received from Scotland Yard.

"Is this your passport?" asked he.

"No, it's my master's."

"And your master is—"

"He stayed on board."

"But he must go to the consul's in person, so as to establish his identity."

"Oh, is that necessary?"

"Quite indispensable[16]."

"And where is the consulate?"

"There, on the corner of the square," said Fix, pointing to a house two hundred steps off.

"I'll go and fetch my master, who won't be much pleased, however, to be disturbed."

The passenger bowed to Fix, and returned to the steamer.

---

[15] 'Visaed' means to be stamped with a visa, which is an official endorsement issued by an authorised official permitting a person to enter or reside in that country.

[16] 'Indispensable' means absolutely necessary or essential.

A Study Guide: Around the World in Eighty Days

Comprehension exercise 6

Q1) Why was Fix particularly anxious about the arrival of the steamer Mongolia?
a) He was expecting a friend on board.
b) He was a passenger on the steamer.
c) He was a detective searching for a criminal.
d) He had business dealings with the Peninsular and Oriental Company.

Q2) What conclusion can be drawn about Fix's attitude towards his task?
a) He was indifferent and lacked dedication.
b) He was relaxed and unconcerned about the outcome.
c) He was impatient and eager for success.
d) He was unsure and hesitant about his abilities.

Q3) How long did the steamer Mongolia stop at Suez?
a) Two hours
b) Three hours
c) Four hours
d) Five hours

Q4) What does the term "importunate" mean as used in the text?
a) Polite and courteous
b) Persistent and insistent
c) Confident and assertive
d) Rude and disrespectful

Q5) What does the word "visaed" imply in the context of the text?
a) Checked for authenticity
b) Rejected for entry
c) Cancelled for travel
d) Modified for identification

Chapter 7

WHICH ONCE MORE DEMONSTRATES THE USELESSNESS OF PASSPORTS AS AIDS TO DETECTIVES

The detective passed down the quay, and rapidly made his way to the consul's office, where he was at once admitted to the presence of that official.

"Consul," said he, without preamble[1], "I have strong reasons for believing that my man is a passenger on the Mongolia." And he narrated what had just passed concerning the passport.

"Well, Mr. Fix," replied the consul, "I shall not be sorry to see the rascal's face; but perhaps he won't come here—that is, if he is the person you suppose him to be. A robber doesn't quite like to leave traces of his flight behind him; and, besides, he is not obliged to have his passport countersigned."

"If he is as shrewd as I think he is, consul, he will come."

"To have his passport visaed?"

"Yes. Passports are only good for annoying honest folks, and aiding in the flight of rogues. I assure you it will be quite the thing for him to do; but I hope you will not visa the passport."

"Why not? If the passport is genuine I have no right to refuse."

"Still, I must keep this man here until I can get a warrant to arrest him from London."

"Ah, that's your look-out. But I cannot—"

The consul did not finish his sentence, for as he spoke a knock was heard at the door, and two strangers entered, one of whom was the servant whom Fix had met on the quay. The other, who was his master, held out his passport with the request that the consul would do him the favour to visa it. The consul took the document and carefully read it, whilst Fix observed, or rather devoured[2], the stranger with his eyes from a corner of the room.

"You are Mr. Phileas Fogg?" said the consul, after reading the passport.

"I am."

---

[1] 'Preamble' means an introduction or an opening statement.
[2] 'Devour' means to consume something completely. Here, the words refer to Mr. Fix staring at Mr. Fogg with great voracity and focus.

"And this man is your servant?"

"He is: a Frenchman, named Passepartout."

"You are from London?"

"Yes."

"And you are going—"

"To Bombay."

"Very good, sir. You know that a visa is useless, and that no passport is required?"

"I know it, sir," replied Phileas Fogg; "but I wish to prove, by your visa, that I came by Suez."

"Very well, sir."

The consul proceeded to sign and date the passport, after which he added his official seal. Mr. Fogg paid the customary fee, coldly bowed, and went out, followed by his servant.

"Well?" queried the detective.

"Well, he looks and acts like a perfectly honest man," replied the consul.

"Possibly; but that is not the question. Do you think, consul, that this phlegmatic[3] gentleman resembles, feature by feature, the robber whose description I have received?"

"I concede[4] that; but then, you know, all descriptions—"

"I'll make certain of it," interrupted Fix. "The servant seems to me less mysterious than the master; besides, he's a Frenchman, and can't help talking. Excuse me for a little while, consul."

Fix started off in search of Passepartout.

Meanwhile Mr. Fogg, after leaving the consulate, repaired to the quay, gave some orders to Passepartout, went off to the Mongolia in a boat, and descended to his cabin. He took up his note-book, which contained the following memoranda:

"Left London, Wednesday, October 2nd, at 8.45 p.m. "Reached Paris, Thursday, October 3rd, at 7.20 a.m. "Left Paris, Thursday, at 8.40 a.m. "Reached Turin by Mont Cenis, Friday, October 4th, at 6.35 a.m. "Left Turin, Friday, at 7.20 a.m. "Arrived at Brindisi, Saturday, October 5th, at 4 p.m. "Sailed on the Mongolia, Saturday, at 5 p.m. "Reached Suez, Wednesday, October 9th, at 11 a.m. "Total of hours spent, 158+; or, in days, six days and a half."

These dates were inscribed in an itinerary divided into columns, indicating the month, the day of the month, and the day for the stipulated and actual arrivals at each principal

---

[3] 'Phlegmatic' means an unemotional and calm disposition.

[4] 'Concede' means to agree to something hesitantly or grudgingly.

point Paris, Brindisi, Suez, Bombay, Calcutta, Singapore, Hong Kong, Yokohama, San Francisco, New York, and London—from the 2nd of October to the 21st of December; and giving a space for setting down the gain made or the loss suffered on arrival at each locality. This methodical record thus contained an account of everything needed, and Mr. Fogg always knew whether he was behind-hand or in advance of his time. On this Friday, October 9th, he noted his arrival at Suez, and observed that he had as yet neither gained nor lost. He sat down quietly to breakfast in his cabin, never once thinking of inspecting the town, being one of those Englishmen who are wont[5] to see foreign countries through the eyes of their domestics.

---

[5] 'Wont' means accustomed to do something.

Comprehension exercise 7

Q1) Why did Fix hope that Phileas Fogg would come to the consulate to have his passport visaed?
a) To avoid leaving traces of his flight behind.
b) To prove that he came by Suez.
c) To seek refuge from the detective.
d) To obtain a false visa for his passport.

Q2) What does the consul's response about Phileas Fogg's honesty imply?
a) The consul is convinced of Fogg's innocence.
b) The consul doubts Fogg's intentions.
c) The consul is indifferent to Fogg's honesty.
d) The consul is certain Fogg is the bank robber.

Q3) What does Mr. Fogg use his notebook for?
a) Sketching portraits of passengers
b) Writing down orders for Passepartout
c) Keeping a record of his journey
d) Drafting letters to the consulate

Q4) What does the word "phlegmatic" mean as used in the text?
a) Impulsive and energetic
b) Calm and composed
c) Sensitive and emotional
d) Aggressive and confrontational

Q5) What does the word "concede" suggest in the context of the text?
a) To accept reluctantly
b) To refuse outrightly
c) To agree wholeheartedly
d) To dispute vigorously

Chapter 8

IN WHICH PASSEPARTOUT TALKS RATHER MORE, PERHAPS, THAN IS PRUDENT

Fix soon rejoined Passepartout, who was lounging and looking about on the quay, as if he did not feel that he, at least, was obliged not to see anything.[1]

"Well, my friend," said the detective, coming up with him, "is your passport visaed?"

"Ah, it's you, is it, monsieur?" responded Passepartout. "Thanks, yes, the passport is all right."

"And you are looking about you?"

"Yes; but we travel so fast that I seem to be journeying in a dream.[2] So this is Suez?"

"Yes."

"In Egypt?"

"Certainly, in Egypt."

"And in Africa?"

"In Africa."

"In Africa!" repeated Passepartout. "Just think, monsieur, I had no idea that we should go farther than Paris; and all that I saw of Paris was between twenty minutes past seven and twenty minutes before nine in the morning, between the Northern and the Lyons stations, through the windows of a car, and in a driving rain! How I regret not having seen once more Pere la Chaise and the circus in the Champs Elysees!"

"You are in a great hurry, then?"

"I am not, but my master is. By the way, I must buy some shoes and shirts. We came away without trunks, only with a carpet-bag."

"I will show you an excellent shop for getting what you want."

"Really, monsieur, you are very kind."

And they walked off together, Passepartout chatting volubly as they went along.

---

[1] Despite Mr. Fogg remaining on board the steamer, Passepartout felt it unnecessary to remain with him and forego the opportunity to enjoy the picturesque sights of the towns and cities they were visiting.

[2] Passepartout suggests that their rapid travel from one city to another is akin to a journey in a dream, where the conventional constraints of time and space do not apply.

"Above all," said he; "don't let me lose the steamer."

"You have plenty of time; it's only twelve o'clock."

Passepartout pulled out his big watch. "Twelve!" he exclaimed; "why, it's only eight minutes before ten."

"Your watch is slow."

"My watch? A family watch, monsieur, which has come down from my great-grandfather! It doesn't vary five minutes in the year. It's a perfect chronometer, look you."

"I see how it is," said Fix. "You have kept London time, which is two hours behind that of Suez. You ought to regulate your watch at noon in each country."[3]

"I regulate my watch? Never!"

"Well, then, it will not agree with the sun."

"So much the worse for the sun, monsieur. The sun will be wrong, then!"[4]

And the worthy fellow returned the watch to its fob with a defiant gesture. After a few minutes silence, Fix resumed: "You left London hastily, then?"

"I rather think so! Last Friday at eight o'clock in the evening, Monsieur Fogg came home from his club, and three-quarters of an hour afterwards we were off."

"But where is your master going?"

"Always straight ahead. He is going round the world."

"Round the world?" cried Fix.

"Yes, and in eighty days! He says it is on a wager; but, between us, I don't believe a word of it. That wouldn't be common sense. There's something else in the wind."

"Ah! Mr. Fogg is a character, is he?"

"I should say he was."

"Is he rich?"

"No doubt, for he is carrying an enormous sum in brand new banknotes with him. And he doesn't spare the money on the way, either: he has offered a large reward to the engineer of the Mongolia if he gets us to Bombay well in advance of time."

---

[3] The detective is referring to the different time zones, and the need to match their watches with the time of the region they are currently in.

As the Earth rotates, different parts of the Earth enter and exit daylight at different times of the day. Scientists have divided the Earth into 24 different time zones so that every area on the planet has its noon (the middle of the day) when the sun is highest. When a person travels from one time zone to another, they are required to set their clocks as per the time of the new zone.

[4] Passepartout may be a very skilled and experienced acrobat, but he is unaware of the basic rule of long-distance travel – adjusting watches to the current time zone.

"And you have known your master a long time?"

"Why, no; I entered his service the very day we left London."

The effect of these replies upon the already suspicious and excited detective may be imagined. The hasty departure from London soon after the robbery; the large sum carried by Mr. Fogg; his eagerness to reach distant countries; the pretext of an eccentric and foolhardy bet—all confirmed Fix in his theory. He continued to pump poor Passepartout, and learned that he really knew little or nothing of his master, who lived a solitary existence in London, was said to be rich, though no one knew whence came his riches, and was mysterious and impenetrable in his affairs and habits. Fix felt sure that Phileas Fogg would not land at Suez, but was really going on to Bombay.

"Is Bombay far from here?" asked Passepartout.

"Pretty far. It is a ten days' voyage by sea."

"And in what country is Bombay?"

"India."

"In Asia?"

"Certainly."

"The deuce! I was going to tell you there's one thing that worries me—my burner!"

"What burner?"

"My gas-burner, which I forgot to turn off, and which is at this moment burning at my expense. I have calculated, monsieur, that I lose two shillings every four and twenty hours, exactly sixpence more than I earn; and you will understand that the longer our journey—"

Did Fix pay any attention to Passepartout's trouble about the gas? It is not probable. He was not listening, but was cogitating[5] a project. Passepartout and he had now reached the shop, where Fix left his companion to make his purchases, after recommending him not to miss the steamer, and hurried back to the consulate. Now that he was fully convinced, Fix had quite recovered his equanimity[6].

"Consul," said he, "I have no longer any doubt. I have spotted my man. He passes himself off as an odd stick who is going round the world in eighty days."

"Then he's a sharp fellow," returned the consul, "and counts on returning to London after putting the police of the two countries off his track."

"We'll see about that," replied Fix.

"But are you not mistaken?"

---

[5] 'Cogitate' means to think or mediate intently.
[6] 'Equanimity' means maintaining calmness and stability, especially in a demanding situation.

"I am not mistaken."

"Why was this robber so anxious to prove, by the visa, that he had passed through Suez?"

"Why? I have no idea; but listen to me."

He reported in a few words the most important parts of his conversation with Passepartout.

"In short," said the consul, "appearances are wholly against this man. And what are you going to do?"

"Send a dispatch to London for a warrant of arrest to be dispatched instantly to Bombay, take passage on board the Mongolia, follow my rogue to India, and there, on English ground, arrest him politely, with my warrant in my hand, and my hand on his shoulder."

Having uttered these words with a cool, careless air, the detective took leave of the consul, and repaired to the telegraph office, whence he sent the dispatch which we have seen to the London police office. A quarter of an hour later found Fix, with a small bag in his hand, proceeding on board the Mongolia; and, ere[7] many moments longer, the noble steamer rode out at full steam upon the waters of the Red Sea.

---

[7] 'Ere' means preceding in time, earlier than.

Comprehension exercise 8

Q1) What does Passepartout's reaction to Fix's question about his passport suggest about him?
a) He is nervous and suspicious.
b) He is oblivious and carefree.
c) He is evasive and deceptive.
d) He is curious and observant.

Q2) Why does Fix become suspicious of Mr. Fogg's intentions?
a) Mr. Fogg carries a large sum of money.
b) Mr. Fogg is always in a hurry.
c) Mr. Fogg enters into eccentric bets.
d) Mr. Fogg lives a solitary life.

Q3) What is Fix's plan after becoming fully convinced of Mr. Fogg's intentions?
a) To arrest Mr. Fogg at the shop.
b) To send a dispatch to London for a warrant of arrest.
c) To follow Mr. Fogg to India and arrest him there.
d) To seek help from the consul in apprehending Mr. Fogg.

Q4) What does the word "equanimity" mean as used in the text?
a) Eagerness and excitement
b) Nervousness and apprehension
c) Calmness and composure
d) Confusion and disarray

Q5) What does the word "cogitating" imply in the context of the text?
a) Reflecting deeply and pondering
b) Rushing and hurrying
c) Speaking confidently and assertively
d) Avoiding and evading

Chapter 9

IN WHICH THE RED SEA AND THE INDIAN OCEAN PROVE PROPITIOUS
TO THE DESIGNS OF PHILEAS FOGG

The distance between Suez and Aden[1] is precisely thirteen hundred and ten miles, and the regulations of the company allow the steamers one hundred and thirty-eight hours in which to traverse it. The Mongolia, thanks to the vigorous exertions of the engineer[2], seemed likely, so rapid was her speed, to reach her destination considerably within that time. The greater part of the passengers from Brindisi were bound for India some for Bombay, others for Calcutta[3] by way of Bombay, the nearest route thither, now that a railway crosses the Indian peninsula. Among the passengers was a number of officials and military officers of various grades, the latter being either attached to the regular British forces or commanding the Sepoy[4] troops, and receiving high salaries ever since the central government has assumed the powers of the East India Company: for the sub-lieutenants get 280 pounds, brigadiers, 2,400 pounds, and generals of divisions, 4,000 pounds. What with the military men, a number of rich young Englishmen on their travels, and the hospitable efforts of the purser, the time passed quickly on the Mongolia. The best of fare was spread upon the cabin tables at breakfast, lunch, dinner, and the eight o'clock supper, and the ladies scrupulously[5] changed their toilets twice a day; and the hours were whirled away, when the sea was tranquil, with music, dancing, and games.

But the Red Sea is full of caprice[6], and often boisterous, like most long and narrow gulfs. When the wind came from the African or Asian coast the Mongolia, with her long hull, rolled fearfully. Then the ladies speedily disappeared below; the pianos were silent; singing and dancing suddenly ceased. Yet the good ship ploughed straight on, unretarded by wind or wave, towards the straits of Bab-el-Mandeb[7]. What was Phileas Fogg doing all this time? It might be thought that, in his anxiety, he would be constantly watching the changes of the wind, the disorderly raging of the billows—every chance, in short, which

---

[1] Aden is a port city in Yemen, which was then governed as part of British India. In 1937, the colony was detached from British India and in 1967 it became the People's Republic of South Yemen.

[2] The engineer worked extra hard to reach the destination on time, probably because of the reward promised to him by Mr. Fogg.

[3] Calcutta, now known as Kolkata, is located on the east bank of the Hooghly River and is the main commercial and cultural centre of Eastern India.

[4] 'A 'sepoy' refers to an Indian soldier who served in the British army during the colonial period.

[5] 'Scrupulous' means having moral integrity or acting in strictness for what is considered right.

[6] 'Caprice' means a sudden change in mood or etiquette.

[7] The Bab-el-Mandeb is a strait that connects the Red Sea to the Gulf of Aden.

might force the Mongolia to slacken her speed, and thus interrupt his journey. But, if he thought of these possibilities, he did not betray the fact by any outward sign.

Always the same impassible member of the Reform Club, whom no incident could surprise, as unvarying as the ship's chronometers[8], and seldom having the curiosity even to go upon the deck, he passed through the memorable scenes of the Red Sea with cold indifference; did not care to recognise the historic towns and villages which, along its borders, raised their picturesque outlines against the sky; and betrayed no fear of the dangers of the Arabic Gulf, which the old historians always spoke of with horror, and upon which the ancient navigators never ventured without propitiating[9] the gods by ample sacrifices. How did this eccentric personage pass his time on the Mongolia? He made his four hearty meals every day, regardless of the most persistent rolling and pitching on the part of the steamer[10]; and he played whist indefatigably[11], for he had found partners as enthusiastic in the game as himself. A tax-collector, on the way to his post at Goa[12]; the Rev. Decimus Smith, returning to his parish at Bombay; and a brigadier-general of the English army, who was about to rejoin his brigade at Benares[13], made up the party, and, with Mr. Fogg, played whist by the hour together in absorbing silence.

As for Passepartout, he, too, had escaped sea-sickness, and took his meals conscientiously[14] in the forward cabin. He rather enjoyed the voyage, for he was well fed and well lodged, took a great interest in the scenes through which they were passing, and consoled himself with the delusion that his master's whim would end at Bombay. He was pleased, on the day after leaving Suez, to find on deck the obliging person with whom he had walked and chatted on the quays.

"If I am not mistaken," said he, approaching this person, with his most amiable smile, "you are the gentleman who so kindly volunteered to guide me at Suez?"

"Ah! I quite recognise you. You are the servant of the strange Englishman—"[15]

"Just so, monsieur—"

"Fix."

"Monsieur Fix," resumed Passepartout, "I'm charmed to find you on board. Where are you bound?"

---

[8] A 'chronometer' is a piece of equipment that measures time very accurately.

[9] 'Propitiate' means to gain goodwill or appease.

[10] Despite being at sea, Mr. Fogg had a hearty appetite and enjoyed his meals, unlike many others who often experience seasickness and must limit their food intake.

[11] 'Indefatigable' means untiring.

[12] Goa is a coastal state in Western India.

[13] *Benares*, or *Benaras*, or Varanasi is the holiest of the Hindu sacred cities on the bank of the River Ganges in North India.

[14] 'Conscientious' means careful and meticulous.

[15] Fix pretends to have come across Passepartout by chance and did not give any hint of him having special interest in him and his master.

"Like you, to Bombay."

"That's capital! Have you made this trip before?"

"Several times. I am one of the agents of the Peninsular Company."

"Then you know India?"

"Why yes," replied Fix, who spoke cautiously.

"A curious place, this India?"

"Oh, very curious. Mosques, minarets, temples, fakirs, pagodas, tigers, snakes, elephants! I hope you will have ample time to see the sights."

"I hope so, Monsieur Fix. You see, a man of sound sense ought not to spend his life jumping from a steamer upon a railway train, and from a railway train upon a steamer again, pretending to make the tour of the world in eighty days! No; all these gymnastics, you may be sure, will cease at Bombay."

"And Mr. Fogg is getting on well?" asked Fix, in the most natural tone in the world.

"Quite well, and I too. I eat like a famished ogre[16]; it's the sea air."

"But I never see your master on deck."

"Never; he hasn't the least curiosity."

"Do you know, Mr. Passepartout, that this pretended tour in eighty days may conceal some secret errand—perhaps a diplomatic mission?"

"Faith, Monsieur Fix, I assure you I know nothing about it, nor would I give half a crown to find out."[17]

After this meeting, Passepartout and Fix got into the habit of chatting together, the latter making it a point to gain the worthy man's confidence. He frequently offered him a glass of whiskey or pale ale in the steamer bar-room, which Passepartout never failed to accept with graceful alacrity[18], mentally pronouncing Fix the best of good fellows.

Meanwhile the Mongolia was pushing forward rapidly; on the 13th, Mocha[19], surrounded by its ruined walls whereon date-trees were growing, was sighted, and on the mountains beyond were espied vast coffee-fields. Passepartout was ravished[20] to behold this celebrated place, and thought that, with its circular walls and dismantled fort, it looked like an immense coffee-cup and saucer. The following night they passed through the Strait of Bab-el-Mandeb, which means in Arabic The Bridge of Tears, and the next day

---

[16] An 'ogre' is a giant in fairy tales that feeds on humans. Here, the word refers to a monster that eats a lot.

[17] Passepartout reassures Mr. Fix that he is not aware of his master's plan, nor is he interested in knowing them.

[18] 'Alacrity' means cheerful readiness.

[19] Mocha is a port city on the Red Sea coast of Yemen and is famous for its coffee.

[20] 'Ravish' means to overcome by emotion.

they put in at Steamer Point, north-west of Aden harbour, to take in coal. This matter of fuelling steamers is a serious one at such distances from the coal-mines; it costs the Peninsular Company some eight hundred thousand pounds a year. In these distant seas, coal is worth three or four pounds sterling a ton.

The Mongolia had still sixteen hundred and fifty miles to traverse before reaching Bombay, and was obliged to remain four hours at Steamer Point to coal up. But this delay, as it was foreseen, did not affect Phileas Fogg's programme; besides, the Mongolia, instead of reaching Aden on the morning of the 15th, when she was due, arrived there on the evening of the 14th, a gain of fifteen hours.

Mr. Fogg and his servant went ashore at Aden to have the passport again visaed; Fix, unobserved, followed them. The visa procured, Mr. Fogg returned on board to resume his former habits[21]; while Passepartout, according to custom, sauntered about among the mixed population of Somalis, Banyans, Parsees, Jews, Arabs, and Europeans who comprise the twenty-five thousand inhabitants of Aden. He gazed with wonder upon the fortifications which make this place the Gibraltar of the Indian Ocean, and the vast cisterns where the English engineers were still at work, two thousand years after the engineers of Solomon.

"Very curious, very curious," said Passepartout to himself, on returning to the steamer. "I see that it is by no means useless to travel, if a man wants to see something new." At six p.m. the Mongolia slowly moved out of the roadstead, and was soon once more on the Indian Ocean. She had a hundred and sixty-eight hours in which to reach Bombay, and the sea was favourable, the wind being in the north-west, and all sails aiding the engine. The steamer rolled but little, the ladies, in fresh toilets, reappeared on deck, and the singing and dancing were resumed. The trip was being accomplished most successfully, and Passepartout was enchanted with the congenial companion which chance had secured him in the person of the delightful Fix. On Sunday, October 20th, towards noon, they came in sight of the Indian coast: two hours later the pilot came on board. A range of hills lay against the sky in the horizon, and soon the rows of palms which adorn Bombay came distinctly into view. The steamer entered the road formed by the islands in the bay, and at half-past four she hauled up at the quays of Bombay.

Phileas Fogg was in the act of finishing the thirty-third rubber of the voyage, and his partner and himself having, by a bold stroke, captured all thirteen of the tricks, concluded this fine campaign with a brilliant victory.

The Mongolia was due at Bombay on the 22nd; she arrived on the 20th. This was a gain to Phileas Fogg of two days since his departure from London, and he calmly entered the fact in the itinerary, in the column of gains.

---

[21] Mr. Fogg's former habits were- eating well and playing cards.

A Study Guide: Around the World in Eighty Days

Comprehension exercise 8

Q1) Why did the passengers on the Mongolia disappear below deck when the Red Sea became boisterous?
a) They were afraid of pirates.
b) They wanted to avoid sea-sickness.
c) They were participating in a safety drill.
d) They were seeking shelter from the wind and waves.

Q2) Why did Passepartout enjoy the voyage despite the rough seas?
a) He liked the challenge of the rough weather.
b) He appreciated the luxurious accommodations.
c) He was fascinated by the sights along the way.
d) He enjoyed the company of his fellow passengers.

Q3) How did Mr. Fogg and his servant spend their time during the voyage?
a) They socialized with other passengers.
b) They explored the historic towns and villages along the Red Sea.
c) They played whist with other passengers.
d) They attended music and dance performances on deck.

Q4) What does the word "alacrity" mean as used in the text?
a) Laziness and reluctance
b) Eagerness and promptness
c) Disinterest and apathy
d) Anxiety and apprehension

Q5) What does the word "ravished" imply in the context of the text?
a) Excited and delighted
b) Annoyed and frustrated
c) Confused and disoriented
d) Disappointed and discouraged

Chapter 10

IN WHICH PASSEPARTOUT IS ONLY TOO GLAD TO GET OFF WITH THE LOSS OF HIS SHOES

Everybody knows that the great reversed triangle of land, with its base in the north and its apex in the south, which is called India, embraces fourteen hundred thousand square miles, upon which is spread unequally a population of one hundred and eighty millions of souls.[1] The British Crown exercises a real and despotic[2] dominion over the larger portion of this vast country, and has a governor-general stationed at Calcutta, governors at Madras, Bombay, and in Bengal, and a lieutenant-governor at Agra.

But British India, properly so called, only embraces seven hundred thousand square miles, and a population of from one hundred to one hundred and ten millions of inhabitants. A considerable portion of India is still free from British authority; and there are certain ferocious rajahs in the interior who are absolutely independent. The celebrated East India Company was all-powerful from 1756, when the English first gained a foothold on the spot where now stands the city of Madras, down to the time of the great Sepoy insurrection[3]. It gradually annexed province after province, purchasing them of the native chiefs, whom it seldom paid, and appointed the governor-general and his subordinates, civil and military. But the East India Company has now passed away, leaving the British possessions in India directly under the control of the Crown. The aspect of the country, as well as the manners and distinctions of race, is daily changing.[4]

Formerly one was obliged to travel in India by the old cumbrous[5] methods of going on foot or on horseback, in palanquins or unwieldy coaches; now fast steamboats ply on the Indus and the Ganges, and a great railway, with branch lines joining the main line at many points on its route, traverses the peninsula from Bombay to Calcutta in three days.

---

[1] The current (2024) population of India is just over 1.4 billion and it is the second most populous country in the world. The country is now spread over 1.2 million sq miles.

[2] 'Despotic' means having unlimited power over other people, and often using it unfairly and cruelly.

[3] '*Sepoy* insurrection' refers to the great Indian Rebellion of 1857-58, also known as India's First War of Independence.

[4] During British rule, India was made up of British India (areas directly under the rule of the British), and the Princely States (areas under local Indian princes and kings). The East India Company arrived in India in 1612 and administered the country until 1858. Following the First War of Independence in 1858, control of India was transferred from the Company to the British Crown, which maintained governance until 1947, when India achieved independence.

[5] 'Cumbrous' means heavy and slow.

This railway does not run in a direct line across India. The distance between Bombay and Calcutta, as the bird flies, is only from one thousand to eleven hundred miles; but the deflections of the road increase this distance by more than a third.

The general route of the Great Indian Peninsula Railway is as follows: Leaving Bombay, it passes through Salcette[6], crossing to the continent opposite Tannah[7], goes over the chain of the Western Ghauts, runs thence north-east as far as Burhampoor, skirts the nearly independent territory of Bundelcund[8], ascends to Allahabad, turns thence eastwardly, meeting the Ganges at Benares, then departs from the river a little, and, descending south-eastward by Burdivan and the French town of Chandernagor, has its terminus at Calcutta.

The passengers of the Mongolia went ashore at half-past four p.m.; at exactly eight the train would start for Calcutta.

Mr. Fogg, after bidding good-bye to his whist partners, left the steamer, gave his servant several errands to do, urged it upon him to be at the station promptly at eight, and, with his regular step, which beat to the second, like an astronomical clock, directed his steps to the passport office. As for the wonders of Bombay—its famous city hall, its splendid library, its forts and docks, its bazaars, mosques, synagogues, its Armenian churches, and the noble pagoda on Malabar Hill, with its two polygonal towers—he cared not a straw to see them. He would not deign to examine even the masterpieces of Elephanta[9], or the mysterious hypogea[10], concealed south-east from the docks, or those fine remains of Buddhist architecture, the Kanherian grottoes of the island of Salcette.

Having transacted his business at the passport office, Phileas Fogg repaired quietly to the railway station, where he ordered dinner. Among the dishes served up to him, the landlord especially recommended a certain giblet of "native rabbit," on which he prided himself.

Mr. Fogg accordingly tasted the dish, but, despite its spiced sauce, found it far from palatable. He rang for the landlord, and, on his appearance, said, fixing his clear eyes upon him, "Is this rabbit, sir?"

"Yes, my lord," the rogue boldly replied, "rabbit from the jungles."

"And this rabbit did not mew when he was killed?"

"Mew, my lord! What, a rabbit mew! I swear to you—"

"Be so good, landlord, as not to swear, but remember this: cats were formerly considered, in India, as sacred animals. That was a good time."

---

[6] Salsette Island is part of the state of Maharashtra, on India's west coast.
[7] Present day Thane, a city in Maharashtra state of India.
[8] Present day Bundelkhand, a region of Central India.
[9] Elephanta Caves, a UNESCO World Heritage Site, is a collection of temples dedicated to Lord Shiva.
[10] A 'hypogeal' is an underground chamber.

"For the cats, my lord?"

"Perhaps for the travellers as well!"

After which Mr. Fogg quietly continued his dinner. Fix had gone on shore shortly after Mr. Fogg, and his first destination was the headquarters of the Bombay police. He made himself known as a London detective, told his business at Bombay, and the position of affairs relative to the supposed robber, and nervously asked if a warrant had arrived from London. It had not reached the office; indeed, there had not yet been time for it to arrive. Fix was sorely disappointed, and tried to obtain an order of arrest from the director of the Bombay police. This the director refused, as the matter concerned the London office, which alone could legally deliver the warrant. Fix did not insist, and was fain[11] to resign himself to await the arrival of the important document; but he was determined not to lose sight of the mysterious rogue as long as he stayed in Bombay. He did not doubt for a moment, any more than Passepartout, that Phileas Fogg would remain there, at least until it was time for the warrant to arrive.

Passepartout, however, had no sooner heard his master's orders on leaving the Mongolia than he saw at once that they were to leave Bombay as they had done Suez and Paris, and that the journey would be extended at least as far as Calcutta, and perhaps beyond that place. He began to ask himself if this bet that Mr. Fogg talked about was not really in good earnest, and whether his fate was not in truth forcing him, despite his love of repose, around the world in eighty days![12]

Having purchased the usual quota of shirts and shoes, he took a leisurely promenade about the streets, where crowds of people of many nationalities—Europeans, Persians with pointed caps, Banyas[13] with round turbans, Sindes[14] with square bonnets, Parsees[15] with black mitres, and long-robed Armenians—were collected. It happened to be the day of a Parsee festival. These descendants of the sect of Zoroaster—the most thrifty, civilised, intelligent, and austere of the East Indians, among whom are counted the richest native merchants of Bombay—were celebrating a sort of religious carnival, with processions and shows, in the midst of which Indian dancing-girls, clothed in rose-coloured gauze, looped up with gold and silver, danced airily, but with perfect modesty, to the sound of viols and the clanging of tambourines. It is needless to say that Passepartout watched these curious ceremonies with staring eyes and gaping mouth, and that his countenance was that of the greenest booby[16] imaginable.

Unhappily for his master, as well as himself, his curiosity drew him unconsciously farther off than he intended to go. At last, having seen the Parsee carnival wind away in the distance, he was turning his steps towards the station, when he happened to espy the

---

[11] 'Fain' means to be happy or glad.
[12] Passepartout believed that it was Mr. Fogg's destiny to go around the world in eighty days, and that the bet was just a medium.
[13] Banya, or *Bania,* is a community of merchants, money lenders and bankers.
[14] Sindes, or *Sindhis,* are natives of Sindh province.
[15] Parsees, or *Parsis*, are Persian migrants of the Zoroastrian community.
[16] 'Booby' refers to a silly person.

splendid pagoda on Malabar Hill, and was seized with an irresistible desire to see its interior. He was quite ignorant that it is forbidden to Christians to enter certain Indian temples, and that even the faithful must not go in without first leaving their shoes outside the door. It may be said here that the wise policy of the British Government severely punishes a disregard of the practices of the native religions.

Passepartout, however, thinking no harm, went in like a simple tourist, and was soon lost in admiration of the splendid Brahmin ornamentation which everywhere met his eyes, when of a sudden he found himself sprawling on the sacred flagging. He looked up to behold three enraged priests, who forthwith fell upon him; tore off his shoes, and began to beat him with loud, savage exclamations. The agile Frenchman was soon upon his feet again, and lost no time in knocking down two of his long-gowned adversaries with his fists and a vigorous application of his toes; then, rushing out of the pagoda as fast as his legs could carry him, he soon escaped the third priest by mingling with the crowd in the streets.

At five minutes before eight, Passepartout, hatless, shoeless, and having in the squabble lost his package of shirts and shoes, rushed breathlessly into the station.

Fix, who had followed Mr. Fogg to the station, and saw that he was really going to leave Bombay, was there, upon the platform. He had resolved to follow the supposed robber to Calcutta, and farther, if necessary. Passepartout did not observe the detective, who stood in an obscure corner; but Fix heard him relate his adventures in a few words to Mr. Fogg.

"I hope that this will not happen again," said Phileas Fogg coldly, as he got into the train. Poor Passepartout, quite crestfallen[17], followed his master without a word. Fix was on the point of entering another carriage, when an idea struck him which induced him to alter his plan.

"No, I'll stay," muttered he. "An offence has been committed on Indian soil. I've got my man."

Just then the locomotive gave a sharp screech, and the train passed out into the darkness of the night.

---

[17] 'Crestfallen' means sad and disappointed.

Comprehension exercise 10

Q1) What is the British Crown's relationship with India, according to the text?
a) It exercises control over the entire country.
b) It only governs British India, leaving the rest to local rulers.
c) It has no authority over India.
d) It shares power with the East India Company.

Q2) How did Mr. Fogg react when he found out the "native rabbit" he was served wasn't actually rabbit?
a) He became angry and demanded a refund.
b) He ignored it and continued eating.
c) He left the restaurant immediately.
d) He scolded the landlord for trying to deceive him.

Q3) Why did Passepartout end up rushing breathlessly into the station?
a) He was late for the train departure.
b) He was being chased by angry priests.
c) He had lost his package of shirts and shoes.
d) He wanted to catch up with Mr. Fogg.

Q4) What does the word "despotic" mean in the context of the text?
a) Authoritative and commanding
b) Benevolent and compassionate
c) Corrupt and oppressive
d) Humble and modest

Q5) What does the word "crestfallen" imply about Passepartout's demeanour?
a) Confident and triumphant
b) Annoyed and frustrated
c) Depressed and disappointed
d) Elated and jubilant

Chapter 11

IN WHICH PHILEAS FOGG SECURES A CURIOUS MEANS OF CONVEYANCE AT A FABULOUS PRICE

The train had started punctually. Among the passengers were a number of officers, Government officials, and opium and indigo merchants, whose business called them to the eastern coast. Passepartout rode in the same carriage with his master, and a third passenger occupied a seat opposite to them. This was Sir Francis Cromarty, one of Mr. Fogg's whist partners on the Mongolia, now on his way to join his corps at Benares. Sir Francis was a tall, fair man of fifty, who had greatly distinguished himself in the last Sepoy revolt. He made India his home, only paying brief visits to England at rare intervals; and was almost as familiar as a native with the customs, history, and character of India and its people. But Phileas Fogg, who was not travelling, but only describing a circumference, took no pains to inquire into these subjects; he was a solid body, traversing an orbit around the terrestrial globe, according to the laws of rational mechanics.[1] He was at this moment calculating in his mind the number of hours spent since his departure from London, and, had it been in his nature to make a useless demonstration, would have rubbed his hands for satisfaction. Sir Francis Cromarty had observed the oddity of his travelling companion—although the only opportunity he had for studying him had been while he was dealing the cards, and between two rubbers—and questioned himself whether a human heart really beat beneath this cold exterior, and whether Phileas Fogg had any sense of the beauties of nature. The brigadier-general was free to mentally confess that, of all the eccentric persons he had ever met, none was comparable to this product of the exact sciences[2].

Phileas Fogg had not concealed from Sir Francis his design of going round the world, nor the circumstances under which he set out; and the general only saw in the wager a useless eccentricity and a lack of sound common sense. In the way this strange gentleman was going on, he would leave the world without having done any good to himself or anybody else.

An hour after leaving Bombay the train had passed the viaducts and the Island of Salcette, and had got into the open country. At Callyan[3] they reached the junction of the

---

[1] Mr. Fogg showed no inclination to explore the local culture or engage with Mr. Cromarty's knowledge about the people. His primary focus was on quickly travelling from one destination to the next, without indulging in the enriching experiences that travel offers.

[2] Mr Cromarty makes a mental note about Mr. Fogg as being an eccentric for whom everything should be exact and precisely measured.

[3] Present day Kalyan, a city in Maharashtra.

branch line which descends towards south-eastern India by Kandallah[4] and Pounah[5]; and, passing Pauwell, they entered the defiles of the mountains, with their basalt bases, and their summits crowned with thick and verdant forests. Phileas Fogg and Sir Francis Cromarty exchanged a few words from time to time, and now Sir Francis, reviving the conversation, observed, "Some years ago, Mr. Fogg, you would have met with a delay at this point which would probably have lost you your wager."

"How so, Sir Francis?"

"Because the railway stopped at the base of these mountains, which the passengers were obliged to cross in palanquins[6] or on ponies to Kandallah, on the other side."

"Such a delay would not have deranged my plans in the least," said Mr. Fogg. "I have constantly foreseen the likelihood of certain obstacles."

"But, Mr. Fogg," pursued Sir Francis, "you run the risk of having some difficulty about this worthy fellow's adventure at the pagoda." Passepartout, his feet comfortably wrapped in his travelling-blanket, was sound asleep and did not dream that anybody was talking about him. "The Government is very severe upon that kind of offence. It takes particular care that the religious customs of the Indians should be respected, and if your servant were caught—"

"Very well, Sir Francis," replied Mr. Fogg; "if he had been caught he would have been condemned and punished, and then would have quietly returned to Europe. I don't see how this affair could have delayed his master."

The conversation fell again. During the night the train left the mountains behind, and passed Nassik, and the next day proceeded over the flat, well-cultivated country of the Khandeish, with its straggling villages, above which rose the minarets of the pagodas. This fertile territory is watered by numerous small rivers and limpid streams, mostly tributaries of the Godavery.

Passepartout, on waking and looking out, could not realise that he was actually crossing India in a railway train. The locomotive, guided by an English engineer and fed with English coal, threw out its smoke upon cotton, coffee, nutmeg, clove, and pepper plantations, while the steam curled in spirals around groups of palm-trees, in the midst of which were seen picturesque bungalows, viharis (sort of abandoned monasteries), and marvellous temples enriched by the exhaustless ornamentation of Indian architecture. Then they came upon vast tracts extending to the horizon, with jungles inhabited by snakes and tigers, which fled at the noise of the train; succeeded by forests penetrated by the railway, and still haunted by elephants which, with pensive eyes, gazed at the train as it passed. The travellers crossed, beyond Milligaum, the fatal country so often stained

---

[4] Present day Khandala, a hill station in the Western Ghats in Maharashtra.
[5] Present day Pune, a city in Maharashtra.
[6] A 'palanquin' is a structure used to carry one person on the shoulders of four bearers.

with blood by the sectaries of the goddess Kali[7]. Not far off rose Ellora[8], with its graceful pagodas, and the famous Aurungabad, capital of the ferocious Aureng-Zeb, now the chief town of one of the detached provinces of the kingdom of the Nizam. It was thereabouts that Feringhea, the Thuggee[9] chief, king of the stranglers, held his sway. These ruffians, united by a secret bond, strangled victims of every age in honour of the goddess Death, without ever shedding blood; there was a period when this part of the country could scarcely be travelled over without corpses being found in every direction. The English Government has succeeded in greatly diminishing these murders, though the Thuggees still exist, and pursue the exercise of their horrible rites.

At half-past twelve the train stopped at Burhampoor[10] where Passepartout was able to purchase some Indian slippers, ornamented with false pearls, in which, with evident vanity, he proceeded to encase his feet. The travellers made a hasty breakfast and started off for Assurghur, after skirting for a little the banks of the small river Tapty, which empties into the Gulf of Cambray, near Surat.

Passepartout was now plunged into absorbing reverie[11]. Up to his arrival at Bombay, he had entertained hopes that their journey would end there; but, now that they were plainly whirling across India at full speed, a sudden change had come over the spirit of his dreams. His old vagabond nature returned to him; the fantastic ideas of his youth once more took possession of him. He came to regard his master's project as intended in good earnest, believed in the reality of the bet, and therefore in the tour of the world and the necessity of making it without fail within the designated period. Already he began to worry about possible delays, and accidents which might happen on the way. He recognised himself as being personally interested in the wager, and trembled at the thought that he might have been the means of losing it by his unpardonable folly of the night before[12]. Being much less cool-headed than Mr. Fogg, he was much more restless, counting and recounting the days passed over, uttering maledictions[13] when the train stopped, and accusing it of sluggishness, and mentally blaming Mr. Fogg for not having bribed the engineer. The worthy fellow was ignorant that, while it was possible by such means to hasten the rate of a steamer, it could not be done on the railway.

The train entered the defiles of the Sutpour Mountains, which separate the Khandeish from Bundelcund[14], towards evening. The next day Sir Francis Cromarty asked Passepartout what time it was; to which, on consulting his watch, he replied that it was

---

[7] *Kali* is the Hindu goddess of destruction and creative powers. She is depicted as black-skinned, red-eyed, blood-stained and wearing a necklace of skulls.

[8] Ellora, a UNESCO World Heritage Site, is a complex of rock cut temple caves.

[9] 'Thugs' are organised criminal gangs, who deceive and murder the travellers for their money and valuables. The Thug cult was very prominent in British India.

[10] Burhampoor, present day Berhampur, is a historical city in Madhya Pradesh state of India.

[11] 'Reverie' is a state of day dreaming.

[12] The folly being referred to is Passepartout entering the pagoda on Malabar Hill while wearing his shoes.

[13] 'Maledictions' are curses or damning words.

[14] Present day Bundelkhand, a historical region in northern Madhya Pradesh.

three in the morning. This famous timepiece, always regulated on the Greenwich meridian, which was now some seventy-seven degrees westward, was at least four hours slow. Sir Francis corrected Passepartout's time, whereupon the latter made the same remark that he had done to Fix; and upon the general insisting that the watch should be regulated in each new meridian, since he was constantly going eastward, that is in the face of the sun, and therefore the days were shorter by four minutes for each degree gone over, Passepartout obstinately refused to alter his watch, which he kept at London time. It was an innocent delusion which could harm no one. [15]

The train stopped, at eight o'clock, in the midst of a glade some fifteen miles beyond Rothal, where there were several bungalows, and workmen's cabins. The conductor, passing along the carriages, shouted, "Passengers will get out here!"

Phileas Fogg looked at Sir Francis Cromarty for an explanation; but the general could not tell what meant a halt in the midst of this forest of dates and acacias.

Passepartout, not less surprised, rushed out and speedily returned, crying: "Monsieur, no more railway!"

"What do you mean?" asked Sir Francis.

"I mean to say that the train isn't going on."

The general at once stepped out, while Phileas Fogg calmly followed him, and they proceeded together to the conductor.

"Where are we?" asked Sir Francis.

"At the hamlet of Kholby."

"Do we stop here?"

"Certainly. The railway isn't finished."

"What! not finished?"

"No. There's still a matter of fifty miles to be laid from here to Allahabad, where the line begins again."

"But the papers announced the opening of the railway throughout."

"What would you have, officer? The papers were mistaken."

"Yet you sell tickets from Bombay to Calcutta," retorted Sir Francis, who was growing warm.

"No doubt," replied the conductor; "but the passengers know that they must provide means of transportation for themselves from Kholby to Allahabad."

---

[15] As they travel, Mr. Fogg and Passepartout move through different time zones; however, as Passepartout is unaware of the concept of 'time zones', he refuses to change the time shown on his watch and continues to refer to British time even while in India.

Sir Francis was furious. Passepartout would willingly have knocked the conductor down, and did not dare to look at his master.

"Sir Francis," said Mr. Fogg quietly, "we will, if you please, look about for some means of conveyance to Allahabad."

"Mr. Fogg, this is a delay greatly to your disadvantage."

"No, Sir Francis; it was foreseen."

"What! You knew that the way—"

"Not at all; but I knew that some obstacle or other would sooner or later arise on my route. Nothing, therefore, is lost. I have two days, which I have already gained[16], to sacrifice. A steamer leaves Calcutta for Hong Kong at noon, on the 25th. This is the 22nd, and we shall reach Calcutta in time."

There was nothing to say to so confident a response.

It was but too true that the railway came to a termination at this point. The papers were like some watches, which have a way of getting too fast, and had been premature in their announcement of the completion of the line. The greater part of the travellers were aware of this interruption, and, leaving the train, they began to engage such vehicles as the village could provide four-wheeled palkigharis[17], waggons[18] drawn by zebus, carriages that looked like perambulating pagodas, palanquins, ponies, and what not.

Mr. Fogg and Sir Francis Cromarty, after searching the village from end to end, came back without having found anything.

"I shall go afoot," said Phileas Fogg.

Passepartout, who had now rejoined his master, made a wry grimace, as he thought of his magnificent, but too frail Indian shoes. Happily he too had been looking about him, and, after a moment's hesitation, said, "Monsieur, I think I have found a means of conveyance."

"What?"

"An elephant! An elephant that belongs to an Indian who lives but a hundred steps from here."

"Let's go and see the elephant," replied Mr. Fogg.

They soon reached a small hut, near which, enclosed within some high palings, was the animal in question. An Indian came out of the hut, and, at their request, conducted them within the enclosure. The elephant, which its owner had reared, not for a beast of

---

[16] These are the two days they gained when they reached Bombay two days earlier than scheduled on Mongolia.

[17] 'Palkigharis' are a type of sedan chair.

[18] A 'waggon' is a four-wheeled vehicle pulled by humped cattle.

burden,[19] but for warlike purposes, was half domesticated. The Indian had begun already, by often irritating him, and feeding him every three months on sugar and butter, to impart to him a ferocity not in his nature, this method being often employed by those who train the Indian elephants for battle. Happily, however, for Mr. Fogg, the animal's instruction in this direction had not gone far, and the elephant still preserved his natural gentleness. Kiouni—this was the name of the beast—could doubtless travel rapidly for a long time, and, in default of any other means of conveyance, Mr. Fogg resolved to hire him. But elephants are far from cheap in India, where they are becoming scarce, the males, which alone are suitable for circus shows, are much sought, especially as but few of them are domesticated. When therefore Mr. Fogg proposed to the Indian to hire Kiouni, he refused point-blank. Mr. Fogg persisted, offering the excessive sum of ten pounds an hour for the loan of the beast to Allahabad. Refused. Twenty pounds? Refused also. Forty pounds? Still refused. Passepartout jumped at each advance; but the Indian declined to be tempted. Yet the offer was an alluring one, for, supposing it took the elephant fifteen hours to reach Allahabad, his owner would receive no less than six hundred pounds sterling.

Phileas Fogg, without getting in the least flurried, then proposed to purchase the animal outright, and at first offered a thousand pounds for him. The Indian, perhaps thinking he was going to make a great bargain, still refused.

Sir Francis Cromarty took Mr. Fogg aside, and begged him to reflect before he went any further; to which that gentleman replied that he was not in the habit of acting rashly, that a bet of twenty thousand pounds was at stake, that the elephant was absolutely necessary to him, and that he would secure him if he had to pay twenty times his value. Returning to the Indian, whose small, sharp eyes, glistening with avarice[20], betrayed that with him it was only a question of how great a price he could obtain. Mr. Fogg offered first twelve hundred, then fifteen hundred, eighteen hundred, two thousand pounds. Passepartout, usually so rubicund[21], was fairly white with suspense.

At two thousand pounds the Indian yielded.

"What a price, good heavens!" cried Passepartout, "for an elephant."

It only remained now to find a guide, which was comparatively easy. A young Parsee, with an intelligent face, offered his services, which Mr. Fogg accepted, promising so generous a reward as to materially stimulate his zeal. The elephant was led out and equipped. The Parsee, who was an accomplished elephant driver, covered his back with a sort of saddle-cloth, and attached to each of his flanks some curiously uncomfortable howdahs[22]. Phileas Fogg paid the Indian with some banknotes which he extracted from the famous carpet-bag, a proceeding that seemed to deprive poor Passepartout of his vitals. Then he offered to carry Sir Francis to Allahabad, which the brigadier gratefully accepted, as one traveller the more would not be likely to fatigue the gigantic beast.

---

[19] A beast of burden is an animal that is used for carrying heavy loads.
[20] 'Avarice' is extreme greed for wealth.
[21] 'Rubicund' means red coloured complexion, mostly associated with outdoor activities.
[22] A 'howdah' is a seat with a canopy and railing that is secured to the back of an elephant.

Provisions were purchased at Kholby, and, while Sir Francis and Mr. Fogg took the howdahs on either side, Passepartout got astride[23] the saddle-cloth between them. The Parsee perched himself on the elephant's neck, and at nine o'clock they set out from the village, the animal marching off through the dense forest of palms by the shortest cut.

---

[23] 'Astride' means to sit across with a leg on each side.

Comprehension exercise 11

Q1) Who was the third passenger in the carriage with Mr. Fogg and Passepartout?
a) A government official
b) An opium merchant
c) An officer
d) Sir Francis Cromarty

Q2) Why was Passepartout particularly worried about possible delays and accidents during the journey?
a) He feared for Mr. Fogg's safety.
b) He was concerned about losing the bet.
c) He was anxious about facing difficulties in unfamiliar territories.
d) He was worried about the condition of the railway tracks.

Q3) Why did the train unexpectedly stop at Kholby?
a) The locomotive malfunctioned.
b) The conductor announced the end of the railway line.
c) There was a problem with the railway tracks.
d) The passengers needed to change trains.

Q4) What does the word "obstinately" mean in the context of the text?
a) Openly and honestly
b) Reluctantly and grudgingly
c) Stubbornly and inflexibly
d) Humbly and modestly

Q5) What does the phrase "deprive poor Passepartout of his vitals" imply about Passepartout's reaction?
a) He felt physically ill.
b) He was angry and frustrated.
c) He was extremely nervous and anxious.
d) He was relieved and relaxed.

Chapter 12

IN WHICH PHILEAS FOGG AND HIS COMPANIONS VENTURE
ACROSS THE INDIAN FORESTS, AND WHAT ENSUED

In order to shorten the journey, the guide passed to the left of the line where the railway was still in process of being built. This line, owing to the capricious[1] turnings of the Vindhia[2] Mountains, did not pursue a straight course. The Parsee, who was quite familiar with the roads and paths in the district, declared that they would gain twenty miles by striking directly through the forest.

Phileas Fogg and Sir Francis Cromarty, plunged to the neck in the peculiar howdahs provided for them, were horribly jostled by the swift trotting of the elephant, spurred on as he was by the skilful Parsee; but they endured the discomfort with true British phlegm[3], talking little, and scarcely able to catch a glimpse of each other. As for Passepartout, who was mounted on the beast's back, and received the direct force of each concussion as he trod along, he was very careful, in accordance with his master's advice, to keep his tongue from between his teeth, as it would otherwise have been bitten off short. The worthy fellow bounced from the elephant's neck to his rump, and vaulted like a clown on a spring-board; yet he laughed in the midst of his bouncing, and from time to time took a piece of sugar out of his pocket, and inserted it in Kiouni's trunk, who received it without in the least slackening his regular trot.

After two hours the guide stopped the elephant, and gave him an hour for rest, during which Kiouni, after quenching his thirst at a neighbouring spring, set to devouring the branches and shrubs round about him. Neither Sir Francis nor Mr. Fogg regretted the delay, and both descended with a feeling of relief. "Why, he's made of iron!" exclaimed the general, gazing admiringly on Kiouni.

"Of forged iron," replied Passepartout, as he set about preparing a hasty breakfast.

At noon the Parsee gave the signal of departure. The country soon presented a very savage aspect. Copses of dates and dwarf-palms succeeded the dense forests; then vast, dry plains, dotted with scanty shrubs, and sown with great blocks of syenite[4]. All this portion of Bundelcund, which is little frequented by travellers, is inhabited by a fanatical population, hardened in the most horrible practices of the Hindoo faith. The English have not been able to secure complete dominion over this territory, which is subjected to the

---

[1] 'Capricious' means unpredictable or unaccountable.
[2] Present day *Vindhya* is a discontinuous range of mountain ridges.
[3] 'Phlegm' is the ability to stay calm and not get emotional even in dangerous or difficult times.
[4] 'Syenite' is a coarsely grained igneous rock.

influence of rajahs, whom it is almost impossible to reach in their inaccessible mountain fastnesses. The travellers several times saw bands of ferocious Indians, who, when they perceived the elephant striding across-country, made angry and threatening motions. The Parsee avoided them as much as possible. Few animals were observed on the route; even the monkeys hurried from their path with contortions[5] and grimaces which convulsed Passepartout with laughter.

In the midst of his gaiety, however, one thought troubled the worthy servant. What would Mr. Fogg do with the elephant when he got to Allahabad? Would he carry him on with him? Impossible! The cost of transporting him would make him ruinously expensive. Would he sell him, or set him free? The estimable beast certainly deserved some consideration. Should Mr. Fogg choose to make him, Passepartout, a present of Kiouni, he would be very much embarrassed; and these thoughts did not cease worrying him for a long time.

The principal chain of the Vindhias was crossed by eight in the evening, and another halt was made on the northern slope, in a ruined bungalow. They had gone nearly twenty-five miles that day, and an equal distance still separated them from the station of Allahabad.

The night was cold. The Parsee lit a fire in the bungalow with a few dry branches, and the warmth was very grateful, provisions purchased at Kholby sufficed for supper, and the travellers ate ravenously[6]. The conversation, beginning with a few disconnected phrases, soon gave place to loud and steady snores. The guide watched Kiouni, who slept standing, bolstering himself against the trunk of a large tree. Nothing occurred during the night to disturb the slumberers, although occasional growls from panthers and chatterings of monkeys broke the silence; the more formidable beasts made no cries or hostile demonstration against the occupants of the bungalow. Sir Francis slept heavily, like an honest soldier overcome with fatigue. Passepartout was wrapped in uneasy dreams of the bouncing of the day before. As for Mr. Fogg, he slumbered as peacefully as if he had been in his serene mansion in Saville Row.

The journey was resumed at six in the morning; the guide hoped to reach Allahabad by evening. In that case, Mr. Fogg would only lose a part of the forty-eight hours saved since the beginning of the tour. Kiouni, resuming his rapid gait, soon descended the lower spurs of the Vindhias, and towards noon they passed by the village of Kallenger, on the Cani, one of the branches of the Ganges. The guide avoided inhabited places, thinking it safer to keep the open country, which lies along the first depressions of the basin of the great river. Allahabad was now only twelve miles to the north-east. They stopped under a clump of bananas, the fruit of which, as healthy as bread and as succulent as cream, was amply partaken of and appreciated.

At two o'clock the guide entered a thick forest which extended several miles; he preferred to travel under cover of the woods. They had not as yet had any unpleasant

---

[5] 'Contortion' is an action of twisting or bending unnaturally into a different shape or form.
[6] 'Ravenously' means to eat greedily or voraciously.

encounters, and the journey seemed on the point of being successfully accomplished, when the elephant, becoming restless, suddenly stopped.

It was then four o'clock.

"What's the matter?" asked Sir Francis, putting out his head.

"I don't know, officer," replied the Parsee, listening attentively to a confused murmur which came through the thick branches.

The murmur soon became more distinct; it now seemed like a distant concert of human voices accompanied by brass instruments. Passepartout was all eyes and ears[7]. Mr. Fogg patiently waited without a word. The Parsee jumped to the ground, fastened the elephant to a tree, and plunged into the thicket. He soon returned, saying:

"A procession of Brahmins is coming this way. We must prevent their seeing us, if possible."

The guide unloosed the elephant and led him into a thicket, at the same time asking the travellers not to stir. He held himself ready to bestride[8] the animal at a moment's notice, should flight become necessary; but he evidently thought that the procession of the faithful would pass without perceiving them amid the thick foliage, in which they were wholly concealed.

The discordant[9] tones of the voices and instruments drew nearer, and now droning songs mingled with the sound of the tambourines and cymbals. The head of the procession soon appeared beneath the trees, a hundred paces away; and the strange figures who performed the religious ceremony were easily distinguished through the branches. First came the priests, with mitres[10] on their heads, and clothed in long lace robes. They were surrounded by men, women, and children, who sang a kind of lugubrious[11] psalm[12], interrupted at regular intervals by the tambourines and cymbals; while behind them was drawn a car with large wheels, the spokes of which represented serpents entwined with each other. Upon the car, which was drawn by four richly caparisoned[13] zebus[14], stood a hideous statue with four arms, the body coloured a dull red, with haggard eyes, dishevelled hair, protruding tongue, and lips tinted with betel. It stood upright upon the figure of a prostrate[15] and headless giant.

Sir Francis, recognising the statue, whispered, "The goddess Kali; the goddess of love and death."

---

[7] To be 'all eyes and ears' is an idiom meaning to listen and watch eagerly and carefully.
[8] 'Bestride' means to sit with a leg on either side of an object or animal.
[9] 'Discordant' means harsh and jarring because of lack of harmony.
[10] A 'mitre' is a type of traditional, ceremonial headgear.
[11] 'Lugubrious' means looking or sounding sad or dismal.
[12] 'Psalm' is a sacred song or a hymn.
[13] 'Caparison' means dressed with decorative clothing.
[14] 'Zebus' is domesticated humped cattle.
[15] 'Prostrate' means lying flat on the ground in submission.

"Of death, perhaps," muttered back Passepartout, "but of love—that ugly old hag? Never!"

The Parsee made a motion to keep silence.

A group of old fakirs were capering[16] and making a wild ado round the statue; these were striped with ochre, and covered with cuts whence their blood issued drop by drop—stupid fanatics, who, in the great Indian ceremonies, still throw themselves under the wheels of Juggernaut[17]. Some Brahmins, clad in all the sumptuousness of Oriental apparel, and leading a woman who faltered at every step, followed. This woman was young, and as fair as a European. Her head and neck, shoulders, ears, arms, hands, and toes were loaded down with jewels and gems with bracelets, earrings, and rings; while a tunic bordered with gold, and covered with a light muslin robe, betrayed the outline of her form.

The guards who followed the young woman presented a violent contrast to her, armed as they were with naked sabres hung at their waists, and long damascened[18] pistols, and bearing a corpse on a palanquin. It was the body of an old man, gorgeously arrayed in the habiliments of a rajah, wearing, as in life, a turban embroidered with pearls, a robe of tissue of silk and gold, a scarf of cashmere sewed with diamonds, and the magnificent weapons of a Hindoo prince. Next came the musicians and a rearguard of capering fakirs, whose cries sometimes drowned the noise of the instruments; these closed the procession.

Sir Francis watched the procession with a sad countenance, and, turning to the guide, said, "A suttee.[19]"

The Parsee nodded, and put his finger to his lips.[20] The procession slowly wound under the trees, and soon its last ranks disappeared in the depths of the wood. The songs gradually died away; occasionally cries were heard in the distance, until at last all was silence again.

Phileas Fogg had heard what Sir Francis said, and, as soon as the procession had disappeared, asked: "What is a suttee?"

"A suttee," returned the general, "is a human sacrifice, but a voluntary one. The woman you have just seen will be burned to-morrow at the dawn of day."

"Oh, the scoundrels!" cried Passepartout, who could not repress his indignation.

---

[16] 'Caper' means to skip and dance in a lively or playful manner.

[17] Present day *Jagannath*, Lord of the Universe. An annual festival called *Jagannath Yatra* (literal translation: procession of Lord Jagannath) is celebrated in Puri, Orissa, and attended by the public with such feverish vigour that it crushes everything that comes in its path.

[18] 'Damascene' is the process of inlaying a metal object with gold or silver decoration.

[19] *Sati*, now an obsolete Indian custom, was a funeral ritual where a widow would self-immolate herself on her husband's pyre. In India, a ban on Sati was issued in 1861.

[20] 'Putting a finger to one's lips' is a way of telling someone to be quiet.

"And the corpse?" asked Mr. Fogg.

"Is that of the prince, her husband," said the guide; "an independent rajah of Bundelcund."

"Is it possible," resumed Phileas Fogg, his voice betraying not the least emotion, "that these barbarous customs still exist in India, and that the English have been unable to put a stop to them?"

"These sacrifices do not occur in the larger portion of India," replied Sir Francis; "but we have no power over these savage territories, and especially here in Bundelcund. The whole district north of the Vindhias is the theatre of incessant[21] murders and pillage."

"The poor wretch!" exclaimed Passepartout, "to be burned alive!"

"Yes," returned Sir Francis, "burned alive. And, if she were not, you cannot conceive what treatment she would be obliged to submit to from her relatives. They would shave off her hair, feed her on a scanty allowance of rice, treat her with contempt; she would be looked upon as an unclean creature, and would die in some corner, like a scurvy dog[22]. The prospect of so frightful an existence drives these poor creatures to the sacrifice much more than love or religious fanaticism. Sometimes, however, the sacrifice is really voluntary, and it requires the active interference of the Government to prevent it. Several years ago, when I was living at Bombay, a young widow asked permission of the governor to be burned along with her husband's body; but, as you may imagine, he refused. The woman left the town, took refuge with an independent rajah, and there carried out her self-devoted purpose."

While Sir Francis was speaking, the guide shook his head several times, and now said: "The sacrifice which will take place to-morrow at dawn is not a voluntary one."

"How do you know?"

"Everybody knows about this affair in Bundelcund."

"But the wretched creature did not seem to be making any resistance," observed Sir Francis.

"That was because they had intoxicated her with fumes of hemp and opium."[23]

"But where are they taking her?"

"To the pagoda of Pillaji, two miles from here; she will pass the night there."

"And the sacrifice will take place—"

"To-morrow, at the first light of dawn."

---

[21] 'Incessant' means continuing without interruption.

[22] 'Scurvy dog' is an idiom referring to someone as contemptible, or despicable.

[23] The widow was drugged to numb her senses to what was happening to her presently. If not drugged, she would have resisted being a Sati.

The guide now led the elephant out of the thicket, and leaped upon his neck. Just at the moment that he was about to urge Kiouni forward with a peculiar whistle, Mr. Fogg stopped him, and, turning to Sir Francis Cromarty, said, "Suppose we save this woman."

"Save the woman, Mr. Fogg!"

"I have yet twelve hours to spare; I can devote them to that."

"Why, you are a man of heart!"

"Sometimes," replied Phileas Fogg, quietly; "when I have the time."

A Study Guide: Around the World in Eighty Days

Comprehension exercise 12

Q1) Why did the guide prefer to travel through the forest rather than follow the line where the railway was still being built?
a) To avoid the noise and commotion of the railway construction.
b) To save time by taking a shorter route.
c) To enjoy the scenic beauty of the forest.
d) To avoid potential dangers posed by the unfinished railway line.

Q2) How did Passepartout ensure his safety while riding on the elephant's back?
a) By holding tightly onto the elephant's neck.
b) By keeping his tongue from between his teeth.
c) By wearing protective gear provided by the guide.
d) By staying close to Mr. Fogg and Sir Francis Cromarty.

Q3) Why did the guide lead the elephant into a thicket and ask the travellers not to stir when they heard the approaching procession?
a) To hide from potential danger posed by the procession.
b) To rest and wait until the procession passed by.
c) To observe the religious ceremony performed by the procession.
d) To seek assistance from the procession in case of an emergency.

Q4) What does the word "phlegm" mean in the context of the text?
a) Enthusiasm or excitement
b) Indifference or calmness
c) Courage or bravery
d) Irritation or annoyance

Q5) What does the word "fanatics" mean in the context of the text?
a) Critics or sceptics
b) Enthusiasts or admirers
c) Devotees or zealots
d) Sceptics or cynics

Chapter 13

IN WHICH PASSEPARTOUT RECEIVES A NEW PROOF THAT FORTUNE FAVORS THE BRAVE

The project was a bold one, full of difficulty, perhaps impracticable. Mr. Fogg was going to risk life, or at least liberty, and therefore the success of his tour. But he did not hesitate, and he found in Sir Francis Cromarty an enthusiastic ally[1].

As for Passepartout, he was ready for anything that might be proposed. His master's idea charmed him; he perceived a heart, a soul, under that icy exterior. He began to love Phileas Fogg.

There remained the guide: what course would he adopt? Would he not take part with the Indians? In default of his assistance, it was necessary to be assured of his neutrality.

Sir Francis frankly put the question to him.

"Officers," replied the guide, "I am a Parsee, and this woman is a Parsee. Command me as you will." [2]

"Excellent!" said Mr. Fogg.

"However," resumed the guide, "it is certain, not only that we shall risk our lives, but horrible tortures, if we are taken."

"That is foreseen," replied Mr. Fogg. "I think we must wait till night before acting."

"I think so," said the guide.

The worthy Indian then gave some account of the victim, who, he said, was a celebrated beauty of the Parsee race, and the daughter of a wealthy Bombay merchant. She had received a thoroughly English education in that city, and, from her manners and intelligence, would be thought a European. Her name was Aouda. Left an orphan, she was married against her will to the old rajah of Bundelcund; and, knowing the fate that awaited her, she escaped, was retaken, and devoted by the rajah's relatives, who had an interest in her death, to the sacrifice from which it seemed she could not escape.

The Parsee's narrative only confirmed Mr. Fogg and his companions in their generous design. It was decided that the guide should direct the elephant towards the pagoda of Pillaji, which he accordingly approached as quickly as possible. They halted, half an hour

---

[1] An 'ally' is a person or a group that provides assistance or support in an ongoing activity.
[2] The guide willingly agreed to support their mission to save the woman as she belonged to his own religious group.

afterwards, in a copse, some five hundred feet from the pagoda, where they were well concealed; but they could hear the groans and cries of the fakirs distinctly.

They then discussed the means of getting at the victim. The guide was familiar with the pagoda of Pillaji, in which, as he declared, the young woman was imprisoned. Could they enter any of its doors while the whole party of Indians was plunged in a drunken sleep, or was it safer to attempt to make a hole in the walls? This could only be determined at the moment and the place themselves; but it was certain that the abduction[3] must be made that night, and not when, at break of day, the victim was led to her funeral pyre. Then no human intervention could save her.

As soon as night fell, about six o'clock, they decided to make a reconnaissance[4] around the pagoda. The cries of the fakirs were just ceasing; the Indians were in the act of plunging themselves into the drunkenness caused by liquid opium mingled with hemp, and it might be possible to slip between them to the temple itself.

The Parsee, leading the others, noiselessly crept through the wood, and in ten minutes they found themselves on the banks of a small stream, whence, by the light of the rosin torches, they perceived a pyre of wood, on the top of which lay the embalmed body of the rajah, which was to be burned with his wife. The pagoda, whose minarets loomed above the trees in the deepening dusk, stood a hundred steps away.

"Come!" whispered the guide.

He slipped more cautiously than ever through the brush, followed by his companions; the silence around was only broken by the low murmuring of the wind among the branches.

Soon the Parsee stopped on the borders of the glade[5], which was lit up by the torches. The ground was covered by groups of the Indians, motionless in their drunken sleep; it seemed a battlefield strewn with the dead. Men, women, and children lay together.

In the background, among the trees, the pagoda of Pillaji loomed distinctly. Much to the guide's disappointment, the guards of the rajah, lighted by torches, were watching at the doors and marching to and fro with naked sabres; probably the priests, too, were watching within.

The Parsee, now convinced that it was impossible to force an entrance to the temple, advanced no farther, but led his companions back again. Phileas Fogg and Sir Francis Cromarty also saw that nothing could be attempted in that direction. They stopped, and engaged in a whispered colloquy[6].

"It is only eight now," said the brigadier, "and these guards may also go to sleep."

---

[3] The 'abduction' refers to Mr. Fogg and his friends taking the woman forcefully from the temple away from her executioners.

[4] 'Reconnaissance' is a preliminary survey to gain information.

[5] A 'glade' is an open space in a forest.

[6] A 'colloquy' is a conversation or conference between people.

"It is not impossible," returned the Parsee.

They lay down at the foot of a tree, and waited.

The time seemed long; the guide ever and anon left them to take an observation on the edge of the wood, but the guards watched steadily by the glare of the torches, and a dim light crept through the windows of the pagoda.

They waited till midnight; but no change took place among the guards, and it became apparent that their yielding to sleep could not be counted on. The other plan must be carried out; an opening in the walls of the pagoda must be made. It remained to ascertain whether the priests were watching by the side of their victim as assiduously[7] as were the soldiers at the door.

After a last consultation, the guide announced that he was ready for the attempt, and advanced, followed by the others. They took a roundabout way, so as to get at the pagoda on the rear. They reached the walls about half-past twelve, without having met anyone; here there was no guard, nor were there either windows or doors.

The night was dark. The moon, on the wane, scarcely left the horizon, and was covered with heavy clouds; the height of the trees deepened the darkness.

It was not enough to reach the walls; an opening in them must be accomplished, and to attain this purpose the party only had their pocket-knives. Happily the temple walls were built of brick and wood, which could be penetrated with little difficulty; after one brick had been taken out, the rest would yield easily.

They set noiselessly to work, and the Parsee on one side and Passepartout on the other began to loosen the bricks so as to make an aperture two feet wide. They were getting on rapidly, when suddenly a cry was heard in the interior of the temple, followed almost instantly by other cries replying from the outside. Passepartout and the guide stopped. Had they been heard? Was the alarm being given? Common prudence[8] urged them to retire, and they did so, followed by Phileas Fogg and Sir Francis. They again hid themselves in the wood, and waited till the disturbance, whatever it might be, ceased, holding themselves ready to resume their attempt without delay. But, awkwardly enough, the guards now appeared at the rear of the temple, and there installed themselves, in readiness to prevent a surprise.

It would be difficult to describe the disappointment of the party, thus interrupted in their work. They could not now reach the victim; how, then, could they save her? Sir Francis shook his fists, Passepartout was beside himself, and the guide gnashed his teeth with rage. The tranquil Fogg waited, without betraying any emotion.

"We have nothing to do but to go away," whispered Sir Francis.

"Nothing but to go away," echoed the guide.

---

[7] 'Assiduous' means showing great care, attention, and effort.
[8] 'Prudence' means the ability to govern by reason.

"Stop," said Fogg. "I am only due at Allahabad tomorrow before noon."[9]

"But what can you hope to do?" asked Sir Francis. "In a few hours it will be daylight, and—"

"The chance which now seems lost may present itself at the last moment."

Sir Francis would have liked to read Phileas Fogg's eyes. What was this cool Englishman thinking of? Was he planning to make a rush for the young woman at the very moment of the sacrifice, and boldly snatch her from her executioners?

This would be utter folly, and it was hard to admit that Fogg was such a fool. Sir Francis consented, however, to remain to the end of this terrible drama. The guide led them to the rear of the glade, where they were able to observe the sleeping groups.

Meanwhile Passepartout, who had perched himself on the lower branches of a tree, was resolving an idea which had at first struck him like a flash, and which was now firmly lodged in his brain.

He had commenced by saying to himself, "What folly!" and then he repeated, "Why not, after all? It's a chance,—perhaps the only one; and with such sots!" Thinking thus, he slipped, with the suppleness of a serpent, to the lowest branches, the ends of which bent almost to the ground.

The hours passed, and the lighter shades now announced the approach of day, though it was not yet light. This was the moment. The slumbering multitude became animated, the tambourines sounded, songs and cries arose; the hour of the sacrifice had come. The doors of the pagoda swung open, and a bright light escaped from its interior, in the midst of which Mr. Fogg and Sir Francis espied the victim. She seemed, having shaken off the stupor of intoxication, to be striving to escape from her executioner. Sir Francis's heart throbbed; and, convulsively seizing Mr. Fogg's hand, found in it an open knife. Just at this moment the crowd began to move. The young woman had again fallen into a stupor caused by the fumes of hemp, and passed among the fakirs, who escorted her with their wild, religious cries.

Phileas Fogg and his companions, mingling in the rear ranks of the crowd, followed; and in two minutes they reached the banks of the stream, and stopped fifty paces from the pyre, upon which still lay the rajah's corpse. In the semi-obscurity they saw the victim, quite senseless, stretched out beside her husband's body. Then a torch was brought, and the wood, heavily soaked with oil, instantly took fire.

At this moment Sir Francis and the guide seized Phileas Fogg, who, in an instant of mad generosity, was about to rush upon the pyre. But he had quickly pushed them aside, when the whole scene suddenly changed. A cry of terror arose. The whole multitude prostrated[10] themselves, terror-stricken, on the ground.

---

[9] Mr. Fogg insisted that they still had some time to wait and save the woman.
[10] 'Prostrate' means to throw oneself on the ground, face downwards.

The old rajah was not dead, then, since he rose of a sudden, like a spectre, took up his wife in his arms, and descended from the pyre in the midst of the clouds of smoke, which only heightened his ghostly appearance.

Fakirs and soldiers and priests, seized with instant terror, lay there, with their faces on the ground, not daring to lift their eyes and behold such a prodigy[11].

The inanimate victim was borne along by the vigorous arms which supported her, and which she did not seem in the least to burden. Mr. Fogg and Sir Francis stood erect, the Parsee bowed his head, and Passepartout was, no doubt, scarcely less stupefied.

The resuscitated rajah approached Sir Francis and Mr. Fogg, and, in an abrupt tone, said, "Let us be off!"

It was Passepartout himself, who had slipped upon the pyre in the midst of the smoke and, profiting by the still overhanging darkness, had delivered the young woman from death! It was Passepartout who, playing his part with a happy audacity[12], had passed through the crowd amid the general terror.

A moment after all four of the party had disappeared in the woods, and the elephant was bearing them away at a rapid pace. But the cries and noise, and a ball which whizzed through Phileas Fogg's hat, apprised[13] them that the trick had been discovered.

The old rajah's body, indeed, now appeared upon the burning pyre; and the priests, recovered from their terror, perceived that an abduction had taken place. They hastened into the forest, followed by the soldiers, who fired a volley after the fugitives; but the latter rapidly increased the distance between them, and ere[14] long found themselves beyond the reach of the bullets and arrows.

---

[11] 'Prodigy' means someone or something that's extraordinary or inexplicable.
[12] 'Audacity' is the willingness to take bold risks.
[13] 'Apprise' means to give notice to.
[14] 'Ere' is an archaic word used to indicate the quickness of the passing hour, something happening before time.

A Study Guide: Around the World in Eighty Days

Comprehension exercise 13

Q1) Why does Passepartout ultimately decide to rescue Aouda?
a) Because he is ordered to do so by Mr. Fogg.
b) Because he wants to impress Sir Francis Cromarty.
c) Because he feels compassion for Aouda and sees an opportunity to help her.
d) Because he wants to prove his bravery to the guide.

Q2) What does Sir Francis Cromarty's reaction to Mr. Fogg's impulse to rush towards the pyre reveal about his character?
a) He is hesitant and lacks courage.
a) He is impulsive and reckless.
c) He is cautious and level-headed.
d) He is indifferent and uninterested.

Q3) How does the group plan to rescue Aouda from the sacrificial ritual?
a) By bribing the guards at the temple.
b) By creating an opening in the walls of the temple.
c) By distracting the priests with a false alarm.
d) By persuading the old rajah to release her.

Q4) What does the word "audacious" mean in the context of Passepartout's actions?
a) Cowardly
b) Brave and daring
c) Uninterested
d) Unworthy

Q5) Which word best describes the old rajah's sudden appearance at the end of the sacrificial ritual?
a) Expected
b) Miraculous
c) Unnecessary
d) Predictable

Chapter 14

IN WHICH PHILEAS FOGG DESCENDS THE WHOLE LENGTH OF THE BEAUTIFUL
VALLEY OF THE GANGES WITHOUT EVER THINKING OF SEEING IT

The rash exploit had been accomplished; and for an hour Passepartout laughed gaily at his success. Sir Francis pressed the worthy fellow's hand, and his master said, "Well done!" which, from him, was high commendation; to which Passepartout replied that all the credit of the affair belonged to Mr. Fogg. As for him, he had only been struck with a "queer" idea; and he laughed to think that for a few moments he, Passepartout, the ex-gymnast, ex-sergeant fireman, had been the spouse of a charming woman, a venerable, embalmed[1] rajah! As for the young Indian woman, she had been unconscious throughout of what was passing, and now, wrapped up in a travelling-blanket, was reposing[2] in one of the howdahs.

The elephant, thanks to the skilful guidance of the Parsee, was advancing rapidly through the still darksome forest, and, an hour after leaving the pagoda, had crossed a vast plain. They made a halt at seven o'clock, the young woman being still in a state of complete prostration[3]. The guide made her drink a little brandy and water, but the drowsiness which stupefied her could not yet be shaken off. Sir Francis, who was familiar with the effects of the intoxication produced by the fumes of hemp, reassured his companions on her account. But he was more disturbed at the prospect of her future fate. He told Phileas Fogg that, should Aouda remain in India, she would inevitably fall again into the hands of her executioners. These fanatics were scattered throughout the county, and would, despite the English police, recover their victim at Madras, Bombay, or Calcutta. She would only be safe by quitting India for ever.

Phileas Fogg replied that he would reflect upon the matter.

The station at Allahabad was reached about ten o'clock, and, the interrupted line of railway being resumed, would enable them to reach Calcutta in less than twenty-four hours. Phileas Fogg would thus be able to arrive in time to take the steamer which left Calcutta the next day, October 25th, at noon, for Hong Kong.

The young woman was placed in one of the waiting-rooms of the station, whilst Passepartout was charged with purchasing for her various articles of toilet, a dress, shawl, and some furs; for which his master gave him unlimited credit. Passepartout started off forthwith, and found himself in the streets of Allahabad, that is, the City of God, one of the most venerated in India, being built at the junction of the two sacred rivers, Ganges

---

[1] An embalmed body refers to a dead human body that has been preserved for religious or funeral purposes.

[2] 'Repose' means to rest or lie.

[3] 'Prostration' means to be extremely exhausted or weakened.

and Jumna[4], the waters of which attract pilgrims from every part of the peninsula. The Ganges, according to the legends of the Ramayana, rises in heaven, whence, owing to Brahma's agency, it descends to the earth.

Passepartout made it a point, as he made his purchases, to take a good look at the city. It was formerly defended by a noble fort, which has since become a state prison; its commerce has dwindled away, and Passepartout in vain looked about him for such a bazaar as he used to frequent in Regent Street. At last he came upon an elderly, crusty Jew, who sold second-hand articles, and from whom he purchased a dress of Scotch stuff, a large mantle, and a fine otter-skin pelisse[5], for which he did not hesitate to pay seventy-five pounds. He then returned triumphantly to the station.

The influence to which the priests of Pillaji had subjected Aouda began gradually to yield, and she became more herself, so that her fine eyes resumed all their soft Indian expression.

When the poet-king, Ucaf Uddaul, celebrates the charms of the queen of Ahmehnagara, he speaks thus:

"Her shining tresses, divided in two parts, encircle the harmonious contour of her white and delicate cheeks, brilliant in their glow and freshness. Her ebony brows have the form and charm of the bow of Kama, the god of love, and beneath her long silken lashes the purest reflections and a celestial light swim, as in the sacred lakes of Himalaya, in the black pupils of her great clear eyes. Her teeth, fine, equal, and white, glitter between her smiling lips like dewdrops in a passion-flower's half-enveloped breast. Her delicately formed ears, her vermilion hands, her little feet, curved and tender as the lotus-bud, glitter with the brilliancy of the loveliest pearls of Ceylon, the most dazzling diamonds of Golconda. Her narrow and supple waist, which a hand may clasp around, sets forth the outline of her rounded figure and the beauty of her bosom, where youth in its flower displays the wealth of its treasures; and beneath the silken folds of her tunic she seems to have been modelled in pure silver by the godlike hand of Vicvarcarma[6], the immortal sculptor."

It is enough to say, without applying this poetical rhapsody to Aouda, that she was a charming woman, in all the European acceptation of the phrase. She spoke English with great purity, and the guide had not exaggerated in saying that the young Parsee had been transformed by her bringing up.

The train was about to start from Allahabad, and Mr. Fogg proceeded to pay the guide the price agreed upon for his service, and not a farthing more[7]; which astonished Passepartout, who remembered all that his master owed to the guide's devotion. He had, indeed, risked his life in the adventure at Pillaji, and, if he should be caught afterwards by

---

[4] Jumna, modern day River Yamuna, is a major tributary of the River Ganges.

[5] A 'pelisse' is a sleeved, ankle-length woman's dress.

[6] Lord Vishwakarma is the deity of all engineers, craftsmen, and artisans.

[7] Mr. Fogg paid the guide for his services and did not offer any tip as a reward for his excellent service.

the Indians, he would with difficulty escape their vengeance. Kiouni, also, must be disposed of. What should be done with the elephant, which had been so dearly purchased? Phileas Fogg had already determined this question.

"Parsee," said he to the guide, "you have been serviceable and devoted. I have paid for your service, but not for your devotion. Would you like to have this elephant? He is yours."

The guide's eyes glistened.

"Your honour is giving me a fortune!" cried he.

"Take him, guide," returned Mr. Fogg, "and I shall still be your debtor."

"Good!" exclaimed Passepartout. "Take him, friend. Kiouni is a brave and faithful beast." And, going up to the elephant, he gave him several lumps of sugar, saying, "Here, Kiouni, here, here."

The elephant grunted out his satisfaction, and, clasping Passepartout around the waist with his trunk, lifted him as high as his head. Passepartout, not in the least alarmed, caressed the animal, which replaced him gently on the ground.

Soon after, Phileas Fogg, Sir Francis Cromarty, and Passepartout, installed in a carriage with Aouda, who had the best seat, were whirling at full speed towards Benares. It was a run of eighty miles, and was accomplished in two hours. During the journey, the young woman fully recovered her senses. What was her astonishment to find herself in this carriage, on the railway, dressed in European habiliments, and with travellers who were quite strangers to her! Her companions first set about fully reviving her with a little liquor, and then Sir Francis narrated to her what had passed, dwelling upon the courage with which Phileas Fogg had not hesitated to risk his life to save her, and recounting the happy sequel of the venture, the result of Passepartout's rash idea. Mr. Fogg said nothing; while Passepartout, abashed[8], kept repeating that "it wasn't worth telling."

Aouda pathetically thanked her deliverers, rather with tears than words; her fine eyes interpreted her gratitude better than her lips. Then, as her thoughts strayed back to the scene of the sacrifice, and recalled the dangers which still menaced her, she shuddered with terror.

Phileas Fogg understood what was passing in Aouda's mind, and offered, in order to reassure her, to escort her to Hong Kong, where she might remain safely until the affair was hushed up—an offer which she eagerly and gratefully accepted. She had, it seems, a Parsee relation, who was one of the principal merchants of Hong Kong, which is wholly an English city,[9] though on an island on the Chinese coast.

---

[8] 'Abash' means embarrassed or humbled.
[9] Hong Kong was a British colony from 1841 to 1941 and again from 1945 to 1997.

At half-past twelve the train stopped at Benares. The Brahmin legends assert that this city is built on the site of the ancient Casi[10], which, like Mahomet's tomb, was once suspended between heaven and earth; though the Benares of to-day, which the Orientalists call the Athens of India, stands quite unpoetically on the solid earth, Passepartout caught glimpses of its brick houses and clay huts, giving an aspect of desolation to the place, as the train entered it.

Benares was Sir Francis Cromarty's destination, the troops he was rejoining being encamped some miles northward of the city. He bade adieu to Phileas Fogg, wishing him all success, and expressing the hope that he would come that way again in a less original but more profitable fashion. Mr. Fogg lightly pressed him by the hand. The parting of Aouda, who did not forget what she owed to Sir Francis, betrayed more warmth; and, as for Passepartout, he received a hearty shake of the hand from the gallant general.

The railway, on leaving Benares, passed for a while along the valley of the Ganges. Through the windows of their carriage the travellers had glimpses of the diversified landscape of Behar[11], with its mountains clothed in verdure, its fields of barley, wheat, and corn, its jungles peopled with green alligators, its neat villages, and its still thickly-leaved forests. Elephants were bathing in the waters of the sacred river, and groups of Indians, despite the advanced season and chilly air, were performing solemnly their pious ablutions[12]. These were fervent Brahmins, the bitterest foes of Buddhism, their deities being Vishnu, the solar god, Shiva, the divine impersonation of natural forces, and Brahma, the supreme ruler of priests and legislators. What would these divinities think of India, anglicised as it is to-day, with steamers whistling and scudding along the Ganges, frightening the gulls which float upon its surface, the turtles swarming along its banks, and the faithful dwelling upon its borders?[13]

The panorama passed before their eyes like a flash, save when the steam concealed it fitfully from the view; the travellers could scarcely discern the fort of Chupenie, twenty miles south-westward from Benares, the ancient stronghold of the rajahs of Behar; or Ghazipur and its famous rose-water factories; or the tomb of Lord Cornwallis, rising on the left bank of the Ganges; the fortified town of Buxar, or Patna, a large manufacturing and trading-place, where is held the principal opium market of India; or Monghir, a more than European town, for it is as English as Manchester or Birmingham, with its iron foundries, edgetool[14] factories, and high chimneys puffing clouds of black smoke heavenward.

Night came on; the train passed on at full speed, in the midst of the roaring of the tigers, bears, and wolves which fled before the locomotive; and the marvels of Bengal,

---

[10] Casi, or *Kashi*, or *Benares, or* present day *Varanasi* is a holy city on the banks of the Ganges in Uttar Pradesh, India.

[11] Present day Bihar, India.

[12] 'Ablution' is a ceremonial act of washing parts of the body or sacred containers.

[13] The author reflects on the impact of British dominance on Indian culture and contemplates how the Indian Gods might perceive the transformed India

[14] An 'edgetool' is a hand or machine operated cutting tool.

Golconda ruined Gour, Murshedabad, the ancient capital, Burdwan, Hugly, and the French town of Chandernagor[15], where Passepartout would have been proud to see his country's flag flying, were hidden from their view in the darkness.

Calcutta was reached at seven in the morning, and the packet left for Hong Kong at noon; so that Phileas Fogg had five hours before him.

According to his journal, he was due at Calcutta on the 25th of October, and that was the exact date of his actual arrival. He was therefore neither behind-hand nor ahead of time. The two days gained between London and Bombay had been lost, as has been seen, in the journey across India. But it is not to be supposed that Phileas Fogg regretted them.[16]

---

[15] Present day Chandannagar city is a former French colony and located about 35 kilometres from Kolkata/ Calcutta.

[16] Mr. Fogg was content with exchanging the gain of two days for saving Auoda's life.

Comprehension exercise 14

Q1) Why does Passepartout attribute the success of the exploit to Mr. Fogg?
a) Because he wants to avoid taking credit for himself.
b) Because he believes Mr. Fogg deserves all the praise.
c) Because he thinks it is not appropriate for him to receive commendation.
d) Because he wants to impress Sir Francis Cromarty.

Q2) What is revealed about Sir Francis Cromarty's character based on his reaction to Aouda's situation?
a) He is indifferent towards Aouda's safety.
b) He is deeply concerned about Aouda's future.
c) He is sceptical about Phileas Fogg's decision-making.
d) He is solely focused on completing the journey to Calcutta.

Q3) Where did Passepartout go to purchase various items for Aouda?
a) Calcutta
b) Allahabad
c) Bombay
d) Benares

Q4) What does the word "prostration" mean in the context of the text?
a) The act of bowing down in reverence
b) The state of complete exhaustion
c) The condition of being unconscious
d) The feeling of intense gratitude

Q5) Which word best describes Phileas Fogg's reaction to the guide's service?
a) Appreciative
b) Indifferent
c) Dismissive
d) Suspicious

Chapter 15

IN WHICH THE BAG OF BANKNOTES DISGORGES SOME THOUSANDS OF POUNDS MORE

The train entered the station, and Passepartout jumping out first, was followed by Mr. Fogg, who assisted his fair companion to descend. Phileas Fogg intended to proceed at once to the Hong Kong steamer, in order to get Aouda comfortably settled for the voyage. He was unwilling to leave her while they were still on dangerous ground.

Just as he was leaving the station a policeman came up to him, and said, "Mr. Phileas Fogg?"

"I am he."

"Is this man your servant?" added the policeman, pointing to Passepartout.

"Yes."

"Be so good, both of you, as to follow me."

Mr. Fogg betrayed no surprise whatever. The policeman was a representative of the law, and law is sacred to an Englishman. Passepartout tried to reason about the matter, but the policeman tapped him with his stick, and Mr. Fogg made him a signal to obey.

"May this young lady go with us?" asked he.

"She may," replied the policeman.

Mr. Fogg, Aouda, and Passepartout were conducted to a palkigahri, a sort of four-wheeled carriage, drawn by two horses, in which they took their places and were driven away. No one spoke during the twenty minutes which elapsed before they reached their destination. They first passed through the "black town," with its narrow streets, its miserable, dirty huts, and squalid population; then through the "European town," which presented a relief in its bright brick mansions, shaded by coconut-trees and bristling with masts, where, although it was early morning, elegantly dressed horsemen and handsome equipages were passing back and forth.

The carriage stopped before a modest-looking house, which, however, did not have the appearance of a private mansion. The policeman having requested his prisoners—for so, truly, they might be called—to descend, conducted them into a room with barred windows, and said: "You will appear before Judge Obadiah at half-past eight."

He then retired, and closed the door.

"Why, we are prisoners!" exclaimed Passepartout, falling into a chair.

Aouda, with an emotion she tried to conceal, said to Mr. Fogg: "Sir, you must leave me to my fate! It is on my account that you receive this treatment, it is for having saved me!"

Phileas Fogg contented himself with saying that it was impossible. It was quite unlikely that he should be arrested for preventing a suttee. The complainants would not dare present themselves with such a charge. There was some mistake. Moreover, he would not, in any event, abandon Aouda, but would escort her to Hong Kong.

"But the steamer leaves at noon!" observed Passepartout, nervously.

"We shall be on board by noon," replied his master, placidly[1].

It was said so positively that Passepartout could not help muttering to himself, "Parbleu[2] that's certain! Before noon we shall be on board." But he was by no means reassured.

At half-past eight the door opened, the policeman appeared, and, requesting them to follow him, led the way to an adjoining hall. It was evidently a court-room, and a crowd of Europeans and natives already occupied the rear of the apartment.

Mr. Fogg and his two companions took their places on a bench opposite the desks of the magistrate and his clerk. Immediately after, Judge Obadiah, a fat, round man, followed by the clerk, entered. He proceeded to take down a wig which was hanging on a nail, and put it hurriedly on his head.

"The first case," said he. Then, putting his hand to his head, he exclaimed, "Heh! This is not my wig!"

"No, your worship," returned the clerk, "it is mine."

"My dear Mr. Oysterpuff, how can a judge give a wise sentence in a clerk's wig?"

The wigs were exchanged.

Passepartout was getting nervous, for the hands on the face of the big clock over the judge seemed to go around with terrible rapidity.[3]

"The first case," repeated Judge Obadiah.

"Phileas Fogg?" demanded Oysterpuff.

"I am here," replied Mr. Fogg.

"Passepartout?"

"Present," responded Passepartout.

---

[1] 'Placid' means peaceful and calm.
[2] 'Parbleu' is an exclamation expressing surprise.
[3] Passepartout was nervous about being delayed and missing the steamer to Hong Kong.

"Good," said the judge. "You have been looked for, prisoners, for two days on the trains from Bombay."

"But of what are we accused?" asked Passepartout, impatiently.

"You are about to be informed."

"I am an English subject, sir," said Mr. Fogg, "and I have the right—"

"Have you been ill-treated?"

"Not at all."

"Very well; let the complainants come in."

A door was swung open by order of the judge, and three Indian priests entered.

"That's it," muttered Passepartout; "these are the rogues who were going to burn our young lady."

The priests took their places in front of the judge, and the clerk proceeded to read in a loud voice a complaint of sacrilege[4] against Phileas Fogg and his servant, who were accused of having violated a place held consecrated by the Brahmin religion.

"You hear the charge?" asked the judge.

"Yes, sir," replied Mr. Fogg, consulting his watch, "and I admit it."

"You admit it?"

"I admit it, and I wish to hear these priests admit, in their turn, what they were going to do at the pagoda of Pillaji."

The priests looked at each other; they did not seem to understand what was said.

"Yes," cried Passepartout, warmly; "at the pagoda of Pillaji, where they were on the point of burning their victim."

The judge stared with astonishment, and the priests were stupefied.

"What victim?" said Judge Obadiah. "Burn whom? In Bombay itself?"

"Bombay?" cried Passepartout.

"Certainly. We are not talking of the pagoda of Pillaji, but of the pagoda of Malabar Hill, at Bombay."

"And as a proof," added the clerk, "here are the desecrator's very shoes, which he left behind him."

Whereupon he placed a pair of shoes on his desk.

---

[4] 'Sacrilege' means violation of what is regarded as sacred.

"My shoes!" cried Passepartout, in his surprise permitting this imprudent[5] exclamation to escape him.

The confusion of master and man, who had quite forgotten the affair at Bombay, for which they were now detained at Calcutta, may be imagined.

Fix the detective, had foreseen the advantage which Passepartout's escapade gave him, and, delaying his departure for twelve hours, had consulted the priests of Malabar Hill. Knowing that the English authorities dealt very severely with this kind of misdemeanour, he promised them a goodly sum in damages, and sent them forward to Calcutta by the next train. Owing to the delay caused by the rescue of the young widow, Fix and the priests reached the Indian capital before Mr. Fogg and his servant, the magistrates having been already warned by a dispatch to arrest them should they arrive. Fix's disappointment when he learned that Phileas Fogg had not made his appearance in Calcutta may be imagined. He made up his mind that the robber had stopped somewhere on the route and taken refuge in the southern provinces. For twenty-four hours Fix watched the station with feverish anxiety; at last he was rewarded by seeing Mr. Fogg and Passepartout arrive, accompanied by a young woman, whose presence he was wholly at a loss to explain. He hastened for a policeman; and this was how the party came to be arrested and brought before Judge Obadiah.

Had Passepartout been a little less preoccupied, he would have espied the detective ensconced in a corner of the court-room, watching the proceedings with an interest easily understood; for the warrant had failed to reach him at Calcutta, as it had done at Bombay and Suez.

Judge Obadiah had unfortunately caught Passepartout's rash exclamation, which the poor fellow would have given the world to recall.

"The facts are admitted?" asked the judge.

"Admitted," replied Mr. Fogg, coldly.

"Inasmuch," resumed the judge, "as the English law protects equally and sternly the religions of the Indian people, and as the man Passepartout has admitted that he violated the sacred pagoda of Malabar Hill, at Bombay, on the 20th of October, I condemn the said Passepartout to imprisonment for fifteen days and a fine of three hundred pounds."

"Three hundred pounds!" cried Passepartout, startled at the largeness of the sum.

"Silence!" shouted the constable.

"And inasmuch," continued the judge, "as it is not proved that the act was not done by the connivance of the master with the servant, and as the master in any case must be held responsible for the acts of his paid servant, I condemn Phileas Fogg to a week's imprisonment and a fine of one hundred and fifty pounds."

---

[5] 'Imprudent' means rash and unwise.

Fix rubbed his hands softly with satisfaction; if Phileas Fogg could be detained in Calcutta a week, it would be more than time for the warrant to arrive. Passepartout was stupefied. This sentence ruined his master. A wager of twenty thousand pounds lost, because he, like a precious fool, had gone into that abominable pagoda!

Phileas Fogg, as self-composed as if the judgment did not in the least concern him, did not even lift his eyebrows while it was being pronounced. Just as the clerk was calling the next case, he rose, and said, "I offer bail[6]."

"You have that right," returned the judge.

Fix's blood ran cold, but he resumed his composure when he heard the judge announce that the bail required for each prisoner would be one thousand pounds.

"I will pay it at once," said Mr. Fogg, taking a roll of bank-bills from the carpet-bag, which Passepartout had by him, and placing them on the clerk's desk.

"This sum will be restored to you upon your release from prison," said the judge. "Meanwhile, you are liberated on bail."

"Come!" said Phileas Fogg to his servant.

"But let them at least give me back my shoes!" cried Passepartout angrily.

"Ah, these are pretty dear shoes!" he muttered, as they were handed to him. "More than a thousand pounds apiece;[7] besides, they pinch my feet."

Mr. Fogg, offering his arm to Aouda, then departed, followed by the crestfallen[8] Passepartout. Fix still nourished hopes that the robber would not, after all, leave the two thousand pounds behind him, but would decide to serve out his week in jail, and issued forth on Mr. Fogg's traces. That gentleman took a carriage, and the party were soon landed on one of the quays[9].

The Rangoon was moored half a mile off in the harbour, its signal of departure hoisted at the mast-head. Eleven o'clock was striking; Mr. Fogg was an hour in advance of time. Fix saw them leave the carriage and push off in a boat for the steamer, and stamped his feet with disappointment.

"The rascal is off, after all!" he exclaimed. "Two thousand pounds sacrificed! He's as prodigal[10] as a thief! I'll follow him to the end of the world if necessary; but, at the rate he is going on, the stolen money will soon be exhausted."

---

[6] 'Bail' is the temporary release of an accused person awaiting trial, on condition that a sum of money is submitted to guarantee their appearance in court.

[7] The shoes cost a thousand pounds apiece, considering Mr. Fogg had to pay two thousand pounds as the bail amount for Passepartout's crime of not removing them before entering a Hindu temple.

[8] 'Crestfallen' means sad and disappointed.

[9] A 'quay' is a platform projecting into water, for loading and unloading ships.

[10] 'Prodigal' refers to a person who is recklessly wasteful.

The detective was not far wrong in making this conjecture. Since leaving London, what with travelling expenses, bribes, the purchase of the elephant, bails, and fines, Mr. Fogg had already spent more than five thousand pounds on the way, and the percentage of the sum recovered from the bank robber promised to the detectives, was rapidly diminishing.

Comprehension exercise 15

Q1) Why does Mr. Fogg offer bail for himself and Passepartout?
a) Because he believes they are innocent and will be acquitted.
b) Because he wants to avoid imprisonment at any cost.
c) Because he wants to ensure their release from custody.
d) Because he is confident that Fix will cover the bail amount.

Q2) How does Fix feel when he sees Mr. Fogg offering bail?
a) Excited
b) Shocked
c) Relieved
d) Indifferent

Q3) Why is Passepartout startled by the judge's sentence?
a) Because he is sentenced to imprisonment for a longer period than expected.
b) Because he is fined a larger amount than he anticipated.
c) Because he realizes the seriousness of the charges against him.
d) Because he is shocked by the unexpected turn of events.

Q4) What does the word "crestfallen" mean in the context of the text?
a) Angry
b) Confused
c) Disappointed
d) Frightened

Q5) Which word best describes Passepartout's reaction to being handed back his shoes?
a) Indignant
b) Grateful
c) Amused
d) Relieved

Chapter 16

IN WHICH FIX DOES NOT SEEM TO UNDERSTAND WHAT IS SAID TO HIM

The Rangoon—one of the Peninsular and Oriental Company's boats plying in the Chinese and Japanese seas—was a screw steamer[1], built of iron, weighing about seventeen hundred and seventy tons, and with engines of four hundred horse-power. She was as fast, but not as well fitted up, as the Mongolia, and Aouda was not as comfortably provided for on board of her as Phileas Fogg could have wished. However, the trip from Calcutta to Hong Kong only comprised some three thousand five hundred miles, occupying from ten to twelve days, and the young woman was not difficult to please.

During the first days of the journey Aouda became better acquainted with her protector, and constantly gave evidence of her deep gratitude for what he had done. The phlegmatic gentleman listened to her, apparently at least, with coldness, neither his voice nor his manner betraying the slightest emotion; but he seemed to be always on the watch that nothing should be wanting to Aouda's comfort. He visited her regularly each day at certain hours, not so much to talk himself, as to sit and hear her talk. He treated her with the strictest politeness, but with the precision of an automaton, the movements of which had been arranged for this purpose. Aouda did not quite know what to make of him, though Passepartout had given her some hints of his master's eccentricity[2], and made her smile by telling her of the wager which was sending him round the world. After all, she owed Phileas Fogg her life, and she always regarded him through the exalting medium of her gratitude.

Aouda confirmed the Parsee guide's narrative of her touching history. She did, indeed, belong to the highest of the native races of India. Many of the Parsee merchants have made great fortunes there by dealing in cotton; and one of them, Sir Jametsee Jeejeebhoy, was made a baronet by the English government. Aouda was a relative of this great man, and it was his cousin, Jeejeeh, whom she hoped to join at Hong Kong. Whether she would find a protector in him she could not tell; but Mr. Fogg essayed to calm her anxieties, and to assure her that everything would be mathematically—he used the very word—arranged. Aouda fastened her great eyes, "clear as the sacred lakes of the Himalaya," upon him; but the intractable[3] Fogg, as reserved as ever, did not seem at all inclined to throw himself into this lake.[4]

---

[1] A screw steamer is a boat powered by a steam engine, where screw refers to its propellers.
[2] 'Eccentricity' refers to the quality of being strange or queer.
[3] 'Intractable' means stubborn or inflexible.
[4] Mr. Fogg did not seem to be affected or influenced by the beauty of Aouda's lovely eyes.

The first few days of the voyage passed prosperously, amid favourable weather and propitious[5] winds, and they soon came in sight of the great Andaman[6], the principal of the islands in the Bay of Bengal, with its picturesque Saddle Peak, two thousand four hundred feet high, looming above the waters. The steamer passed along near the shores, but the savage Papuans, who are in the lowest scale of humanity, but are not, as has been asserted, cannibals, did not make their appearance.

The panorama of the islands, as they steamed by them, was superb. Vast forests of palms, arecs, bamboo, teakwood, of the gigantic mimosa, and tree-like ferns covered the foreground, while behind, the graceful outlines of the mountains were traced against the sky; and along the coasts swarmed by thousands the precious swallows whose nests furnish a luxurious dish to the tables of the Celestial Empire[7]. The varied landscape afforded by the Andaman Islands was soon passed, however, and the Rangoon rapidly approached the Straits of Malacca[8], which gave access to the China seas.

What was detective Fix, so unluckily drawn on from country to country, doing all this while? He had managed to embark on the Rangoon at Calcutta without being seen by Passepartout, after leaving orders that, if the warrant should arrive, it should be forwarded to him at Hong Kong; and he hoped to conceal his presence to the end of the voyage. It would have been difficult to explain why he was on board without awakening Passepartout's suspicions, who thought him still at Bombay. But necessity impelled[9] him, nevertheless, to renew his acquaintance with the worthy servant, as will be seen.

All the detective's hopes and wishes were now centred on Hong Kong; for the steamer's stay at Singapore would be too brief to enable him to take any steps there. The arrest must be made at Hong Kong, or the robber would probably escape him for ever. Hong Kong[10] was the last English ground on which he would set foot; beyond, China, Japan, America offered to Fogg an almost certain refuge. If the warrant should at last make its appearance at Hong Kong, Fix could arrest him and give him into the hands of the local police, and there would be no further trouble. But beyond Hong Kong, a simple warrant would be of no avail; an extradition[11] warrant would be necessary, and that

---

[5] 'Propitious' means favourable or promising.

[6] The Andaman Islands are an archipelago in the Bay of Bengal and are part of the Union Territory of India. Until the late 18th century, the natives of these islands, the Andamanese, had had very little contact with the outside world. There were about 10 main tribes, with their respective languages, but now only 2 tribes remain, and their cultural identities have been lost, as they now mostly speak Hindi, an Indian language.

[7] The 'Celestial Empire' is an old name used to refer to China.

[8] The Strait of Malacca is a narrow stretch of water between the Peninsular Malaysia and the Indonesian island of Sumatra.

[9] 'Impel' means to urge someone to do something.

[10] Hong Kong was formerly a British colony until 1997 (except during the Second World War), after that it was returned to China.

[11] 'Extradition' is a formal process for requesting the surrender of a person from one territory to another for prosecution.

would result in delays and obstacles, of which the rascal would take advantage to elude[12] justice.

Fix thought over these probabilities during the long hours which he spent in his cabin, and kept repeating to himself, "Now, either the warrant will be at Hong Kong, in which case I shall arrest my man, or it will not be there; and this time it is absolutely necessary that I should delay his departure. I have failed at Bombay, and I have failed at Calcutta; if I fail at Hong Kong, my reputation is lost: Cost what it may, I must succeed! But how shall I prevent his departure, if that should turn out to be my last resource?"

Fix made up his mind that, if worst came to worst, he would make a confidant of Passepartout, and tell him what kind of a fellow his master really was. That Passepartout was not Fogg's accomplice, he was very certain. The servant, enlightened by his disclosure, and afraid of being himself implicated in the crime, would doubtless become an ally of the detective. But this method was a dangerous one, only to be employed when everything else had failed. A word from Passepartout to his master would ruin all. The detective was therefore in a sore strait[13]. But suddenly a new idea struck him. The presence of Aouda on the Rangoon, in company with Phileas Fogg, gave him new material for reflection.

Who was this woman? What combination of events had made her Fogg's travelling companion? They had evidently met somewhere between Bombay and Calcutta; but where? Had they met accidentally, or had Fogg gone into the interior purposely in quest of this charming damsel? Fix was fairly puzzled. He asked himself whether there had not been a wicked elopement; and this idea so impressed itself upon his mind that he determined to make use of the supposed intrigue[14]. Whether the young woman were married or not, he would be able to create such difficulties for Mr. Fogg at Hong Kong that he could not escape by paying any amount of money.

But could he even wait till they reached Hong Kong? Fogg had an abominable way of jumping from one boat to another, and, before anything could be effected, might get full under way again for Yokohama[15]. [16]

Fix decided that he must warn the English authorities, and signal the Rangoon before her arrival. This was easy to do, since the steamer stopped at Singapore, whence there is a telegraphic wire[17] to Hong Kong. He finally resolved, moreover, before acting more

---

[12] 'Elude' means to escape in a cunning or skilful way.

[13] 'Sore straits' or 'dire straits' are idioms meaning a very difficult situation.

[14] 'Supposed intrigue' refers to the curiosity that has stemmed from Fix's assumption that the lady had in fact eloped with Mr. Fogg.

[15] Yokohama is a Japanese city.

[16] Fix was desperate to arrest Mr. Fogg as soon as possible, as he feared that Mr. Fogg will escape given the slightest of chance.

[17] 'Telegraphic wire' is a wire that transmits messages over telegraphs and telephone signals using electricity or radio signals.

positively, to question Passepartout. It would not be difficult to make him talk; and, as there was no time to lose, Fix prepared to make himself known.

It was now the 30th of October, and on the following day the Rangoon was due at Singapore.

Fix emerged from his cabin and went on deck. Passepartout was promenading up and down in the forward part of the steamer. The detective rushed forward with every appearance of extreme surprise, and exclaimed, "You here, on the Rangoon?"

"What, Monsieur Fix, are you on board?" returned the really astonished Passepartout, recognising his crony[18] of the Mongolia. "Why, I left you at Bombay, and here you are, on the way to Hong Kong! Are you going round the world too?"

"No, no," replied Fix; "I shall stop at Hong Kong—at least for some days."

"Hum!" said Passepartout, who seemed for an instant perplexed. "But how is it I have not seen you on board since we left Calcutta?"

"Oh, a trifle of sea-sickness—I've been staying in my berth. The Gulf of Bengal does not agree with me as well as the Indian Ocean. And how is Mr. Fogg?"

"As well and as punctual as ever, not a day behind time! But, Monsieur Fix, you don't know that we have a young lady with us."

"A young lady?" replied the detective, not seeming to comprehend what was said.[19]

Passepartout thereupon recounted Aouda's history, the affair at the Bombay pagoda, the purchase of the elephant for two thousand pounds, the rescue, the arrest, and sentence of the Calcutta court, and the restoration of Mr. Fogg and himself to liberty on bail. Fix, who was familiar with the last events, seemed to be equally ignorant of all that Passepartout related; and the later was charmed to find so interested a listener.

"But does your master propose to carry this young woman to Europe?"

"Not at all. We are simply going to place her under the protection of one of her relatives, a rich merchant at Hong Kong."

"Nothing to be done there," said Fix to himself, concealing his disappointment.[20] "A glass of gin, Mr. Passepartout?"

"Willingly, Monsieur Fix. We must at least have a friendly glass on board the Rangoon."

---

[18] A 'crony' is a friend or a companion.
[19] Fix pretended as if he was unaware of their lady friend.
[20] Mr. Fix is disappointed to know that there has been no elopement or kidnapping, and that the lady is onboard with her own wish and on her way to live with her relatives. There was now no reason for him to arrest Mr. Fogg.

Comprehension exercise 16

Q1) What can be inferred about Phileas Fogg's attitude towards Aouda based on the text?
a) He is indifferent towards her and does not care about her well-being.
b) He is deeply grateful for her presence and ensures her comfort.
c) He is hesitant to interact with her and avoids conversation.
d) He is suspicious of her motives and keeps his distance.

Q2) Why did Detective Fix decide to question Passepartout?
a) To gather more information about Mr. Fogg's whereabouts.
b) To seek assistance in apprehending Mr. Fogg.
c) To confirm his suspicions about Aouda.
d) To discuss his plans to warn the English authorities.

Q3) Where did Detective Fix hope to arrest Mr. Fogg?
a) Bombay
b) Calcutta
c) Singapore
d) Hong Kong

Q4) What does the word "phlegmatic" mean in the context of the text?
a) Enthusiastic
b) Indifferent
c) Emotional
d) Agitated

Q5) What does the word "automaton" imply about Phileas Fogg's behaviour towards Aouda?
a) He is unpredictable
b) He is mechanical
c) He is compassionate
d) He is impulsive

Chapter 17

SHOWING WHAT HAPPENED ON THE VOYAGE FROM SINGAPORE TO HONG KONG

The detective and Passepartout met often on deck after this interview, though Fix was reserved, and did not attempt to induce his companion to divulge any more facts concerning Mr. Fogg. He caught a glimpse of that mysterious gentleman once or twice; but Mr. Fogg usually confined himself to the cabin, where he kept Aouda company, or, according to his inveterate[1] habit, took a hand at whist.

Passepartout began very seriously to conjecture[2] what strange chance kept Fix still on the route that his master was pursuing. It was really worth considering why this certainly very amiable and complacent person, whom he had first met at Suez, had then encountered on board the Mongolia, who disembarked at Bombay, which he announced as his destination, and now turned up so unexpectedly on the Rangoon, was following Mr. Fogg's tracks step by step. What was Fix's object? Passepartout was ready to wager his Indian shoes—which he religiously preserved—that Fix would also leave Hong Kong at the same time with them, and probably on the same steamer.

Passepartout might have cudgelled[3] his brain for a century without hitting upon the real object which the detective had in view. He never could have imagined that Phileas Fogg was being tracked as a robber around the globe. But, as it is in human nature to attempt the solution of every mystery, Passepartout suddenly discovered an explanation of Fix's movements, which was in truth far from unreasonable. Fix, he thought, could only be an agent of Mr. Fogg's friends at the Reform Club, sent to follow him up, and to ascertain that he really went round the world as had been agreed upon.

"It's clear!" repeated the worthy servant to himself, proud of his shrewdness. "He's a spy sent to keep us in view! That isn't quite the thing, either, to be spying Mr. Fogg, who is so honourable a man! Ah, gentlemen of the Reform, this shall cost you dear!"

Passepartout, enchanted with his discovery, resolved to say nothing to his master, lest he should be justly offended at this mistrust on the part of his adversaries. But he determined to chaff[4] Fix, when he had the chance, with mysterious allusions[5], which, however, need not betray his real suspicions.

---

[1] 'Inveterate' means a confirmed habit.
[2] 'Conjecture' means to form an opinion about something based on incomplete information.
[3] 'Cudgel' means to beat with a short stout stick.
[4] 'Chaff' means to tease or make fun of.
[5] 'Allusion' means an indirect or passing reference.

During the afternoon of Wednesday, 30th October, the Rangoon entered the Strait of Malacca, which separates the peninsula of that name from Sumatra. The mountainous and craggy islets intercepted the beauties of this noble island from the view of the travellers. The Rangoon weighed anchor at Singapore the next day at four a.m., to receive coal, having gained half a day on the prescribed time of her arrival. Phileas Fogg noted this gain in his journal, and then, accompanied by Aouda, who betrayed a desire for a walk on shore, disembarked.

Fix, who suspected Mr. Fogg's every movement, followed them cautiously, without being himself perceived; while Passepartout, laughing in his sleeve at Fix's manoeuvres, went about his usual errands.

The island of Singapore is not imposing in aspect, for there are no mountains; yet its appearance is not without attractions. It is a park checkered by pleasant highways and avenues. A handsome carriage, drawn by a sleek pair of New Holland horses, carried Phileas Fogg and Aouda into the midst of rows of palms with brilliant foliage, and of clove-trees, whereof the cloves form the heart of a half-open flower. Pepper plants replaced the prickly hedges of European fields; sago-bushes, large ferns with gorgeous branches, varied the aspect of this tropical clime; while nutmeg-trees in full foliage filled the air with a penetrating perfume. Agile and grinning bands of monkeys skipped about in the trees, nor were tigers wanting in the jungles.

After a drive of two hours through the country, Aouda and Mr. Fogg returned to the town, which is a vast collection of heavy-looking, irregular houses, surrounded by charming gardens rich in tropical fruits and plants; and at ten o'clock they re-embarked, closely followed by the detective, who had kept them constantly in sight.

Passepartout, who had been purchasing several dozen mangoes—a fruit as large as good-sized apples, of a dark-brown colour outside and a bright red within, and whose white pulp, melting in the mouth, affords gourmands a delicious sensation—was waiting for them on deck. He was only too glad to offer some mangoes to Aouda, who thanked him very gracefully for them.

At eleven o'clock the Rangoon rode out of Singapore harbour, and in a few hours the high mountains of Malacca, with their forests, inhabited by the most beautifully-furred tigers[6] in the world, were lost to view. Singapore is distant some thirteen hundred miles from the island of Hong Kong, which is a little English colony near the Chinese coast. Phileas Fogg hoped to accomplish the journey in six days, so as to be in time for the steamer which would leave on the 6th of November for Yokohama, the principal Japanese port.

The Rangoon had a large quota of passengers, many of whom disembarked at Singapore, among them a number of Indians, Ceylonese, Chinamen, Malays, and Portuguese, mostly second-class travellers.

---

[6] The Malayan Tigers have been classified as Critically Endangered on the IUCN Red List since 2015.

The weather, which had hitherto been fine, changed with the last quarter of the moon. The sea rolled heavily, and the wind at intervals rose almost to a storm, but happily blew from the south-west, and thus aided the steamer's progress. The captain as often as possible put up his sails, and under the double action of steam and sail the vessel made rapid progress along the coasts of Anam and Cochin China. Owing to the defective construction of the Rangoon, however, unusual precautions became necessary in unfavourable weather; but the loss of time which resulted from this cause, while it nearly drove Passepartout out of his senses, did not seem to affect his master in the least. Passepartout blamed the captain, the engineer, and the crew, and consigned all who were connected with the ship to the land where the pepper grows. Perhaps the thought of the gas, which was remorselessly burning at his expense in Saville Row, had something to do with his hot impatience.

"You are in a great hurry, then," said Fix to him one day, "to reach Hong Kong?"

"A very great hurry!"

"Mr. Fogg, I suppose, is anxious to catch the steamer for Yokohama?"

"Terribly anxious."

"You believe in this journey around the world, then?"

"Absolutely. Don't you, Mr. Fix?"

"I? I don't believe a word of it."

"You're a sly dog!" said Passepartout, winking at him.[7]

This expression rather disturbed Fix, without his knowing why. Had the Frenchman guessed his real purpose? He knew not what to think. But how could Passepartout have discovered that he was a detective? Yet, in speaking as he did, the man evidently meant more than he expressed.[8]

Passepartout went still further the next day; he could not hold his tongue.

"Mr. Fix," said he, in a bantering tone, "shall we be so unfortunate as to lose you when we get to Hong Kong?"

"Why," responded Fix, a little embarrassed, "I don't know; perhaps—"

"Ah, if you would only go on with us! An agent of the Peninsular Company, you know, can't stop on the way! You were only going to Bombay, and here you are in China. America is not far off, and from America to Europe is only a step."

---

[7] Passepartout believes he has uncovered the true purpose of Mr. Fix's journey, which was to trail Mr. Fogg on his global travels.

[8] Passepartout engages in banter with Mr. Fix, intending to confuse him. This leaves Mr. Fix worried and unsure if Passepartout already knows his true identity.

Fix looked intently at his companion, whose countenance was as serene as possible, and laughed with him. But Passepartout persisted in chaffing him by asking him if he made much by his present occupation.

"Yes, and no," returned Fix; "there is good and bad luck in such things. But you must understand that I don't travel at my own expense."

"Oh, I am quite sure of that!" cried Passepartout, laughing heartily.[9]

Fix, fairly puzzled, descended to his cabin and gave himself up to his reflections. He was evidently suspected; somehow or other the Frenchman had found out that he was a detective. But had he told his master? What part was he playing in all this: was he an accomplice or not? Was the game, then, up? Fix spent several hours turning these things over in his mind, sometimes thinking that all was lost, then persuading himself that Fogg was ignorant of his presence, and then undecided what course it was best to take.

Nevertheless, he preserved his coolness of mind, and at last resolved to deal plainly with Passepartout. If he did not find it practicable to arrest Fogg at Hong Kong, and if Fogg made preparations to leave that last foothold of English territory, he, Fix, would tell Passepartout all. Either the servant was the accomplice of his master, and in this case the master knew of his operations, and he should fail; or else the servant knew nothing about the robbery, and then his interest would be to abandon the robber.

Such was the situation between Fix and Passepartout. Meanwhile Phileas Fogg moved about above them in the most majestic and unconscious indifference. He was passing methodically in his orbit around the world, regardless of the lesser stars which gravitated around him. Yet there was near by what the astronomers would call a disturbing star, which might have produced an agitation in this gentleman's heart. But no! the charms of Aouda failed to act, to Passepartout's great surprise; and the disturbances, if they existed, would have been more difficult to calculate than those of Uranus which led to the discovery of Neptune.[10]

It was every day an increasing wonder to Passepartout, who read in Aouda's eyes the depths of her gratitude to his master. Phileas Fogg, though brave and gallant, must be, he thought, quite heartless. As to the sentiment which this journey might have awakened in

---

[9] Passepartout assumed that the members of the Reform Club were paying Fix to go around following Mr. Fogg.

[10] The location of Planet Neptune was mathematically predicted before it was directly observed. Planet Uranus was discovered in 1781, and the planet had completed its one full orbit by 1847; however, a series of irregularities were observed by the astronomers which hinted at the presence of another planet whose gravity may be disturbing Uranus's path around the Sun. These calculations determined the position and nature of planet Neptune before it was discovered in 1846.

The writer employs an analogy with the planets and the sun to illustrate the characters' positions in the story. In this analogy, the world represents the sun, Mr. Fogg is likened to a planet, and Lady Aouda is compared to a disrupting star. However, despite her presence, she appears to have minimal influence on Mr. Fogg's trajectory.

him, there was clearly no trace of such a thing; while poor Passepartout existed in perpetual reveries[11].

One day he was leaning on the railing of the engine-room, and was observing the engine, when a sudden pitch of the steamer threw the screw out of the water. The steam came hissing out of the valves; and this made Passepartout indignant[12].

"The valves are not sufficiently charged!" he exclaimed. "We are not going. Oh, these English! If this was an American craft, we should blow up, perhaps, but we should at all events go faster!"

---

[11] 'Reverie' is a state of being lost in daydreams.
[12] 'Indignant' means annoyed or angry.

A Study Guide: Around the World in Eighty Days

Comprehension exercise 17

Q1) Why does Fix decide to make himself known to Passepartout?
a) He wants to warn Passepartout about Mr. Fogg's true nature.
b) He needs Passepartout's help to apprehend Mr. Fogg.
c) He wants to gather information about Mr. Fogg's plans.
d) He hopes to gain Passepartout's trust to achieve his own objectives.

Q2) Why does Fix feign ignorance about Aouda when Passepartout recounts her history?
a) Because he wants to see if Passepartout will reveal more information.
b) Because he genuinely doesn't remember encountering Aouda before.
c) Because he is trying to maintain his cover and conceal his true intentions.
d) Because he is preoccupied with other thoughts and not paying attention.

Q3) What does Fix plan to do before acting more positively in his pursuit of Mr. Fogg?
a) Warn the English authorities
b) Question Passepartout
c) Signal the Rangoon before her arrival at Singapore
d) Signal the Rangoon before her departure from Hong Kong

Q4) What does the word "punctual" mean in the context of the text?
a) Strict
b) Precise
c) Timely
d) Disorganized

Q5) Which word best describes Fix's reaction to Passepartout's recounting of events?
a) Disinterested
b) Enthusiastic
c) Surprised
d) Amused

Chapter 18

IN WHICH PHILEAS FOGG, PASSEPARTOUT, AND FIX GO EACH ABOUT HIS BUSINESS

The weather was bad during the latter days of the voyage. The wind, obstinately remaining in the north-west, blew a gale, and retarded the steamer. The Rangoon rolled heavily and the passengers became impatient of the long, monstrous waves which the wind raised before their path. A sort of tempest[1] arose on the 3rd of November, the squall knocking the vessel about with fury, and the waves running high. The Rangoon reefed all her sails[2], and even the rigging proved too much, whistling and shaking amid the squall. The steamer was forced to proceed slowly, and the captain estimated that she would reach Hong Kong twenty hours behind time, and more if the storm lasted.

Phileas Fogg gazed at the tempestuous sea, which seemed to be struggling especially to delay him, with his habitual tranquillity. He never changed countenance for an instant, though a delay of twenty hours, by making him too late for the Yokohama boat, would almost inevitably cause the loss of the wager. But this man of nerve manifested neither impatience nor annoyance; it seemed as if the storm were a part of his programme, and had been foreseen. Aouda was amazed to find him as calm as he had been from the first time she saw him.

Fix did not look at the state of things in the same light. The storm greatly pleased him.[3] His satisfaction would have been complete had the Rangoon been forced to retreat before the violence of wind and waves. Each delay filled him with hope, for it became more and more probable that Fogg would be obliged to remain some days at Hong Kong; and now the heavens themselves became his allies, with the gusts and squalls. It mattered not that they made him sea-sick—he made no account of this inconvenience; and, whilst his body was writhing under their effects, his spirit bounded with hopeful exultation.

Passepartout was enraged beyond expression by the unpropitious[4] weather. Everything had gone so well till now! Earth and sea had seemed to be at his master's service; steamers and railways obeyed him; wind and steam united to speed his journey. Had the hour of adversity come? Passepartout was as much excited as if the twenty thousand pounds were to come from his own pocket. The storm exasperated him, the

---

[1] 'Tempest' is a violent windy storm.
[2] 'Reefing of sails' means reducing the area of a sail by either folding or rolling its canvas.
[3] Fix was pleased by this turn of events because it would potentially cause a delay in Mr. Fogg's travel plans. This delay would provide Fix with a better opportunity to arrest Mr. Fogg and achieve his objective.
[4] 'Unpropitious' means unfavourable or unsympathetic.

gale[5] made him furious, and he longed to lash the obstinate sea into obedience. Poor fellow! Fix carefully concealed from him his own satisfaction, for, had he betrayed it, Passepartout could scarcely have restrained himself from personal violence.[6]

Passepartout remained on deck as long as the tempest lasted, being unable to remain quiet below, and taking it into his head to aid the progress of the ship by lending a hand with the crew. He overwhelmed the captain, officers, and sailors, who could not help laughing at his impatience, with all sorts of questions. He wanted to know exactly how long the storm was going to last; whereupon he was referred to the barometer[7], which seemed to have no intention of rising. Passepartout shook it, but with no perceptible effect; for neither shaking nor maledictions[8] could prevail upon it to change its mind.[9]

On the 4th, however, the sea became more calm, and the storm lessened its violence; the wind veered southward, and was once more favourable. Passepartout cleared up with the weather. Some of the sails were unfurled, and the Rangoon resumed its most rapid speed. The time lost could not, however, be regained. Land was not signalled until five o'clock on the morning of the 6th; the steamer was due on the 5th. Phileas Fogg was twenty-four hours behind-hand, and the Yokohama steamer would, of course, be missed.

The pilot went on board at six, and took his place on the bridge, to guide the Rangoon through the channels to the port of Hong Kong. Passepartout longed to ask him if the steamer had left for Yokohama; but he dared not, for he wished to preserve the spark of hope, which still remained till the last moment. He had confided his anxiety to Fix who—the sly rascal!—tried to console him by saying that Mr. Fogg would be in time if he took the next boat; but this only put Passepartout in a passion.

Mr. Fogg, bolder than his servant, did not hesitate to approach the pilot, and tranquilly ask him if he knew when a steamer would leave Hong Kong for Yokohama.

"At high tide to-morrow morning," answered the pilot.

"Ah!" said Mr. Fogg, without betraying any astonishment.

Passepartout, who heard what passed, would willingly have embraced the pilot, while Fix would have been glad to twist his neck.

"What is the steamer's name?" asked Mr. Fogg.

"The Carnatic."

"Ought she not to have gone yesterday?"

---

[5] A 'gale' is a strong wind.
[6] Passepartout was so angry and irritated at the storm causing the delay that if Fix had not hidden his satisfaction, Passepartout would have squabbled with him.
[7] A 'barometer' is an instrument used in forecasting the weather and determining the altitude by measuring atmospheric pressure.
[8] 'Malediction' is a magical word or phrase uttered with the intention of bringing evil, a curse.
[9] In his agitation, Passepartout was forcefully jerking the barometer, cursing it all the while.

"Yes, sir; but they had to repair one of her boilers, and so her departure was postponed till to-morrow."

"Thank you," returned Mr. Fogg, descending mathematically to the saloon.

Passepartout clasped the pilot's hand and shook it heartily in his delight, exclaiming, "Pilot, you are the best of good fellows!"

The pilot probably does not know to this day why his responses won him this enthusiastic greeting. He remounted the bridge, and guided the steamer through the flotilla of junks, tankas[10], and fishing boats which crowd the harbour of Hong Kong.

At one o'clock the Rangoon was at the quay, and the passengers were going ashore.

Chance had strangely favoured Phileas Fogg, for had not the Carnatic been forced to lie over for repairing her boilers, she would have left on the 6th of November, and the passengers for Japan would have been obliged to await for a week the sailing of the next steamer. Mr. Fogg was, it is true, twenty-four hours behind his time; but this could not seriously imperil the remainder of his tour.

The steamer which crossed the Pacific from Yokohama to San Francisco made a direct connection with that from Hong Kong, and it could not sail until the latter reached Yokohama; and if Mr. Fogg was twenty-four hours late on reaching Yokohama, this time would no doubt be easily regained in the voyage of twenty-two days across the Pacific. He found himself, then, about twenty-four hours behind-hand, thirty-five days after leaving London.

The Carnatic was announced to leave Hong Kong at five the next morning. Mr. Fogg had sixteen hours in which to attend to his business there, which was to deposit Aouda safely with her wealthy relative.

On landing, he conducted her to a palanquin, in which they repaired to the Club Hotel. A room was engaged for the young woman, and Mr. Fogg, after seeing that she wanted for nothing, set out in search of her cousin Jeejeeh. He instructed Passepartout to remain at the hotel until his return, that Aouda might not be left entirely alone.

Mr. Fogg repaired to the Exchange, where, he did not doubt, every one would know so wealthy and considerable a personage as the Parsee merchant. Meeting a broker, he made the inquiry, to learn that Jeejeeh had left China two years before, and, retiring from business with an immense fortune, had taken up his residence in Europe—in Holland the broker thought, with the merchants of which country he had principally traded. Phileas Fogg returned to the hotel, begged a moment's conversation with Aouda, and without more ado, apprised her that Jeejeeh was no longer at Hong Kong, but probably in Holland.

Aouda at first said nothing. She passed her hand across her forehead, and reflected a few moments. Then, in her sweet, soft voice, she said: "What ought I to do, Mr. Fogg?"

---

[10] The Tankas, also known as the boat people, are an ethnic group in Southern China, who live on boats with fishing as their livelihoods.

"It is very simple," responded the gentleman. "Go on to Europe."

"But I cannot intrude—"

"You do not intrude, nor do you in the least embarrass my project. Passepartout!"

"Monsieur."

"Go to the Carnatic, and engage three cabins."

Passepartout, delighted that the young woman, who was very gracious to him, was going to continue the journey with them, went off at a brisk gait to obey his master's order.

Comprehension exercise 18

Q1) How did Phileas Fogg react to the delay caused by the storm?
a) He became anxious and irritable, fearing the loss of the wager.
b) He expressed frustration and impatience towards the captain.
c) He remained calm and composed, as if the delay was expected.
d) He blamed the crew and demanded they speed up the journey.

Q2) Why did Fix feel pleased about the storm?
a) He enjoyed the excitement and danger it brought.
b) He saw it as an opportunity to prevent Fogg from winning the wager.
c) He believed it would speed up the journey to Hong Kong.
d) He thought it would provide valuable experience for the crew.

Q3) What was the name of the steamer that Phileas Fogg inquired about with the pilot?
a) The Rangoon
b) The Carnatic
c) The Yokohama
d) The Pacific

Q4) What does the word "obstinate" mean in the context of the text?
a) Unpredictable
b) Stubborn
c) Unyielding
d) Fickle

Q5) What does the word "maledictions" imply about Passepartout's actions?
a) He was praying fervently for the storm to end.
b) He was shouting curses at the barometer for not changing.
c) He was offering blessings to the crew for their hard work.
d) He was expressing gratitude to the captain for his leadership.

Chapter 19

IN WHICH PASSEPARTOUT TAKES A TOO GREAT INTEREST IN HIS MASTER,
AND WHAT COMES OF IT

Hong Kong is an island which came into the possession of the English by the Treaty of Nankin, after the war of 1842; and the colonising genius of the English has created upon it an important city and an excellent port. The island is situated at the mouth of the Canton River, and is separated by about sixty miles from the Portuguese town of Macao, on the opposite coast. Hong Kong has beaten Macao in the struggle for the Chinese trade, and now the greater part of the transportation of Chinese goods finds its depot at the former place. Docks, hospitals, wharves, a Gothic cathedral, a government house, macadamised streets[1], give to Hong Kong the appearance of a town in Kent or Surrey transferred by some strange magic to the antipodes[2].

Passepartout wandered, with his hands in his pockets, towards the Victoria port, gazing as he went at the curious palanquins and other modes of conveyance, and the groups of Chinese, Japanese, and Europeans who passed to and fro in the streets. Hong Kong seemed to him not unlike Bombay, Calcutta, and Singapore, since, like them, it betrayed[3] everywhere the evidence of English supremacy. At the Victoria port he found a confused mass of ships of all nations: English, French, American, and Dutch, men-of-war and trading vessels, Japanese and Chinese junks, sempas, tankas, and flower-boats, which formed so many floating parterres[4]. Passepartout noticed in the crowd a number of the natives who seemed very old and were dressed in yellow. On going into a barber's to get shaved he learned that these ancient men were all at least eighty years old, at which age they are permitted to wear yellow, which is the Imperial colour. Passepartout, without exactly knowing why, thought this very funny.[5]

On reaching the quay where they were to embark on the Carnatic, he was not astonished to find Fix walking up and down. The detective seemed very much disturbed and disappointed.

---

[1] 'Macadam' is a type of road construction, in which crushed stones are placed and compacted thoroughly, and then covered with a binding layer of stone dust and cement or bituminous binder.

[2] The antipodes are two diametrically opposite places on the Earth.

[3] 'Betray' means to reveal or show evidence.

[4] 'Parterres' are the ornamental arrangement of flower beds.

[5] Yellow, the colour of the Sun, was regarded as the costume colour of the esteemed emperors of Imperial China.

"This is bad," muttered Passepartout, "for the gentlemen of the Reform Club!" He accosted[6] Fix with a merry smile, as if he had not perceived that gentleman's chagrin.[7] The detective had, indeed, good reasons to inveigh[8] against the bad luck which pursued him. The warrant had not come! It was certainly on the way, but as certainly it could not now reach Hong Kong for several days; and, this being the last English territory on Mr. Fogg's route, the robber would escape, unless he could manage to detain him.

"Well, Monsieur Fix," said Passepartout, "have you decided to go with us so far as America?"

"Yes," returned Fix, through his set teeth.

"Good!" exclaimed Passepartout, laughing heartily. "I knew you could not persuade yourself to separate from us. Come and engage your berth."

They entered the steamer office and secured cabins for four persons. The clerk, as he gave them the tickets, informed them that, the repairs on the Carnatic having been completed, the steamer would leave that very evening, and not next morning, as had been announced.

"That will suit my master all the better," said Passepartout. "I will go and let him know."

Fix now decided to make a bold move; he resolved to tell Passepartout all. It seemed to be the only possible means of keeping Phileas Fogg several days longer at Hong Kong. He accordingly invited his companion into a tavern which caught his eye on the quay. On entering, they found themselves in a large room handsomely decorated, at the end of which was a large camp-bed furnished with cushions. Several persons lay upon this bed in a deep sleep. At the small tables which were arranged about the room some thirty customers were drinking English beer, porter, gin, and brandy; smoking, the while, long red clay pipes stuffed with little balls of opium mingled with essence of rose. From time to time one of the smokers, overcome with the narcotic, would slip under the table, whereupon the waiters, taking him by the head and feet, carried and laid him upon the bed. The bed already supported twenty of these stupefied sots[9].

Fix and Passepartout saw that they were in a smoking-house haunted by those wretched[10], cadaverous[11], idiotic creatures to whom the English merchants sell every year the miserable drug called opium, to the amount of one million four hundred thousand pounds—thousands devoted to one of the most despicable vices which afflict humanity! The Chinese government has in vain attempted to deal with the evil by stringent laws. It passed gradually from the rich, to whom it was at first exclusively reserved, to the lower

---

[6] 'Accost' means to approach or address someone.
[7] Passepartout approached Mr. Fix boldly, pretending to be unaware of his annoyance or anger.
[8] 'Inveigh' means to protest or criticise something.
[9] A sot is a habitual drunkard.
[10] 'Wretched' means miserable and unhappy.
[11] 'Cadaverous' means very pale and sickly thin.

classes, and then its ravages could not be arrested.[12] Opium is smoked everywhere, at all times, by men and women, in the Celestial Empire; and, once accustomed to it, the victims cannot dispense with it, except by suffering horrible bodily contortions and agonies. A great smoker can smoke as many as eight pipes a day; but he dies in five years. It was in one of these dens that Fix and Passepartout, in search of a friendly glass, found themselves. Passepartout had no money, but willingly accepted Fix's invitation in the hope of returning the obligation at some future time.

They ordered two bottles of port, to which the Frenchman did ample justice, whilst Fix observed him with close attention. They chatted about the journey, and Passepartout was especially merry at the idea that Fix was going to continue it with them. When the bottles were empty, however, he rose to go and tell his master of the change in the time of the sailing of the Carnatic.

Fix caught him by the arm, and said, "Wait a moment."

"What for, Mr. Fix?"

"I want to have a serious talk with you."

"A serious talk!" cried Passepartout, drinking up the little wine that was left in the bottom of his glass. "Well, we'll talk about it to-morrow; I haven't time now."

"Stay! What I have to say concerns your master."

Passepartout, at this, looked attentively at his companion. Fix's face seemed to have a singular expression. He resumed his seat.

"What is it that you have to say?"

Fix placed his hand upon Passepartout's arm, and, lowering his voice, said, "You have guessed who I am?"

"Parbleu!" said Passepartout, smiling.

"Then I'm going to tell you everything—"

"Now that I know everything, my friend! Ah! that's very good. But go on, go on. First, though, let me tell you that those gentlemen have put themselves to a useless expense."

"Useless!" said Fix. "You speak confidently. It's clear that you don't know how large the sum is."

"Of course I do," returned Passepartout. "Twenty thousand pounds."[13]

"Fifty-five thousand!" answered Fix, pressing his companion's hand. [14]

---

[12] English traders had started selling opium first to the wealthy as a mark of riches and class; however, the poison soon passed on to the middle and lower classes.

[13] Passepartout is referring to the amount that the bet has been placed for - twenty thousand pounds, as he thinks that's the reason Fix is following them around on instructions of the Reform Club members.

[14] Fix is referring to the amount stolen from the Bank of England – fifty-five thousand pounds.

"What!" cried the Frenchman. "Has Monsieur Fogg dared—fifty-five thousand pounds! Well, there's all the more reason for not losing an instant," he continued, getting up hastily.

Fix pushed Passepartout back in his chair, and resumed: "Fifty-five thousand pounds; and if I succeed, I get two thousand pounds. If you'll help me, I'll let you have five hundred of them."

"Help you?" cried Passepartout, whose eyes were standing wide open.

"Yes; help me keep Mr. Fogg here for two or three days."

"Why, what are you saying? Those gentlemen are not satisfied with following my master and suspecting his honour, but they must try to put obstacles in his way! I blush for them![15]"

"What do you mean?"

"I mean that it is a piece of shameful trickery. They might as well waylay[16] Mr. Fogg and put his money in their pockets!"

"That's just what we count on doing."

"It's a conspiracy, then," cried Passepartout, who became more and more excited as the liquor mounted in his head, for he drank without perceiving it. "A real conspiracy! And gentlemen, too. Bah!"

Fix began to be puzzled.

"Members of the Reform Club!" continued Passepartout. "You must know, Monsieur Fix, that my master is an honest man, and that, when he makes a wager, he tries to win it fairly!"

"But who do you think I am?" asked Fix, looking at him intently.

"Parbleu[17]! An agent of the members of the Reform Club, sent out here to interrupt my master's journey. But, though I found you out some time ago, I've taken good care to say nothing about it to Mr. Fogg."

"He knows nothing, then?"

"Nothing," replied Passepartout, again emptying his glass.

The detective passed his hand across his forehead, hesitating before he spoke again. What should he do? Passepartout's mistake seemed sincere, but it made his design more difficult. It was evident that the servant was not the master's accomplice, as Fix had been inclined to suspect.

---

[15] 'I blush for them'- Passepartout refers to the embarrassment these men should feel when thinking of such ideas.

[16] 'Waylay' means to interrupt or trouble someone.

[17] 'Parbleu' is a French term used to express disbelief or surprise.

"Well," said the detective to himself, "as he is not an accomplice, he will help me."

He had no time to lose: Fogg must be detained at Hong Kong, so he resolved to make a clean breast of it.[18]

"Listen to me," said Fix abruptly. "I am not, as you think, an agent of the members of the Reform Club—"

"Bah!" retorted Passepartout, with an air of raillery[19].

"I am a police detective, sent out here by the London office."

"You, a detective?"

"I will prove it. Here is my commission[20]."

Passepartout was speechless with astonishment when Fix displayed this document, the genuineness of which could not be doubted.

"Mr. Fogg's wager," resumed Fix, "is only a pretext, of which you and the gentlemen of the Reform are dupes. He had a motive for securing your innocent complicity."

"But why?"

"Listen. On the 28th of last September a robbery of fifty-five thousand pounds was committed at the Bank of England by a person whose description was fortunately secured. Here is his description; it answers exactly to that of Mr. Phileas Fogg."

"What nonsense!" cried Passepartout, striking the table with his fist. "My master is the most honourable of men!"

"How can you tell? You know scarcely anything about him. You went into his service the day he came away; and he came away on a foolish pretext, without trunks, and carrying a large amount in banknotes. And yet you are bold enough to assert that he is an honest man!"

"Yes, yes," repeated the poor fellow, mechanically.

"Would you like to be arrested as his accomplice?"

Passepartout, overcome by what he had heard, held his head between his hands, and did not dare to look at the detective. Phileas Fogg, the saviour of Aouda, that brave and generous man, a robber! And yet how many presumptions there were against him! Passepartout essayed to reject the suspicions which forced themselves upon his mind; he did not wish to believe that his master was guilty.

"Well, what do you want of me?" said he, at last, with an effort.

---

[18] 'To make a clean breast of something' is an idiom that means to speak openly and honestly about something that has been lied about previously.

[19] 'Raillery' means to banter or joke with someone in good nature.

[20] A 'commission' here refers to a document that authorizes a person with the authority to do or produce something.

"See here," replied Fix; "I have tracked Mr. Fogg to this place, but as yet I have failed to receive the warrant of arrest for which I sent to London. You must help me to keep him here in Hong Kong—"

"I! But I—"

"I will share with you the two thousand pounds reward offered by the Bank of England."

"Never!" replied Passepartout, who tried to rise, but fell back, exhausted in mind and body.

"Mr. Fix," he stammered, "even should what you say be true—if my master is really the robber you are seeking for—which I deny—I have been, am, in his service; I have seen his generosity and goodness; and I will never betray him—not for all the gold in the world. I come from a village where they don't eat that kind of bread!"

"You refuse?"

"I refuse."

"Consider that I've said nothing," said Fix; "and let us drink."

"Yes; let us drink!"

Passepartout felt himself yielding more and more to the effects of the liquor. Fix, seeing that he must, at all hazards, be separated from his master, wished to entirely overcome him. Some pipes full of opium lay upon the table. Fix slipped one into Passepartout's hand. He took it, put it between his lips, lit it, drew several puffs, and his head, becoming heavy under the influence of the narcotic, fell upon the table.

"At last!" said Fix, seeing Passepartout unconscious. "Mr. Fogg will not be informed of the Carnatic's departure;[21] and, if he is, he will have to go without this cursed Frenchman!"

And, after paying his bill, Fix left the tavern.

---

[21] Mr. Fogg remained unaware that the steamer would depart that very evening, not the following morning.

A Study Guide: Around the World in Eighty Days

Comprehension exercise 19

Q1) Why did Passepartout find Hong Kong similar to other cities like Bombay, Calcutta, and Singapore?
a) Because it was dominated by English influence.
b) Because it had a diverse population of Chinese, Japanese, and Europeans.
c) Because it was located at the mouth of a river.
d) Because it had a large port with ships of various nations.

Q2) What is the reason behind the old Chinese men wearing yellow clothing?
a) Because it is their traditional attire.
b) Because it indicates their age, being at least eighty years old.
c) Because yellow is considered lucky in Chinese culture.
d) Because it signifies their occupation as barbers.

Q3) What does the word "stupefied" mean in the context of the text?
a) Angry
b) Confused
c) Overwhelmed
d) Drugged

Q4) What does the word "cadaverous" suggest about the appearance of the opium smokers?
a) Joyful
b) Healthy
c) Pale and emaciated
d) Energetic

Q5) What does the word "raillery" mean as used in the sentence "Bah!" retorted Passepartout, with an air of raillery.
a) Sarcasm or mockery
b) Sympathy or understanding
c) Seriousness or solemnity
d) Eagerness or excitement

Chapter 20

IN WHICH FIX COMES FACE TO FACE WITH PHILEAS FOGG

While these events were passing at the opium-house, Mr. Fogg, unconscious of the danger he was in of losing the steamer, was quietly escorting Aouda about the streets of the English quarter, making the necessary purchases for the long voyage before them. It was all very well for an Englishman like Mr. Fogg to make the tour of the world with a carpet-bag; a lady could not be expected to travel comfortably under such conditions. He acquitted his task with characteristic serenity, and invariably replied to the remonstrances[1] of his fair companion, who was confused by his patience and generosity:

"It is in the interest of my journey—a part of my programme."

The purchases made, they returned to the hotel, where they dined at a sumptuously served table-d'hote[2]; after which Aouda, shaking hands with her protector after the English fashion, retired to her room for rest. Mr. Fogg absorbed himself throughout the evening in the perusal of The Times and Illustrated London News.

Had he been capable of being astonished at anything, it would have been not to see his servant return at bedtime. But, knowing that the steamer was not to leave for Yokohama until the next morning, he did not disturb himself about the matter. When Passepartout did not appear the next morning to answer his master's bell, Mr. Fogg, not betraying the least vexation, contented himself with taking his carpet-bag, calling Aouda, and sending for a palanquin.

It was then eight o'clock; at half-past nine, it being then high tide, the Carnatic would leave the harbour. Mr. Fogg and Aouda got into the palanquin, their luggage being brought after on a wheelbarrow, and half an hour later stepped upon the quay whence they were to embark. Mr. Fogg then learned that the Carnatic had sailed the evening before. He had expected to find not only the steamer, but his domestic, and was forced to give up both; but no sign of disappointment appeared on his face, and he merely remarked to Aouda, "It is an accident, madam; nothing more."

At this moment a man who had been observing him attentively approached. It was Fix, who, bowing, addressed Mr. Fogg: "Were you not, like me, sir, a passenger by the Rangoon, which arrived yesterday?"

"I was, sir," replied Mr. Fogg coldly. "But I have not the honour—"

---

[1] 'Remonstrance' means an earnest opposition towards someone or something.
[2] Table-d'hôte is a French term used for a set multi-course menu offered at a fixed price in a restaurant. Back then, the French restaurants offered two choices to their diners - one was a là carte, where dishes were ordered and paid for individually; and the other was table-d'hôte.

"Pardon me; I thought I should find your servant here."

"Do you know where he is, sir?" asked Aouda anxiously.

"What!" responded Fix, feigning[3] surprise. "Is he not with you?"

"No," said Aouda. "He has not made his appearance since yesterday. Could he have gone on board the Carnatic without us?"

"Without you, madam?" answered the detective. "Excuse me, did you intend to sail in the Carnatic?"

"Yes, sir."

"So did I, madam, and I am excessively disappointed. The Carnatic, its repairs being completed, left Hong Kong twelve hours before the stated time, without any notice being given; and we must now wait a week for another steamer."

As he said "a week" Fix felt his heart leap for joy. Fogg detained at Hong Kong for a week! There would be time for the warrant to arrive, and fortune at last favoured the representative of the law. His horror may be imagined when he heard Mr. Fogg say, in his placid voice, "But there are other vessels besides the Carnatic, it seems to me, in the harbour of Hong Kong."

And, offering his arm to Aouda, he directed his steps toward the docks in search of some craft about to start. Fix, stupefied, followed; it seemed as if he were attached to Mr. Fogg by an invisible thread. Chance, however, appeared really to have abandoned the man it had hitherto served so well. For three hours Phileas Fogg wandered about the docks, with the determination, if necessary, to charter a vessel to carry him to Yokohama; but he could only find vessels which were loading or unloading, and which could not therefore set sail. Fix began to hope again.[4]

But Mr. Fogg, far from being discouraged, was continuing his search, resolved not to stop if he had to resort to Macao, when he was accosted[5] by a sailor on one of the wharves.

"Is your honour looking for a boat?"

"Have you a boat ready to sail?"

"Yes, your honour; a pilot-boat—No. 43—the best in the harbour."

"Does she go fast?"

"Between eight and nine knots the hour. Will you look at her?"

"Yes."

"Your honour will be satisfied with her. Is it for a sea excursion?"

---

[3] 'Feign' means to give a false appearance of something.
[4] Mr. Fogg couldn't find a single vessel that was ready to set sail.
[5] 'Accost' means to confront someone or speak to someone in an aggressive way.

"No; for a voyage."

"A voyage?"

"Yes, will you agree to take me to Yokohama?"

The sailor leaned on the railing, opened his eyes wide, and said, "Is your honour joking?"

"No. I have missed the Carnatic, and I must get to Yokohama by the 14th at the latest, to take the boat for San Francisco."

"I am sorry," said the sailor; "but it is impossible."

"I offer you a hundred pounds per day, and an additional reward of two hundred pounds if I reach Yokohama in time."

"Are you in earnest?"

"Very much so."

The pilot walked away a little distance, and gazed out to sea, evidently struggling between the anxiety to gain a large sum and the fear of venturing so far. Fix was in mortal suspense.

Mr. Fogg turned to Aouda and asked her, "You would not be afraid, would you, madam?"

"Not with you, Mr. Fogg," was her answer.

The pilot now returned, shuffling his hat in his hands.

"Well, pilot?" said Mr. Fogg.

"Well, your honour," replied he, "I could not risk myself, my men, or my little boat of scarcely twenty tons on so long a voyage at this time of year. Besides, we could not reach Yokohama in time, for it is sixteen hundred and sixty miles from Hong Kong."

"Only sixteen hundred," said Mr. Fogg.

"It's the same thing."

Fix breathed more freely.

"But," added the pilot, "it might be arranged another way."

Fix ceased to breathe at all.

"How?" asked Mr. Fogg.

"By going to Nagasaki, at the extreme south of Japan, or even to Shanghai, which is only eight hundred miles from here. In going to Shanghai we should not be forced to sail wide of the Chinese coast, which would be a great advantage, as the currents run northward, and would aid us."

"Pilot," said Mr. Fogg, "I must take the American steamer at Yokohama, and not at Shanghai or Nagasaki."

"Why not?" returned the pilot. "The San Francisco steamer does not start from Yokohama. It puts in at Yokohama and Nagasaki, but it starts from Shanghai."

"You are sure of that?"

"Perfectly."

"And when does the boat leave Shanghai?"

"On the 11th, at seven in the evening. We have, therefore, four days before us, that is ninety-six hours; and in that time, if we had good luck and a south-west wind, and the sea was calm, we could make those eight hundred miles to Shanghai."

"And you could go—"

"In an hour; as soon as provisions could be got aboard and the sails put up."

"It is a bargain. Are you the master of the boat?"

"Yes; John Bunsby, master of the Tankadere."

"Would you like some earnest-money[6]?"

"If it would not put your honour out—"

"Here are two hundred pounds on account sir," added Phileas Fogg, turning to Fix, "if you would like to take advantage—"

"Thanks, sir; I was about to ask the favour."

"Very well. In half an hour we shall go on board."

"But poor Passepartout?" urged Aouda, who was much disturbed by the servant's disappearance.

"I shall do all I can to find him," replied Phileas Fogg.

While Fix, in a feverish, nervous state, repaired to the pilot-boat, the others directed their course to the police-station at Hong Kong. Phileas Fogg there gave Passepartout's description, and left a sum of money to be spent in the search for him. The same formalities having been gone through at the French consulate, and the palanquin having stopped at the hotel for the luggage, which had been sent back there, they returned to the wharf.

It was now three o'clock; and pilot-boat No. 43, with its crew on board, and its provisions stored away, was ready for departure.

The Tankadere was a neat little craft of twenty tons, as gracefully built as if she were a racing yacht. Her shining copper sheathing, her galvanised iron-work, her deck, white as

---

[6] 'Earnest-money' is a sum of money that is deposited to demonstrate one's seriousness about buying a product or service.

ivory, betrayed the pride taken by John Bunsby in making her presentable. Her two masts leaned a trifle backward; she carried brigantine[7], foresail[8], storm-jib[9], and standing-jib[10], and was well rigged for running before the wind; and she seemed capable of brisk speed, which, indeed, she had already proved by gaining several prizes in pilot-boat races. The crew of the Tankadere was composed of John Bunsby, the master, and four hardy mariners, who were familiar with the Chinese seas. John Bunsby, himself, a man of forty-five or thereabouts, vigorous, sunburnt, with a sprightly expression of the eye, and energetic and self-reliant countenance, would have inspired confidence in the most timid.

Phileas Fogg and Aouda went on board, where they found Fix already installed. Below deck was a square cabin, of which the walls bulged out in the form of cots, above a circular divan; in the centre was a table provided with a swinging lamp. The accommodation was confined, but neat.

"I am sorry to have nothing better to offer you," said Mr. Fogg to Fix, who bowed without responding.

The detective had a feeling akin to humiliation in profiting by the kindness of Mr. Fogg.

"It's certain," thought he, "though rascal as he is, he is a polite one!"

The sails and the English flag were hoisted at ten minutes past three. Mr. Fogg and Aouda, who were seated on deck, cast a last glance at the quay, in the hope of espying Passepartout. Fix was not without his fears lest chance should direct the steps of the unfortunate servant, whom he had so badly treated, in this direction; in which case an explanation the reverse of satisfactory to the detective must have ensued. But the Frenchman did not appear, and, without doubt, was still lying under the stupefying influence of the opium.

John Bunsby, master, at length gave the order to start, and the Tankadere, taking the wind under her brigantine, foresail, and standing-jib, bounded briskly forward over the waves.

---

[7] 'Brigantine' is a two-masted sailing vessel with a square-rigged foremast and at least two sails on the main mast.

[8] 'Foresail' is a type of sail set on the foremast mast of a sailing vessel.

[9] A 'Storm-jib' is a small, robust jib used in stormy weather to maintain manoeuvrability of a vessel.

[10] A 'Standing-jib' is a triangular sail that sets ahead of the foremast of a sailing vessel.

Comprehension exercise 20

Q1) Why did Mr. Fogg and Aouda return to the hotel after making their purchases in the English quarter?
a) To prepare for their voyage
b) To meet Passepartout
c) To have dinner at a sumptuous table-d'hote
d) To rest before their departure

Q2) Why did Fix feel hopeful when Mr. Fogg mentioned looking for other vessels in the harbour?
a) Because he thought Mr. Fogg would give up and return to England
b) Because he believed Mr. Fogg would not find a suitable vessel for his journey
c) Because he anticipated Mr. Fogg's disappointment and frustration
d) Because he hoped Mr. Fogg would be delayed in finding another means of travel

Q3) What was the profession of the man who approached Mr. Fogg at the quay?
a) Detective
b) Sailor
c) Pilot
d) Ship Captain

Q4) What does the word "stated" mean in the sentence "the Carnatic had sailed the evening before the stated time"?
a) Recorded or mentioned
b) Fixed or declared
c) Unchanged or unaltered
d) Scheduled or planned

Q5) What does the word "profiting" imply about Fix's feelings towards Mr. Fogg?
a) Satisfaction or contentment
b) Gratitude or indebtedness
c) Ambivalence or indifference
d) Humiliation or discomfort

Chapter 21

IN WHICH THE MASTER OF THE "TANKADERE" RUNS GREAT RISK OF LOSING A REWARD OF TWO HUNDRED POUNDS

This voyage of eight hundred miles was a perilous venture on a craft of twenty tons, and at that season of the year. The Chinese seas are usually boisterous, subject to terrible gales of wind, and especially during the equinoxes[1]; and it was now early November.

It would clearly have been to the master's advantage to carry his passengers to Yokohama, since he was paid a certain sum per day; but he would have been rash to attempt such a voyage, and it was imprudent even to attempt to reach Shanghai. But John Bunsby believed in the Tankadere, which rode on the waves like a seagull; and perhaps he was not wrong.

Late in the day they passed through the capricious channels of Hong Kong, and the Tankadere, impelled by favourable winds, conducted herself admirably.

"I do not need, pilot," said Phileas Fogg, when they got into the open sea, "to advise you to use all possible speed."[2]

"Trust me, your honour. We are carrying all the sail the wind will let us. The poles would add nothing, and are only used when we are going into port."

"It's your trade, not mine, pilot, and I confide in you."

Phileas Fogg, with body erect and legs wide apart, standing like a sailor, gazed without staggering at the swelling waters. The young woman, who was seated aft[3], was profoundly affected as she looked out upon the ocean, darkening now with the twilight, on which she had ventured in so frail a vessel. Above her head rustled the white sails, which seemed like great white wings. The boat, carried forward by the wind, seemed to be flying in the air.[4]

Night came. The moon was entering her first quarter, and her insufficient light would soon die out in the mist on the horizon. Clouds were rising from the east, and already overcast a part of the heavens.

---

[1] Equinoxes are the two days in the year (22nd September and 20th March) when the sun crosses the equator and, as a result, the day and night are of equal length.

[2] Mr. Fogg urges the pilot to be as quick as possible in their travels.

[3] 'Aft' means towards the stern or rear of the ship.

[4] The boat was propelled by the high speed of the air and hence it seemed to be flying.

The pilot had hung out his lights, which was very necessary in these seas crowded with vessels bound landward; for collisions are not uncommon occurrences, and, at the speed she was going, the least shock would shatter the gallant little craft.

Fix, seated in the bow, gave himself up to meditation. He kept apart from his fellow-travellers, knowing Mr. Fogg's taciturn[5] tastes; besides, he did not quite like to talk to the man whose favours he had accepted. He was thinking, too, of the future. It seemed certain that Fogg would not stop at Yokohama, but would at once take the boat for San Francisco; and the vast extent of America would ensure him impunity and safety. Fogg's plan appeared to him the simplest in the world. Instead of sailing directly from England to the United States, like a common villain, he had traversed three quarters of the globe, so as to gain the American continent more surely; and there, after throwing the police off his track, he would quietly enjoy himself with the fortune stolen from the bank. But, once in the United States, what should he, Fix, do? Should he abandon this man? No, a hundred times no! Until he had secured his extradition, he would not lose sight of him for an hour. It was his duty, and he would fulfil it to the end. At all events, there was one thing to be thankful for; Passepartout was not with his master; and it was above all important, after the confidences Fix had imparted to him, that the servant should never have speech with his master.

Phileas Fogg was also thinking of Passepartout, who had so strangely disappeared. Looking at the matter from every point of view, it did not seem to him impossible that, by some mistake, the man might have embarked on the Carnatic at the last moment; and this was also Aouda's opinion, who regretted very much the loss of the worthy fellow to whom she owed so much. They might then find him at Yokohama; for, if the Carnatic was carrying him thither, it would be easy to ascertain if he had been on board.

A brisk breeze arose about ten o'clock; but, though it might have been prudent to take in a reef[6], the pilot, after carefully examining the heavens, let the craft remain rigged as before. The Tankadere bore sail admirably, as she drew a great deal of water, and everything was prepared for high speed in case of a gale.

Mr. Fogg and Aouda descended into the cabin at midnight, having been already preceded by Fix, who had lain down on one of the cots. The pilot and crew remained on deck all night.

At sunrise the next day, which was 8th November, the boat had made more than one hundred miles. The log indicated a mean speed of between eight and nine miles. The Tankadere still carried all sail, and was accomplishing her greatest capacity of speed. If the wind held as it was, the chances would be in her favour. During the day she kept along the coast, where the currents were favourable; the coast, irregular in profile, and visible sometimes across the clearings, was at most five miles distant. The sea was less boisterous, since the wind came off land—a fortunate circumstance for the boat, which would suffer, owing to its small tonnage, by a heavy surge on the sea.

---

[5] 'Taciturn' means uncommunicative or untalkative.
[6] 'To take in a reef' means to reduce the size of a sail by rolling up or folding in a reef.

The breeze subsided a little towards noon, and set in from the south-west. The pilot put up his poles, but took them down again within two hours, as the wind freshened up anew.

Mr. Fogg and Aouda, happily unaffected by the roughness of the sea, ate with a good appetite, Fix being invited to share their repast, which he accepted with secret chagrin[7]. To travel at this man's expense and live upon his provisions was not palatable to him. Still, he was obliged to eat, and so he ate.

When the meal was over, he took Mr. Fogg apart, and said, "sir"—this "sir" scorched his lips, and he had to control himself to avoid collaring this "gentleman"—"sir, you have been very kind to give me a passage on this boat. But, though my means will not admit of my expending them as freely as you, I must ask to pay my share—"

"Let us not speak of that, sir," replied Mr. Fogg.

"But, if I insist—"

"No, sir," repeated Mr. Fogg, in a tone which did not admit of a reply. "This enters into my general expenses."

Fix, as he bowed, had a stifled feeling, and, going forward, where he ensconced[8] himself, did not open his mouth for the rest of the day.

Meanwhile they were progressing famously, and John Bunsby was in high hope. He several times assured Mr. Fogg that they would reach Shanghai in time; to which that gentleman responded that he counted upon it. The crew set to work in good earnest, inspired by the reward to be gained. There was not a sheet which was not tightened, not a sail which was not vigorously hoisted; not a lurch could be charged to the man at the helm. They worked as desperately as if they were contesting in a Royal yacht regatta[9].

By evening, the log showed that two hundred and twenty miles had been accomplished from Hong Kong, and Mr. Fogg might hope that he would be able to reach Yokohama without recording any delay in his journal; in which case, the many misadventures which had overtaken him since he left London would not seriously affect his journey.

The Tankadere entered the Straits of Fo-Kien, which separate the island of Formosa from the Chinese coast, in the small hours of the night, and crossed the Tropic of Cancer[10]. The sea was very rough in the straits, full of eddies formed by the counter-currents, and the chopping waves broke her course, whilst it became very difficult to stand on deck.

---

[7] 'Chagrin' means humiliation or disappointment.
Fix feels humiliated for taking advantage of Mr. Fogg, as he believes Mr. Fogg to be a robber.

[8] 'Ensconce' means to hide or conceal securely.

[9] A 'regatta' is a series of boat races.

[10] The Tropic of Cancer, also known as Northern Tropic, is the northern most latitude circle on the Earth at which the Sun can be directly overhead.

At daybreak the wind began to blow hard again, and the heavens seemed to predict a gale. The barometer announced a speedy change, the mercury rising and falling capriciously[11]; the sea also, in the south-east, raised long surges which indicated a tempest. The sun had set the evening before in a red mist, in the midst of the phosphorescent scintillations of the ocean[12].

John Bunsby long examined the threatening aspect of the heavens, muttering indistinctly between his teeth. At last he said in a low voice to Mr. Fogg, "Shall I speak out to your honour?"

"Of course."

"Well, we are going to have a squall[13]."

"Is the wind north or south?" asked Mr. Fogg quietly.

"South. Look! a typhoon is coming up."

"Glad it's a typhoon from the south, for it will carry us forward."

"Oh, if you take it that way," said John Bunsby, "I've nothing more to say." John Bunsby's suspicions were confirmed. At a less advanced season of the year the typhoon, according to a famous meteorologist, would have passed away like a luminous cascade of electric flame; but in the winter equinox it was to be feared that it would burst upon them with great violence.

The pilot took his precautions in advance. He reefed all sail, the pole-masts were dispensed with; all hands went forward to the bows. A single triangular sail, of strong canvas, was hoisted as a storm-jib, so as to hold the wind from behind. Then they waited.

John Bunsby had requested his passengers to go below; but this imprisonment in so narrow a space, with little air, and the boat bouncing in the gale, was far from pleasant. Neither Mr. Fogg, Fix, nor Aouda consented to leave the deck.

The storm of rain and wind descended upon them towards eight o'clock. With but its bit of sail, the Tankadere was lifted like a feather by a wind, an idea of whose violence can scarcely be given. To compare her speed to four times that of a locomotive going on full steam would be below the truth.

The boat scudded thus northward during the whole day, borne on by monstrous waves, preserving always, fortunately, a speed equal to theirs. Twenty times she seemed almost to be submerged by these mountains of water which rose behind her; but the adroit[14] management of the pilot saved her. The passengers were often bathed in spray, but they submitted to it philosophically. Fix cursed it, no doubt; but Aouda, with her eyes

---

[11] 'Capricious' means impulsive or unpredictable.
[12] Sometimes a flash of light or glow can be observed at night by the sea or ocean. This phenomenon is usually caused by the algae suspended in the water. When the algae are rubbed against each other, they emit a glow, flash or sparkle of light.
[13] A 'squall' is a sudden violent gust of wind or storm.
[14] 'Adroit' means skilful or clever.

fastened upon her protector, whose coolness amazed her, showed herself worthy of him, and bravely weathered the storm. As for Phileas Fogg, it seemed just as if the typhoon were a part of his programme.

Up to this time the Tankadere had always held her course to the north; but towards evening the wind, veering three quarters, bore down from the north-west. The boat, now lying in the trough of the waves, shook and rolled terribly; the sea struck her with fearful violence. At night the tempest increased in violence. John Bunsby saw the approach of darkness and the rising of the storm with dark misgivings[15]. He thought awhile, and then asked his crew if it was not time to slacken speed. After a consultation he approached Mr. Fogg, and said, "I think, your honour, that we should do well to make for one of the ports on the coast."

"I think so too."

"Ah!" said the pilot. "But which one?"

"I know of but one," returned Mr. Fogg tranquilly.

"And that is—"

"Shanghai."

The pilot, at first, did not seem to comprehend; he could scarcely realise so much determination and tenacity. Then he cried, "Well—yes! Your honour is right. To Shanghai!"[16]

So the Tankadere kept steadily on her northward track.

The night was really terrible; it would be a miracle if the craft did not founder. Twice it could have been all over with her if the crew had not been constantly on the watch. Aouda was exhausted, but did not utter a complaint. More than once Mr. Fogg rushed to protect her from the violence of the waves.

Day reappeared. The tempest still raged with undiminished fury; but the wind now returned to the south-east. It was a favourable change, and the Tankadere again bounded forward on this mountainous sea, though the waves crossed each other, and imparted shocks and counter-shocks which would have crushed a craft less solidly built. From time to time the coast was visible through the broken mist, but no vessel was in sight. The Tankadere was alone upon the sea.

---

[15] The pilot has strong doubts about the violent storm and the damage it could do to the sailing party.

[16] Given the severe weather conditions, the pilot sought Mr. Fogg's approval to make a stop at a nearby port. However, Mr. Fogg consents to only one stop, Shanghai, their intended destination. This illustrates Mr. Fogg's unwavering determination to win his bet, regardless of the obstacles.

There were some signs of a calm at noon, and these became more distinct as the sun descended toward the horizon. The tempest had been as brief as terrific. The passengers, thoroughly exhausted, could now eat a little, and take some repose.

The night was comparatively quiet. Some of the sails were again hoisted, and the speed of the boat was very good. The next morning at dawn they espied the coast, and John Bunsby was able to assert that they were not one hundred miles from Shanghai. A hundred miles, and only one day to traverse them! That very evening Mr. Fogg was due at Shanghai, if he did not wish to miss the steamer to Yokohama. Had there been no storm, during which several hours were lost, they would be at this moment within thirty miles of their destination.

The wind grew decidedly calmer, and happily the sea fell with it. All sails were now hoisted, and at noon the Tankadere was within forty-five miles of Shanghai. There remained yet six hours in which to accomplish that distance. All on board feared that it could not be done, and every one—Phileas Fogg, no doubt, excepted—felt his heart beat with impatience. The boat must keep up an average of nine miles an hour, and the wind was becoming calmer every moment! It was a capricious breeze, coming from the coast, and after it passed the sea became smooth. Still, the Tankadere was so light, and her fine sails caught the fickle zephyrs so well, that, with the aid of the currents John Bunsby found himself at six o'clock not more than ten miles from the mouth of Shanghai River. Shanghai itself is situated at least twelve miles up the stream. At seven they were still three miles from Shanghai. The pilot swore an angry oath; the reward of two hundred pounds was evidently on the point of escaping him. He looked at Mr. Fogg. Mr. Fogg was perfectly tranquil; and yet his whole fortune was at this moment at stake.

At this moment, also, a long black funnel, crowned with wreaths of smoke, appeared on the edge of the waters. It was the American steamer, leaving for Yokohama at the appointed time.

"Confound her!"[17] cried John Bunsby, pushing back the rudder with a desperate jerk.

"Signal her!" said Phileas Fogg quietly.

A small brass cannon stood on the forward deck of the Tankadere, for making signals in the fogs. It was loaded to the muzzle; but just as the pilot was about to apply a red-hot coal to the touchhole[18], Mr. Fogg said, "Hoist your flag!"

The flag was run up at half-mast, and, this being the signal of distress, it was hoped that the American steamer, perceiving it, would change her course a little, so as to succour[19] the pilot-boat.

"Fire!" said Mr. Fogg. And the booming of the little cannon resounded in the air.

---

[17] 'Confound her!' is a cry of curse in desperation.
[18] 'To apply a red-hot coal to the touchhole' means to ignite the cannon or fire it.
[19] 'Succour' means to offer help to someone in need.

Comprehension exercise 21

Q1) Why did the passengers refuse to go below deck during the storm?
a) They preferred to be on deck to observe the storm.
b) The cabin was too cramped and uncomfortable.
c) They wanted to assist the crew in managing the boat.
d) They were afraid of being trapped below deck if the boat foundered.

Q2) Why did Mr. Fogg insist on signalling the American steamer?
a) To ask for directions to Shanghai
b) To request assistance due to the storm
c) To offer assistance to the American steamer
d) To notify the steamer of their safe passage

Q3) What was the purpose of hoisting the flag at half-mast on the Tankadere?
a) To signal that they were about to fire the cannon
b) To indicate distress and request assistance
c) To celebrate their successful navigation through the storm
d) To warn other vessels to keep a safe distance

Q4) What does the word "capricious" mean in the sentence "It was a capricious breeze, coming from the coast"?
a) Erratic or unpredictable
b) Strong or forceful
c) Gentle or mild
d) Steady or consistent

Q5) What does the word "desperate" imply about John Bunsby's action of pushing back the rudder?
a) Courageous or bold
b) Desperate or hopeless
c) Calm or composed
d) Cautious or prudent

Chapter 22

IN WHICH PASSEPARTOUT FINDS OUT THAT, EVEN AT THE ANTIPODES, IT IS CONVENIENT TO HAVE SOME MONEY IN ONE'S POCKET

The Carnatic, setting sail from Hong Kong at half-past six on the 7th of November, directed her course at full steam towards Japan. She carried a large cargo and a well-filled cabin of passengers. Two state-rooms in the rear were, however, unoccupied—those which had been engaged by Phileas Fogg.

The next day a passenger with a half-stupefied eye, staggering gait, and disordered hair, was seen to emerge from the second cabin, and to totter to a seat on deck.

It was Passepartout; and what had happened to him was as follows: Shortly after Fix left the opium den, two waiters had lifted the unconscious Passepartout, and had carried him to the bed reserved for the smokers. Three hours later, pursued even in his dreams by a fixed idea, the poor fellow awoke, and struggled against the stupefying influence of the narcotic. The thought of a duty unfulfilled shook off his torpor[1], and he hurried from the abode of drunkenness. Staggering and holding himself up by keeping against the walls, falling down and creeping up again, and irresistibly impelled[2] by a kind of instinct, he kept crying out, "The Carnatic! the Carnatic!"

The steamer lay puffing alongside the quay, on the point of starting. Passepartout had but few steps to go; and, rushing upon the plank, he crossed it, and fell unconscious on the deck, just as the Carnatic was moving off. Several sailors, who were evidently accustomed to this sort of scene, carried the poor Frenchman down into the second cabin, and Passepartout did not wake until they were one hundred and fifty miles away from China. Thus he found himself the next morning on the deck of the Carnatic, and eagerly inhaling the exhilarating sea-breeze[3]. The pure air sobered him. He began to collect his sense, which he found a difficult task; but at last he recalled the events of the evening before, Fix's revelation, and the opium-house.

"It is evident," said he to himself, "that I have been abominably drunk! What will Mr. Fogg say? At least I have not missed the steamer, which is the most important thing."[4]

Then, as Fix occurred to him: "As for that rascal, I hope we are well rid of him, and that he has not dared, as he proposed, to follow us on board the Carnatic. A detective on

---

[1] 'Torpor' means a state of mental or physical inactivity.
[2] 'Impel' means to be inspired or compelled to do something.
[3] 'Eagerly inhaling the exhilarating sea-breeze' means taking deep breaths of fresh air.
[4] Passepartout assumes that Mr. Fogg and Aouda are already aboard the Carnatic.

the track of Mr. Fogg, accused of robbing the Bank of England! Pshaw! Mr. Fogg is no more a robber than I am a murderer."[5]

Should he divulge Fix's real errand to his master? Would it do to tell the part the detective was playing? Would it not be better to wait until Mr. Fogg reached London again, and then impart to him that an agent of the metropolitan police had been following him round the world, and have a good laugh over it? No doubt; at least, it was worth considering. The first thing to do was to find Mr. Fogg, and apologise for his singular behaviour.

Passepartout got up and proceeded, as well as he could with the rolling of the steamer, to the after-deck. He saw no one who resembled either his master or Aouda. "Good!" muttered he; "Aouda has not got up yet, and Mr. Fogg has probably found some partners at whist."

He descended to the saloon. Mr. Fogg was not there. Passepartout had only, however, to ask the purser the number of his master's state-room. The purser replied that he did not know any passenger by the name of Fogg.

"I beg your pardon," said Passepartout persistently. "He is a tall gentleman, quiet, and not very talkative, and has with him a young lady—"

"There is no young lady on board," interrupted the purser. "Here is a list of the passengers; you may see for yourself."

Passepartout scanned the list, but his master's name was not upon it. All at once an idea struck him.

"Ah! am I on the Carnatic?"

"Yes."

"On the way to Yokohama?"

"Certainly."

Passepartout had for an instant feared that he was on the wrong boat; but, though he was really on the Carnatic, his master was not there.

He fell thunderstruck on a seat. He saw it all now. He remembered that the time of sailing had been changed, that he should have informed his master of that fact, and that he had not done so. It was his fault, then, that Mr. Fogg and Aouda had missed the steamer. Yes, but it was still more the fault of the traitor who, in order to separate him from his master, and detain the latter at Hong Kong, had inveigled[6] him into getting drunk! He now saw the detective's trick; and at this moment Mr. Fogg was certainly ruined, his bet was lost, and he himself perhaps arrested and imprisoned! At this thought

---

[5] The phrase 'no more than' is used to emphasize the limited possibility for something to happen.

[6] 'Inveigle' means to persuade someone by means of deception.

A Study Guide: Around the World in Eighty Days

Passepartout tore his hair[7]. Ah, if Fix ever came within his reach, what a settling of accounts[8] there would be![9]

After his first depression, Passepartout became calmer, and began to study his situation. It was certainly not an enviable one. He found himself on the way to Japan, and what should he do when he got there? His pocket was empty; he had not a solitary shilling, not so much as a penny. His passage had fortunately been paid for in advance; and he had five or six days in which to decide upon his future course. He fell to at meals with an appetite, and ate for Mr. Fogg, Aouda, and himself. He helped himself as generously as if Japan were a desert, where nothing to eat was to be looked for.[10]

At dawn on the 13th the Carnatic entered the port of Yokohama. This is an important port of call in the Pacific, where all the mail-steamers, and those carrying travellers between North America, China, Japan, and the Oriental islands put in. It is situated in the bay of Yeddo, and at but a short distance from that second capital of the Japanese Empire, and the residence of the Tycoon, the civil Emperor, before the Mikado, the spiritual Emperor, absorbed his office in his own. The Carnatic anchored at the quay near the custom-house, in the midst of a crowd of ships bearing the flags of all nations.

Passepartout went timidly ashore on this so curious territory of the Sons of the Sun[11]. He had nothing better to do than, taking chance for his guide, to wander aimlessly through the streets of Yokohama. He found himself at first in a thoroughly European quarter, the houses having low fronts, and being adorned with verandas, beneath which he caught glimpses of neat peristyles[12]. This quarter occupied, with its streets, squares, docks, and warehouses, all the space between the "promontory[13] of the Treaty"[14] and the river. Here, as at Hong Kong and Calcutta, were mixed crowds of all races, Americans and English, Chinamen and Dutchmen, mostly merchants ready to buy or sell anything. The

---

[7] 'To tear one's hair' is an idiom used to express extreme anxiety or grief.

[8] 'To settle one's account' is an idiom meaning to avenge a wicked or an evil act.

[9] Passepartout is deeply distressed when he realises that his master has missed the Carnatic, and most probably lost his wager due to his mistake. He is angry and takes a mental note to avenge Fix's evil deeds.

[10] Passepartout ate a lot, as if to prepare himself for when he lands in Yokohama penniless and may have to go without food for days.

[11] The sun is an iconic Japanese symbol, and the 'Sons of the Sun' refers to the Japanese people. According to a myth, the goddess of the sun founded Japan and all the Japanese emperors are known as the 'Sons of the Sun' to denote their status as direct descendants of the goddess.

[12] The 'Peristyle' is a continuous porch formed by a row of columns and was used a lot in Roman and Greek architecture.

[13] 'Promontory' is a high point of land that juts out into the sea or a river.

[14] 'Promontory of the Treaty' refers to the Convention of Kanagawa, or the Japan-US treaty of peace and Amity. The treaty effectively meant the end of Japan's 220-year-old policy of national seclusion by opening two of its ports to American vessels.

Frenchman felt himself as much alone among them as if he had dropped down in the midst of Hottentots[15].

He had, at least, one resource,—to call on the French and English consuls at Yokohama for assistance. But he shrank from telling the story of his adventures, intimately connected as it was with that of his master; and, before doing so, he determined to exhaust all other means of aid. As chance did not favour him in the European quarter, he penetrated that inhabited by the native Japanese, determined, if necessary, to push on to Yeddo[16].

The Japanese quarter of Yokohama is called Benten[17], after the goddess of the sea, who is worshipped on the islands round about. There Passepartout beheld beautiful fir and cedar groves, sacred gates of a singular architecture, bridges half hid in the midst of bamboos and reeds, temples shaded by immense cedar-trees, holy retreats where were sheltered Buddhist priests and sectaries of Confucius[18], and interminable streets, where a perfect harvest of rose-tinted and red-cheeked children, who looked as if they had been cut out of Japanese screens, and who were playing in the midst of short-legged poodles and yellowish cats, might have been gathered.

The streets were crowded with people. Priests were passing in processions, beating their dreary tambourines; police and custom-house officers with pointed hats encrusted with lac and carrying two sabres hung to their waists; soldiers, clad in blue cotton with white stripes, and bearing guns; the Mikado's[19] guards, enveloped in silken doubles, hauberks[20] and coats of mail; and numbers of military folk of all ranks—for the military profession is as much respected in Japan as it is despised in China—went hither and thither in groups and pairs. Passepartout saw, too, begging friars, long-robed pilgrims, and simple civilians, with their warped and jet-black hair, big heads, long busts, slender legs, short stature, and complexions varying from copper-colour to a dead white, but never yellow, like the Chinese, from whom the Japanese widely differ. He did not fail to observe the curious equipages—carriages and palanquins, barrows supplied with sails, and litters made of bamboo; nor the women—whom he thought not especially handsome—who took little steps with their little feet, whereon they wore canvas shoes, straw sandals, and clogs of worked wood, and who displayed tight-looking eyes, flat chests, teeth fashionably blackened, and gowns crossed with silken scarfs, tied in an enormous knot behind an ornament which the modern Parisian ladies seem to have borrowed from the dames of Japan.

---

[15] Hottentots, also known as Khoikhoi, are the nomadic people of southwestern Africa. The writer compares a European with an African person to express how out of place Passepartout felt.

[16] Yeddo is the former name of Tokyo.

[17] Benten, also known as *Benzaiten* in Japanese mythology, is one of the Seven Goddesses of Luck. She is a patron of literature and music and is generally associated with the sea.

[18] 'Sectaries of Confucius' refer to the followers of the teachings of Confucius, who was a Chinese philosopher and teacher.

[19] Mikado, now an obsolete term, was used for the Emperor of Japan.

[20] A 'hauberk' is a full-length military tunic.

Passepartout wandered for several hours in the midst of this motley[21] crowd, looking in at the windows of the rich and curious shops, the jewellery establishments glittering with quaint Japanese ornaments, the restaurants decked with streamers and banners, the tea-houses, where the odorous beverage was being drunk with saki, a liquor concocted from the fermentation of rice, and the comfortable smoking-houses, where they were puffing, not opium, which is almost unknown in Japan, but a very fine, stringy tobacco. He went on till he found himself in the fields, in the midst of vast rice plantations. There he saw dazzling camellias expanding themselves, with flowers which were giving forth their last colours and perfumes, not on bushes, but on trees, and within bamboo enclosures, cherry, plum, and apple trees, which the Japanese cultivate rather for their blossoms than their fruit, and which queerly-fashioned, grinning scarecrows protected from the sparrows, pigeons, ravens, and other voracious birds. On the branches of the cedars were perched large eagles; amid the foliage of the weeping willows were herons, solemnly standing on one leg; and on every hand were crows, ducks, hawks, wild birds, and a multitude of cranes, which the Japanese consider sacred, and which to their minds symbolise long life and prosperity.

As he was strolling along, Passepartout espied some violets among the shrubs.

"Good!" said he; "I'll have some supper."[22]

But, on smelling them, he found that they were odourless.

"No chance there," thought he.

The worthy fellow had certainly taken good care to eat as hearty a breakfast as possible before leaving the Carnatic; but, as he had been walking about all day, the demands of hunger were becoming importunate. He observed that the butchers stalls contained neither mutton, goat, nor pork; and, knowing also that it is a sacrilege to kill cattle, which are preserved solely for farming, he made up his mind that meat was far from plentiful in Yokohama—nor was he mistaken; and, in default of butcher's meat, he could have wished for a quarter of wild boar or deer, a partridge, or some quails, some game or fish, which, with rice, the Japanese eat almost exclusively. But he found it necessary to keep up a stout heart, and to postpone the meal he craved till the following morning. Night came, and Passepartout re-entered the native quarter, where he wandered through the streets, lit by vari-coloured lanterns, looking on at the dancers, who were executing skilful steps and boundings, and the astrologers who stood in the open air with their telescopes. Then he came to the harbour, which was lit up by the resin torches of the fishermen, who were fishing from their boats.

The streets at last became quiet, and the patrol, the officers of which, in their splendid costumes, and surrounded by their suites, Passepartout thought seemed like ambassadors, succeeded the bustling crowd. Each time a company passed, Passepartout chuckled, and said to himself: "Good! another Japanese embassy departing for Europe!"

---

[21] 'Motley' means diverse and varied.
[22] Violet flowers and leaves are edible and can be cooked or used as salads.

Comprehension exercise 22

Q1) Why was Passepartout dishevelled when he woke up in a cabin of the Carnatic?
a) He was shaken awake by the crew.
b) He was startled by the sound of the ship's horn.
c) He struggled against the effects of the opium he had ingested.
d) He was disturbed by the commotion of other passengers.

Q2) Why did Passepartout fear that Mr. Fogg was ruined?
a) He believed Mr. Fogg had missed the steamer.
b) He thought Mr. Fogg might have been arrested.
c) He was concerned about the lost bet.
d) All the above

Q3) What resource did Passepartout decide to use before seeking assistance from the consuls?
a) He planned to explore the European quarter of Yokohama.
b) He intended to exhaust all other means of aid.
c) He would consult the Japanese police for help.
d) He wanted to find Mr. Fogg and apologize first.

Q4) What does the word "motley" mean as used in the sentence "Passepartout wandered for several hours in the midst of this motley crowd"?
a) Diverse or varied
b) Unruly or disorderly
c) Cheerful or merry
d) Hostile or aggressive

Q5) What does the phrase "stout heart" mean in the context of the sentence "But he found it necessary to keep up a stout heart"?
a) A courageous attitude
b) A physically strong heart
c) A heart capable of enduring hardship
d) A determined mindset

Chapter 23

IN WHICH PASSEPARTOUT'S NOSE BECOMES OUTRAGEOUSLY LONG

The next morning poor, jaded, famished Passepartout said to himself that he must get something to eat at all hazards, and the sooner he did so the better. He might, indeed, sell his watch; but he would have starved first.[1] Now or never he must use the strong, if not melodious voice which nature had bestowed upon him. He knew several French and English songs, and resolved to try them upon the Japanese, who must be lovers of music, since they were for ever pounding on their cymbals, tam-tams, and tambourines, and could not but appreciate European talent.

It was, perhaps, rather early in the morning to get up a concert, and the audience prematurely aroused from their slumbers, might not possibly pay their entertainer with coin bearing the Mikado's features. Passepartout therefore decided to wait several hours; and, as he was sauntering along, it occurred to him that he would seem rather too well dressed for a wandering artist. The idea struck him to change his garments for clothes more in harmony with his project; by which he might also get a little money to satisfy the immediate cravings of hunger. The resolution taken, it remained to carry it out.

It was only after a long search that Passepartout discovered a native dealer in old clothes, to whom he applied for an exchange. The man liked the European costume, and ere long Passepartout issued from his shop accoutred in an old Japanese coat, and a sort of one-sided turban, faded with long use. A few small pieces of silver, moreover, jingled in his pocket.

"Good!" thought he. "I will imagine I am at the Carnival!"

His first care, after being thus "Japanesed," was to enter a tea-house of modest appearance, and, upon half a bird and a little rice, to breakfast like a man for whom dinner was as yet a problem to be solved.[2]

"Now," thought he, when he had eaten heartily, "I mustn't lose my head. I can't sell this costume again for one still more Japanese. I must consider how to leave this country of the Sun, of which I shall not retain the most delightful of memories, as quickly as possible."

It occurred to him to visit the steamers which were about to leave for America. He would offer himself as a cook or servant, in payment of his passage and meals. Once at

---

[1] Passepartout cherished his watch so deeply that he wouldn't part with it even in exchange for food.

[2] Passepartout had full breakfast and ate like he might not get dinner.

San Francisco, he would find some means of going on. The difficulty was, how to traverse the four thousand seven hundred miles of the Pacific which lay between Japan and the New World[3].

Passepartout was not the man to let an idea go begging, and directed his steps towards the docks. But, as he approached them, his project, which at first had seemed so simple, began to grow more and more formidable to his mind. What need would they have of a cook or servant on an American steamer, and what confidence would they put in him, dressed as he was? What references could he give?

As he was reflecting in this wise, his eyes fell upon an immense placard which a sort of clown was carrying through the streets. This placard, which was in English, read as follows:

ACROBATIC JAPANESE TROUPE,
HONOURABLE WILLIAM BATULCAR, PROPRIETOR,
LAST REPRESENTATIONS,
PRIOR TO THEIR DEPARTURE TO THE UNITED STATES, OF THE
LONG NOSES! LONG NOSES!
UNDER THE DIRECT PATRONAGE OF THE GOD TINGOU! GREAT ATTRACTION!

"The United States!" said Passepartout; "that's just what I want!"

He followed the clown, and soon found himself once more in the Japanese quarter. A quarter of an hour later he stopped before a large cabin, adorned with several clusters of streamers, the exterior walls of which were designed to represent, in violent colours and without perspective, a company of jugglers.

This was the Honourable William Batulcar's establishment. That gentleman was a sort of Barnum[4], the director of a troupe of mountebanks, jugglers, clowns, acrobats, equilibrists, and gymnasts, who, according to the placard, was giving his last performances before leaving the Empire of the Sun for the States of the Union.

Passepartout entered and asked for Mr. Batulcar, who straightway appeared in person.

"What do you want?" said he to Passepartout, whom he at first took for a native.

"Would you like a servant, sir?" asked Passepartout.

"A servant!" cried Mr. Batulcar, caressing the thick grey beard which hung from his chin. "I already have two who are obedient and faithful, have never left me, and serve me for their nourishment and here they are," added he, holding out his two robust arms, furrowed with veins as large as the strings of a bass-viol.

---

[3] 'New World' refers to the American land.
[4] The reference is to Phineas T Barnum, an American showman and a businessman.

"So I can be of no use to you?"

"None."

"The devil! I should so like to cross the Pacific with you!"

"Ah!" said the Honourable Mr. Batulcar. "You are no more a Japanese than I am a monkey! Who are you dressed up in that way?"

"A man dresses as he can."

"That's true. You are a Frenchman, aren't you?"

"Yes; a Parisian of Paris."

"Then you ought to know how to make grimaces[5]?"

"Why," replied Passepartout, a little vexed that his nationality should cause this question, "we Frenchmen know how to make grimaces, it is true but not any better than the Americans do."

"True. Well, if I can't take you as a servant, I can as a clown. You see, my friend, in France they exhibit foreign clowns, and in foreign parts French clowns."

"Ah!"

"You are pretty strong, eh?"

"Especially after a good meal."

"And you can sing?"

"Yes," returned Passepartout, who had formerly been wont to sing in the streets.

"But can you sing standing on your head, with a top spinning on your left foot, and a sabre balanced on your right?"

"Humph! I think so," replied Passepartout, recalling the exercises of his younger days.

"Well, that's enough," said the Honourable William Batulcar.

The engagement was concluded there and then.

Passepartout had at last found something to do. He was engaged to act in the celebrated Japanese troupe. It was not a very dignified position, but within a week he would be on his way to San Francisco.

The performance, so noisily announced by the Honourable Mr. Batulcar, was to commence at three o'clock, and soon the deafening instruments of a Japanese orchestra resounded at the door. Passepartout, though he had not been able to study or rehearse a part, was designated to lend the aid of his sturdy shoulders in the great exhibition of

---

[5] 'Grimaces' are the twisted expressions on a face to express a variety of feelings, like pain, amusement, disgust etc.

the "human pyramid," executed by the Long Noses of the god Tingou[6]. This "great attraction" was to close the performance.

Before three o'clock the large shed was invaded by the spectators, comprising Europeans and natives, Chinese and Japanese, men, women and children, who precipitated themselves upon the narrow benches and into the boxes opposite the stage. The musicians took up a position inside, and were vigorously performing on their gongs, tam-tams, flutes, bones, tambourines, and immense drums.

The performance was much like all acrobatic displays; but it must be confessed that the Japanese are the first equilibrists[7] in the world.[8]

One, with a fan and some bits of paper, performed the graceful trick of the butterflies and the flowers; another traced in the air, with the odorous smoke of his pipe, a series of blue words, which composed a compliment to the audience; while a third juggled with some lighted candles, which he extinguished successively as they passed his lips, and relit again without interrupting for an instant his juggling. Another reproduced the most singular combinations with a spinning-top; in his hands the revolving tops seemed to be animated with a life of their own in their interminable whirling; they ran over pipe-stems, the edges of sabres, wires and even hairs stretched across the stage; they turned around on the edges of large glasses, crossed bamboo ladders, dispersed into all the corners, and produced strange musical effects by the combination of their various pitches of tone. The jugglers tossed them in the air, threw them like shuttlecocks with wooden battledores, and yet they kept on spinning; they put them into their pockets, and took them out still whirling as before.

It is useless to describe the astonishing performances of the acrobats and gymnasts. The turning on ladders, poles, balls, barrels, &c., was executed with wonderful precision.

But the principal attraction was the exhibition of the Long Noses, a show to which Europe is as yet a stranger.

The Long Noses form a peculiar company, under the direct patronage of the god Tingou. Attired after the fashion of the Middle Ages, they bore upon their shoulders a splendid pair of wings; but what especially distinguished them was the long noses which were fastened to their faces, and the uses which they made of them. These noses were made of bamboo, and were five, six, and even ten feet long, some straight, others curved, some ribboned, and some having imitation warts upon them. It was upon these appendages, fixed tightly on their real noses, that they performed their gymnastic exercises. A dozen of these sectaries of Tingou lay flat upon their backs, while others,

---

[6] Tingou, or Tengu, are a type of legendary creature found in Japanese religion. Tengu appear in a variety of shapes, often with wings and an unusually long nose.

[7] An 'equilibrist' is someone who performs difficult feats of balancing.

[8] Passepartout is in awe of the Japanese performing balancing feats and expresses that by exclaiming that 'the Japanese are the first equilibrists in the world'.

dressed to represent lightning-rods, came and frolicked on their noses, jumping from one to another, and performing the most skilful leapings and somersaults.

As a last scene, a "human pyramid" had been announced, in which fifty Long Noses were to represent the Car of Juggernaut[9]. But, instead of forming a pyramid by mounting each other's shoulders, the artists were to group themselves on top of the noses. It happened that the performer who had hitherto formed the base of the Car had quitted the troupe, and as, to fill this part, only strength and adroitness[10] were necessary, Passepartout had been chosen to take his place.

The poor fellow really felt sad when—melancholy reminiscence of his youth!—he donned his costume, adorned with vari-coloured wings, and fastened to his natural feature a false nose six feet long. But he cheered up when he thought that this nose was winning him something to eat.

He went upon the stage, and took his place beside the rest who were to compose the base of the Car of Juggernaut. They all stretched themselves on the floor, their noses pointing to the ceiling. A second group of artists disposed themselves on these long appendages, then a third above these, then a fourth, until a human monument reaching to the very cornices of the theatre soon arose on top of the noses. This elicited loud applause, in the midst of which the orchestra was just striking up a deafening air, when the pyramid tottered, the balance was lost, one of the lower noses vanished from the pyramid, and the human monument was shattered like a castle built of cards!

It was Passepartout's fault. Abandoning his position, clearing the footlights without the aid of his wings, and, clambering up to the right-hand gallery, he fell at the feet of one of the spectators, crying, "Ah, my master! my master!"

"You here?"

"Myself."

"Very well; then let us go to the steamer, young man!"

Mr. Fogg, Aouda, and Passepartout passed through the lobby of the theatre to the outside, where they encountered the Honourable Mr. Batulcar, furious with rage. He demanded damages for the "breakage" of the pyramid; and Phileas Fogg appeased him by giving him a handful of banknotes.

At half-past six, the very hour of departure, Mr. Fogg and Aouda, followed by Passepartout, who in his hurry had retained his wings, and nose six feet long, stepped upon the American steamer.

---

[9] The reference is to the *Lord Jaggannath Yatra*, which is an annual procession of chariots carrying the idol of *Lord Jaggannath* in Puri, India.

[10] 'Adroitness' means cleverness or skill.

Comprehension exercise 23

Q1) Why did Passepartout decide to change his clothes before trying to earn money?
a) He wanted to appear more Japanese.
b) He wanted to wear something warm.
c) He thought he looked too well-dressed.
d) He hoped to blend in better with the locals.

Q2) How did Passepartout ultimately secure a position with the Japanese troupe?
a) He worked as a servant Mr. to Batulcar.
b) He demonstrated his singing skills to Mr. Batulcar.
c) He volunteered to act as a clown in the troupe's performance.
d) He showed off his acrobatic abilities to the troupe members.

Q3) What role did Passepartout play in the troupe's performance?
a) He was part of the great 'human pyramid'.
b) He juggled with lighted candles.
c) He balanced spinning-tops on various objects.
d) He executed graceful tricks with a fan and bits of paper.

Q4) What does the word "adroitness" mean in the sentence "as, to fill this part, only strength and adroitness were necessary"?
a) Skilfulness and agility
b) Boldness and bravery
c) Intelligence and cleverness
d) Precision and accuracy

Q5) What does the phrase "deafening air" mean in the context of the sentence "this elicited loud applause, in the midst of which the orchestra was just striking up a deafening air"?
a) A noisy piece of music
b) A tune played softly
c) A silent interlude
d) A musical performance without instruments

Chapter 24

DURING WHICH MR. FOGG AND PARTY CROSS THE PACIFIC OCEAN

What happened when the pilot-boat came in sight of Shanghai will be easily guessed. The signals made by the Tankadere had been seen by the captain of the Yokohama steamer, who, espying the flag at half-mast, had directed his course towards the little craft. Phileas Fogg, after paying the stipulated price of his passage to John Busby, and rewarding that worthy with the additional sum of five hundred and fifty pounds, ascended the steamer with Aouda and Fix; and they started at once for Nagasaki and Yokohama.

They reached their destination on the morning of the 14th of November. Phileas Fogg lost no time in going on board the Carnatic, where he learned, to Aouda's great delight—and perhaps to his own, though he betrayed no emotion—that Passepartout, a Frenchman, had really arrived on her the day before.

The San Francisco steamer was announced to leave that very evening, and it became necessary to find Passepartout, if possible, without delay. Mr. Fogg applied in vain to the French and English consuls, and, after wandering through the streets a long time, began to despair of finding his missing servant. Chance, or perhaps a kind of presentiment[1], at last led him into the Honourable Mr. Batulcar's theatre. He certainly would not have recognised Passepartout in the eccentric mountebank's costume; but the latter, lying on his back, perceived his master in the gallery. He could not help starting, which so changed the position of his nose as to bring the "pyramid" pell-mell[2] upon the stage.

All this Passepartout learned from Aouda, who recounted to him what had taken place on the voyage from Hong Kong to Shanghai on the Tankadere, in company with one Mr. Fix.

Passepartout did not change countenance on hearing this name. He thought that the time had not yet arrived to divulge to his master what had taken place between the detective and himself; and, in the account he gave of his absence, he simply excused himself for having been overtaken by drunkenness, in smoking opium at a tavern in Hong Kong.

Mr. Fogg heard this narrative coldly, without a word; and then furnished his man with funds necessary to obtain clothing more in harmony with his position. Within an hour the

---

[1] A 'presentiment' is a kind of intuitive feeling about what may happen in the future.
[2] 'Pell-mell' refers to a confused or disorganised state of matter.

Frenchman had cut off his nose and parted with his wings, and retained nothing about him which recalled the sectary[3] of the god Tingou.

The steamer which was about to depart from Yokohama to San Francisco belonged to the Pacific Mail Steamship Company, and was named the General Grant. She was a large paddle-wheel steamer of two thousand five hundred tons; well equipped and very fast. The massive walking-beam rose and fell above the deck; at one end a piston-rod worked up and down; and at the other was a connecting-rod which, in changing the rectilinear motion to a circular one, was directly connected with the shaft of the paddles. The General Grant was rigged with three masts, giving a large capacity for sails, and thus materially aiding the steam power. By making twelve miles an hour, she would cross the ocean in twenty-one days. Phileas Fogg was therefore justified in hoping that he would reach San Francisco by the 2nd of December, New York by the 11th, and London on the 20th—thus gaining several hours on the fatal date of the 21st of December.

There was a full complement of passengers on board, among them English, many Americans, a large number of coolies on their way to California, and several East Indian officers, who were spending their vacation in making the tour of the world. Nothing of moment happened on the voyage; the steamer, sustained on its large paddles, rolled but little, and the Pacific almost justified its name[4]. Mr. Fogg was as calm and taciturn as ever. His young companion felt herself more and more attached to him by other ties than gratitude; his silent but generous nature impressed her more than she thought; and it was almost unconsciously that she yielded to emotions which did not seem to have the least effect upon her protector.[5] Aouda took the keenest interest in his plans, and became impatient at any incident which seemed likely to retard his journey.

She often chatted with Passepartout, who did not fail to perceive the state of the lady's heart; and, being the most faithful of domestics, he never exhausted his eulogies of Phileas Fogg's honesty, generosity, and devotion. He took pains to calm Aouda's doubts of a successful termination of the journey, telling her that the most difficult part of it had passed, that now they were beyond the fantastic countries of Japan and China, and were fairly on their way to civilised places again. A railway train from San Francisco to New York, and a transatlantic steamer from New York to Liverpool, would doubtless bring them to the end of this impossible journey round the world within the period agreed upon.

On the ninth day after leaving Yokohama, Phileas Fogg had traversed exactly one half of the terrestrial globe. The General Grant passed, on the 23rd of November, the one hundred and eightieth meridian, and was at the very antipodes of London.[6] Mr. Fogg had, it is true, exhausted fifty-two of the eighty days in which he was to complete the tour, and

---

[3] A 'sectary' is a religious or political group of followers.

[4] It refers to the Pacific Ocean. The phrase 'Pacific almost justified its name' suggests that the water was calm and free from wind, as the word Pacific means peaceful or mild.

[5] Aouda initially felt gratitude towards Mr. Fogg. As she spends more time with him, she starts to feel deep affection or liking for him; however, the same could not be said for Mr. Fogg.

[6] Mr. Fogg and party had now reached the antipode, the diametrically opposite point of London.

there were only twenty-eight left. But, though he was only half-way by the difference of meridians, he had really gone over two-thirds of the whole journey; for he had been obliged to make long circuits from London to Aden, from Aden to Bombay, from Calcutta to Singapore, and from Singapore to Yokohama. Could he have followed without deviation the fiftieth parallel, which is that of London, the whole distance would only have been about twelve thousand miles; whereas he would be forced, by the irregular methods of locomotion, to traverse twenty-six thousand, of which he had, on the 23rd of November, accomplished seventeen thousand five hundred. And now the course was a straight one, and Fix was no longer there to put obstacles in their way!

It happened also, on the 23rd of November, that Passepartout made a joyful discovery. It will be remembered that the obstinate fellow had insisted on keeping his famous family watch at London time, and on regarding that of the countries he had passed through as quite false and unreliable. Now, on this day, though he had not changed the hands, he found that his watch exactly agreed with the ship's chronometers. His triumph was hilarious. He would have liked to know what Fix would say if he were aboard!

"The rogue told me a lot of stories," repeated Passepartout, "about the meridians, the sun, and the moon! Moon, indeed! moonshine more likely! If one listened to that sort of people, a pretty sort of time one would keep! I was sure that the sun would some day regulate itself by my watch!"

Passepartout was ignorant that, if the face of his watch had been divided into twenty-four hours, like the Italian clocks, he would have no reason for exultation; for the hands of his watch would then, instead of as now indicating nine o'clock in the morning, indicate nine o'clock in the evening, that is, the twenty-first hour after midnight precisely the difference between London time and that of the one hundred and eightieth meridian. But if Fix had been able to explain this purely physical effect, Passepartout would not have admitted, even if he had comprehended it. Moreover, if the detective had been on board at that moment, Passepartout would have joined issue with him on a quite different subject, and in an entirely different manner.[7]

Where was Fix at that moment?

He was actually on board the General Grant.

On reaching Yokohama, the detective, leaving Mr. Fogg, whom he expected to meet again during the day, had repaired at once to the English consulate, where he at last found the warrant of arrest. It had followed him from Bombay, and had come by the Carnatic, on which steamer he himself was supposed to be. Fix's disappointment may be imagined when he reflected that the warrant was now useless. Mr. Fogg had left English ground, and it was now necessary to procure his extradition!

---

[7] Passepartout still could not understand the principle of time differences between different time zones.

"Well," thought Fix, after a moment of anger, "my warrant is not good here, but it will be in England. The rogue evidently intends to return to his own country, thinking he has thrown the police off his track. Good! I will follow him across the Atlantic. As for the money, heaven grant there may be some left! But the fellow has already spent in travelling, rewards, trials, bail, elephants, and all sorts of charges, more than five thousand pounds. Yet, after all, the Bank is rich!"

His course decided on, he went on board the General Grant, and was there when Mr. Fogg and Aouda arrived. To his utter amazement, he recognised Passepartout, despite his theatrical disguise. He quickly concealed himself in his cabin, to avoid an awkward explanation, and hoped—thanks to the number of passengers—to remain unperceived by Mr. Fogg's servant.

On that very day, however, he met Passepartout face to face on the forward deck. The latter, without a word, made a rush for him, grasped him by the throat, and, much to the amusement of a group of Americans, who immediately began to bet on him, administered to the detective a perfect volley of blows, which proved the great superiority of French over English pugilistic[8] skill.[9]

When Passepartout had finished, he found himself relieved and comforted. Fix got up in a somewhat rumpled condition, and, looking at his adversary, coldly said, "Have you done?"

"For this time—yes."

"Then let me have a word with you."

"But I—"

"In your master's interests."

Passepartout seemed to be vanquished[10] by Fix's coolness, for he quietly followed him, and they sat down aside from the rest of the passengers.

"You have given me a thrashing," said Fix. "Good, I expected it. Now, listen to me. Up to this time I have been Mr. Fogg's adversary. I am now in his game."

"Aha!" cried Passepartout; "you are convinced he is an honest man?"

"No," replied Fix coldly, "I think him a rascal. Sh! don't budge, and let me speak. As long as Mr. Fogg was on English ground, it was for my interest to detain him there until my warrant of arrest arrived. I did everything I could to keep him back. I sent the Bombay priests after him, I got you intoxicated at Hong Kong, I separated you from him, and I made him miss the Yokohama steamer."

Passepartout listened, with closed fists.

---

[8] 'Pugilism' means boxing.
[9] After an exchange of blows, Passepartout, a Frenchman, won over Mr. Fix, an Englishman.
[10] 'Vanquish' means to be defeated.

"Now," resumed Fix, "Mr. Fogg seems to be going back to England. Well, I will follow him there. But hereafter I will do as much to keep obstacles out of his way as I have done up to this time to put them in his path. I've changed my game, you see, and simply because it was for my interest to change it. Your interest is the same as mine; for it is only in England that you will ascertain whether you are in the service of a criminal or an honest man."

Passepartout listened very attentively to Fix, and was convinced that he spoke with entire good faith.

"Are we friends?" asked the detective.

"Friends?—no," replied Passepartout; "but allies, perhaps. At the least sign of treason, however, I'll twist your neck for you."

"Agreed," said the detective quietly.

Eleven days later, on the 3rd of December, the General Grant entered the bay of the Golden Gate, and reached San Francisco.

Mr. Fogg had neither gained nor lost a single day.

Comprehension exercise 24

Q1) What was Phileas Fogg's reaction upon learning that Passepartout had arrived in Yokohama?
a) He expressed excitement and joy.
b) He remained indifferent and silent.
c) He showed disappointment and frustration.
d) He was surprised but remained composed.

Q2) Where did Phileas Fogg eventually find Passepartout?
a) At the French consulate in Yokohama.
b) At the local tavern in Hong Kong.
c) In a theatre owned by Mr. Batulcar.
d) On board the San Francisco steamer.

Q3) How did Passepartout explain his absence to Mr. Fogg?
a) He claimed to have been kidnapped by pirates.
b) He confessed to getting lost in the streets of Hong Kong.
c) He blamed his absence on drunkenness and opium smoking.
d) He fabricated a story about joining a circus troupe.

Q4) Why did Mr. Fogg provide funds to Passepartout?
a) To bribe officials for information.
b) To repay his debts from opium dens.
c) To purchase new clothing fitting for his position.
d) To finance a secret mission for Mr. Fogg.

Q5) Where did Fix hide upon recognizing Passepartout on board the General Grant?
a) In the cargo hold of the ship.
b) In his cabin to avoid detection.
c) Among a group of American passengers.
d) On the forward deck of the ship.

Chapter 25

IN WHICH A SLIGHT GLIMPSE IS HAD OF SAN FRANCISCO

It was seven in the morning when Mr. Fogg, Aouda, and Passepartout set foot upon the American continent, if this name can be given to the floating quay upon which they disembarked. These quays, rising and falling with the tide, thus facilitate the loading and unloading of vessels. Alongside them were clippers of all sizes, steamers of all nationalities, and the steamboats, with several decks rising one above the other, which ply on the Sacramento and its tributaries. There were also heaped up the products of a commerce which extends to Mexico, Chili, Peru, Brazil, Europe, Asia, and all the Pacific islands.

Passepartout, in his joy on reaching at last the American continent, thought he would manifest it by executing a perilous[1] vault in fine style; but, tumbling upon some worm-eaten planks, he fell through them. Put out of countenance by the manner in which he thus "set foot" upon the New World, he uttered a loud cry, which so frightened the innumerable cormorants and pelicans that are always perched upon these movable quays, that they flew noisily away[2].

Mr. Fogg, on reaching shore, proceeded to find out at what hour the first train left for New York, and learned that this was at six o'clock p.m.; he had, therefore, an entire day to spend in the Californian capital. Taking a carriage at a charge of three dollars, he and Aouda entered it, while Passepartout mounted the box beside the driver, and they set out for the International Hotel.

From his exalted position Passepartout observed with much curiosity the wide streets, the low, evenly ranged houses, the Anglo-Saxon Gothic churches, the great docks, the palatial wooden and brick warehouses, the numerous conveyances, omnibuses, horse-cars, and upon the side-walks, not only Americans and Europeans, but Chinese and Indians. Passepartout was surprised at all he saw. San Francisco was no longer the legendary city of 1849[3]—a city of banditti, assassins, and incendiaries, who had flocked hither in crowds in pursuit of plunder; a paradise of outlaws, where they gambled with

---

[1] 'Perilous' means risky or hazardous.

[2] Passepartout was delighted to finally reach America and wanted to mark his entry by leaping onto the land in a rather wild style. Instead, he landed on some decomposed planks and slid through them into the water, crying out loud.

[3] San Francisco, California was the base of the gold rush of 1849. It became the largest and the most important centre in the American West, but it also led to a large boom in the population and immigration. The rapid growth could not keep up with the city planning and the social climate soon became chaotic, corrupt and crime driven by an active militia movement.

gold-dust, a revolver in one hand and a bowie-knife in the other: it was now a great commercial emporium.

The lofty tower of its City Hall overlooked the whole panorama of the streets and avenues, which cut each other at right-angles, and in the midst of which appeared pleasant, verdant squares, while beyond appeared the Chinese quarter, seemingly imported from the Celestial Empire in a toy-box. Sombreros and red shirts and plumed Indians were rarely to be seen; but there were silk hats and black coats everywhere worn by a multitude of nervously active, gentlemanly-looking men. Some of the streets—especially Montgomery Street, which is to San Francisco what Regent Street is to London, the Boulevard des Italiens to Paris, and Broadway to New York—were lined with splendid and spacious stores, which exposed in their windows the products of the entire world.

When Passepartout reached the International Hotel, it did not seem to him as if he had left England at all.

The ground floor of the hotel was occupied by a large bar, a sort of restaurant freely open to all passers-by, who might partake[4] of dried beef, oyster soup, biscuits, and cheese, without taking out their purses. Payment was made only for the ale, porter, or sherry which was drunk. This seemed "very American" to Passepartout. The hotel refreshment-rooms were comfortable, and Mr. Fogg and Aouda, installing themselves at a table, were abundantly served on diminutive[5] plates by negroes[6] of darkest hue.

After breakfast, Mr. Fogg, accompanied by Aouda, started for the English consulate to have his passport visaed. As he was going out, he met Passepartout, who asked him if it would not be well, before taking the train, to purchase some dozens of Enfield rifles and Colt's revolvers. He had been listening to stories of attacks upon the trains by the Sioux and Pawnees[7]. Mr. Fogg thought it a useless precaution, but told him to do as he thought best, and went on to the consulate.

He had not proceeded two hundred steps, however, when, "by the greatest chance in the world," he met Fix. The detective seemed wholly taken by surprise. What! Had Mr. Fogg and himself crossed the Pacific together, and not met on the steamer! At least Fix felt honoured to behold once more the gentleman to whom he owed so much, and, as his business recalled him to Europe, he should be delighted to continue the journey in such pleasant company.

---

[4] To 'partake' means to eat or drink.

[5] 'Diminutive' means petite or small.

[6] The word 'Negro' was used to denote a person of Negroid heritage, loosely meaning a person of dark skin colour. The word 'Negro' was earlier considered as normal. However, during the 1950s and 1960s, the word was considered offensive as it was associated with segregation, slavery and discrimination that the Afro-Americans were being treated to. The word 'Negro' has now been censored by many newspapers and other media. It is a derogatory and offensive term.

[7] Sioux (also known as Lakotas) and Pawnees are two different American Indian tribes. Cruel and violent warfare had been practiced between them for centuries since the mid 1700s; however, the Massacre of Canyon battle that took place in Nebraska in 1873 was the deadliest attack.

Mr. Fogg replied that the honour would be his; and the detective—who was determined not to lose sight of him—begged permission to accompany them in their walk about San Francisco—a request which Mr. Fogg readily granted.

They soon found themselves in Montgomery Street, where a great crowd was collected; the side-walks, street, horsecar rails, the shop-doors, the windows of the houses, and even the roofs, were full of people. Men were going about carrying large posters, and flags and streamers were floating in the wind; while loud cries were heard on every hand.

"Hurrah for Camerfield!"

"Hurrah for Mandiboy!"

It was a political meeting; at least so Fix conjectured, who said to Mr. Fogg, "Perhaps we had better not mingle with the crowd. There may be danger in it."

"Yes," returned Mr. Fogg; "and blows, even if they are political are still blows."

Fix smiled at this remark; and, in order to be able to see without being jostled about, the party took up a position on the top of a flight of steps situated at the upper end of Montgomery Street. Opposite them, on the other side of the street, between a coal wharf and a petroleum warehouse, a large platform had been erected in the open air, towards which the current of the crowd seemed to be directed.

For what purpose was this meeting? What was the occasion of this excited assemblage? Phileas Fogg could not imagine. Was it to nominate some high official—a governor or member of Congress? It was not improbable, so agitated was the multitude before them.

Just at this moment there was an unusual stir in the human mass. All the hands were raised in the air. Some, tightly closed, seemed to disappear suddenly in the midst of the cries—an energetic way, no doubt, of casting a vote. The crowd swayed back, the banners and flags wavered, disappeared an instant, then reappeared in tatters. The undulations of the human surge reached the steps, while all the heads floundered on the surface like a sea agitated by a squall. Many of the black hats disappeared, and the greater part of the crowd seemed to have diminished in height.

"It is evidently a meeting," said Fix, "and its object must be an exciting one. I should not wonder if it were about the Alabama, despite the fact that that question is settled."

"Perhaps," replied Mr. Fogg, simply.

"At least, there are two champions in presence of each other, the Honourable Mr. Camerfield and the Honourable Mr. Mandiboy."

Aouda, leaning upon Mr. Fogg's arm, observed the tumultuous scene with surprise, while Fix asked a man near him what the cause of it all was. Before the man could reply, a fresh agitation arose; hurrahs and excited shouts were heard; the staffs of the banners began to be used as offensive weapons; and fists flew about in every direction. Thumps were exchanged from the tops of the carriages and omnibuses which had been blocked up in the crowd. Boots and shoes went whirling through the air, and Mr. Fogg thought he even heard the crack of revolvers mingling in the din[8], the rout approached the stairway, and flowed over the lower step. One of the parties had evidently been repulsed; but the mere lookers-on could not tell whether Mandiboy or Camerfield had gained the upper hand.

"It would be prudent for us to retire," said Fix, who was anxious that Mr. Fogg should not receive any injury, at least until they got back to London. "If there is any question about England in all this, and we were recognised, I fear it would go hard with us."

"An English subject—" began Mr. Fogg.

He did not finish his sentence; for a terrific hubbub[9] now arose on the terrace behind the flight of steps where they stood, and there were frantic shouts of, "Hurrah for Mandiboy! Hip, hip, hurrah!"

It was a band of voters coming to the rescue of their allies, and taking the Camerfield forces in flank. Mr. Fogg, Aouda, and Fix found themselves between two fires; it was too late to escape. The torrent of men, armed with loaded canes and sticks, was irresistible. Phileas Fogg and Fix were roughly hustled in their attempts to protect their fair companion; the former, as cool as ever, tried to defend himself with the weapons which nature has placed at the end of every Englishman's arm, but in vain. A big brawny fellow with a red beard, flushed face, and broad shoulders, who seemed to be the chief of the band, raised his clenched fist to strike Mr. Fogg, whom he would have given a crushing blow, had not Fix rushed in and received it in his stead. An enormous bruise immediately made its appearance under the detective's silk hat, which was completely smashed in.

"Yankee[10]!" exclaimed Mr. Fogg, darting a contemptuous look at the ruffian.

"Englishman!" returned the other. "We will meet again!"

"When you please."

"What is your name?"

"Phileas Fogg. And yours?"

"Colonel Stamp Proctor."

The human tide now swept by, after overturning Fix, who speedily got upon his feet again, though with tattered clothes. Happily, he was not seriously hurt. His travelling overcoat was divided into two unequal parts, and his trousers resembled those of certain Indians, which fit less compactly than they are easy to put on. Aouda had escaped unharmed, and Fix alone bore marks of the fray in his black and blue bruise.

---

[8] 'Din' is a loud, unpleasant, and prolonged noise.
[9] 'Hubbub' is a chaotic, noisy situation.
[10] The word 'Yankee' typically refers to a native or inhabitant of the United States, especially from the northern states. It carries historical connotations, particularly during the American Civil War when it was used as a term for Union soldiers, but it is now considered derogatory.

"Thanks," said Mr. Fogg to the detective, as soon as they were out of the crowd.

"No thanks are necessary," replied. Fix; "but let us go."

"Where?"

"To a tailor's."

Such a visit was, indeed, opportune. The clothing of both Mr. Fogg and Fix was in rags, as if they had themselves been actively engaged in the contest between Camerfield and Mandiboy. An hour after, they were once more suitably attired, and with Aouda returned to the International Hotel.

Passepartout was waiting for his master, armed with half a dozen six-barrelled revolvers. When he perceived Fix, he knit his brows; but Aouda having, in a few words, told him of their adventure, his countenance resumed its placid expression. Fix evidently was no longer an enemy, but an ally; he was faithfully keeping his word.

Dinner over, the coach which was to convey the passengers and their luggage to the station drew up to the door. As he was getting in, Mr. Fogg said to Fix, "You have not seen this Colonel Proctor again?"

"No."

"I will come back to America to find him," said Phileas Fogg calmly. "It would not be right for an Englishman to permit himself to be treated in that way, without retaliating."

The detective smiled, but did not reply. It was clear that Mr. Fogg was one of those Englishmen who, while they do not tolerate duelling at home, fight abroad when their honour is attacked.

At a quarter before six the travellers reached the station, and found the train ready to depart. As he was about to enter it, Mr. Fogg called a porter, and said to him: "My friend, was there not some trouble to-day in San Francisco?"

"It was a political meeting, sir," replied the porter.

"But I thought there was a great deal of disturbance in the streets."

"It was only a meeting assembled for an election."

"The election of a general-in-chief, no doubt?" asked Mr. Fogg.

"No, sir; of a justice of the peace."[11]

Phileas Fogg got into the train, which started off at full speed.

---

[11] 'Justice of the Peace' is a lay magistrate appointed to hear minor cases in a town, or a local district.

Comprehension exercise 25

Q1) Why does Passepartout find San Francisco surprising?
a) He expected it to be more chaotic and dangerous.
b) It reminded him of the legendary city of 1849.
c) The architecture was different from what he had heard.
d) The streets were devoid of any activity.

Q2) How did Mr. Fogg react when Colonel Stamp Proctor attempted to strike him?
a) He retaliated with physical force.
b) He calmly exchanged words with Colonel Proctor.
c) He called for assistance from the crowd.
d) He ignored the attack and walked away.

Q3) What did Mr. Fogg and Fix do after being attacked during the political meeting?
a) They fought back against the assailants.
b) They fled the scene to avoid further confrontation.
c) They sought medical assistance for their injuries.
d) They proceeded to a tailor's to repair their torn clothing.

Q4) How did Mr. Fogg plan to retaliate against Colonel Stamp Proctor for the attack?
a) By reporting the incident to the authorities
b) By challenging him to a duel
c) By avoiding him in the future
d) By taking legal action against him

Q5) What does the term "perilous" mean as used in the text?
a) Safe
b) Dangerous
c) Pleasant
d) Secure

Chapter 26

IN WHICH PHILEAS FOGG AND PARTY TRAVEL BY THE PACIFIC RAILROAD

"From ocean to ocean"[1]—so say the Americans; and these four words compose the general designation of the "great trunk line" which crosses the entire width of the United States. The Pacific Railroad[2] is, however, really divided into two distinct lines: the Central Pacific, between San Francisco and Ogden, and the Union Pacific, between Ogden and Omaha. Five main lines connect Omaha with New York.

New York and San Francisco are thus united by an uninterrupted metal ribbon[3], which measures no less than three thousand seven hundred and eighty-six miles. Between Omaha and the Pacific the railway crosses a territory which is still infested by Indians and wild beasts, and a large tract which the Mormons[4], after they were driven from Illinois in 1845, began to colonise.

The journey from New York to San Francisco consumed, formerly, under the most favourable conditions, at least six months. It is now accomplished in seven days.

It was in 1862 that, in spite of the Southern Members of Congress, who wished a more southerly route, it was decided to lay the road between the forty-first and forty-second parallels. President Lincoln himself fixed the end of the line at Omaha, in Nebraska. The work was at once commenced, and pursued with true American energy; nor did the rapidity with which it went on injuriously affect its good execution. The road grew, on the prairies, a mile and a half a day. A locomotive, running on the rails laid down the evening before, brought the rails to be laid on the morrow, and advanced upon them as fast as they were put in position.

The Pacific Railroad is joined by several branches in Iowa, Kansas, Colorado, and Oregon. On leaving Omaha, it passes along the left bank of the Platte River as far as the junction of its northern branch, follows its southern branch, crosses the Laramie territory and the Wahsatch Mountains, turns the Great Salt Lake, and reaches Salt Lake City, the Mormon capital, plunges into the Tuilla Valley, across the American Desert, Cedar and Humboldt Mountains, the Sierra Nevada, and descends, via Sacramento, to the Pacific—

---

[1] The two oceans referred to here are the Pacific and the Atlantic Ocean on either side of the American landmass.

[2] The Pacific Railroad was North America's first transcontinental railroad. It was a 1,911 mile continuous railroad constructed between 1863 and 1869.

[3] 'Metal ribbon' refers to the rail tracks.

[4] Mormons are a religious and cultural group that follow the Latter Day Saint movement of Restorationist Christianity initiated by Joseph Smith Jr. during the 1820s, with Utah as the centre of its cultural influence.

its grade, even on the Rocky Mountains, never exceeding one hundred and twelve feet to the mile.

Such was the road to be traversed in seven days, which would enable Phileas Fogg—at least, so he hoped—to take the Atlantic steamer at New York on the 11th for Liverpool.

The car[5] which he occupied was a sort of long omnibus on eight wheels, and with no compartments in the interior. It was supplied with two rows of seats, perpendicular to the direction of the train on either side of an aisle which conducted to the front and rear platforms. These platforms were found throughout the train, and the passengers were able to pass from one end of the train to the other. It was supplied with saloon cars, balcony cars, restaurants, and smoking-cars; theatre cars alone were wanting[6], and they will have these some day.

Book and news dealers, sellers of edibles, drinkables, and cigars, who seemed to have plenty of customers, were continually circulating in the aisles.

The train left Oakland station at six o'clock. It was already night, cold and cheerless, the heavens being overcast with clouds which seemed to threaten snow. The train did not proceed rapidly; counting the stoppages, it did not run more than twenty miles an hour, which was a sufficient speed, however, to enable it to reach Omaha within its designated time.

There was but little conversation in the car, and soon many of the passengers were overcome with sleep. Passepartout found himself beside the detective; but he did not talk to him. After recent events, their relations with each other had grown somewhat cold; there could no longer be mutual sympathy or intimacy between them. Fix's manner had not changed; but Passepartout was very reserved, and ready to strangle his former friend on the slightest provocation.

Snow began to fall an hour after they started, a fine snow, however, which happily could not obstruct the train; nothing could be seen from the windows but a vast, white sheet, against which the smoke of the locomotive had a greyish aspect.

At eight o'clock a steward entered the car and announced that the time for going to bed had arrived; and in a few minutes the car was transformed into a dormitory. The backs of the seats were thrown back, bedsteads carefully packed were rolled out by an ingenious system, berths were suddenly improvised, and each traveller had soon at his disposition a comfortable bed, protected from curious eyes by thick curtains. The sheets were clean and the pillows soft. It only remained to go to bed and sleep which everybody did—while the train sped on across the State of California.

The country between San Francisco and Sacramento is not very hilly. The Central Pacific, taking Sacramento for its starting-point, extends eastward to meet the road from Omaha. The line from San Francisco to Sacramento runs in a north-easterly direction,

---

[5] The word 'car' refers to the railway wagon or carriage.

[6] The railway had separate carriages for smoking, restaurants etc, but still lacked one that was exclusively for theatre or cinema.

along the American River, which empties into San Pablo Bay. The one hundred and twenty miles between these cities were accomplished in six hours, and towards midnight, while fast asleep, the travellers passed through Sacramento; so that they saw nothing of that important place, the seat of the State government, with its fine quays, its broad streets, its noble hotels, squares, and churches.

The train, on leaving Sacramento, and passing the junction, Roclin, Auburn, and Colfax, entered the range of the Sierra Nevada. 'Cisco was reached at seven in the morning; and an hour later the dormitory was transformed into an ordinary car, and the travellers could observe the picturesque beauties of the mountain region through which they were steaming[7]. The railway track wound in and out among the passes, now approaching the mountain-sides, now suspended over precipices[8], avoiding abrupt angles by bold curves, plunging into narrow defiles[9], which seemed to have no outlet. The locomotive, its great funnel emitting a weird light, with its sharp bell, and its cow-catcher[10] extended like a spur[11], mingled its shrieks and bellowings with the noise of torrents and cascades, and twined its smoke among the branches of the gigantic pines.

There were few or no bridges or tunnels on the route. The railway turned around the sides of the mountains, and did not attempt to violate nature by taking the shortest cut from one point to another.[12]

The train entered the State of Nevada through the Carson Valley about nine o'clock, going always northeasterly; and at midday reached Reno, where there was a delay of twenty minutes for breakfast.

From this point the road, running along Humboldt River, passed northward for several miles by its banks; then it turned eastward, and kept by the river until it reached the Humboldt Range[13], nearly at the extreme eastern limit of Nevada.

Having breakfasted, Mr. Fogg and his companions resumed their places in the car, and observed the varied landscape which unfolded itself as they passed along the vast prairies, the mountains lining the horizon, and the creeks, with their frothy, foaming streams. Sometimes a great herd of buffaloes, massing together in the distance, seemed like a moveable dam. These innumerable multitudes of ruminating[14] beasts often form an

---

[7] The train was powered by a steam locomotive and hence the use of the word- steaming.

[8] 'Precipice' is a very steep rock face or cliff.

[9] A 'Defile' is a steep- sided narrow gorge or passage.

[10] A Cowcatcher is a metal frame in front of a locomotive for pushing aside cattle or other obstacles on the line.

[11] A spur is an appointed device worn on the heel by the rider of a horse and used to urge the horse forward.

[12] The train line wound around the mountains and did not cut into them (through tunnels) to reach its destination, even though it meant taking the longer route.

[13] The Humboldt Range is a range of mountains in northwest Nevada, USA.

[14] To 'ruminate' means to chew over and over again. The stomach of buffaloes, like other ruminants, has four chambers and when the ruminant has finished chewing, the food is brought back and re-chewed.

insurmountable obstacle to the passage of the trains; thousands of them have been seen passing over the track for hours together, in compact ranks. The locomotive is then forced to stop and wait till the road is once more clear.[15]

This happened, indeed, to the train in which Mr. Fogg was travelling. About twelve o'clock a troop of ten or twelve thousand head of buffalo encumbered the track. The locomotive, slackening its speed, tried to clear the way with its cow-catcher; but the mass of animals was too great. The buffaloes marched along with a tranquil gait, uttering now and then deafening bellowings. There was no use of interrupting them, for, having taken a particular direction, nothing can moderate and change their course; it is a torrent of living flesh which no dam could contain.

The travellers gazed on this curious spectacle from the platforms; but Phileas Fogg, who had the most reason of all to be in a hurry, remained in his seat, and waited philosophically until it should please the buffaloes to get out of the way.

Passepartout was furious at the delay they occasioned, and longed to discharge his arsenal of revolvers upon them.

"What a country!" cried he. "Mere cattle stop the trains, and go by in a procession, just as if they were not impeding travel! Parbleu! I should like to know if Mr. Fogg foresaw this mishap in his programme! And here's an engineer who doesn't dare to run the locomotive into this herd of beasts!"

The engineer did not try to overcome the obstacle, and he was wise. He would have crushed the first buffaloes, no doubt, with the cow-catcher; but the locomotive, however powerful, would soon have been checked, the train would inevitably have been thrown off the track, and would then have been helpless.

The best course was to wait patiently, and regain the lost time by greater speed when the obstacle was removed. The procession of buffaloes lasted three full hours, and it was night before the track was clear. The last ranks of the herd were now passing over the rails, while the first had already disappeared below the southern horizon.

It was eight o'clock when the train passed through the defiles of the Humboldt Range, and half-past nine when it penetrated Utah, the region of the Great Salt Lake, the singular colony of the Mormons[16].

---

[15] Large groups of buffaloes (thousands in number) often block the trains' passage when they pass over their tracks.

[16] Mormons are a religious and cultural group that follow Latter Day Saint movement of Restorationist Christianity initiated by Joseph Smith Jr. during 1820s, with Utah as the centre of its cultural influence.

A Study Guide: Around the World in Eighty Days

Comprehension exercise 26

Q1) How did the passengers transform the train car at bedtime?
a) By rearranging the seats.
b) By rolling out bedsteads and improvising berths.
c) By folding up the tables and chairs.
d) By converting it into a restaurant car.

Q2) What is the main purpose of the Pacific Railroad described in the passage?
a) To transport goods between Omaha and Sacramento.
b) To connect New York and San Francisco by rail.
c) To facilitate travel across the Sierra Nevada mountains.
d) To serve as a tourist attraction for scenic views.

Q3) What was the major obstacle encountered by the train during its journey?
a) A snowstorm
b) A herd of buffaloes
c) Mechanical failure
d) Indian attacks

Q4) What is the meaning of the term "dormitory" as used in the passage?
a) A large dining hall.
b) A communal bathroom.
c) A place for sleeping.
d) A room for recreation.

Q5) What does the phrase "insurmountable obstacle" suggest about the buffaloes?
a) They are easily avoided.
b) They are impossible to control.
c) They are dangerous predators.
d) They are friendly creatures.

Chapter 27

IN WHICH PASSEPARTOUT UNDERGOES, AT A SPEED OF TWENTY MILES AN HOUR,
A COURSE OF MORMON HISTORY

During the night of the 5th of December, the train ran south-easterly for about fifty miles; then rose an equal distance in a north-easterly direction, towards the Great Salt Lake.

Passepartout, about nine o'clock, went out upon the platform to take the air. The weather was cold, the heavens grey, but it was not snowing. The sun's disc, enlarged by the mist, seemed an enormous ring of gold, and Passepartout was amusing himself by calculating its value in pounds sterling, when he was diverted from this interesting study by a strange-looking personage who made his appearance on the platform.

This personage, who had taken the train at Elko, was tall and dark, with black moustache, black stockings, a black silk hat, a black waistcoat, black trousers, a white cravat[1], and dogskin gloves. He might have been taken for a clergyman. He went from one end of the train to the other, and affixed to the door of each car a notice written in manuscript.

Passepartout approached and read one of these notices, which stated that Elder William Hitch, Mormon missionary, taking advantage of his presence on train No. 48, would deliver a lecture on Mormonism in car No. 117, from eleven to twelve o'clock; and that he invited all who were desirous of being instructed concerning the mysteries of the religion of the "Latter Day Saints" to attend.

"I'll go," said Passepartout to himself. He knew nothing of Mormonism except the custom of polygamy,[2] which is its foundation.

The news quickly spread through the train, which contained about one hundred passengers, thirty of whom, at most, attracted by the notice, ensconced themselves in car No. 117. Passepartout took one of the front seats. Neither Mr. Fogg nor Fix cared to attend.

At the appointed hour Elder William Hitch rose, and, in an irritated voice, as if he had already been contradicted, said, "I tell you that Joe Smith is a martyr, that his brother

---

[1] A 'cravat' is a neckband.

[2] 'Polygamy' is the practice of marrying many spouses at the same time. It was practiced by the leaders of the Latter Day Saints Church for more than half of the 19th century, and practiced publicly from 1852 to 1890.

Hiram is a martyr, and that the persecutions of the United States Government against the prophets will also make a martyr of Brigham Young. Who dares to say the contrary?"

No one ventured to gainsay the missionary, whose excited tone contrasted curiously with his naturally calm visage. No doubt his anger arose from the hardships to which the Mormons were actually subjected. The government had just succeeded, with some difficulty, in reducing these independent fanatics to its rule. It had made itself master of Utah, and subjected that territory to the laws of the Union, after imprisoning Brigham Young[3] on a charge of rebellion and polygamy.[4] The disciples of the prophet had since redoubled their efforts, and resisted, by words at least, the authority of Congress. Elder Hitch, as is seen, was trying to make proselytes on the very railway trains.

Then, emphasising his words with his loud voice and frequent gestures, he related the history of the Mormons from Biblical times: how that, in Israel, a Mormon prophet of the tribe of Joseph published the annals[5] of the new religion, and bequeathed them to his son Mormon; how, many centuries later, a translation of this precious book, which was written in Egyptian, was made by Joseph Smith, junior, a Vermont farmer, who revealed himself as a mystical prophet in 1825; and how, in short, the celestial messenger appeared to him in an illuminated forest, and gave him the annals of the Lord.

Several of the audience, not being much interested in the missionary's narrative, here left the car; but Elder Hitch, continuing his lecture, related how Smith, junior, with his father, two brothers, and a few disciples, founded the church of the "Latter Day Saints," which, adopted not only in America, but in England, Norway and Sweden, and Germany, counts many artisans, as well as men engaged in the liberal professions, among its members; how a colony was established in Ohio, a temple erected there at a cost of two hundred thousand dollars, and a town built at Kirkland; how Smith became an enterprising banker, and received from a simple mummy showman a papyrus scroll written by Abraham and several famous Egyptians.

The Elder's story became somewhat wearisome, and his audience grew gradually less, until it was reduced to twenty passengers. But this did not disconcert the enthusiast, who proceeded with the story of Joseph Smith's bankruptcy in 1837, and how his ruined creditors gave him a coat of tar and feathers; his reappearance some years afterwards, more honourable and honoured than ever, at Independence, Missouri, the chief of a flourishing colony of three thousand disciples, and his pursuit thence by outraged Gentiles, and retirement into the Far West.

---

[3] Brigham Young was an American religious leader, politician, a polygamist and the second president of The Church of Jesus Christ of Latter-day Saints (LDS Church) until his death in 1877.

[4] The LDS Church and the US government disagreed over the matter of polygamy. While the government wanted to put an end to it, the LDS church defended the practice of polygamy as a matter of religious freedom. In 1857-58, the US forces entered the Utah Territory, resulting in an armed confrontation between the Mormon settlers and the US government. In the end, Utah's governorship was transferred from the LDS Church president to a non-Mormon leader.

[5] 'Annals' are historical records of events year by year.

Ten hearers only were now left, among them honest Passepartout, who was listening with all his ears. Thus he learned that, after long persecutions, Smith reappeared in Illinois, and in 1839 founded a community at Nauvoo, on the Mississippi, numbering twenty-five thousand souls, of which he became mayor, chief justice, and general-in-chief; that he announced himself, in 1843, as a candidate for the Presidency of the United States; and that finally, being drawn into ambuscade at Carthage, he was thrown into prison, and assassinated by a band of men disguised in masks.

Passepartout was now the only person left in the car, and the Elder, looking him full in the face, reminded him that, two years after the assassination of Joseph Smith, the inspired prophet, Brigham Young, his successor, left Nauvoo for the banks of the Great Salt Lake, where, in the midst of that fertile region, directly on the route of the emigrants who crossed Utah on their way to California, the new colony, thanks to the polygamy practised by the Mormons, had flourished beyond expectations.

"And this," added Elder William Hitch, "this is why the jealousy of Congress has been aroused against us! Why have the soldiers of the Union invaded the soil of Utah? Why has Brigham Young, our chief, been imprisoned, in contempt of all justice? Shall we yield to force? Never! Driven from Vermont, driven from Illinois, driven from Ohio, driven from Missouri, driven from Utah, we shall yet find some independent territory on which to plant our tents. And you, my brother," continued the Elder, fixing his angry eyes upon his single auditor, "will you not plant yours there, too, under the shadow of our flag?"

"No!" replied Passepartout courageously, in his turn retiring from the car, and leaving the Elder to preach to vacancy.

During the lecture the train had been making good progress, and towards half-past twelve it reached the northwest border of the Great Salt Lake. Thence the passengers could observe the vast extent of this interior sea, which is also called the Dead Sea, and into which flows an American Jordan. It is a picturesque expanse, framed in lofty crags in large strata, encrusted with white salt—a superb sheet of water, which was formerly of larger extent than now, its shores having encroached with the lapse of time, and thus at once reduced its breadth and increased its depth.

The Salt Lake, seventy miles long and thirty-five wide, is situated three miles eight hundred feet above the sea. Quite different from Lake Asphaltite, whose depression is twelve hundred feet below the sea, it contains considerable salt, and one quarter of the weight of its water is solid matter, its specific weight being 1,170, and, after being distilled, 1,000. Fishes are, of course, unable to live in it, and those which descend through the Jordan, the Weber, and other streams soon perish.

The country around the lake was well cultivated, for the Mormons are mostly farmers; while ranches and pens for domesticated animals, fields of wheat, corn, and other cereals, luxuriant prairies, hedges of wild rose, clumps of acacias and milk-wort[6], would have been seen six months later. Now the ground was covered with a thin powdering of snow.

---

[6] A milkwort is a small plant, whose consumption is believed to increase the milk yield of cows.

The train reached Ogden at two o'clock, where it rested for six hours, Mr. Fogg and his party had time to pay a visit to Salt Lake City, connected with Ogden by a branch road; and they spent two hours in this strikingly American town, built on the pattern of other cities of the Union, like a checker-board, "with the sombre sadness of right-angles," as Victor Hugo[7] expresses it. The founder of the City of the Saints could not escape from the taste for symmetry which distinguishes the Anglo-Saxons. In this strange country, where the people are certainly not up to the level of their institutions, everything is done "squarely"[8]—cities, houses, and follies.

The travellers, then, were promenading, at three o'clock, about the streets of the town built between the banks of the Jordan and the spurs of the Wahsatch Range. They saw few or no churches, but the prophet's mansion, the court-house, and the arsenal, blue-brick houses with verandas and porches, surrounded by gardens bordered with acacias, palms, and locusts[9]. A clay and pebble wall, built in 1853, surrounded the town; and in the principal street were the market and several hotels adorned with pavilions. The place did not seem thickly populated. The streets were almost deserted, except in the vicinity of the temple, which they only reached after having traversed several quarters surrounded by palisades. There were many women, which was easily accounted for by the "peculiar institution" of the Mormons;[10] but it must not be supposed that all the Mormons are polygamists. They are free to marry or not, as they please; but it is worth noting that it is mainly the female citizens of Utah who are anxious to marry, as, according to the Mormon religion, maiden ladies are not admitted to the possession of its highest joys. These poor creatures seemed to be neither well off nor happy. Some—the more well-to-do, no doubt—wore short, open, black silk dresses, under a hood or modest shawl; others were habited in Indian fashion.

Passepartout could not behold without a certain fright these women, charged, in groups, with conferring happiness on a single Mormon. His common sense pitied, above all, the husband. It seemed to him a terrible thing to have to guide so many wives at once across the vicissitudes of life, and to conduct them, as it were, in a body to the Mormon paradise with the prospect of seeing them in the company of the glorious Smith[11], who doubtless was the chief ornament of that delightful place, to all eternity. He felt decidedly repelled from such a vocation, and he imagined—perhaps he was mistaken—that the fair ones of Salt Lake City cast rather alarming glances on his person. Happily, his stay there was but brief. At four the party found themselves again at the station, took their places

---

[7] Victor Marie Hugo, 1802-1885, is the most prominent and well known French poet, novelist and dramatist. *Les Misérables* and *The Hunchback of Notre-Dame* are his most famous works.

[8] The word 'squarely' is used to mean: a) the square shape when describing the grid streets of Salt Lake City and its houses; and b) as an act done directly, without deviating when describing the people and their behaviour.

[9] Locusts are short-horned grasshoppers belonging to the Acrididae family.

[10] The author is hinting at the culture of polygamy for there being more women than men, as in this culture one man may marry more than one woman.

[11] 'Glorious Smith' refers to Joseph Smith Jr., who initiated the Mormon religion.

in the train, and the whistle sounded for starting. Just at the moment, however, that the locomotive wheels began to move, cries of "Stop! stop!" were heard.

Trains, like time and tide, stop for no one. The gentleman who uttered the cries was evidently a belated Mormon. He was breathless with running. Happily for him, the station had neither gates nor barriers. He rushed along the track, jumped on the rear platform of the train, and fell, exhausted, into one of the seats.

Passepartout, who had been anxiously watching this amateur gymnast, approached him with lively interest, and learned that he had taken flight after an unpleasant domestic scene.

When the Mormon had recovered his breath, Passepartout ventured to ask him politely how many wives he had; for, from the manner in which he had decamped[12], it might be thought that he had twenty at least.

"One, sir," replied the Mormon, raising his arms heavenward —"one, and that was enough!"

---

[12] To 'decamp' means to abscond or flee secretly.

A Study Guide: Around the World in Eighty Days

Comprehension exercise 27

Q1) Why did Passepartout find himself amused while on the train platform?
a) He was calculating the train's speed.
b) He was studying the weather patterns.
c) He was observing the peculiar attire of a stranger.
d) He was enjoying the scenery of the Great Salt Lake.

Q2) What can be inferred about Passepartout's attitude towards attending the lecture on Mormonism?
a) He was curious and eager to learn.
b) He was indifferent and uninterested.
c) He was apprehensive but decided to attend.
d) He was sceptical and hesitant.

Q3) What announcement did Passepartout read on the notice affixed to the train car?
a) A schedule change for the next stop.
b) A lecture on Mormonism by Elder William Hitch.
c) A warning about the weather conditions.
d) A promotion for a local restaurant.

Q4) Why did the audience for Elder William Hitch's lecture gradually diminish?
a) The train reached its destination.
b) The lecture became repetitive and boring.
c) Passengers were called for meals.
d) The weather conditions worsened.

Q5) What is the meaning of the word "ensconced" as used in the passage?
a) Covered in fur.
b) Concealed or hidden.
c) Seated comfortably or securely.
d) Entertained with music.

Chapter 28

IN WHICH PASSEPARTOUT DOES NOT SUCCEED IN MAKING ANYBODY LISTEN TO REASON

The train, on leaving Great Salt Lake at Ogden, passed northward for an hour as far as Weber River, having completed nearly nine hundred miles from San Francisco. From this point it took an easterly direction towards the jagged Wahsatch Mountains. It was in the section included between this range and the Rocky Mountains that the American engineers found the most formidable difficulties in laying the road, and that the government granted a subsidy of forty-eight thousand dollars per mile, instead of sixteen thousand allowed for the work done on the plains. But the engineers, instead of violating nature, avoided its difficulties by winding around, instead of penetrating the rocks. One tunnel only, fourteen thousand feet in length, was pierced in order to arrive at the great basin.

The track up to this time had reached its highest elevation at the Great Salt Lake. From this point it described a long curve, descending towards Bitter Creek Valley, to rise again to the dividing ridge of the waters between the Atlantic and the Pacific. There were many creeks in this mountainous region, and it was necessary to cross Muddy Creek, Green Creek, and others, upon culverts[13].

Passepartout grew more and more impatient as they went on, while Fix longed to get out of this difficult region, and was more anxious than Phileas Fogg himself to be beyond the danger of delays and accidents, and set foot on English soil.

At ten o'clock at night the train stopped at Fort Bridger station, and twenty minutes later entered Wyoming Territory, following the valley of Bitter Creek throughout. The next day, 7th December, they stopped for a quarter of an hour at Green River station. Snow had fallen abundantly during the night, but, being mixed with rain, it had half melted, and did not interrupt their progress. The bad weather, however, annoyed Passepartout; for the accumulation of snow, by blocking the wheels of the cars, would certainly have been fatal to Mr. Fogg's tour.

"What an idea!" he said to himself. "Why did my master make this journey in winter? Couldn't he have waited for the good season to increase his chances?"

While the worthy Frenchman was absorbed in the state of the sky and the depression of the temperature[14], Aouda was experiencing fears from a totally different cause.

Several passengers had got off at Green River, and were walking up and down the platforms; and among these Aouda recognised Colonel Stamp Proctor, the same who had

---

[13] A 'culvert' is a tunnel that is built under railways or roads to allow a passage for flowing water.

[14] 'The state of the sky and the depression of the temperature' refers to the wet and cold weather that was annoying Passepartout.

so grossly insulted Phileas Fogg at the San Francisco meeting. Not wishing to be recognised, the young woman drew back from the window, feeling much alarm at her discovery. She was attached to the man who, however coldly, gave her daily evidences of the most absolute devotion. She did not comprehend, perhaps, the depth of the sentiment with which her protector inspired her, which she called gratitude, but which, though she was unconscious of it, was really more than that. Her heart sank within her when she recognised the man whom Mr. Fogg desired, sooner or later, to call to account for his conduct. Chance alone, it was clear, had brought Colonel Proctor on this train; but there he was, and it was necessary, at all hazards, that Phileas Fogg should not perceive his adversary. [15]

Aouda seized a moment when Mr. Fogg was asleep to tell Fix and Passepartout whom she had seen.

"That Proctor on this train!" cried Fix. "Well, reassure yourself, madam; before he settles with Mr. Fogg; he has got to deal with me! It seems to me that I was the more insulted of the two."

"And, besides," added Passepartout, "I'll take charge of him, colonel as he is."

"Mr. Fix," resumed Aouda, "Mr. Fogg will allow no one to avenge him. He said that he would come back to America to find this man. Should he perceive Colonel Proctor, we could not prevent a collision which might have terrible results. He must not see him."

"You are right, madam," replied Fix; "a meeting between them might ruin all. Whether he were victorious or beaten, Mr. Fogg would be delayed, and—"

"And," added Passepartout, "that would play the game of the gentlemen of the Reform Club. In four days we shall be in New York. Well, if my master does not leave this car during those four days, we may hope that chance will not bring him face to face with this confounded American. We must, if possible, prevent his stirring out of it."

The conversation dropped. Mr. Fogg had just woke up, and was looking out of the window. Soon after Passepartout, without being heard by his master or Aouda, whispered to the detective, "Would you really fight for him?"

"I would do anything," replied Fix, in a tone which betrayed determined will, "to get him back living to Europe!"

Passepartout felt something like a shudder shoot through his frame, but his confidence in his master remained unbroken.

Was there any means of detaining Mr. Fogg in the car, to avoid a meeting between him and the colonel? It ought not to be a difficult task, since that gentleman was naturally sedentary and little curious. The detective, at least, seemed to have found a way; for,

---

[15] Aouda didn't realise it herself at the time, but she had greater sentiments for Mr. Fogg than just gratitude. Her affection towards him worried her about Mr. Fogg's safety, especially when she saw Colonel Stamp onboard the same train.

after a few moments, he said to Mr. Fogg, "These are long and slow hours, sir, that we are passing on the railway."

"Yes," replied Mr. Fogg; "but they pass."

"You were in the habit of playing whist," resumed Fix, "on the steamers."

"Yes; but it would be difficult to do so here. I have neither cards nor partners."

"Oh, but we can easily buy some cards, for they are sold on all the American trains. And as for partners, if madam plays—"

"Certainly, sir," Aouda quickly replied; "I understand whist. It is part of an English education."

"I myself have some pretensions to playing a good game. Well, here are three of us, and a dummy—"[16]

"As you please, sir," replied Phileas Fogg, heartily glad to resume his favourite pastime even on the railway.

Passepartout was dispatched in search of the steward, and soon returned with two packs of cards, some pins, counters, and a shelf covered with cloth.

The game commenced. Aouda understood whist sufficiently well, and even received some compliments on her playing from Mr. Fogg. As for the detective, he was simply an adept[17], and worthy of being matched against his present opponent.

"Now," thought Passepartout, "we've got him. He won't budge."

At eleven in the morning the train had reached the dividing ridge of the waters at Bridger Pass, seven thousand five hundred and twenty-four feet above the level of the sea, one of the highest points attained by the track in crossing the Rocky Mountains. After going about two hundred miles, the travellers at last found themselves on one of those vast plains which extend to the Atlantic, and which nature has made so propitious[18] for laying the iron road[19].

On the declivity[20] of the Atlantic basin the first streams, branches of the North Platte River, already appeared. The whole northern and eastern horizon was bounded by the immense semi-circular curtain which is formed by the southern portion of the Rocky Mountains, the highest being Laramie Peak. Between this and the railway extended vast plains, plentifully irrigated. On the right rose the lower spurs of the mountainous mass

---

[16] Fix is proposing a game of Dummy whist, which is a variant of classic game of Whist. Dummy whist is played by only three players and a dummy hand is dealt to be on the team of the winning player.

[17] 'Adept' means to be proficient at something.

[18] 'Propitious' means favourable or advantageous.

[19] The 'iron road' refers to the railway track they are all travelling on.

[20] 'Declivity' means a downward slope.

which extends southward to the sources of the Arkansas River, one of the great tributaries of the Missouri[21].[22]

At half-past twelve the travellers caught sight for an instant of Fort Halleck, which commands that section; and in a few more hours the Rocky Mountains were crossed. There was reason to hope, then, that no accident would mark the journey through this difficult country. The snow had ceased falling, and the air became crisp and cold. Large birds, frightened by the locomotive, rose and flew off in the distance. No wild beast appeared on the plain. It was a desert in its vast nakedness.[23]

After a comfortable breakfast, served in the car, Mr. Fogg and his partners had just resumed whist, when a violent whistling was heard, and the train stopped. Passepartout put his head out of the door, but saw nothing to cause the delay; no station was in view.

Aouda and Fix feared that Mr. Fogg might take it into his head to get out; but that gentleman contented himself with saying to his servant, "See what is the matter."

Passepartout rushed out of the car. Thirty or forty passengers had already descended, amongst them Colonel Stamp Proctor.

The train had stopped before a red signal which blocked the way. The engineer and conductor were talking excitedly with a signal-man, whom the station-master at Medicine Bow, the next stopping place, had sent on before. The passengers drew around and took part in the discussion, in which Colonel Proctor, with his insolent manner, was conspicuous.[24]

Passepartout, joining the group, heard the signal-man say, "No! you can't pass. The bridge at Medicine Bow is shaky, and would not bear the weight of the train."

This was a suspension-bridge thrown over some rapids, about a mile from the place where they now were. According to the signal-man, it was in a ruinous condition, several of the iron wires being broken; and it was impossible to risk the passage. He did not in any way exaggerate the condition of the bridge. It may be taken for granted that, rash as the Americans usually are, when they are prudent[25] there is good reason for it.

Passepartout, not daring to apprise his master of what he heard, listened with set teeth, immovable as a statue.

"Hum!" cried Colonel Proctor; "but we are not going to stay here, I imagine, and take root in the snow[26]?"

---

[21] The Missouri River is the longest river in the United States. It flows for approximately 2,500 miles before it enters the Mississippi River.
[22] The Arkansas River is the second-longest tributary in the Mississippi-Missouri river system.
[23] The vast desert looked naked as it was devoid of any coverage of plant life.
[24] Colonel Proctor's rude and arrogant nature made him more noticeable than the others.
[25] 'Prudent' means to be sensible and sagacious about the future.
[26] The phrase 'to take root in' means to stay in an area long enough to establish oneself there.

"Colonel," replied the conductor, "we have telegraphed to Omaha for a train, but it is not likely that it will reach Medicine Bow in less than six hours."

"Six hours!" cried Passepartout.

"Certainly," returned the conductor, "besides, it will take us as long as that to reach Medicine Bow on foot."

"But it is only a mile from here," said one of the passengers.

"Yes, but it's on the other side of the river."

"And can't we cross that in a boat?" asked the colonel.

"That's impossible. The creek is swelled by the rains. It is a rapid, and we shall have to make a circuit of ten miles to the north to find a ford."

The colonel launched a volley of oaths, denouncing the railway company and the conductor; and Passepartout, who was furious, was not disinclined to make common cause with him. Here was an obstacle, indeed, which all his master's banknotes could not remove.

There was a general disappointment among the passengers, who, without reckoning the delay, saw themselves compelled to trudge[27] fifteen miles over a plain covered with snow. They grumbled and protested, and would certainly have thus attracted Phileas Fogg's attention if he had not been completely absorbed in his game.

Passepartout found that he could not avoid telling his master what had occurred, and, with hanging head, he was turning towards the car, when the engineer, a true Yankee, named Forster called out, "Gentlemen, perhaps there is a way, after all, to get over."

"On the bridge?" asked a passenger.

"On the bridge."

"With our train?"

"With our train."

Passepartout stopped short, and eagerly listened to the engineer.

"But the bridge is unsafe," urged the conductor.

"No matter," replied Forster; "I think that by putting on the very highest speed we might have a chance of getting over."

"The devil!" muttered Passepartout.

But a number of the passengers were at once attracted by the engineer's proposal, and Colonel Proctor was especially delighted, and found the plan a very feasible one. He told stories about engineers leaping their trains over rivers without bridges, by putting on full steam; and many of those present avowed themselves of the engineer's mind.

---

[27] To 'trudge' means to walk slowly with heavy steps due to exhaustion or harsh conditions.

"We have fifty chances out of a hundred of getting over," said one.

"Eighty! ninety!"

Passepartout was astounded, and, though ready to attempt anything to get over Medicine Creek, thought the experiment proposed a little too American. "Besides," thought he, "there's a still more simple way, and it does not even occur to any of these people! Sir," said he aloud to one of the passengers, "the engineer's plan seems to me a little dangerous, but—"

"Eighty chances!" replied the passenger, turning his back on him.

"I know it," said Passepartout, turning to another passenger, "but a simple idea—"

"Ideas are no use," returned the American, shrugging his shoulders, "as the engineer assures us that we can pass."

"Doubtless," urged Passepartout, "we can pass, but perhaps it would be more prudent—"

"What! Prudent!" cried Colonel Proctor, whom this word seemed to excite prodigiously. "At full speed, don't you see, at full speed!"

"I know—I see," repeated Passepartout; "but it would be, if not more prudent, since that word displeases you, at least more natural—"

"Who! What! What's the matter with this fellow?" cried several.

The poor fellow did not know to whom to address himself.

"Are you afraid?" asked Colonel Proctor.

"I afraid? Very well; I will show these people that a Frenchman can be as American as they!"

"All aboard!" cried the conductor.

"Yes, all aboard!" repeated Passepartout, and immediately. "But they can't prevent me from thinking that it would be more natural for us to cross the bridge on foot, and let the train come after!"

But no one heard this sage[28] reflection, nor would anyone have acknowledged its justice. The passengers resumed their places in the cars. Passepartout took his seat without telling what had passed. The whist-players were quite absorbed in their game.

The locomotive whistled vigorously; the engineer, reversing the steam, backed the train for nearly a mile—retiring, like a jumper, in order to take a longer leap.[29] Then, with

---

[28] 'Sage' refers to something that's profoundly wise.

[29] Long jumpers take a running start before they propel themselves in the air from a take-off point to achieve maximum distance in the air. The runway is a very important part of a long jump. The engineer prepared the locomotive for the jump over the bridge by taking a mile-long runway to build its speed.

another whistle, he began to move forward; the train increased its speed, and soon its rapidity became frightful; a prolonged screech issued from the locomotive; the piston worked up and down twenty strokes to the second. They perceived that the whole train, rushing on at the rate of a hundred miles an hour, hardly bore upon the rails at all.

And they passed over! It was like a flash. No one saw the bridge. The train leaped, so to speak, from one bank to the other, and the engineer could not stop it until it had gone five miles beyond the station.[30] But scarcely had the train passed the river, when the bridge, completely ruined, fell with a crash into the rapids of Medicine Bow.

---

[30] The train was travelling at such high speed that it took a much longer distance for it to finally come to a halt.

Comprehension exercise 28

Q1) In the text, what was Passepartout's main concern?
a) Avoiding a dangerous meeting with Colonel Proctor.
b) Ensuring Mr. Fogg's comfort during the journey.
c) Finding a way to entertain himself during the train ride.
d) Resolving a dispute with the conductor over the train delay.

Q2) What caused the delay in the train's journey?
a) A mechanical failure in the locomotive.
b) Weather conditions affecting the train tracks.
c) A dispute between passengers and the conductor.
d) A red signal indicating an unsafe bridge ahead.

Q3) What is the primary reason for the passengers' dissatisfaction during the delay?
a) They feared missing their connections.
b) They were tired of the long journey.
c) They disliked the inconvenience of walking.
d) They were upset about the lack of communication from the conductor.

Q4) What does the word "sedentary" mean in the context of the passage?
a) Active and energetic.
b) Relaxed and calm.
c) Fond of sitting; characterized by much sitting.
d) Engaged in physical exercise.

Q5) Which word best describes the passengers' reaction to the engineer's proposal to cross the bridge?
a) Enthusiastic
b) Indifferent
c) Apprehensive
d) Aggressive

Chapter 29

IN WHICH CERTAIN INCIDENTS ARE NARRATED WHICH
ARE ONLY TO BE MET WITH ON AMERICAN RAILROADS

The train pursued its course, that evening, without interruption, passing Fort Saunders, crossing Cheyne Pass, and reaching Evans Pass. The road here attained the highest elevation of the journey, eight thousand and ninety-two feet above the level of the sea. The travellers had now only to descend to the Atlantic by limitless plains, levelled by nature. A branch of the "grand trunk" led off southward to Denver, the capital of Colorado. The country round about is rich in gold and silver, and more than fifty thousand inhabitants are already settled there.

Thirteen hundred and eighty-two miles had been passed over from San Francisco, in three days and three nights; four days and nights more would probably bring them to New York. Phileas Fogg was not as yet behind-hand.

During the night Camp Walbach was passed on the left; Lodge Pole Creek ran parallel with the road, marking the boundary between the territories of Wyoming and Colorado. They entered Nebraska at eleven, passed near Sedgwick, and touched at Julesburg, on the southern branch of the Platte River.

It was here that the Union Pacific Railroad was inaugurated on the 23rd of October, 1867, by the chief engineer, General Dodge. Two powerful locomotives, carrying nine cars of invited guests, amongst whom was Thomas C. Durant, vice-president of the road, stopped at this point; cheers were given, the Sioux and Pawnees performed an imitation Indian battle, fireworks were let off, and the first number of the Railway Pioneer was printed by a press brought on the train. Thus was celebrated the inauguration of this great railroad, a mighty instrument of progress and civilisation, thrown across the desert, and destined to link together cities and towns which do not yet exist. The whistle of the locomotive, more powerful than Amphion's lyre[1], was about to bid them rise from American soil.

Fort McPherson was left behind at eight in the morning, and three hundred and fifty-seven miles had yet to be traversed before reaching Omaha. The road followed the capricious windings of the southern branch of the Platte River, on its left bank. At nine the train stopped at the important town of North Platte, built between the two arms of

---

[1] Amphion and Zethus were twin brothers in Greek mythology who constructed the city walls of Thebes. It is believed that as Amphion played his Lyre (a musical string instrument), the rocks followed him and set themselves into place. The myth is that the strings of the Lyre, when continuously played, will cause the construction works to complete themselves.

the river, which rejoin each other around it and form a single artery, a large tributary, whose waters empty into the Missouri a little above Omaha.

The one hundred and first meridian was passed.

Mr. Fogg and his partners had resumed their game; no one—not even the dummy—complained of the length of the trip. Fix had begun by winning several guineas, which he seemed likely to lose; but he showed himself a not less eager whist-player than Mr. Fogg. During the morning, chance distinctly favoured that gentleman. Trumps and honours were showered upon his hands.

Once, having resolved on a bold stroke, he was on the point of playing a spade, when a voice behind him said, "I should play a diamond."

Mr. Fogg, Aouda, and Fix raised their heads, and beheld Colonel Proctor.

Stamp Proctor and Phileas Fogg recognised each other at once.

"Ah! it's you, is it, Englishman?" cried the colonel; "it's you who are going to play a spade!"

"And who plays it," replied Phileas Fogg coolly, throwing down the ten of spades.

"Well, it pleases me to have it diamonds," replied Colonel Proctor, in an insolent tone.

He made a movement as if to seize the card which had just been played, adding, "You don't understand anything about whist."[2]

"Perhaps I do, as well as another," said Phileas Fogg, rising.

"You have only to try, son of John Bull[3]," replied the colonel.

Aouda turned pale, and her blood ran cold. She seized Mr. Fogg's arm and gently pulled him back. Passepartout was ready to pounce upon the American, who was staring insolently at his opponent. But Fix got up, and, going to Colonel Proctor said, "You forget that it is I with whom you have to deal, sir; for it was I whom you not only insulted, but struck!"

"Mr. Fix," said Mr. Fogg, "pardon me, but this affair is mine, and mine only. The colonel has again insulted me, by insisting that I should not play a spade, and he shall give me satisfaction for it."

"When and where you will," replied the American, "and with whatever weapon you choose."

---

[2] The Colonel suggests that Mr. Fogg didn't know anything about whist, as he should have played a diamond instead of a spades card.

[3] 'John Bull' is a term and a character used to personify the United Kingdom (England more specifically). He is usually illustrated as a middle-aged, stout, and jolly natured man in cartoons and other graphic works.

Aouda in vain attempted to retain Mr. Fogg; as vainly did the detective endeavour to make the quarrel his[4]. Passepartout wished to throw the colonel out of the window, but a sign from his master checked him. Phileas Fogg left the car, and the American followed him upon the platform. "Sir," said Mr. Fogg to his adversary, "I am in a great hurry to get back to Europe, and any delay whatever will be greatly to my disadvantage."

"Well, what's that to me?" replied Colonel Proctor.

"Sir," said Mr. Fogg, very politely, "after our meeting at San Francisco, I determined to return to America and find you as soon as I had completed the business which called me to England."

"Really!"

"Will you appoint a meeting for six months hence?"

"Why not ten years hence?"[5]

"I say six months," returned Phileas Fogg; "and I shall be at the place of meeting promptly."

"All this is an evasion," cried Stamp Proctor. "Now or never!"

"Very good. You are going to New York?"

"No."

"To Chicago?"

"No."

"To Omaha?"

"What difference is it to you? Do you know Plum Creek?"

"No," replied Mr. Fogg.

"It's the next station. The train will be there in an hour, and will stop there ten minutes. In ten minutes several revolver-shots could be exchanged."

"Very well," said Mr. Fogg. "I will stop at Plum Creek."

"And I guess you'll stay there too," added the American insolently[6].

"Who knows?" replied Mr. Fogg, returning to the car as coolly as usual. He began to reassure Aouda, telling her that blusterers were never to be feared, and begged Fix to be his second at the approaching duel, a request which the detective could not refuse. Mr. Fogg resumed the interrupted game with perfect calmness.

---

[4] Mr. Fix hinted that he was the one struck by the Colonel, implying that it was their altercation, rather than involving Mr. Fogg.

[5] The American mocks Mr. Fogg's suggestion to delay their duel, implying Mr. Fogg is afraid to confront the challenge in six months.

[6] 'Insolent' means disrespectful or rude in speech or conduct.

A Study Guide: Around the World in Eighty Days

At eleven o'clock the locomotive's whistle announced that they were approaching Plum Creek station. Mr. Fogg rose, and, followed by Fix, went out upon the platform. Passepartout accompanied him, carrying a pair of revolvers. Aouda remained in the car, as pale as death[7].

The door of the next car opened, and Colonel Proctor appeared on the platform, attended by a Yankee of his own stamp[8] as his second.[9] But just as the combatants were about to step from the train, the conductor hurried up, and shouted, "You can't get off, gentlemen!"

"Why not?" asked the colonel.

"We are twenty minutes late, and we shall not stop."

"But I am going to fight a duel with this gentleman."

"I am sorry," said the conductor; "but we shall be off at once. There's the bell ringing now."

The train started.

"I'm really very sorry, gentlemen," said the conductor. "Under any other circumstances I should have been happy to oblige you. But, after all, as you have not had time to fight here, why not fight as we go along?"

"That wouldn't be convenient, perhaps, for this gentleman," said the colonel, in a jeering[10] tone.

"It would be perfectly so," replied Phileas Fogg.

"Well, we are really in America," thought Passepartout, "and the conductor is a gentleman of the first order!"[11]

So muttering, he followed his master.

The two combatants, their seconds, and the conductor passed through the cars to the rear of the train. The last car was only occupied by a dozen passengers, whom the conductor politely asked if they would not be so kind as to leave it vacant for a few moments, as two gentlemen had an affair of honour to settle. The passengers granted the request with alacrity[12], and straightway disappeared on the platform.

---

[7] 'As pale as death' is an idiom meaning exceptionally pale in colour due to nausea or fear.

[8] 'To put one's own stamp' means to influence someone or something in their own unique ways.

[9] The Colonel stepped onto the platform with another American who behaved very similarly to him.

[10] Once more, the American ridicules Mr. Fogg, insinuating that Mr. Fogg might use this as a pretext to avoid the confrontation.

[11] The writer uses sarcasm to show how rude the conductor's behaviour was in suggesting the men fight while on the train.

[12] 'Alacrity' means cheerful readiness.

166

The car, which was some fifty feet long, was very convenient for their purpose. The adversaries might march on each other in the aisle, and fire at their ease. Never was duel more easily arranged. Mr. Fogg and Colonel Proctor, each provided with two six-barrelled revolvers, entered the car. The seconds, remaining outside, shut them in. They were to begin firing at the first whistle of the locomotive. After an interval of two minutes, what remained of the two gentlemen would be taken from the car.

Nothing could be more simple. Indeed, it was all so simple that Fix and Passepartout felt their hearts beating as if they would crack. They were listening for the whistle agreed upon, when suddenly savage cries resounded in the air, accompanied by reports which certainly did not issue from the car where the duellists were. The reports continued in front and the whole length of the train. Cries of terror proceeded from the interior of the cars.

Colonel Proctor and Mr. Fogg, revolvers in hand, hastily quitted their prison[13], and rushed forward where the noise was most clamorous[14]. They then perceived that the train was attacked by a band of Sioux[15].

This was not the first attempt of these daring Indians, for more than once they had waylaid[16] trains on the road. A hundred of them had, according to their habit, jumped upon the steps without stopping the train, with the ease of a clown mounting a horse at full gallop.

The Sioux were armed with guns, from which came the reports, to which the passengers, who were almost all armed, responded by revolver-shots.

The Indians had first mounted the engine, and half stunned the engineer and stoker with blows from their muskets. A Sioux chief, wishing to stop the train, but not knowing how to work the regulator, had opened wide instead of closing the steam-valve, and the locomotive was plunging forward with terrific velocity.

The Sioux had at the same time invaded the cars, skipping like enraged monkeys over the roofs, thrusting open the doors, and fighting hand to hand with the passengers. Penetrating the baggage-car, they pillaged it, throwing the trunks out of the train. The cries and shots were constant. The travellers defended themselves bravely; some of the cars were barricaded, and sustained a siege, like moving forts, carried along at a speed of a hundred miles an hour.

Aouda behaved courageously from the first. She defended herself like a true heroine with a revolver, which she shot through the broken windows whenever a savage made his appearance. Twenty Sioux had fallen mortally wounded[17] to the ground, and the

---

[13] 'Prison' refers to the railway car that Mr. Fogg and the American were locked in for their fight.
[14] 'Clamorous' means a loud and confused noise.
[15] The Sioux are a group of Native American Indian tribes.
[16] 'Waylay' means to stop or interrupt someone or something.
[17] A 'mortal wound' refers to a wound that has caused the death of a person or an animal.

wheels crushed those who fell upon the rails as if they had been worms. Several passengers, shot or stunned, lay on the seats.

It was necessary to put an end to the struggle, which had lasted for ten minutes, and which would result in the triumph of the Sioux if the train was not stopped. Fort Kearney station, where there was a garrison, was only two miles distant; but, that once passed, the Sioux would be masters of the train between Fort Kearney and the station beyond.

The conductor was fighting beside Mr. Fogg, when he was shot and fell. At the same moment he cried, "Unless the train is stopped in five minutes, we are lost!"

"It shall be stopped," said Phileas Fogg, preparing to rush from the car.

"Stay, monsieur," cried Passepartout; "I will go."

Mr. Fogg had not time to stop the brave fellow, who, opening a door unperceived by the Indians, succeeded in slipping under the car; and while the struggle continued and the balls[18] whizzed across each other over his head, he made use of his old acrobatic experience, and with amazing agility worked his way under the cars, holding on to the chains, aiding himself by the brakes and edges of the sashes, creeping from one car to another with marvellous skill, and thus gaining the forward end of the train.

There, suspended by one hand between the baggage-car and the tender, with the other he loosened the safety chains; but, owing to the traction[19], he would never have succeeded in unscrewing the yoking-bar[20], had not a violent concussion jolted this bar out. The train, now detached from the engine, remained a little behind, whilst the locomotive rushed forward with increased speed.

Carried on by the force already acquired, the train still moved for several minutes; but the brakes were worked and at last they stopped, less than a hundred feet from Kearney station.

The soldiers of the fort, attracted by the shots, hurried up; the Sioux had not expected them, and decamped[21] in a body before the train entirely stopped.

But when the passengers counted each other on the station platform several were found missing; among others the courageous Frenchman, whose devotion had just saved them.

---

[18] 'Balls' here refer to the gun bullets that are being shot around.
[19] 'Traction' is the force between the wheels and the rails.
[20] A 'yoking bar' is a frame used to tie and distribute the weight equally in two parts.
[21] 'Decamping' means to abscond or leave secretly.

Comprehension exercise 29

Q1) What was the primary reason for the delay in the train's journey at Plum Creek station?
a) Mechanical failure in the locomotive.
b) A duel arranged between Mr. Fogg and Colonel Proctor.
c) Indian attacks on the train.
d) Passenger altercation with the conductor.

Q2) which statement about Aouda's behaviour during the confrontation with the Sioux is most accurate?
a) Aouda retreated to safety and avoided confrontation with the Sioux.
b) Aouda showed bravery by engaging in physical combat with the Sioux.
c) Aouda sought help from the garrison at Fort Kearney to handle the situation.
d) Aouda used a revolver to defend herself and the passengers against the Sioux.

Q3) What did the conductor suggest as an alternative to stopping the train for the duel?
a) To fight the duel while the train was moving.
b) To postpone the duel until they reached their destination.
c) To hold the duel at the next station.
d) To resolve their conflict peacefully.

Q4) What prevented the Indians from capturing the train entirely during the attack?
a) Proximity to the fort garrison.
b) The passengers barricaded themselves inside the cars.
c) Passepartout's acrobatic manoeuvres delayed them.
d) The train's increased speed confused the attackers.

Q5) What does the word "acrobatic" mean in the context of the passage?
a) Swift and agile movement.
b) Courageous and brave action.
c) Intelligent and strategic thinking.
d) Skilful and precise coordination.

Chapter 30

IN WHICH PHILEAS FOGG SIMPLY DOES HIS DUTY

Three passengers including Passepartout had disappeared. Had they been killed in the struggle? Were they taken prisoners by the Sioux? It was impossible to tell.

There were many wounded, but none mortally. Colonel Proctor was one of the most seriously hurt; he had fought bravely, and a ball had entered his groin. He was carried into the station with the other wounded passengers, to receive such attention as could be of avail.

Aouda was safe; and Phileas Fogg, who had been in the thickest of the fight, had not received a scratch. Fix was slightly wounded in the arm. But Passepartout was not to be found, and tears coursed down Aouda's cheeks.

All the passengers had got out of the train, the wheels of which were stained with blood. From the tyres and spokes hung ragged pieces of flesh. As far as the eye could reach on the white plain behind, red trails were visible. The last Sioux were disappearing in the south, along the banks of Republican River.

Mr. Fogg, with folded arms, remained motionless. He had a serious decision to make. Aouda, standing near him, looked at him without speaking, and he understood her look. If his servant was a prisoner, ought he not to risk everything to rescue him from the Indians? "I will find him, living or dead," said he quietly to Aouda.

"Ah, Mr.—Mr. Fogg!" cried she, clasping his hands and covering them with tears.

"Living," added Mr. Fogg, "if we do not lose a moment."

Phileas Fogg, by this resolution, inevitably sacrificed himself; he pronounced his own doom. The delay of a single day would make him lose the steamer at New York, and his bet would be certainly lost. But as he thought, "It is my duty," he did not hesitate.

The commanding officer of Fort Kearney was there. A hundred of his soldiers had placed themselves in a position to defend the station, should the Sioux attack it.

"Sir," said Mr. Fogg to the captain, "three passengers have disappeared."

"Dead?" asked the captain.

"Dead or prisoners; that is the uncertainty which must be solved. Do you propose to pursue the Sioux?"

"That's a serious thing to do, sir," returned the captain. "These Indians may retreat beyond the Arkansas, and I cannot leave the fort unprotected."

"The lives of three men are in question, sir," said Phileas Fogg.

"Doubtless; but can I risk the lives of fifty men to save three?"

"I don't know whether you can, sir; but you ought to do so."

"Nobody here," returned the other, "has a right to teach me my duty."

"Very well," said Mr. Fogg, coldly. "I will go alone."

"You, sir!" cried Fix, coming up; "you go alone in pursuit of the Indians?"

"Would you have me leave this poor fellow to perish—him to whom every one present owes his life? I shall go."

"No, sir, you shall not go alone," cried the captain, touched in spite of himself. "No! you are a brave man. Thirty volunteers!" he added, turning to the soldiers.

The whole company started forward at once. The captain had only to pick his men. Thirty were chosen, and an old sergeant placed at their head.

"Thanks, captain," said Mr. Fogg.

"Will you let me go with you?" asked Fix.

"Do as you please, sir. But if you wish to do me a favour, you will remain with Aouda. In case anything should happen to me—"

A sudden pallor overspread the detective's face. Separate himself from the man whom he had so persistently followed step by step! Leave him to wander about in this desert! Fix gazed attentively at Mr. Fogg, and, despite his suspicions and of the struggle which was going on within him, he lowered his eyes before that calm and frank look.

"I will stay," said he.

A few moments after, Mr. Fogg pressed the young woman's hand, and, having confided to her his precious carpet-bag, went off with the sergeant and his little squad. But, before going, he had said to the soldiers, "My friends, I will divide five thousand dollars among you, if we save the prisoners."

It was then a little past noon.

Aouda retired to a waiting-room, and there she waited alone, thinking of the simple and noble generosity, the tranquil courage of Phileas Fogg. He had sacrificed his fortune, and was now risking his life, all without hesitation, from duty, in silence.

Fix did not have the same thoughts, and could scarcely conceal his agitation. He walked feverishly up and down the platform, but soon resumed his outward composure. He now saw the folly of which he had been guilty in letting Fogg go alone. What! This man, whom he had just followed around the world, was permitted now to separate himself from him! He began to accuse and abuse himself, and, as if he were director of police, administered to himself a sound lecture for his greenness[1].

"I have been an idiot!" he thought, "and this man will see it. He has gone, and won't come back! But how is it that I, Fix, who have in my pocket a warrant for his arrest, have been so fascinated by him? Decidedly, I am nothing but an ass!"

So reasoned the detective, while the hours crept by all too slowly. He did not know what to do. Sometimes he was tempted to tell Aouda all; but he could not doubt how the young woman would receive his confidences. What course should he take? He thought of pursuing Fogg across the vast white plains; it did not seem impossible that he might overtake him. Footsteps were easily printed on the snow! But soon, under a new sheet, every imprint would be effaced.[2]

Fix became discouraged. He felt a sort of insurmountable longing[3] to abandon the game altogether. He could now leave Fort Kearney station, and pursue his journey homeward in peace.

Towards two o'clock in the afternoon, while it was snowing hard, long whistles were heard approaching from the east. A great shadow, preceded by a wild light, slowly advanced, appearing still larger through the mist, which gave it a fantastic aspect. No train was expected from the east, neither had there been time for the succour[4] asked for by telegraph to arrive; the train from Omaha to San Francisco was not due till the next day. The mystery was soon explained.

The locomotive, which was slowly approaching with deafening whistles, was that which, having been detached from the train, had continued its route with such terrific rapidity, carrying off the unconscious engineer and stoker. It had run several miles, when, the fire becoming low for want of fuel, the steam had slackened; and it had finally stopped an hour after, some twenty miles beyond Fort Kearney. Neither the engineer nor the stoker was dead, and, after remaining for some time in their swoon[5], had come to themselves. The train had then stopped. The engineer, when he found himself in the desert, and the locomotive without cars, understood what had happened. He could not imagine how the locomotive had become separated from the train; but he did not doubt that the train left behind was in distress.

He did not hesitate what to do. It would be prudent to continue on to Omaha, for it would be dangerous to return to the train, which the Indians might still be engaged in pillaging. Nevertheless, he began to rebuild the fire in the furnace; the pressure again

---

[1] 'Greenness' here refers to Fix's inexperience or lack of maturity. He is reprimanding himself for his own perceived shortcoming.

[2] A new fall of snow will cover all the foot marks and all previous prints will be erased.

[3] 'Insurmountable longing' means an overwhelming or an invincible desire.

[4] 'Succour' means assistance and here refers to the train requested by the stranded passengers to carry them to their destination.

[5] 'Swoon' means an occurrence of fainting.

mounted, and the locomotive returned, running backwards to Fort Kearney. This it was which was whistling in the mist.

The travellers were glad to see the locomotive resume its place at the head of the train. They could now continue the journey so terribly interrupted.

Aouda, on seeing the locomotive come up, hurried out of the station, and asked the conductor, "Are you going to start?"

"At once, madam."

"But the prisoners, our unfortunate fellow-travellers—"

"I cannot interrupt the trip," replied the conductor. "We are already three hours behind time."

"And when will another train pass here from San Francisco?"

"To-morrow evening, madam."

"To-morrow evening! But then it will be too late! We must wait—"

"It is impossible," responded the conductor. "If you wish to go, please get in."

"I will not go," said Aouda.

Fix had heard this conversation. A little while before, when there was no prospect of proceeding on the journey, he had made up his mind to leave Fort Kearney; but now that the train was there, ready to start, and he had only to take his seat in the car, an irresistible influence held him back. The station platform burned his feet, and he could not stir. The conflict in his mind again began; anger and failure stifled him. He wished to struggle on to the end.

Meanwhile the passengers and some of the wounded, among them Colonel Proctor, whose injuries were serious, had taken their places in the train. The buzzing of the over-heated boiler was heard, and the steam was escaping from the valves. The engineer whistled, the train started, and soon disappeared, mingling its white smoke with the eddies[6] of the densely falling snow.

The detective had remained behind.

Several hours passed. The weather was dismal, and it was very cold. Fix sat motionless on a bench in the station; he might have been thought asleep. Aouda, despite the storm, kept coming out of the waiting-room, going to the end of the platform, and peering through the tempest of snow, as if to pierce the mist which narrowed the horizon around her, and to hear, if possible, some welcome sound. She heard and saw nothing. Then she would return, chilled through, to issue out again after the lapse of a few moments, but always in vain.[7]

---

[6] 'Eddies' are the circular movements, like swirls or whirls, of the snow, smoke, or wind.

[7] Aouda was restless and her impatience was making her feel nervous and anxious about Mr. Fogg's and Passepartout's return.

Evening came, and the little band had not returned. Where could they be? Had they found the Indians, and were they having a conflict with them, or were they still wandering amid the mist? The commander of the fort was anxious, though he tried to conceal his apprehensions. As night approached, the snow fell less plentifully, but it became intensely cold. Absolute silence rested on the plains. Neither flight of bird nor passing of beast troubled the perfect calm.

Throughout the night Aouda, full of sad forebodings[8], her heart stifled with anguish, wandered about on the verge of the plains. Her imagination carried her far off, and showed her innumerable dangers. What she suffered through the long hours it would be impossible to describe.

Fix remained stationary in the same place, but did not sleep. Once a man approached and spoke to him, and the detective merely replied by shaking his head.

Thus the night passed. At dawn, the half-extinguished disc of the sun rose above a misty horizon; but it was now possible to recognise objects two miles off. Phileas Fogg and the squad had gone southward; in the south all was still vacancy. It was then seven o'clock.

The captain, who was really alarmed, did not know what course to take.

Should he send another detachment to the rescue of the first? Should he sacrifice more men, with so few chances of saving those already sacrificed? His hesitation did not last long, however. Calling one of his lieutenants, he was on the point of ordering a reconnaissance[9], when gunshots were heard. Was it a signal? The soldiers rushed out of the fort, and half a mile off they perceived a little band returning in good order.

Mr. Fogg was marching at their head, and just behind him were Passepartout and the other two travellers, rescued from the Sioux.

They had met and fought the Indians ten miles south of Fort Kearney. Shortly before the detachment arrived, Passepartout and his companions had begun to struggle with their captors, three of whom the Frenchman had felled with his fists, when his master and the soldiers hastened up to their relief.

All were welcomed with joyful cries. Phileas Fogg distributed the reward he had promised to the soldiers, while Passepartout, not without reason, muttered to himself, "It must certainly be confessed that I cost my master dear!"

Fix, without saying a word, looked at Mr. Fogg, and it would have been difficult to analyse the thoughts which struggled within him. As for Aouda, she took her protector's hand and pressed it in her own, too much moved to speak.

---

[8] 'Foreboding' refers to a sad and fearful anxiety that something bad is about to happen. These feelings can arise from intuition, observation of ominous signs, or past experiences.

[9] 'Reconnaissance' means to survey or observe a region.

Meanwhile, Passepartout was looking about for the train; he thought he should find it there, ready to start for Omaha, and he hoped that the time lost might be regained.

"The train! the train!" cried he.

"Gone," replied Fix.

"And when does the next train pass here?" said Phileas Fogg.

"Not till this evening."

"Ah!" returned the impassible[10] gentleman quietly.

---

[10] 'Impassible' is an archaic word used for someone incapable of expressing their emotions.

A Study Guide: Around the World in Eighty Days

Comprehension exercise 30:

Q1) How does Fix react to the idea of leaving Fort Kearney without pursuing Mr. Fogg?
a) He feels relieved and eager to return home.
b) He becomes determined to continue following Mr. Fogg.
c) He feels regretful and blames himself for allowing Mr. Fogg to go alone.
d) He decides to abandon his pursuit of Mr. Fogg and remain at Fort Kearney.

Q2) What was the fate of the unconscious engineer and stoker after the locomotive became separated from the train?
a) They were left behind and rescued by the soldiers.
b) They were killed by the Indians during the attack.
c) They remained unconscious until the locomotive returned.
d) They woke up and continued operating the locomotive.

Q3) Why did Aouda refuse to board the train when it was ready to depart from Fort Kearney?
a) She was waiting for Mr. Fogg to return.
b) She was concerned about the wounded passengers.
c) She wanted to wait for the next train from San Francisco.
d) She preferred to remain at the station until morning.

Q4) What does the word "reconnaissance" as used in the text mean?
a) To retreat from danger.
b) To send a rescue team.
c) To survey or explore an area.
d) To engage in combat with enemies.

Q5) In the context of the passage, what does the word "impassible" most likely mean?
a) Unemotional or unaffected by feelings.
b) Impervious to physical harm or damage.
c) Incapable of making decisions.
d) Unable to be stopped or hindered.

Chapter 31

IN WHICH FIX, THE DETECTIVE, CONSIDERABLY FURTHERS THE INTERESTS OF PHILEAS FOGG

Phileas Fogg found himself twenty hours behind time. Passepartout, the involuntary cause of this delay, was desperate. He had ruined his master!

At this moment the detective approached Mr. Fogg, and, looking him intently in the face, said:

"Seriously, sir, are you in great haste?"

"Quite seriously."

"I have a purpose in asking," resumed Fix. "Is it absolutely necessary that you should be in New York on the 11th, before nine o'clock in the evening, the time that the steamer leaves for Liverpool?"

"It is absolutely necessary."

"And, if your journey had not been interrupted by these Indians, you would have reached New York on the morning of the 11th?"

"Yes; with eleven hours to spare before the steamer left."

"Good! you are therefore twenty hours behind. Twelve from twenty leaves eight. You must regain eight hours. Do you wish to try to do so?"

"On foot?" asked Mr. Fogg.

"No; on a sledge," replied Fix. "On a sledge with sails. A man has proposed such a method to me."

It was the man who had spoken to Fix during the night, and whose offer he had refused.

Phileas Fogg did not reply at once; but Fix, having pointed out the man, who was walking up and down in front of the station, Mr. Fogg went up to him. An instant after, Mr. Fogg and the American, whose name was Mudge, entered a hut built just below the fort.

There Mr. Fogg examined a curious vehicle, a kind of frame on two long beams, a little raised in front like the runners of a sledge, and upon which there was room for five or six persons. A high mast was fixed on the frame, held firmly by metallic lashings[1], to which was attached a large brigantine[2] sail. This mast held an iron stay upon which to hoist a jib-sail[3]. Behind, a sort of rudder served to guide the vehicle. It was, in short, a sledge rigged like a sloop[4]. During the winter, when the trains are blocked up by the snow, these sledges make extremely rapid journeys across the frozen plains from one station to another. Provided with more sails than a cutter, and with the wind behind them, they slip over the surface of the prairies[5] with a speed equal if not superior to that of the express trains.

Mr. Fogg readily made a bargain with the owner of this land-craft. The wind was favourable, being fresh, and blowing from the west. The snow had hardened, and Mudge was very confident of being able to transport Mr. Fogg in a few hours to Omaha. Thence the trains eastward run frequently to Chicago and New York. It was not impossible that the lost time might yet be recovered; and such an opportunity was not to be rejected.

Not wishing to expose Aouda to the discomforts of travelling in the open air, Mr. Fogg proposed to leave her with Passepartout at Fort Kearney, the servant taking upon himself to escort her to Europe by a better route and under more favourable conditions. But Aouda refused to separate from Mr. Fogg, and Passepartout was delighted with her decision; for nothing could induce him to leave his master while Fix was with him.

It would be difficult to guess the detective's thoughts. Was this conviction shaken by Phileas Fogg's return, or did he still regard him as an exceedingly shrewd rascal, who, his journey round the world completed, would think himself absolutely safe in England? Perhaps Fix's opinion of Phileas Fogg was somewhat modified; but he was nevertheless resolved to do his duty, and to hasten the return of the whole party to England as much as possible.

At eight o'clock the sledge was ready to start. The passengers took their places on it, and wrapped themselves up closely in their travelling-cloaks. The two great sails were hoisted, and under the pressure of the wind the sledge slid over the hardened snow with a velocity of forty miles an hour.

The distance between Fort Kearney and Omaha, as the birds fly[6], is at most two hundred miles. If the wind held good, the distance might be traversed in five hours; if no accident happened the sledge might reach Omaha by one o'clock.

What a journey! The travellers, huddled close together, could not speak for the cold, intensified by the rapidity at which they were going. The sledge sped on as lightly as a

---

[1] In nautical terminology, 'lashings' are often used to secure objects on a ship or boat, such as cargo or equipment, to prevent them from shifting or moving during rough seas.

[2] A 'brigantine' is a two-masted sailing ship.

[3] A 'jib-sail' is a triangular staysail set forward of the mast.

[4] A 'sloop' is a sailing boat.

[5] 'Prairies' are large expanses of flat or gently rolling grasslands, typically characterized by fertile soil and few trees. They are found in various parts of the world, including North America, particularly in the central United States and Canada.

[6] 'As the crow (or bird) flies' is the measurement of distance in a straight line.

boat over the waves. When the breeze came skimming the earth the sledge seemed to be lifted off the ground by its sails. Mudge, who was at the rudder, kept in a straight line, and by a turn of his hand checked the lurches[7] which the vehicle had a tendency to make. All the sails were up, and the jib was so arranged as not to screen the brigantine. A topmast was hoisted, and another jib, held out to the wind, added its force to the other sails. Although the speed could not be exactly estimated, the sledge could not be going at less than forty miles an hour.

"If nothing breaks," said Mudge, "we shall get there!"

Mr. Fogg had made it for Mudge's interest to reach Omaha within the time agreed on, by the offer of a handsome reward.

The prairie, across which the sledge was moving in a straight line, was as flat as a sea. It seemed like a vast frozen lake. The railroad which ran through this section ascended from the south-west to the north-west by Great Island, Columbus, an important Nebraska town, Schuyler, and Fremont, to Omaha. It followed throughout the right bank of the Platte River. The sledge, shortening this route, took a chord of the arc described by the railway.[8] Mudge was not afraid of being stopped by the Platte River, because it was frozen. The road, then, was quite clear of obstacles, and Phileas Fogg had but two things to fear—an accident to the sledge, and a change or calm in the wind.

But the breeze, far from lessening its force, blew as if to bend the mast, which, however, the metallic lashings held firmly. These lashings, like the chords of a stringed instrument, resounded as if vibrated by a violin bow. The sledge slid along in the midst of a plaintively intense melody.

"Those chords give the fifth and the octave,"[9] said Mr. Fogg.

These were the only words he uttered during the journey. Aouda, cosily packed in furs and cloaks, was sheltered as much as possible from the attacks of the freezing wind. As for Passepartout, his face was as red as the sun's disc when it sets in the mist, and he laboriously inhaled the biting air. With his natural buoyancy of spirits, he began to hope again. They would reach New York on the evening, if not on the morning, of the 11th, and there was still some chances that it would be before the steamer sailed for Liverpool.

Passepartout even felt a strong desire to grasp his ally, Fix, by the hand. He remembered that it was the detective who procured the sledge, the only means of reaching Omaha in time; but, checked by some presentiment, he kept his usual reserve. One thing, however, Passepartout would never forget, and that was the sacrifice which

---

[7] 'Lurches' are unsteady and abrupt movements. Mudge adjusted the rudder to steer the sledge back on its course whenever it came off due to these sudden movements.

[8] An arc is a curved segment between two points, whereas a chord length is the straight line between two points. While the railway line was laid along the curved segment, the sledge took the chord line, which was the shorter distance.

[9] The Fifth and the Octave refer to the musical notes, and Mr. Fogg is comparing the sound made by lashes/ chords against the wind to that of the musical notes from a stringed instrument.

Mr. Fogg had made, without hesitation, to rescue him from the Sioux. Mr. Fogg had risked his fortune and his life. No! His servant would never forget that!

While each of the party was absorbed in reflections so different, the sledge flew past over the vast carpet of snow. The creeks it passed over were not perceived. Fields and streams disappeared under the uniform whiteness. The plain was absolutely deserted. Between the Union Pacific road and the branch which unites Kearney with Saint Joseph it formed a great uninhabited island. Neither village, station, nor fort appeared. From time to time they sped by some phantom-like tree, whose white skeleton twisted and rattled in the wind. Sometimes flocks of wild birds rose, or bands of gaunt[10], famished, ferocious prairie-wolves[11] ran howling after the sledge. Passepartout, revolver in hand, held himself ready to fire on those which came too near. Had an accident then happened to the sledge, the travellers, attacked by these beasts, would have been in the most terrible danger; but it held on its even course, soon gained on the wolves, and ere long left the howling band at a safe distance behind.

About noon Mudge perceived by certain landmarks that he was crossing the Platte River. He said nothing, but he felt certain that he was now within twenty miles of Omaha. In less than an hour he left the rudder and furled his sails, whilst the sledge, carried forward by the great impetus the wind had given it, went on half a mile further with its sails unspread.

It stopped at last, and Mudge, pointing to a mass of roofs white with snow, said: "We have got there!"

Arrived! Arrived at the station which is in daily communication, by numerous trains, with the Atlantic seaboard!

Passepartout and Fix jumped off, stretched their stiffened limbs, and aided Mr. Fogg and the young woman to descend from the sledge. Phileas Fogg generously rewarded Mudge, whose hand Passepartout warmly grasped[12], and the party directed their steps to the Omaha railway station.

The Pacific Railroad proper finds its terminus at this important Nebraska town. Omaha is connected with Chicago by the Chicago and Rock Island Railroad, which runs directly east, and passes fifty stations.

A train was ready to start when Mr. Fogg and his party reached the station, and they only had time to get into the cars. They had seen nothing of Omaha; but Passepartout

---

[10] 'Gaunt' means skinny and scraggy looking.

[11] A 'prairie wolf' is a native, medium sized, North American coyote.

[12] This action expresses Passepartout's gratitude towards Mudge for getting them to Omaha on time.

confessed to himself that this was not to be regretted, as they were not travelling to see the sights.[13]

The train passed rapidly across the State of Iowa, by Council Bluffs, Des Moines, and Iowa City. During the night it crossed the Mississippi at Davenport, and by Rock Island entered Illinois. The next day, which was the 10th, at four o'clock in the evening, it reached Chicago, already risen from its ruins, and more proudly seated than ever on the borders of its beautiful Lake Michigan.

Nine hundred miles separated Chicago from New York; but trains are not wanting at Chicago[14]. Mr. Fogg passed at once from one to the other, and the locomotive of the Pittsburgh, Fort Wayne, and Chicago Railway left at full speed, as if it fully comprehended that that gentleman had no time to lose. It traversed Indiana, Ohio, Pennsylvania, and New Jersey like a flash, rushing through towns with antique names, some of which had streets and car-tracks, but as yet no houses. At last the Hudson came into view; and, at a quarter-past eleven in the evening of the 11th, the train stopped in the station on the right bank of the river, before the very pier of the Cunard line.

The China, for Liverpool, had started three-quarters of an hour before!

---

[13] Passepartout's perception of their travels has now changed. While earlier he wanted to see the sights and enjoy the new cities that they were passing by, now his whole focus was to complete their trip around the world within eighty days. All he wanted was for his master to win his bet.

[14] The phrase "trains are not wanting at Chicago" means that there is no shortage of trains available in Chicago. In other words, Chicago has ample availability of trains, suggesting that it is well-connected by rail transportation.

A Study Guide: Around the World in Eighty Days

Comprehension exercise 31:

Q1) How did Phileas Fogg plan to regain the lost time caused by the Indian interruption?
a) By traveling on foot
b) By sailing on a ship
c) By riding on a sledge with sails
d) By taking a faster train

Q2) How did Phileas Fogg plan to travel from Omaha to New York?
a) By train
b) By horse-drawn carriage
c) By sailing on a ship
d) By walking

Q3) What did Mr. Fogg compare the sound of the metallic lashings on the sledge to?
a) A violin bow on strings
b) A roaring lion
c) A chirping bird
d) A howling wolf

Q4) In the context of the passage, what does the word "lurches" mean?
a) Rapid movements
b) Sudden stops
c) Swinging motions
d) Unsteady movements

Q5) What is the meaning of the phrase "as the birds fly" in the passage?
a) Following a straight path
b) Flying in flocks
c) Flying at a slow pace
d) Flying high above the ground

Chapter 32

IN WHICH PHILEAS FOGG ENGAGES IN A DIRECT STRUGGLE WITH BAD FORTUNE

The China, in leaving, seemed to have carried off Phileas Fogg's last hope. None of the other steamers were able to serve his projects. The Pereire, of the French Transatlantic Company, whose admirable steamers are equal to any in speed and comfort, did not leave until the 14th; the Hamburg boats did not go directly to Liverpool or London, but to Havre; and the additional trip from Havre to Southampton would render Phileas Fogg's last efforts of no avail. The Inman steamer[1] did not depart till the next day, and could not cross the Atlantic in time to save the wager.

Mr. Fogg learned all this in consulting his Bradshaw, which gave him the daily movements of the trans-Atlantic steamers.

Passepartout was crushed; it overwhelmed him to lose the boat by three-quarters of an hour. It was his fault, for, instead of helping his master, he had not ceased putting obstacles in his path! And when he recalled all the incidents of the tour, when he counted up the sums expended in pure loss and on his own account, when he thought that the immense stake, added to the heavy charges of this useless journey, would completely ruin Mr. Fogg, he overwhelmed himself with bitter self-accusations. Mr. Fogg, however, did not reproach him; and, on leaving the Cunard pier, only said: "We will consult about what is best to-morrow. Come."

The party crossed the Hudson in the Jersey City ferryboat, and drove in a carriage to the St. Nicholas Hotel, on Broadway. Rooms were engaged, and the night passed, briefly to Phileas Fogg, who slept profoundly, but very long to Aouda and the others, whose agitation did not permit them to rest.

The next day was the 12th of December. From seven in the morning of the 12th to a quarter before nine in the evening of the 21st there were nine days, thirteen hours, and forty-five minutes. If Phileas Fogg had left in the China, one of the fastest steamers on the Atlantic, he would have reached Liverpool, and then London, within the period agreed upon.

Mr. Fogg left the hotel alone, after giving Passepartout instructions to await his return, and inform Aouda to be ready at an instant's notice. He proceeded to the banks of the Hudson, and looked about among the vessels moored or anchored in the river, for

---

[1] The Inman steamer refers to the fleet of the Inman Line, called such after its founding member, William Inman. It was one of the largest 19th century British passenger shipping companies.

any that were about to depart. Several had departure signals, and were preparing to put to sea at morning tide; for in this immense and admirable port there is not one day in a hundred that vessels do not set out for every quarter of the globe. But they were mostly sailing vessels, of which, of course, Phileas Fogg could make no use.

He seemed about to give up all hope, when he espied, anchored at the Battery, a cable's length off at most, a trading vessel, with a screw, well-shaped, whose funnel, puffing a cloud of smoke, indicated that she was getting ready for departure.

Phileas Fogg hailed a boat, got into it, and soon found himself on board the Henrietta, iron-hulled, wood-built above. He ascended to the deck, and asked for the captain, who forthwith presented himself. He was a man of fifty, a sort of sea-wolf, with big eyes, a complexion of oxidised copper, red hair and thick neck, and a growling voice.

"The captain?" asked Mr. Fogg.

"I am the captain."

"I am Phileas Fogg, of London."

"And I am Andrew Speedy, of Cardiff."

"You are going to put to sea[2]?"

"In an hour."

"You are bound for—"

"Bordeaux[3]."

"And your cargo?"

"No freight. Going in ballast."

"Have you any passengers?"

"No passengers. Never have passengers. Too much in the way."[4]

"Is your vessel a swift one?"

"Between eleven and twelve knots. The Henrietta, well known."

"Will you carry me and three other persons to Liverpool?"

"To Liverpool? Why not to China?"

"I said Liverpool."

---

[2] 'To put to sea' is an idiom meaning to leave a port and begin sea travel.

[3] Bordeaux is a port city in the southwest of France and is the world's major wine industry capital. The historic part of the city is on the UNESCO World Heritage List as an outstanding urban and architectural ensemble.

[4] This expression shows the captain's dislike of carrying passengers on board, and instead his preference for cargo.

"No!"

"No?"

"No. I am setting out for Bordeaux, and shall go to Bordeaux."

"Money is no object?"

"None."

The captain spoke in a tone which did not admit of a reply.

"But the owners of the Henrietta—" resumed Phileas Fogg.

"The owners are myself," replied the captain. "The vessel belongs to me."

"I will freight it for you."

"No."

"I will buy it of you."

"No."

Phileas Fogg did not betray the least disappointment; but the situation was a grave one. It was not at New York as at Hong Kong, nor with the captain of the Henrietta as with the captain of the Tankadere. Up to this time money had smoothed away every obstacle. Now money failed.

Still, some means must be found to cross the Atlantic on a boat, unless by balloon— which would have been venturesome, besides not being capable of being put in practice. It seemed that Phileas Fogg had an idea, for he said to the captain, "Well, will you carry me to Bordeaux?"

"No, not if you paid me two hundred dollars."

"I offer you two thousand."

"Apiece?"

"Apiece."

"And there are four of you?"

"Four."

Captain Speedy began to scratch his head. There were eight thousand dollars to gain, without changing his route; for which it was well worth conquering the repugnance[5] he had for all kinds of passengers. Besides, passengers at two thousand dollars are no longer passengers, but valuable merchandise. "I start at nine o'clock," said Captain Speedy, simply. "Are you and your party ready?"

"We will be on board at nine o'clock," replied, no less simply, Mr. Fogg.

---

[5] 'Repugnance' means intense disgust towards someone or something.

It was half-past eight. To disembark from the Henrietta, jump into a hack, hurry to the St. Nicholas, and return with Aouda, Passepartout, and even the inseparable Fix was the work of a brief time, and was performed by Mr. Fogg with the coolness which never abandoned him. They were on board when the Henrietta made ready to weigh anchor.

When Passepartout heard what this last voyage was going to cost, he uttered a prolonged "Oh!" which extended throughout his vocal gamut[6].

As for Fix, he said to himself that the Bank of England would certainly not come out of this affair well indemnified.[7] When they reached England, even if Mr. Fogg did not throw some handfuls of bank-bills into the sea, more than seven thousand pounds would have been spent!

---

[6] The term 'vocal gamut' refers to the full range of sounds or pitches that a person's voice can produce. Here it suggests that Passepartout's reaction was expressed through a wide range of vocal sounds or tones, indicating a strong, emotional response.

[7] Even if the robber was caught, this whole affair would be a big loss to the Bank of England as a large portion of the stolen money would have been spent by Mr. Fogg (the assumed robber).

Comprehension exercise 32

Q1) Why did Phileas Fogg approach the vessels anchored in the river?
a) To seek alternative transportation after missing the China
b) To inspect their cargo and speed capabilities
c) To inquire about their departure schedule
d) To offer them money for passage to Liverpool

Q2) How did Phileas Fogg convince Captain Speedy to change his mind and agree to take them to Liverpool?
a) By offering to buy the ship
b) By offering a significantly higher amount of money
c) By threatening legal action
d) By promising to bring valuable cargo

Q3) What was Passepartout's reaction upon hearing the cost of the last voyage?
a) He expressed disbelief
b) He felt relieved
c) He was indifferent
d) He was overjoyed

Q4) What does the word "repugnance" as used in the passage mean?
a) Hostility
b) Eagerness
c) Attraction
d) Disgust

Q5) What does the phrase "vocal gamut" suggest about Passepartout's reaction?
a) It was brief
b) It was loud and varied
c) It was controlled
d) It was emotional

Chapter 33

IN WHICH PHILEAS FOGG SHOWS HIMSELF EQUAL TO THE OCCASION

An hour after, the Henrietta passed the lighthouse which marks the entrance of the Hudson, turned the point of Sandy Hook, and put to sea. During the day she skirted Long Island, passed Fire Island, and directed her course rapidly eastward.

At noon the next day, a man mounted the bridge to ascertain the vessel's position. It might be thought that this was Captain Speedy. Not the least in the world. It was Phileas Fogg, Esquire. As for Captain Speedy, he was shut up in his cabin under lock and key, and was uttering loud cries, which signified an anger at once pardonable and excessive.

What had happened was very simple. Phileas Fogg wished to go to Liverpool, but the captain would not carry him there. Then Phileas Fogg had taken passage for Bordeaux, and, during the thirty hours he had been on board, had so shrewdly managed with his banknotes that the sailors and stokers[1], who were only an occasional crew, and were not on the best terms with the captain, went over to him in a body[2]. This was why Phileas Fogg was in command instead of Captain Speedy; why the captain was a prisoner in his cabin; and why, in short, the Henrietta was directing her course towards Liverpool. It was very clear, to see Mr. Fogg manage the craft, that he had been a sailor.

How the adventure ended will be seen anon. Aouda was anxious, though she said nothing. As for Passepartout, he thought Mr. Fogg's manoeuvre simply glorious. The captain had said "between eleven and twelve knots," and the Henrietta confirmed his prediction.

If, then—for there were "ifs" still—the sea did not become too boisterous, if the wind did not veer round to the east, if no accident happened to the boat or its machinery, the Henrietta might cross the three thousand miles from New York to Liverpool in the nine days, between the 12th and the 21st of December. It is true that, once arrived, the affair on board the Henrietta, added to that of the Bank of England, might create more difficulties for Mr. Fogg than he imagined or could desire.

---

[1] A 'stoker' is a person who tends to the furnace of a steam engine.
[2] 'To go over in a body' means to act as a group. Mr. Fogg bribed all the sailors and other workers to change their sides and accept him as their Captain.

During the first days, they went along smoothly enough. The sea was not very unpropitious[3], the wind seemed stationary in the north-east, the sails were hoisted, and the Henrietta ploughed across the waves like a real trans-Atlantic steamer.[4]

Passepartout was delighted. His master's last exploit, the consequences of which he ignored, enchanted him. Never had the crew seen so jolly and dexterous a fellow. He formed warm friendships with the sailors, and amazed them with his acrobatic feats. He thought they managed the vessel like gentlemen, and that the stokers fired up like heroes. His loquacious[5] good-humour infected everyone. He had forgotten the past, its vexations and delays. He only thought of the end, so nearly accomplished; and sometimes he boiled over with impatience, as if heated by the furnaces of the Henrietta. Often, also, the worthy fellow revolved around Fix, looking at him with a keen, distrustful eye; but he did not speak to him, for their old intimacy no longer existed.

Fix, it must be confessed, understood nothing of what was going on. The conquest of the Henrietta, the bribery of the crew, Fogg managing the boat like a skilled seaman, amazed and confused him. He did not know what to think. For, after all, a man who began by stealing fifty-five thousand pounds might end by stealing a vessel; and Fix was not unnaturally inclined to conclude that the Henrietta under Fogg's command, was not going to Liverpool at all, but to some part of the world where the robber, turned into a pirate, would quietly put himself in safety. The conjecture was at least a plausible one, and the detective began to seriously regret that he had embarked on the affair.

As for Captain Speedy, he continued to howl and growl in his cabin; and Passepartout, whose duty it was to carry him his meals, courageous as he was, took the greatest precautions. Mr. Fogg did not seem even to know that there was a captain on board.

On the 13th they passed the edge of the Banks of Newfoundland, a dangerous locality; during the winter, especially, there are frequent fogs and heavy gales of wind. Ever since the evening before the barometer, suddenly falling, had indicated an approaching change in the atmosphere; and during the night the temperature varied, the cold became sharper, and the wind veered to the south-east.

This was a misfortune. Mr. Fogg, in order not to deviate from his course, furled his sails and increased the force of the steam; but the vessel's speed slackened, owing to the state of the sea, the long waves of which broke against the stern. She pitched violently, and this retarded her progress. The breeze little by little swelled into a tempest, and it was to be feared that the Henrietta might not be able to maintain herself upright on the waves.

Passepartout's visage[6] darkened with the skies, and for two days the poor fellow experienced constant fright. But Phileas Fogg was a bold mariner, and knew how to

---

[3] 'Unpropitious' means unfavourable or not conducive to success.
[4] The conditions were favourable and offered a good chance of success for them to reach Liverpool on time.
[5] 'Loquacious' means talkative or chatty.
[6] 'Visage' refers to the face or facial features of a person.

maintain headway against the sea; and he kept on his course, without even decreasing his steam. The Henrietta, when she could not rise upon the waves, crossed them, swamping her deck, but passing safely. Sometimes the screw[7] rose out of the water, beating its protruding end, when a mountain of water raised the stern above the waves; but the craft always kept straight ahead.

The wind, however, did not grow as boisterous as might have been feared; it was not one of those tempests which burst, and rush on with a speed of ninety miles an hour. It continued fresh, but, unhappily, it remained obstinately in the south-east, rendering the sails useless.

The 16th of December was the seventy-fifth day since Phileas Fogg's departure from London, and the Henrietta had not yet been seriously delayed. Half of the voyage was almost accomplished, and the worst localities had been passed. In summer, success would have been well-nigh certain. In winter, they were at the mercy of the bad season. Passepartout said nothing; but he cherished hope in secret, and comforted himself with the reflection that, if the wind failed them, they might still count on the steam.

On this day the engineer came on deck, went up to Mr. Fogg, and began to speak earnestly with him. Without knowing why it was a presentiment, perhaps Passepartout became vaguely uneasy. He would have given one of his ears to hear with the other what the engineer was saying. He finally managed to catch a few words, and was sure he heard his master say, "You are certain of what you tell me?"

"Certain, sir," replied the engineer. "You must remember that, since we started, we have kept up hot fires in all our furnaces, and, though we had coal enough to go on short steam from New York to Bordeaux, we haven't enough to go with all steam from New York to Liverpool." "I will consider," replied Mr. Fogg.

Passepartout understood it all; he was seized with mortal anxiety. The coal was giving out! "Ah, if my master can get over that," muttered he, "he'll be a famous man!" He could not help imparting to Fix what he had overheard.

"Then you believe that we really are going to Liverpool?"

"Of course."

"Ass!" replied the detective, shrugging his shoulders and turning on his heel.[8]

Passepartout was on the point of vigorously resenting the epithet[9], the reason of which he could not for the life of him comprehend; but he reflected that the unfortunate

---

[7] 'Screw' refers to the boat's propellers, which are located under the boat, submerged in water. The waves were so strong that they made the boat convulse and wobble to the extent that its propellers rose above the water.

[8] Fix believed that Mr. Fogg was a robber turned into a pirate and the boat was heading towards Mr. Fogg's secret hideout and not to Liverpool.

[9] An 'epithet' is a derogatory label or an abuse. Here, Passepartout uses the term for Fix.

Fix was probably very much disappointed and humiliated in his self-esteem, after having so awkwardly followed a false scent around the world, and refrained.

And now what course would Phileas Fogg adopt? It was difficult to imagine. Nevertheless he seemed to have decided upon one, for that evening he sent for the engineer, and said to him, "Feed all the fires until the coal is exhausted."

A few moments after, the funnel of the Henrietta vomited forth torrents of smoke. The vessel continued to proceed with all steam on; but on the 18th, the engineer, as he had predicted, announced that the coal would give out in the course of the day.

"Do not let the fires go down," replied Mr. Fogg. "Keep them up to the last. Let the valves be filled."

Towards noon Phileas Fogg, having ascertained their position, called Passepartout, and ordered him to go for Captain Speedy. It was as if the honest fellow had been commanded to unchain a tiger. He went to the poop[10], saying to himself, "He will be like a madman!"

In a few moments, with cries and oaths, a bomb appeared on the poop-deck. The bomb was Captain Speedy. It was clear that he was on the point of bursting. "Where are we?" were the first words his anger permitted him to utter. Had the poor man been an apoplectic[11], he could never have recovered from his paroxysm of wrath[12].

"Where are we?" he repeated, with purple face.

"Seven hundred and seven miles from Liverpool," replied Mr. Fogg, with imperturbable calmness.

"Pirate!" cried Captain Speedy.

"I have sent for you, sir—"

"Pickaroon!"[13]

"—sir," continued Mr. Fogg, "to ask you to sell me your vessel."

"No! By all the devils, no!"

"But I shall be obliged to burn her."

"Burn the Henrietta!"

"Yes; at least the upper part of her. The coal has given out."

"Burn my vessel!" cried Captain Speedy, who could scarcely pronounce the words. "A vessel worth fifty thousand dollars!"

---

[10] A 'poop' is the highest deck of a sailing ship; this is where the captain was kept locked.
[11] 'Apoplectic' means prone to stroke.
[12] 'Paroxysm of wrath' means sudden and uncontrollable outburst of anger or rage.
[13] The term 'Pickaroon', or 'picaroon' refers to a pirate or a thief.

"Here are sixty thousand," replied Phileas Fogg, handing the captain a roll of bank-bills. This had a prodigious effect on Andrew Speedy. An American can scarcely remain unmoved at the sight of sixty thousand dollars. The captain forgot in an instant his anger, his imprisonment, and all his grudges against his passenger. The Henrietta was twenty years old; it was a great bargain. The bomb would not go off after all. Mr. Fogg had taken away the match.

"And I shall still have the iron hull," said the captain in a softer tone.

"The iron hull and the engine. Is it agreed?"

"Agreed."

And Andrew Speedy, seizing the banknotes, counted them and consigned them to his pocket.

During this colloquy[14], Passepartout was as white as a sheet, and Fix seemed on the point of having an apoplectic fit. Nearly twenty thousand pounds had been expended, and Fogg left the hull and engine to the captain, that is, near the whole value of the craft! It was true, however, that fifty-five thousand pounds had been stolen from the Bank.

When Andrew Speedy had pocketed the money, Mr. Fogg said to him, "Don't let this astonish you, sir. You must know that I shall lose twenty thousand pounds, unless I arrive in London by a quarter before nine on the evening of the 21st of December. I missed the steamer at New York, and as you refused to take me to Liverpool—"

"And I did well!" cried Andrew Speedy; "for I have gained at least forty thousand dollars by it!" He added, more sedately, "Do you know one thing, Captain—"

"Fogg."

"Captain Fogg, you've got something of the Yankee about you."

And, having paid his passenger what he considered a high compliment, he was going away, when Mr. Fogg said, "The vessel now belongs to me?"

"Certainly, from the keel to the truck of the masts—all the wood, that is."

"Very well. Have the interior seats, bunks, and frames pulled down, and burn them."

It was necessary to have dry wood to keep the steam up to the adequate pressure, and on that day the poop, cabins, bunks, and the spare deck were sacrificed. On the next day, the 19th of December, the masts, rafts, and spars were burned; the crew worked lustily, keeping up the fires. Passepartout hewed, cut, and sawed away with all his might. There was a perfect rage for demolition.

The railings, fittings, the greater part of the deck, and top sides disappeared on the 20th, and the Henrietta was now only a flat hulk. But on this day they sighted the Irish coast and Fastnet Light. By ten in the evening they were passing Queenstown. Phileas Fogg had only twenty-four hours more in which to get to London; that length of time was

---

[14] 'Colloquy' means conversation or a dialogue between two people.

necessary to reach Liverpool, with all steam on. And the steam was about to give out altogether!

"Sir," said Captain Speedy, who was now deeply interested in Mr. Fogg's project, "I really commiserate you. Everything is against you. We are only opposite Queenstown."

"Ah," said Mr. Fogg, "is that place where we see the lights Queenstown?"

"Yes."

"Can we enter the harbour?"

"Not under three hours. Only at high tide."

"Stay," replied Mr. Fogg calmly, without betraying in his features that by a supreme inspiration he was about to attempt once more to conquer ill-fortune.

Queenstown is the Irish port at which the trans-Atlantic steamers stop to put off the mails. These mails are carried to Dublin by express trains always held in readiness to start; from Dublin they are sent on to Liverpool by the most rapid boats, and thus gain twelve hours on the Atlantic steamers.

Phileas Fogg counted on gaining twelve hours in the same way. Instead of arriving at Liverpool the next evening by the Henrietta, he would be there by noon, and would therefore have time to reach London before a quarter before nine in the evening.

The Henrietta entered Queenstown Harbour at one o'clock in the morning, it then being high tide; and Phileas Fogg, after being grasped heartily by the hand by Captain Speedy, left that gentleman on the levelled hulk of his craft, which was still worth half what he had sold it for.

The party went on shore at once. Fix was greatly tempted to arrest Mr. Fogg on the spot; but he did not. Why? What struggle was going on within him? Had he changed his mind about "his man"? Did he understand that he had made a grave mistake? He did not, however, abandon Mr. Fogg. They all got upon the train, which was just ready to start, at half-past one; at dawn of day they were in Dublin; and they lost no time in embarking on a steamer which, disdaining to rise upon the waves, invariably cut through them.

Phileas Fogg at last disembarked on the Liverpool quay, at twenty minutes before twelve, 21st December. He was only six hours distant from London.

But at this moment Fix came up, put his hand upon Mr. Fogg's shoulder, and, showing his warrant, said, "You are really Phileas Fogg?"

"I am."

"I arrest you in the Queen's name!"

A Study Guide: Around the World in Eighty Days

Comprehension exercise 33

Q1) From the text, what can be inferred about the crew's opinion of Phileas Fogg?
a) They resent his presence on board.
b) They admire his sailing skills and management.
c) They fear him due to his strict discipline.
d) They suspect him of being a pirate.

Q2) What was Phileas Fogg's original destination before he decided to head towards Liverpool?
a) Bordeaux
b) New York
c) London
d) Dublin

Q3) How much time did Phileas Fogg have left to reach London after disembarking in Liverpool?
a) 6 hours
b) 12 hours
c) 24 hours
d) 48 hours

Q4) What does the word "lustrously" as used in the text most likely mean?
a) Softly
b) Shimmeringly
c) Dimly
d) Heavily

Q5) What does the word "colloquy" as used in the text mean?
a) A dispute or argument
b) A casual conversation or dialogue
c) A formal speech or presentation
d) A written agreement or contract

Chapter 34

IN WHICH PHILEAS FOGG AT LAST REACHES LONDON

Phileas Fogg was in prison. He had been shut up in the Custom House, and he was to be transferred to London the next day.

Passepartout, when he saw his master arrested, would have fallen upon Fix had he not been held back by some policemen. Aouda was thunderstruck at the suddenness of an event which she could not understand. Passepartout explained to her how it was that the honest and courageous Fogg was arrested as a robber. The young woman's heart revolted against so heinous a charge, and when she saw that she could attempt to do nothing to save her protector, she wept bitterly.

As for Fix, he had arrested Mr. Fogg because it was his duty, whether Mr. Fogg were guilty or not.

The thought then struck Passepartout, that he was the cause of this new misfortune! Had he not concealed Fix's errand from his master? When Fix revealed his true character and purpose, why had he not told Mr. Fogg? If the latter had been warned, he would no doubt have given Fix proof of his innocence, and satisfied him of his mistake; at least, Fix would not have continued his journey at the expense and on the heels of his master, only to arrest him the moment he set foot on English soil. Passepartout wept till he was blind, and felt like blowing his brains out.

Aouda and he had remained, despite the cold, under the portico of the Custom House. Neither wished to leave the place; both were anxious to see Mr. Fogg again.

That gentleman was really ruined, and that at the moment when he was about to attain his end. This arrest was fatal. Having arrived at Liverpool at twenty minutes before twelve on the 21st of December, he had till a quarter before nine that evening to reach the Reform Club, that is, nine hours and a quarter; the journey from Liverpool to London was six hours.

If anyone, at this moment, had entered the Custom House, he would have found Mr. Fogg seated, motionless, calm, and without apparent anger, upon a wooden bench. He was not, it is true, resigned; but this last blow failed to force him into an outward betrayal of any emotion. Was he being devoured by one of those secret rages, all the more terrible because contained, and which only burst forth, with an irresistible force, at the last moment? No one could tell. There he sat, calmly waiting—for what? Did he still cherish hope? Did he still believe, now that the door of this prison was closed upon him, that he would succeed?

However that may have been, Mr. Fogg carefully put his watch upon the table, and observed its advancing hands. Not a word escaped his lips, but his look was singularly set and stern. The situation, in any event, was a terrible one, and might be thus stated: if Phileas Fogg was honest he was ruined; if he was a knave[1], he was caught.

Did escape occur to him? Did he examine to see if there were any practicable outlet from his prison? Did he think of escaping from it? Possibly; for once he walked slowly around the room. But the door was locked, and the window heavily barred with iron rods. He sat down again, and drew his journal from his pocket. On the line where these words were written, "21st December, Saturday, Liverpool," he added, "80th day, 11.40 a.m.," and waited.

The Custom House clock struck one. Mr. Fogg observed that his watch was two hours too fast.

Two hours! Admitting that he was at this moment taking an express train, he could reach London and the Reform Club by a quarter before nine, p.m. His forehead slightly wrinkled.

At thirty-three minutes past two he heard a singular noise outside, then a hasty opening of doors. Passepartout's voice was audible, and immediately after that of Fix. Phileas Fogg's eyes brightened for an instant.

The door swung open, and he saw Passepartout, Aouda, and Fix, who hurried towards him.

Fix was out of breath, and his hair was in disorder. He could not speak. "Sir," he stammered, "sir—forgive me—most—unfortunate resemblance—robber arrested three days ago—you are free!"

Phileas Fogg was free! He walked to the detective, looked him steadily in the face, and with the only rapid motion he had ever made in his life, or which he ever would make, drew back his arms, and with the precision of a machine knocked Fix down.

"Well hit!" cried Passepartout, "Parbleu! that's what you might call a good application of English fists!"

Fix, who found himself on the floor, did not utter a word. He had only received his deserts[2]. Mr. Fogg, Aouda, and Passepartout left the Custom House without delay, got into a cab, and in a few moments descended at the station.

Phileas Fogg asked if there was an express train about to leave for London. It was forty minutes past two. The express train had left thirty-five minutes before. Phileas Fogg then ordered a special train.

There were several rapid locomotives on hand; but the railway arrangements did not permit the special train to leave until three o'clock.

---

[1] A 'knave' is a dishonest man.
[2] 'Desert' means the state of deserving a reward or punishment (in this case punishment).

At that hour Phileas Fogg, having stimulated the engineer by the offer of a generous reward, at last set out towards London with Aouda and his faithful servant.

It was necessary to make the journey in five hours and a half; and this would have been easy on a clear road throughout. But there were forced delays, and when Mr. Fogg stepped from the train at the terminus, all the clocks in London were striking ten minutes before nine.

Having made the tour of the world, he was behind-hand[3] five minutes. He had lost the wager!

---

[3] 'Hand' here refers to the minute hand of a clock or a watch.

A Study Guide: Around the World in Eighty Days

Comprehension exercise 34

Q1) Why was Phileas Fogg sitting calmly and motionless in the Custom House?
a) He was resigned to his fate.
b) He was secretly raging with anger.
c) He was contemplating his next move.
d) He was waiting patiently, with a stern look.

Q2) What was Phileas Fogg's reaction when Fix informed him that he was free?
a) He shouted with joy.
b) He hugged Fix in gratitude.
c) He knocked Fix down with precise, rapid motion.
d) He expressed disbelief and confusion.

Q3) What action did Phileas Fogg take to ensure he reached London on time after missing the express train?
a) He hailed a cab and drove to London.
b) He ordered a special train to depart immediately.
c) He waited for the next available train.
d) He decided to continue his journey on foot.

Q4) What does the word "resigned" mean in the context of the passage?
a) Angry
b) Accepting defeat or fate
c) Relieved
d) Determined

Q5) What is the meaning of the phrase "received his deserts" as used in the passage?
a) Got what he deserved
b) Was unfairly treated
c) Was praised
d) Received a reward

Chapter 35

IN WHICH PHILEAS FOGG DOES NOT HAVE TO REPEAT HIS ORDERS TO PASSEPARTOUT TWICE

The dwellers in Saville Row would have been surprised the next day, if they had been told that Phileas Fogg had returned home. His doors and windows were still closed, no appearance of change was visible.

After leaving the station, Mr. Fogg gave Passepartout instructions to purchase some provisions, and quietly went to his domicile.

He bore his misfortune with his habitual tranquillity[1]. Ruined! And by the blundering of the detective! After having steadily traversed that long journey, overcome a hundred obstacles, braved many dangers, and still found time to do some good on his way, to fail near the goal by a sudden event which he could not have foreseen, and against which he was unarmed; it was terrible! But a few pounds were left of the large sum he had carried with him. There only remained of his fortune the twenty thousand pounds deposited at Barings, and this amount he owed to his friends of the Reform Club. So great had been the expense of his tour that, even had he won, it would not have enriched him; and it is probable that he had not sought to enrich himself, being a man who rather laid wagers for honour's sake than for the stake proposed. But this wager totally ruined him.

Mr. Fogg's course, however, was fully decided upon; he knew what remained for him to do.

A room in the house in Saville Row was set apart for Aouda, who was overwhelmed with grief at her protector's misfortune. From the words which Mr. Fogg dropped, she saw that he was meditating some serious project.

Knowing that Englishmen governed by a fixed idea sometimes resort to the desperate expedient of suicide, Passepartout kept a narrow watch upon his master, though he carefully concealed the appearance of so doing.

First of all, the worthy fellow had gone up to his room, and had extinguished the gas burner, which had been burning for eighty days. He had found in the letter-box a bill from the gas company, and he thought it more than time to put a stop to this expense, which he had been doomed to bear.

The night passed. Mr. Fogg went to bed, but did he sleep? Aouda did not once close her eyes. Passepartout watched all night, like a faithful dog, at his master's door.

---

[1] 'Tranquillity' is the state of being calm and peaceful.

Mr. Fogg called him in the morning, and told him to get Aouda's breakfast, and a cup of tea and a chop for himself. He desired Aouda to excuse him from breakfast and dinner, as his time would be absorbed all day in putting his affairs to rights. In the evening he would ask permission to have a few moment's conversation with the young lady.

Passepartout, having received his orders, had nothing to do but obey them. He looked at his imperturbable[2] master, and could scarcely bring his mind to leave him. His heart was full, and his conscience tortured by remorse; for he accused himself more bitterly than ever of being the cause of the irretrievable disaster. Yes! if he had warned Mr. Fogg, and had betrayed Fix's projects to him, his master would certainly not have given the detective passage to Liverpool, and then—

Passepartout could hold in no longer.

"My master! Mr. Fogg!" he cried, "why do you not curse me? It was my fault that—"

"I blame no one," returned Phileas Fogg, with perfect calmness. "Go!"

Passepartout left the room, and went to find Aouda, to whom he delivered his master's message.

"Madam," he added, "I can do nothing myself—nothing! I have no influence over my master; but you, perhaps—"

"What influence could I have?" replied Aouda. "Mr. Fogg is influenced by no one. Has he ever understood that my gratitude to him is overflowing? Has he ever read my heart? My friend, he must not be left alone an instant! You say he is going to speak with me this evening?"

"Yes, madam; probably to arrange for your protection and comfort in England."

"We shall see," replied Aouda, becoming suddenly pensive.

Throughout this day (Sunday) the house in Saville Row was as if uninhabited, and Phileas Fogg, for the first time since he had lived in that house, did not set out for his club when Westminster clock struck half-past eleven.

Why should he present himself at the Reform? His friends no longer expected him there. As Phileas Fogg had not appeared in the saloon on the evening before (Saturday, the 21st of December, at a quarter before nine), he had lost his wager. It was not even necessary that he should go to his bankers for the twenty thousand pounds; for his antagonists[3] already had his cheque in their hands, and they had only to fill it out and send it to the Barings to have the amount transferred to their credit.

Mr. Fogg, therefore, had no reason for going out, and so he remained at home. He shut himself up in his room, and busied himself putting his affairs in order. Passepartout continually ascended and descended the stairs. The hours were long for him. He listened at his master's door, and looked through the keyhole, as if he had a perfect right so to do,

---

[2] 'Imperturbable' means calm and composed.
[3] An 'antagonist' is the opponent or the rival.

and as if he feared that something terrible might happen at any moment. Sometimes he thought of Fix, but no longer in anger. Fix, like all the world, had been mistaken in Phileas Fogg, and had only done his duty in tracking and arresting him; while he, Passepartout. . . . This thought haunted him, and he never ceased cursing his miserable folly.

Finding himself too wretched to remain alone, he knocked at Aouda's door, went into her room, seated himself, without speaking, in a corner, and looked ruefully at the young woman. Aouda was still pensive.

About half-past seven in the evening Mr. Fogg sent to know if Aouda would receive him, and in a few moments he found himself alone with her.

Phileas Fogg took a chair, and sat down near the fireplace, opposite Aouda. No emotion was visible on his face. Fogg returned was exactly the Fogg who had gone away; there was the same calm, the same impassibility.

He sat several minutes without speaking; then, bending his eyes on Aouda, "Madam," said he, "will you pardon me for bringing you to England?"

"I, Mr. Fogg!" replied Aouda, checking the pulsations of her heart.

"Please let me finish," returned Mr. Fogg. "When I decided to bring you far away from the country which was so unsafe for you, I was rich, and counted on putting a portion of my fortune at your disposal; then your existence would have been free and happy. But now I am ruined."

"I know it, Mr. Fogg," replied Aouda; "and I ask you in my turn, will you forgive me for having followed you, and—who knows?—for having, perhaps, delayed you, and thus contributed to your ruin?"

"Madam, you could not remain in India, and your safety could only be assured by bringing you to such a distance that your persecutors could not take you."

"So, Mr. Fogg," resumed Aouda, "not content with rescuing me from a terrible death, you thought yourself bound to secure my comfort in a foreign land?"

"Yes, madam; but circumstances have been against me. Still, I beg to place the little I have left at your service."

"But what will become of you, Mr. Fogg?"

"As for me, madam," replied the gentleman, coldly, "I have need of nothing."

"But how do you look upon the fate, sir, which awaits you?"

"As I am in the habit of doing."

"At least," said Aouda, "want should not overtake a man like you. Your friends—"

"I have no friends, madam."

"Your relatives—"

"I have no longer any relatives."

"I pity you, then, Mr. Fogg, for solitude is a sad thing, with no heart to which to confide your griefs. They say, though, that misery itself, shared by two sympathetic souls, may be borne with patience."

"They say so, madam."

"Mr. Fogg," said Aouda, rising and seizing his hand, "do you wish at once a kinswoman and friend? Will you have me for your wife?"

Mr. Fogg, at this, rose in his turn. There was an unwonted[4] light in his eyes, and a slight trembling of his lips. Aouda looked into his face. The sincerity, rectitude, firmness, and sweetness of this soft glance of a noble woman, who could dare all to save him to whom she owed all, at first astonished, then penetrated him. He shut his eyes for an instant, as if to avoid her look. When he opened them again, "I love you!" he said, simply. "Yes, by all that is holiest, I love you, and I am entirely yours!"[5]

"Ah!" cried Aouda, pressing his hand to her heart.

Passepartout was summoned and appeared immediately. Mr. Fogg still held Aouda's hand in his own; Passepartout understood, and his big, round face became as radiant as the tropical sun at its zenith.

Mr. Fogg asked him if it was not too late to notify the Reverend Samuel Wilson, of Marylebone parish, that evening.[6]

Passepartout smiled his most genial smile, and said, "Never too late."

It was five minutes past eight.

"Will it be for to-morrow, Monday?"

"For to-morrow, Monday," said Mr. Fogg, turning to Aouda.

"Yes; for to-morrow, Monday," she replied.

Passepartout hurried off as fast as his legs could carry him.

---

[4] 'Unwonted' means strange or unusual.

[5] This passage describes a moment of emotional revelation and vulnerability for Mr. Fogg. When Aouda looks at him with sincerity and affection, it stirs something deep within him. He is moved by her expression and feels a surge of emotion. By affirming his love and declaring himself entirely hers, Mr. Fogg reveals a vulnerable and emotional side that contrasts with his usual stoic demeanour.

[6] Mr. Fix wanted Reverend Samuel Wilson to bless his marriage with Aouda.

Comprehension exercise 35

Q1) Question: Why did Mr. Fogg remain at home after returning from the station?
a) He was too exhausted to go out.
b) He wanted to avoid his friends at the Reform Club.
c) He needed to organize his affairs.
d) He was awaiting a visit from the detective.

Q2) How did Mr. Fogg's return home surprise the dwellers in Saville Row?
a) His doors and windows were open.
b) He arrived with a large crowd of people.
c) His house showed no signs of change.
d) He was accompanied by police officers.

Q3) What task did Mr. Fogg give to Passepartout after returning home?
a) To fetch his luggage from the station.
b) To inform his friends at the Reform Club.
c) To purchase provisions.
d) To prepare a bath for him.

Q4) Question: What does the word "unwonted" mean in the context of the passage?
a) Ordinary
b) Unexpected
c) Uninteresting
d) Unusual

Q5) In the passage, what does the word "tranquillity" imply about Mr. Fogg's demeanour?
a) He was restless and agitated.
b) He was calm and composed.
c) He was excited and jubilant.
d) He was sad and despondent.

Chapter 36

IN WHICH PHILEAS FOGG'S NAME IS ONCE MORE AT A PREMIUM ON 'CHANGE

It is time to relate what a change took place in English public opinion when it transpired that the real bankrobber, a certain James Strand, had been arrested, on the 17th day of December, at Edinburgh. Three days before, Phileas Fogg had been a criminal, who was being desperately followed up by the police; now he was an honourable gentleman, mathematically pursuing his eccentric journey round the world.

The papers resumed their discussion about the wager; all those who had laid bets, for or against him, revived their interest, as if by magic; the "Phileas Fogg bonds" again became negotiable, and many new wagers were made. Phileas Fogg's name was once more at a premium on 'Change.

His five friends of the Reform Club passed these three days in a state of feverish suspense. Would Phileas Fogg, whom they had forgotten, reappear before their eyes! Where was he at this moment? The 17th of December, the day of James Strand's arrest, was the seventy-sixth since Phileas Fogg's departure, and no news of him had been received. Was he dead? Had he abandoned the effort, or was he continuing his journey along the route agreed upon? And would he appear on Saturday, the 21st of December, at a quarter before nine in the evening, on the threshold of the Reform Club saloon?

The anxiety in which, for three days, London society existed, cannot be described. Telegrams were sent to America and Asia for news of Phileas Fogg. Messengers were dispatched to the house in Saville Row morning and evening. No news. The police were ignorant what had become of the detective, Fix, who had so unfortunately followed up a false scent. Bets increased, nevertheless, in number and value. Phileas Fogg, like a racehorse, was drawing near his last turning-point. The bonds were quoted, no longer at a hundred below par, but at twenty, at ten, and at five[1]; and paralytic old Lord Albemarle bet even in his favour.[2]

---

[1] The mention of bonds being quoted at values closer to their original worth indicates a resurgence of confidence in Fogg's success.

In financial terms, "below par" refers to the value of a bond being less than its face value. When the text says, 'no longer at a hundred below par", it means that the bonds associated with Phileas Fogg were previously valued significantly lower than their face value (100 below par), but now they are quoted at higher values such as twenty, ten, and five, indicating an increase in their worth.

[2] To "bet even in someone's favour" means to place a bet or wager that supports that person's outcome or success.

A great crowd was collected in Pall Mall and the neighbouring streets on Saturday evening; it seemed like a multitude of brokers permanently established around the Reform Club. Circulation was impeded, and everywhere disputes, discussions, and financial transactions were going on. The police had great difficulty in keeping back the crowd, and as the hour when Phileas Fogg was due approached, the excitement rose to its highest pitch.

The five antagonists of Phileas Fogg had met in the great saloon of the club. John Sullivan and Samuel Fallentin, the bankers, Andrew Stuart, the engineer, Gauthier Ralph, the director of the Bank of England, and Thomas Flanagan, the brewer, one and all waited anxiously.

When the clock indicated twenty minutes past eight, Andrew Stuart got up, saying, "Gentlemen, in twenty minutes the time agreed upon between Mr. Fogg and ourselves will have expired."

"What time did the last train arrive from Liverpool?" asked Thomas Flanagan.

"At twenty-three minutes past seven," replied Gauthier Ralph; "and the next does not arrive till ten minutes after twelve."

"Well, gentlemen," resumed Andrew Stuart, "if Phileas Fogg had come in the 7:23 train, he would have got here by this time. We can, therefore, regard the bet as won."

"Wait; don't let us be too hasty," replied Samuel Fallentin. "You know that Mr. Fogg is very eccentric. His punctuality is well known; he never arrives too soon, or too late; and I should not be surprised if he appeared before us at the last minute."

"Why," said Andrew Stuart nervously, "if I should see him, I should not believe it was he."[3]

"The fact is," resumed Thomas Flanagan, "Mr. Fogg's project was absurdly foolish. Whatever his punctuality, he could not prevent the delays which were certain to occur; and a delay of only two or three days would be fatal to his tour."

"Observe, too," added John Sullivan, "that we have received no intelligence from him, though there are telegraphic lines all along his route."

"He has lost, gentleman," said Andrew Stuart, "he has a hundred times lost! You know, besides, that the China the only steamer he could have taken from New York to get here in time arrived yesterday. I have seen a list of the passengers, and the name of Phileas Fogg is not among them. Even if we admit that fortune has favoured him, he can scarcely have reached America. I think he will be at least twenty days behind-hand, and that Lord Albemarle will lose a cool five thousand[4]."

---

[3] Andrew Stuart's statement implies scepticism or disbelief. He is expressing doubt that if he were to see Phileas Fogg, he wouldn't believe it was actually him, possibly because he finds the situation improbable.

[4] Lord Albemarle was an old gentleman who bet five thousand pounds in favour of Mr. Fogg.

"It is clear," replied Gauthier Ralph; "and we have nothing to do but to present Mr. Fogg's cheque at Barings to-morrow."

At this moment, the hands of the club clock pointed to twenty minutes to nine.

"Five minutes more," said Andrew Stuart.

The five gentlemen looked at each other. Their anxiety was becoming intense; but, not wishing to betray it, they readily assented to Mr. Fallentin's proposal of a rubber[5].

"I wouldn't give up my four thousand of the bet," said Andrew Stuart, as he took his seat, "for three thousand nine hundred and ninety-nine."[6]

The clock indicated eighteen minutes to nine.

The players took up their cards, but could not keep their eyes off the clock. Certainly, however secure they felt, minutes had never seemed so long to them!

"Seventeen minutes to nine," said Thomas Flanagan, as he cut the cards which Ralph handed to him.

Then there was a moment of silence. The great saloon was perfectly quiet; but the murmurs of the crowd outside were heard, with now and then a shrill cry. The pendulum beat the seconds, which each player eagerly counted, as he listened, with mathematical regularity.

"Sixteen minutes to nine!" said John Sullivan, in a voice which betrayed his emotion.

One minute more, and the wager would be won. Andrew Stuart and his partners suspended their game. They left their cards, and counted the seconds.

At the fortieth second, nothing. At the fiftieth, still nothing.

At the fifty-fifth, a loud cry was heard in the street, followed by applause, hurrahs, and some fierce growls.

The players rose from their seats.

At the fifty-seventh second the door of the saloon opened; and the pendulum had not beat the sixtieth second when Phileas Fogg appeared, followed by an excited crowd who had forced their way through the club doors, and in his calm voice, said, "Here I am, gentlemen!" [7]

---

[5] 'Rubber' refers to a game of cards, typically bridge or whist. Here, it suggests that the gentlemen agreed to play a game of cards to distract themselves from their intense anxiety.

[6] Andrew Stuart values his bet at four thousand pounds so highly that he would not accept even one pound less. He is emphasizing his confidence in his bet and expressing that he believes it is worth every penny of the four thousand pounds.

[7] Mr. Fogg had arrived at the Reform Club with a couple of seconds to spare.

Comprehension exercise 36

Q1) How did the English public opinion change when the real bank robber was arrested?
a) They lost interest in Phileas Fogg's journey.
b) They considered Phileas Fogg an honourable gentleman.
c) They became more suspicious of Phileas Fogg.
d) They continued to believe Phileas Fogg was a criminal.

Q2) Why were Phileas Fogg's friends at the Reform Club anxious in the days leading up to the 21st of December?
a) They were worried about Phileas Fogg's safety.
b) They were apprehensive about Phileas Fogg fulfilling his wager.
c) They were concerned about their own financial investments.
d) They were anticipating Phileas Fogg's return with excitement.

Q3) What did the gentlemen of the Reform Club do to pass the time while waiting for Phileas Fogg?
a) They engaged in discussions about Phileas Fogg's wager.
b) They played a game of cards.
c) They sent messengers to find information about Phileas Fogg.
d) They discussed the latest news articles about Phileas Fogg.

Q4) What does the word "eccentric" mean in the context of the passage?
a) Predictable and routine
b) Unusual and unconventional
c) Common and ordinary
d) Stable and consistent

Q5) What does the word "suspended" imply about Andrew Stuart and his partners?
a) They stopped playing the game.
b) They hesitated in their actions.
c) They held their breath in anticipation.
d) They elevated their game to a higher level.

Chapter 37

IN WHICH IT IS SHOWN THAT PHILEAS FOGG GAINED NOTHING BY HIS TOUR AROUND THE WORLD, UNLESS IT WERE HAPPINESS

Yes; Phileas Fogg in person.

The reader will remember that at five minutes past eight in the evening—about five and twenty hours after the arrival of the travellers in London—Passepartout had been sent by his master to engage the services of the Reverend Samuel Wilson in a certain marriage ceremony, which was to take place the next day.

Passepartout went on his errand enchanted. He soon reached the clergyman's house, but found him not at home. Passepartout waited a good twenty minutes, and when he left the reverend gentleman, it was thirty-five minutes past eight. But in what a state he was! With his hair in disorder, and without his hat, he ran along the street as never man was seen to run before, overturning passers-by, rushing over the sidewalk like a waterspout.

In three minutes he was in Saville Row again, and staggered back into Mr. Fogg's room.

He could not speak.

"What is the matter?" asked Mr. Fogg.

"My master!" gasped Passepartout—"marriage—impossible—"

"Impossible?"

"Impossible—for to-morrow."

"Why so?"

"Because to-morrow—is Sunday!"

"Monday," replied Mr. Fogg.

"No—to-day is Saturday."

"Saturday? Impossible!"

"Yes, yes, yes, yes!" cried Passepartout. "You have made a mistake of one day! We arrived twenty-four hours ahead of time; but there are only ten minutes left!"

Passepartout had seized his master by the collar, and was dragging him along with irresistible force.

Phileas Fogg, thus kidnapped, without having time to think, left his house, jumped into a cab, promised a hundred pounds to the cabman, and, having run over two dogs and overturned five carriages, reached the Reform Club.

The clock indicated a quarter before nine when he appeared in the great saloon.

Phileas Fogg had accomplished the journey round the world in eighty days!

Phileas Fogg had won his wager of twenty thousand pounds!

How was it that a man so exact and fastidious could have made this error of a day? How came he to think that he had arrived in London on Saturday, the twenty-first day of December, when it was really Friday, the twentieth, the seventy-ninth day only from his departure?

The cause of the error is very simple.

Phileas Fogg had, without suspecting it, gained one day on his journey, and this merely because he had travelled constantly eastward; he would, on the contrary, have lost a day had he gone in the opposite direction, that is, westward.

In journeying eastward he had gone towards the sun, and the days therefore diminished for him as many times four minutes as he crossed degrees in this direction. There are three hundred and sixty degrees on the circumference of the earth; and these three hundred and sixty degrees, multiplied by four minutes, gives precisely twenty-four hours—that is, the day unconsciously gained. In other words, while Phileas Fogg, going eastward, saw the sun pass the meridian eighty times, his friends in London only saw it pass the meridian seventy-nine times. This is why they awaited him at the Reform Club on Saturday, and not Sunday, as Mr. Fogg thought.[1]

And Passepartout's famous family watch, which had always kept London time, would have betrayed this fact, if it had marked the days as well as the hours and the minutes![2]

Phileas Fogg, then, had won the twenty thousand pounds; but, as he had spent nearly nineteen thousand on the way, the pecuniary gain was small. His object was, however, to be victorious, and not to win money. He divided the one thousand pounds that remained between Passepartout and the unfortunate Fix, against whom he cherished no grudge. He deducted, however, from Passepartout's share the cost of the gas which had burned in his room for nineteen hundred and twenty hours, for the sake of regularity.

---

[1] Scientifically, this phenomenon is called "daylight saving time." It refers to the discrepancy in the passage of time between two observers due to differences in their relative motion or gravitational fields. In this case, Phileas Fogg experienced time dilation as a result of his eastward travel, causing him to gain one day on his journey compared to observers in London.

[2] Passepartout did not adjust his watch to the different time zones they were travelling through, so his watch should have maintained the right date and time. And it did. However, his watch only displayed time, not date and day, hence the gain of one day (exactly 24 hours) was not evident from his watch display.

That evening, Mr. Fogg, as tranquil and phlegmatic as ever, said to Aouda: "Is our marriage still agreeable to you?"

"Mr. Fogg," replied she, "it is for me to ask that question. You were ruined, but now you are rich again."

"Pardon me, madam; my fortune belongs to you. If you had not suggested our marriage, my servant would not have gone to the Reverend Samuel Wilson's, I should not have been apprised of my error, and—"

"Dear Mr. Fogg!" said the young woman.

"Dear Aouda!" replied Phileas Fogg.

It need not be said that the marriage took place forty-eight hours after, and that Passepartout, glowing and dazzling, gave the bride away[3]. Had he not saved her, and was he not entitled to this honour?

The next day, as soon as it was light, Passepartout rapped vigorously at his master's door. Mr. Fogg opened it, and asked, "What's the matter, Passepartout?"

"What is it, sir? Why, I've just this instant found out—"

"What?"

"That we might have made the tour of the world in only seventy-eight days."

"No doubt," returned Mr. Fogg, "by not crossing India. But if I had not crossed India, I should not have saved Aouda; she would not have been my wife, and—"

Mr. Fogg quietly shut the door.

Phileas Fogg had won his wager, and had made his journey around the world in eighty days. To do this he had employed every means of conveyance—steamers, railways, carriages, yachts, trading-vessels, sledges, elephants. The eccentric gentleman had throughout displayed all his marvellous qualities of coolness and exactitude. But what then? What had he really gained by all this trouble? What had he brought back from this long and weary journey?

Nothing, say you? Perhaps so; nothing but a charming woman, who, strange as it may appear, made him the happiest of men!

Truly, would you not for less than that make the tour around the world?

The End

---

[3] Giving a bride away is an age-old tradition, in which the bride is given away by her father to her to-be husband. Centuries ago, daughters were considered to be the father's property and the wedding was a ceremony when this right was supposedly passed on to her husband. Nowadays there is no such legal requirement.

In this story, since Aouda didn't have her father to give her away, Passepartout did the honours as he was her life saviour.

Comprehension exercise 37

Q1) Why did Passepartout rush through the street "like a waterspout"?
a) He was late for an appointment.
b) He was excited about possibly winning the wager.
c) He was trying to avoid someone.
d) He was looking for someone.

Q2) Why did Phileas Fogg leave his house in a rush?
a) He received an urgent message.
b) He wanted to reach the Reform Club as soon as possible.
c) He wanted to avoid meeting someone.
d) He decided to take a spontaneous trip.

Q3) How did Phileas Fogg manage to win his wager?
a) By using various means of transportation.
b) By completing the journey in exactly 80 days.
c) By making accurate calculations.
d) By reaching the Reform Club before the deadline.

Q4) What does Phileas Fogg do with the remainder of the money he won?
a) He donates it to charity.
b) He divides it between Passepartout and Fix.
c) He invests it in a business venture.
d) He saves it for his future travels.

Q5) What does the word "phlegmatic" most likely mean in the context of the passage?
a) Energetic
b) Emotional
c) Calm
d) Agitated

A Study Guide: Around the World in Eighty Days

Answers to comprehension exercises

Chapter 1

Q1) Why did Phileas Fogg live such a secluded life in Saville Row?
    Answer: b) Because he preferred solitude and had specific routines.
Q2) How did Phileas Fogg come to be a member of the Reform Club?
    Answer: d) He was sponsored by the Barings due to his financial credibility.
Q3) What did Phileas Fogg do with his winnings from playing whist?
    Answer: c) He donated them to charitable causes.
Q4) What was Phileas Fogg's attitude towards charity?
    Answer: b) He donated anonymously and generously.
Q5) What does the word "enigmatical" mean in the context of the passage?
    Answer: a) Mysterious.

Chapter 2

Q1) How does Phileas Fogg's behaviour towards his servants contribute to his character?
    Answer: b) It suggests that he is demanding and expects perfection.
Q2) What is the significance of the card hung over the clock in Phileas Fogg's house?
    Answer: a) It contains instructions for the servant's daily routine.
Q3) How does Passepartout react to the discovery of Fogg's daily routine?
    Answer: b) He is impressed by its precision and detail.
Q4) What is the meaning of the term "repose" as used in the text?
    Answer: b) Rest and tranquillity
Q13) How would you define the word "vagrant" as described in Passepartout's backstory?
    Answer: a) A person who travels aimlessly or wanders without a home

Chapter 3

Q1) Based on the conversation among the members of the Reform Club, what can be inferred about their social status?
    Answer: b) They are influential individuals with substantial wealth.
Q2) What is included in Phileas Fogg's breakfast at the Reform Club?
    Answer: c) Broiled fish and roast beef
Q3) How does Phileas Fogg spend his time before dinner at the Reform Club?
    Answer: a) Reading newspapers
Q4) How does Phileas Fogg plan to travel around the world?
    Answer: c) By steamship and railway

Q12) What is the meaning of the term "scruples" as used in the text?
Answer: a) Doubts or hesitation about the morality of an action

Chapter 4

Q1) What can be inferred about Phileas Fogg's character from his actions at the railway station?
Answer: a) He is generous towards those in need.
Q2) How does Passepartout feel about Phileas Fogg's sudden decision to embark on a journey around the world?
Answer: b) He is confused and bewildered.
Q3) What time did Phileas Fogg leave the Reform Club?
Answer: b) At twenty-five minutes past seven
Q4) What does the word "stupefaction" as used in the text mean?
Answer: b) Confusion
Q5) Which word could best replace "susceptible" in the sentence: "Passepartout had a moist sensation about the eyes; his master's action touched his susceptible heart."
Answer: c) Vulnerable

Chapter 5

Q1) How did the public react to Phileas Fogg's wager to travel around the world?
Answer: b) They were divided in their opinions.
Q2) What effect did the telegraphic dispatch about Phileas Fogg have on public perception?
Answer: a) It confirmed their suspicions about him.
Q3) Who was the only remaining advocate of Phileas Fogg after the decline in public support?
Answer: a) Lord Albemarle
Q4) What does the term "aberration" as used in the text mean?
Answer: a) A deviation from the norm or expected course
Q5) What is the meaning of the word "paralytic" in the context of the text?
Answer: a) In a state of paralysis or immobility

Chapter 6

Q1) Why was Fix particularly anxious about the arrival of the steamer Mongolia?
Answer: c) He was a detective searching for a criminal.
Q2) What conclusion can be drawn about Fix's attitude towards his task?
Answer: c) He was impatient and eager for success.
Q3) How long did the steamer Mongolia stop at Suez?
Answer: c) Four hours
Q4) What does the term "importunate" mean as used in the text?

Answer: b) Persistent and insistent
Q5) What does the word "visaed" imply in the context of the text?
Answer: a) Checked for authenticity

Chapter 7

Q1) Why did Fix hope that Phileas Fogg would come to the consulate to have his passport visaed?
Answer: b) To prove that he came by Suez.
Q2) What does the consul's response about Phileas Fogg's honesty imply?
Answer: a) The consul is convinced of Fogg's innocence.
Q3) What does Mr. Fogg use his notebook for?
Answer: c) Keeping a record of his journey
Q4) What does the word "phlegmatic" mean as used in the text?
Answer: b) Calm and composed
Q5) What does the word "concede" suggest in the context of the text?
Answer: a) To accept reluctantly

Chapter 8

Q1) What does Passepartout's reaction to Fix's question about his passport suggest?
Answer: b) He is oblivious and carefree.
Q2) Why does Fix become suspicious of Mr. Fogg's intentions?
Answer: a) Mr. Fogg carries a large sum of money.
Q3) What is Fix's plan after becoming fully convinced of Mr. Fogg's intentions?
Answer: b) To send a dispatch to London for a warrant of arrest.
Q4) What does the word "equanimity" mean as used in the text?
Answer: c) Calmness and composure
Q5) What does the word "cogitating" imply in the context of the text?
Answer: a) Reflecting deeply and pondering

Chapter 9

Q1) Why did the passengers on the Mongolia disappear below deck when the Red Sea became boisterous?
Answer: d) They were seeking shelter from the wind and waves.
Q2) Why did Passepartout enjoy the voyage despite the rough seas?
Answer: c) He was fascinated by the sights along the way.
Q3) How did Mr. Fogg and his servant spend their time during the voyage?
Answer: c) They played whist with other passengers.
Q4) What does the word "alacrity" mean as used in the text?
Answer: b) Eagerness and promptness

Q5) What does the word "ravished" imply in the context of the text?
	Answer: a) Excited and delighted

Chapter 10

Q1) What is the British Crown's relationship with India, according to the text?
	Answer: b) It only governs British India, leaving the rest to local rulers.
Q2) How did Mr. Fogg react when he found out the "native rabbit" he was served wasn't actually rabbit?
	Answer: b) He ignored it and continued eating.
Q3) Why did Passepartout end up rushing breathlessly into the station?
	Answer: a) He was late for the train departure.
Q4) What does the word "despotic" mean in the context of the text?
	Answer: c) Corrupt and oppressive
Q5) What does the word "crestfallen" imply about Passepartout's demeanour?
	Answer: c) Depressed and disappointed

Chapter 11

Q1) Who was the third passenger in the carriage with Mr. Fogg and Passepartout?

	Answer: d) Sir Francis Cromarty
Q2) Why was Passepartout particularly worried about possible delays and accidents during the journey?
	Answer: b) He was concerned about losing the bet.
Q3) Why did the train unexpectedly stop at Kholby?
	Answer: b) The conductor announced the end of the railway line.
Q4) What does the word "obstinately" mean in the context of the text?
	Answer: c) Stubbornly and inflexibly
Q5) What does the phrase "deprive poor Passepartout of his vitals" imply about Passepartout's reaction?
	Answer: c) He was extremely nervous and anxious.

Chapter 12

Q1) Why did the guide prefer to travel through the forest rather than follow the line where the railway was still being built?
	Answer: b) To save time by taking a shorter route.
Q2) How did Passepartout ensure his safety while riding on the elephant's back?
	Answer: b) By keeping his tongue from between his teeth.
Q3) Why did the guide lead the elephant into a thicket and ask the travellers not to stir when they heard the approaching procession?
	Answer: a) To hide from potential danger posed by the procession.

A Study Guide: Around the World in Eighty Days

Q4) What does the word "phlegm" mean in the context of the text?
    Answer: b) Indifference or calmness
Q5) What does the word "fanatics" mean in the context of the text?
    Answer: c) Devotees or zealots

Chapter 13

Q1) Why does Passepartout ultimately decide to rescue Aouda?
    Answer: c) Because he feels compassion for Aouda and sees an opportunity to help her.
Q2) What does Sir Francis Cromarty's reaction to Mr. Fogg's impulse to rush towards the pyre reveal about his character?
    Answer: c) He is cautious and level-headed.
Q3) How does the group plan to rescue Aouda from the sacrificial ritual?
    Answer: b) By creating an opening in the walls of the temple.
Q4) What does the word "audacious" mean in the context of Passepartout's actions?
    Answer: b) Brave and daring
Q5) Which word best describes the old rajah's sudden appearance at the end of the sacrificial ritual?
    Answer: b) Miraculous

Chapter 14

Q1) Why does Passepartout attribute the success of the exploit to Mr. Fogg?
    Answer: b) Because he believes Mr. Fogg deserves all the praise.
Q2) What is revealed about Sir Francis Cromarty's character based on his reaction to Aouda's situation?
    Answer: b) He is deeply concerned about Aouda's future.
Q3) Where did Passepartout go to purchase various items for Aouda?
    Answer: b) Allahabad
Q4) What does the word "prostration" mean in the context of the text?
    Answer: b) The state of complete exhaustion
Q5) Which word best describes Phileas Fogg's reaction to the guide's service?
    Answer: a) Appreciative

Chapter 15

Q1) Why does Mr. Fogg offer bail for himself and Passepartout?
    Answer: c) Because he wants to ensure their release from custody.
Q2) How does Fix feel when he sees Mr. Fogg offering bail?
    Answer: b) Shocked
Q3) Why is Passepartout startled by the judge's sentence?
    Answer: b) Because he is fined a larger amount than he anticipated.

Q4) What does the word "crestfallen" mean in the context of the text?
    Answer: c) Disappointed
Q5) Which word best describes Passepartout's reaction to being handed back his shoes?
    Answer: a) Indignant

Chapter 16

Q1) What can be inferred about Phileas Fogg's attitude towards Aouda based on the text?
    Answer: b) He is deeply grateful for her presence and ensures her comfort.
Q2) Why did Detective Fix decide to question Passepartout?
    Answer: a) To gather more information about Mr. Fogg's whereabouts
Q3) Where did Detective Fix hope to arrest Mr. Fogg?
    Answer: d) Hong Kong
Q4) What does the word "phlegmatic" mean in the context of the text?
    Answer: b) Indifferent
Q5) What does the word "automaton" imply about Phileas Fogg's behaviour towards Aouda?
    Answer: b) He is mechanical

Chapter 17

Q1) Why does Fix decide to make himself known to Passepartout?
    Answer: d) He hopes to gain Passepartout's trust to achieve his own objectives.
Q2) Why does Fix feign ignorance about Aouda when Passepartout recounts her history?
    Answer: c) Because he is trying to maintain his cover and conceal his true intentions.
Q3) What does Fix plan to do before acting more positively in his pursuit of Mr. Fogg?
    Answer: b) Question Passepartout
Q4) What does the word "punctual" mean in the context of the text?
    Answer: c) Timely
Q5) Which word best describes Fix's reaction to Passepartout's recounting of events?
    Answer: b) Enthusiastic

Chapter 18

Q1) How did Phileas Fogg react to the delay caused by the storm?
    Answer: b) He saw it as an opportunity to prevent Fogg from winning the wager.
Q2) Why did Fix feel pleased about the storm?
    Answer b) He saw it as an opportunity to prevent Fogg from winning the wager.
Q3) What was the name of the steamer that Phileas Fogg inquired about with the pilot?
    Answer: b) The Carnatic
Q4) What does the word "obstinate" mean in the context of the text?
    Answer: c) Unyielding

A Study Guide: Around the World in Eighty Days

Q5) What does the word "maledictions" imply about Passepartout's actions?
   Answer: b) He was shouting curses at the barometer for not changing.

Chapter 19

Q1) Why did Passepartout find Hong Kong similar to other cities like Bombay, Calcutta, and Singapore?
   Answer: a) Because it was dominated by English influence.
Q2) What is the reason behind the old Chinese men wearing yellow clothing?
   Answer: b) Because it indicates their age, being at least eighty years old.
Q3) What does the word "stupefied" mean in the context of the text?
   Answer: d) Drugged
Q4) What does the word "cadaverous" suggest about the appearance of the opium smokers?
   Answer: c) Pale and emaciated
Q5) What does the word "raillery" mean as used in the sentence "Bah!" retorted Passepartout, with an air of raillery.
   Answer: a) Sarcasm or mockery

Chapter 20

Q1) Why did Mr. Fogg and Aouda return to the hotel after making their purchases in the English quarter?
   Answer: c) To have dinner at a sumptuously served table-d'hote
Q2) Why did Fix feel hopeful when Mr. Fogg mentioned looking for other vessels in the harbour?
   Answer: d) Because he hoped Mr. Fogg would be delayed in finding another means of travel
Q3) What was the profession of the man who approached Mr. Fogg at the quay?
   Answer: c) Pilot
Q4) What does the word "stated" mean in the sentence "the Carnatic had sailed the evening before the stated time"?
   Answer: d) Scheduled or planned
Q5) What does the word "profiting" imply about Fix's feelings towards Mr. Fogg?
   Answer: d) Humiliation or discomfort

Chapter 21

Q1) Why did the passengers refuse to go below deck during the storm?
   Answer: b) The cabin was too cramped and uncomfortable.
Q2) Why did Mr. Fogg insist on signalling the American steamer?
   Answer: b) To request assistance due to the storm
Q3) What was the purpose of hoisting the flag at half-mast on the Tankadere?
   Answer: b) To indicate distress and request assistance

Q4) What does the word "capricious" mean?
> Answer: a) Erratic or unpredictable

Q5) What does the word "desperate" imply about John Bunsby's action of pushing back the rudder?
> Answer: b) Desperate or hopeless

Chapter 22

Q1) Why was Passepartout dishevelled when he woke up in a cabin of the Carnatic?
> Answer: c) He struggled against the effects of the opium he had ingested.

Q2) Why did Passepartout fear that Mr. Fogg was ruined?
> Answer: d) All the above.

Q3) What resource did Passepartout decide to use before seeking assistance from the consuls?
> Answer: b) He intended to exhaust all other means of aid.

Q4) What does the word "motley" mean as used in the sentence "Passepartout wandered for several hours in the midst of this motley crowd"?
> Answer: a) Diverse or varied

Q5) What does the phrase "stout heart" mean in the context of the sentence "But he found it necessary to keep up a stout heart"?
> Answer: a) A courageous attitude

Chapter 23

Q1) Why did Passepartout decide to change his clothes before trying to earn money?
> Answer: c) He thought he would look too well-dressed.

Q2) How did Passepartout ultimately secure a position with the Japanese troupe?
> Answer: c) He volunteered to act as a clown in the troupe's performance.

Q3) What role did Passepartout play in the troupe's performance?
> Answer: a) He was part of the great 'human pyramid'.

Q4) What does the word "adroitness" mean in the sentence "as, to fill this part, only strength and adroitness were necessary"?
> Answer: a) Skilfulness and agility

Q5) What does the phrase "deafening air" mean in the context of the sentence "this elicited loud applause, in the midst of which the orchestra was just striking up a deafening air"?
> Answer: a) A noisy piece of music

Chapter 24

Q1) What was Phileas Fogg's reaction upon learning that Passepartout had arrived in Yokohama?
> Answer: b) He remained indifferent and silent.

A Study Guide: Around the World in Eighty Days

Q2) Where did Phileas Fogg eventually find Passepartout?
    Answer: c) In a theatre owned by Mr. Batulcar.
Q3) How did Passepartout explain his absence to Mr. Fogg?
    Answer: c) He blamed his absence on drunkenness and opium smoking.
Q4) Why did Mr. Fogg provide funds to Passepartout?
    Answer: c) To purchase new clothing fitting for his position.
Q5) Where did Fix hide upon recognizing Passepartout on board the General Grant?
    Answer: b) In his cabin to avoid detection.

Chapter 25

Q1) Why does Passepartout find San Francisco surprising?
    Answer: a) He expected it to be more chaotic and dangerous.
Q2) How did Mr. Fogg react when Colonel Stamp Proctor attempted to strike him?
    Answer: b) He calmly exchanged words with Colonel Proctor.
Q3) What did Mr. Fogg and Fix do after being attacked during the political meeting?
    Answer: d) They proceeded to a tailor's to repair their torn clothing.
Q4) How did Mr. Fogg plan to retaliate against Colonel Stamp Proctor for the attack?
    Answer: b) By challenging him to a duel
Q5) What does the term "perilous" mean as used in the text?
    Answer: b) Dangerous

Chapter 26

Q1) How did the passengers transform the train car at bedtime?
    Correct Answer: b) By rolling out bedsteads and improvising berths.
Q2) What is the main purpose of the Pacific Railroad described in the passage?
    Correct Answer: b) To connect New York and San Francisco by rail.
Q3) What was the major obstacle encountered by the train during its journey?
    Correct Answer: b) A herd of buffaloes
Q4) What is the meaning of the term "dormitory" as used in the passage?
    Correct Answer: c) A place for sleeping.
Q5) What does the phrase "insurmountable obstacle" suggest about the buffaloes?
    Correct Answer: b) They are impossible to control.

Chapter 27

Q1) Why did Passepartout find himself amused while on the train platform?
    Answer: c) He was observing the peculiar attire of a stranger.
Q2) What can be inferred about Passepartout's attitude towards attending the lecture on Mormonism?
    Correct Answer: a) He was curious and eager to learn.
Q3) What announcement did Passepartout read on the notice affixed to the train car?
    Correct Answer: b) A lecture on Mormonism by Elder William Hitch.

Q4) Why did the audience for Elder William Hitch's lecture gradually diminish?
	Answer: b) The lecture became repetitive and boring.
Q5) What is the meaning of the word "ensconced" as used in the passage?
	Answer: c) Seated comfortably or securely.

Chapter 28

Q1) In the text, what was Passepartout's main concern?
	Answer: a) Avoiding a dangerous meeting with Colonel Proctor.
Q2) What caused the delay in the train's journey?
	Answer: d) A red signal indicating an unsafe bridge ahead.
Q3) What is the primary reason for the passengers' dissatisfaction during the delay?
	Answer: c) They disliked the inconvenience of walking.
Q4) What does the word "sedentary" mean in the context of the passage?
	Answer: c) Fond of sitting; characterized by much sitting.
Q5) Which word best describes the passengers' reaction to the engineer's proposal to cross the bridge?
	Answer: a) Enthusiastic

Chapter 29

Q1) What was the primary reason for the delay in the train's journey at Plum Creek station?
	Answer: b) A duel arranged between Mr. Fogg and Colonel Proctor.
Q2) which statement about Aouda's behaviour during the confrontation with the Sioux is most accurate?
	Answer: d) Aouda used a revolver to defend herself and the passengers against the Sioux.
Q3) What did the conductor suggest as an alternative to stopping the train for the duel?
	Answer: a) To fight the duel while the train was moving.
Q4) What prevented the Indians from capturing the train entirely during the attack?
	Answer: a) Proximity to the fort garrison.
Q5) What does the word "acrobatic" mean in the context of the passage?
	Answer: a) Swift and agile movement.

Chapter 30

Q1) How does Fix react to the idea of leaving Fort Kearney without pursuing Mr. Fogg?
	Answer: c) He feels regretful and blames himself for allowing Mr. Fogg to go alone.
Q2) What was the fate of the unconscious engineer and stoker after the locomotive became separated from the train?
	Answer: c) They remained unconscious until the locomotive returned.

Q3) Why did Aouda refuse to board the train when it was ready to depart from Fort Kearney?
    Answer: a) She was waiting for Mr. Fogg to return.
Q4) What does the word "reconnaissance" as used in the text mean?
    Answer: c) To survey or explore an area.
Q5) In the context of the passage, what does the word "impassible" most likely mean?
    Answer: a) Unemotional or unaffected by feelings.

Chapter 31

Q1) How did Phileas Fogg plan to regain the lost time caused by the Indian interruption?
    Answer: c) By riding on a sledge with sails
Q2) How did Phileas Fogg plan to travel from Omaha to New York?
    Answer: a) By train
Q3) What did Mr. Fogg compare the sound of the metallic lashings on the sledge to?
    Answer: a) A violin bow on strings
Q4) In the context of the passage, what does the word "lurches" mean?
    Answer: d) Unsteady movements
Q5) What is the meaning of the phrase "as the birds fly" in the passage?
    Answer: a) Following a straight path

Chapter 32

Q1) Why did Phileas Fogg approach the vessels anchored in the river?
    Answer: a) To seek alternative transportation after missing the China
Q2) How did Phileas Fogg convince Captain Speedy to change his mind and agree to take them to Liverpool?
    Answer: b) By offering a significantly higher amount of money
Q3) What was Passepartout's reaction upon hearing the cost of the last voyage?
    Answer: a) He expressed disbelief
Q4) What does the word "repugnance" as used in the passage mean?
    Answer: d) Disgust
Q5) What does the phrase "vocal gamut" suggest about Passepartout's reaction?
    Answer: b) It was loud and varied

Chapter 33

Q1) From the text, what can be inferred about the crew's opinion of Phileas Fogg?
    Answer: b) They admire his sailing skills and management.
Q2) What was Phileas Fogg's original destination before he decided to head towards Liverpool?
    Answer: a) Bordeaux

Q3) How much time did Phileas Fogg have left to reach London after disembarking in Liverpool?
	Answer: a) 6 hours
Q4) What does the word "lustrously" as used in the text most likely mean?
	Answer: b) Shimmeringly
Q5) What does the word "colloquy" as used in the text mean?
	Answer: b) A casual conversation or dialogue

Chapter 34

Q1) Why was Phileas Fogg sitting calmly and motionless in the Custom House?
	Answer: d) He was waiting patiently, with a stern look.
Q2) What was Phileas Fogg's reaction when Fix informed him that he was free?
	Answer: c) He knocked Fix down with precise, rapid motion.
Q3) What action did Phileas Fogg take to ensure he reached London on time after missing the express train?
	Answer: b) He ordered a special train to depart immediately.
Q4) What does the word "resigned" mean in the context of the passage?
	Answer: b) Accepting defeat or fate
Q5) What is the meaning of the phrase "received his deserts" as used in the passage?
	Answer: a) Got what he deserved

Chapter 35

Q1) Question: Why did Mr. Fogg remain at home after returning from the station?
	Answer: c) He needed to organize his affairs.
Q2) How did Mr. Fogg's return home surprise the dwellers in Saville Row?
	Answer: c) His house showed no signs of change.
Q3) What task did Mr. Fogg give to Passepartout after returning home?
	Answer: c) To purchase provisions.
Q4) Question: What does the word "unwonted" mean in the context of the passage?
	Answer: d) Unusual
Q5) In the passage, what does the word "tranquillity" imply about Mr. Fogg's demeanour?
	Answer: B) He was calm and composed.

Chapter 36

Q1) How did the English public opinion change when the real bank robber was arrested?
	Answer: b) They considered Phileas Fogg an honourable gentleman.
Q2) Why were Phileas Fogg's friends at the Reform Club anxious in the days leading up to the 21st of December?
	Answer: b) They were apprehensive about Phileas Fogg fulfilling his wager.
Q3) What did the gentlemen of the Reform Club do to pass the time while waiting for Phileas Fogg?
	Answer: b) They played a game of cards.

A Study Guide: Around the World in Eighty Days

Q4) What does the word "eccentric" mean in the context of the passage?
   Answer: b) Unusual and unconventional
Q5) What does the word "suspended" imply about Andrew Stuart and his partners?
   Answer: a) They stopped playing the game.

Chapter 37

Q1) Why did Passepartout rush through the street "like a waterspout"?
   Answer: b) He was excited about possibly winning the wager.
Q2) Why did Phileas Fogg leave his house in a rush?
   Answer: b) He wanted to reach the Reform Club as soon as possible.
Q3) How did Phileas Fogg manage to win his wager?
   Answer: a) By using various means of transportation.
Q4) What does Phileas Fogg do with the remainder of the money he won?
   Answer: b) He divides it between Passepartout and Fix.
Q5) What does the word "phlegmatic" most likely mean in the context of the passage?
   Answer: c) Calm

Printed in Great Britain
by Amazon